SECOND WIND

by Marilinne Cooper

CHAPTER ONE

September 2017
Tortola, British Virgin Islands

"I hear all de prison inmates escaped."

After standing for what seemed like hours in the dense heat of the midday sun, Tucker thought he might be hallucinating. He turned his head in the direction of the voice that had spoken. Bloodshot eyes in a round dark face gazed expectantly at him.

"Dat's right," the woman said when he didn't respond. "De prison destroyed in de storm and dey all get out."

Tucker took a few steps as the line inched forward. "Well." He cleared his throat, realizing he hadn't actually talked to anyone in twenty-four hours. His tongue felt dry. "Should we be worried?"

"Worried?" Her raucous laughter dissolved into a coughing fit. "What world you from, boy? We talking about murderers, robbers, rapists...dey hardened *criminals*, boy. And yes, mon, you should be worryin' your white ass about it. What Irma didn't take from us, deese men, dey will. Lord help us."

The man in front of Tucker spoke up now for the first time since joining the queue. His heritage could not be determined by his weathered brown skin and wispy white hair, but it was clear that he was a longtime islander. "It's going to get worse before it gets better here, that's for certain. Been here for thirty years and all I've got left to show for it is three walls and a pile of rubble."

"I'm – I'm so sorry." Tucker didn't know what to say to anybody. He was hot and tired and miserable; he just wanted to get his two bottles of water and MRE rations and go sit down somewhere to eat. Like nearly everyone else on

3

Tortola, his whole life had blown away with the Category 5 winds of Hurricane Irma.

"How'd your place come through?" the old man asked Tucker.

"I was crewing on a sailboat. We'd been waiting for parts. The owners evacuated and left me to watch it..." He was overcome once again with a sudden dizziness, the weight and responsibility of the situation bearing down on him like a careening drop in barometric pressure.

"And..."

Tucker gave a desolate, half-hearted wave towards the water. "Destroyed." Every time he relived his first view of the harbor after the storm, his chest tightened up and he could barely breathe. "A total loss."

An hour later, sitting on a broken cement wall and choking down the nearly inedible food in the "Meals Ready to Eat" box, Tucker tried to reassure himself that "total loss" was probably not entirely accurate. If he could get to the yacht there might still be something salvageable in the cabin. He knew there were long-term provisions in the pantry; cans of soup, tins of peaches. But in his dazed and hungry state, he could not even remember what else could be of any use now. There were valuable navigational charts that would no longer be needed by a boat with a hole the size of pickup truck in its hull.

Once his hunger was somewhat satiated, his other senses seemed to revive. Despite the lack of electricity, running water, and drivable roads, life was beginning to resume on the island. Somewhere nearby, a diesel generator was droning, loud and unrelenting, echoed by another not far off. There was the high-pitched whine of a chainsaw slicing through fallen branches, a baby crying, a woman shouting, and at least three dogs barking incessantly from different locations. An underlying smell of rotting vegetation and sewage pervaded his nostrils and he suspected it would get much worse before it got better.

From his vantage point on the side of a hill, the devastation of the yachts once anchored in Paraquita Bay was horrific to behold. Where just a few days earlier, dozens of cheerful white sailboats had been moored in placid turquoise waters, there was now a mass of broken and battered vessels, wedged together and piled atop one another at odd angles. Millions of dollars in fiberglass had been transformed from sleek floating crafts into a junkyard of worthless dreams.

The boats were so close to each other they appeared to be one giant amorphous creature that had washed up against a jagged shoreline of rocks and denuded mangrove trees. In the midst of this colossal traffic jam of destruction, he could just pick out what he thought was the mast of the Second Wind. If he could get down there somehow, he could probably climb from deck to deck until he reached the Kronenberg's yacht.

With a sudden sense of purpose, he scrambled up onto the wall and shaded his eyes, trying to scope out the ruined landscape.

"Want some?"

Tucker nearly lost his footing at the sound of a voice next to him. He had not heard anyone approaching. A man was standing a few feet away holding out a candy bar. He was wearing only neon green running shorts, plastic flip-flops and aviator sunglasses; tied over his head was a brand-new, royal blue bandana that still had folded creases in it. But what Tucker noticed most was the man's bare chest, as pale as moonlight beneath a thick mat of graying hair. It would not have seemed unusual except (and now Tucker's brain slid into its strange yet familiar mode of logical puzzle-solving), A) this was the Caribbean, B) the sun was shining mercilessly, and C) the man didn't have a shirt on. His skin should have been burnt to a crisp.

"You're not allergic to nuts, are you? Because I might have something else. Would you mind if I had a swig of that water? It's a frickin' hot day." Shoving a wispy ponytail of a nondescript color up into his headscarf, he used the back of his hand to wipe the sweat from his neck.

Feeling as though he was probably making a major mistake, Tucker traded a bottle of water for the candy bar.

"Thanks, you're saving a life here." Taking a few giant gulps, the stranger nodded towards the harbor. "So is that the biggest clusterfuck you've ever seen, or what. It would be awesome if it wasn't so awful."

Overcome by unnamable emotions, Tucker took a big bite of chocolate covered nougat, filling his mouth with the sweetness of the half-melted chewy confection.

"Wait – you speak English? You understand what I've been saying?"

For a moment Tucker was tempted to pretend he was Swedish or German, unsure of this spontaneous companionship with a total stranger. But then he realized he was being ridiculous. He'd weathered out the hurricane in a boarded-up house with two women and three men, owners of other yachts, whom he'd only known by sight. They'd insisted he lock up the Second Wind and hunker down with them for the duration of Irma. He'd been glad he hadn't been alone for that terrifying twenty-four hours, even though they'd turned out to be a detestable group of drunks who had argued over the howling winds and thunderous rain, continuing to shout about American politics even after all of the Jack Daniels and Absolut had been consumed. He'd been happy to get out of there as soon as it was safe to leave. He'd slept on the floor of the emergency shelter for the last two nights, in welcome anonymity.

Now he swallowed the candy and ran his tongue over his teeth before finally replying. "Yes, English, yes." Although he could not see the man's eyes behind the dark polarized lenses of his sunglasses, Tucker could tell he was sizing him up. As they stood there assessing each other, Tucker wondered how he himself looked after not bathing or changing clothes for three days. He could only imagine how he must appear, from the sweaty dampness of his cropped sun-bleached curls, flattened beneath the faded canvas of his sailing cap, to the dirty tanned toes clenched nervously against mud-encrusted flip-flops.

Thinking about his own appearance made him realize a few things – for a man on an island full of washed-out roads that in some places were only passable through filthy ankle-deep water, the stranger's own rubber footwear was remarkably clean. As were his fluorescent shorts. Like they had just been bought or something. Like tumblers on a combination lock, the gears of his brain began clicking again. A) there were no stores open, B) maybe he had just changed into fresh clothing, and C) something was off here.

Tucker coughed self-consciously. "So how'd your house come through the storm? Any damage?" It was the way people introduced themselves now, instead of asking where someone was from.

"My house?" The man gave a hoarse bark of a laugh as he rummaged in a large plastic shopping tote, the exterior of which featured a photo-printed fish and a coral reef. His meaty hand finally emerged with a small bag of peanuts. "Not too good. Let's just say I'm homeless now. How about you?"

"I was crewing on one of those boats down there. So I guess we're both shit out of luck."

"Well, now I wouldn't say that." A handful of nuts was offered in what seemed like an almost cheerful gesture. "So you're a sailor, then?"

Tucker hesitated for a moment. "Yeah, for about a year now. Did a trans-Atlantic crossing with some Brits who kept a yacht in the Greek islands. We were planning to sail the Caribbean, but after a major engine failure, it needed an overhaul before we could go on. The owners decided to fly home for hurricane season and left me to look after the boat while we waited for parts. And now..." He sank back down to his original perch on the wall. "I should have tried to move it somehow. Somewhere."

"Hey. Kid. The hurricane was not your fault. You need to get over it. Move on to the next solution." He wiped his palm on the side of his shorts before extending it to Tucker. "Flush."

"What?"

"That's my name. It's actually John Royal. But they call me Flush."

He knew his reaction was juvenile, but Tucker could not suppress a grin. "Like a toilet?"

"No, like a really good poker hand. A royal one. And you are?"

"Tucker. But some people call me Stone now."

"Stone?" Flush mimicked the look on Tucker's face. "Like stoned out of your mind? Or stone sober?"

"Okay, that's fair. But no, it's actually part of my middle name." He shook the outstretched hand. "Tucker Mackenzie. Tucker Brookstone Mackenzie."

Getting to the shoreline had looked almost impossible, but it was even harder than it appeared. It turned out that Flush had a bad knee and just walking was a slow, laborious process for him. By the time the two of them hauled themselves up the forty-five-degree angle of the first stranded boat, their limbs were scratched and bleeding. Flush had a diagonal cut bisecting his bare chest, which heaved up and down with the effort of his exertions. Wrapping an arm around the metal deck railing to keep himself from sliding down the inclined surface, he rested for a moment, watching Tucker climb nimbly to the fiberglass summit and drop onto the neighboring sloop.

"Which one is yours again?" Flush called breathlessly.

Tucker didn't answer; he was staring at the dangling padlock on the open hatch of the boat's cabin. "Shit," he muttered.

"You okay?"

"Yeah, I'm fine. It just looks like somebody's broken into this one." Warily he peered into the darkness of the interior. Somehow Flush materialized at his side in seconds, peeking over his shoulder.

"Are you going in or should I?"

Tucker gave him a disgusted look. "This is private property. We'd be trespassing."

"Don't be absurd. All's fair in love and war. And hurricanes." Flush pushed past him. "Well, it looks like the pantry was their first target. Didn't leave much for us." He held up a can of sliced beets before tossing it into his shopping tote. "Apparently not very fond of vegetables." He glanced up at Tucker, noted his stern stance and shrugged. "Don't go all judgmental on me, kid. If you want to survive, you need to shift into survival mode."

"I'm not a freakin' pirate!"

He turned to go but a sudden swell in the bay rocked the boat, catching them both by surprise. Tucker caught himself on the door frame, but Flush lost his balance, landing hard on the galley floor. He lay there with his eyes closed for a few seconds and for a terrifying instant Tucker thought maybe he'd been knocked unconscious. What would he do if...

Flush sputtered and propped himself up on one elbow. "Help me up, will you? Apparently I don't have my sea legs yet. And look in there and see if you can find me a T-shirt. I'm bleeding all over the place."

He should just walk away now. But it was a strange new world and he did not want to be left alone in it, so Tucker did what he was asked to do.

It was not easy maneuvering Flush from one deck to the next. During the frequent rest periods along the way, he pumped Tucker for personal information in a persistent but conversational manner.

"Stoney, your parents must be worried about you. You able to get any message to them?"

"No and no. A) I haven't talked to my parents in nearly two years, B) even if I had a phone there is no cell service now, and C) I'm not as young as you think."

"Really?" He could see that Flush was trying not to laugh. "So how old is not as young as I think?"

"Old enough." Tucker glared at him. "Let's go." He stood up again and held out a steadying hand to help Flush move onto the next boat.

"You married?"

He glanced self-consciously at the cheap gold band on his fourth finger. "I was. She left me a while ago."

"But you still wear the ring. Sorry, just curious."

"It's a long story."

"Really. How long could it be at your age?"

"Fuck you. Why don't you just go back to shore and crawl into whatever hole you came out of?" He didn't need to hang with this guy. He'd been alone for weeks already; he'd manage somehow.

"Sensitive subject, I guess. What – you just going to leave me here? After we've come all this way together, buddy?" When Flush realized that Tucker was seriously going to leave him behind, he called after him. "I've got a proposition that will make it worth your while, sailor!"

"Unless you've got a million dollars in that shopping bag of yours, nothing would make it worth my while!" Tucker called over his shoulder. He could see Second Wind now, just two yachts away – he wasn't going to be able to lose Flush that easily.

Reluctantly he waited for the older man to catch up. "What if..." Flush coughed several times and then spit some phlegm into the harbor waters. "What if I told you I had access to that much money, if you can help me get to it?"

Tucker laughed. At least Flush was entertaining.

"This boat is toast, kid." Flush stared dubiously at the murky ankle-deep water that Tucker was wading through inside the cabin. "You better get whatever shit you want to save and then we need to find somewhere else to sleep. I think she's taking more on every minute."

Much as he hated to admit that Flush was right, Tucker had to agree. He grabbed his duffle off a hook in his narrow aft cabin where the disgusting water was almost lapping at his berth. Hastily stuffing his possessions inside,

10

he waded back out to where Flush was filling his bag with any edible rations he could find. "Ahh, now this is beautiful." He gazed lovingly at a bottle of aged Macallan Scotch before tucking it carefully into the overstuffed tote. "Anything else important or valuable we should rescue?"

Tucker opened an overhead compartment and grabbed a couple of paperback books and a box containing a 1000 piece jigsaw puzzle. "Don't judge," he warned as he saw Flush's questioning look.

"What – who me? Got any playing cards up there?"

"Of course." Tucker tossed him a couple of decks, glancing around nervously, trying to think of what else he should be saving. In the stifling heat of a closed-up cabin on a slowly sinking ship, he could barely wrap his mind around whatever this new reality meant for him. Any shreds of security he might have felt in his day-to-day existence had vanished in the aftermath of Irma.

As if reading his thoughts, Flush said, "Look, let it go. Your only responsibility is to yourself right now. Well, and maybe a little bit to me. Come on – we need to find someplace seaworthy where we can camp for the night. It'll be dark before we know it."

Unhooking a collapsible solar lantern from the ceiling, Tucker glumly splashed his way back to the steps. "Here, put this around your neck." He threw an inflatable life vest at Flush. "You might need it."

They made camp on an ostentatious multi-level motor cruiser with covered outdoor decks and built-in bench seating. Wedged between a heeled-over ketch and a couple of smaller sailing vessels tight against the prow, there was little chance of anyone disturbing them for the night. Just before dusk, a coast guard helicopter flew low over the harbor, assessing for damage and possible distress situations as it circled the island. Tucker and Flush pressed themselves against the cabin wall, beneath a deep overhang until the aircraft had passed.

Flush smacked his bare thigh, cursing. "Didn't think the mosquitos would be so bad out here. But the bay is like a freakin' cesspool now. Okay, you are a saint," he said as Tucker handed him a plastic spray bottle of Off. "How did you even remember this?"

"How could I not." Using his duffle as a backrest, Tucker adjusted his LCD headlamp and then pulled out one of the books he had retrieved and a ballpoint pen.

"What – you're doing a crossword puzzle right now? Why not, I guess." Flush untied his bandana, using it as rag to wipe the sweat off his face. Tucker was surprised to see that, unlike the shiny bald pate he had imagined, Flush actually had a full head of wavy hair in some nondescript shade between brown and gray. "Maybe we can play some cards later. You know how to play poker?"

"Yeah, I'm familiar with it." He pretended to be engrossed in the black and white graphics on the page in front of him, but really he was just tired of conversing. The afternoon had been proof that Flush could keep up a nonstop stream of conversation, whether Tucker was participating or not.

"So, tell me, Stoney. Are you a decent sailor?" Flush unscrewed the cap on the bottle of scotch and tipped it up into his mouth. "Oh, my. Yes. Holy fuck, that is good." Even in the fading daylight, Tucker could see the hot color the liquor brought to his companion's cheeks. "Oh, whiskey, how I've missed thee..."

"I'm good enough. No thanks." He waved his hand at the proffered bottle. "You need that more than I do."

"Ever tried it? Just have one swig. So we can say we had a toast. Look at this..." he swept his arm at the rich twilight colors of the darkening sky and waters. "It's worth celebrating."

"Okay." Even in these depressing circumstances, there was something strangely infectious about Flush's good humor. Tucker held the Macallan bottle up. "To being alive." He swallowed a mouthful of the smooth, fiery liquor before passing it back.

12

"Hear, hear. To freedom."

And that was when the pieces all fell into place.

Tucker was unsure of what to do with his newly realized knowledge about Flush. In his mind he could see a whole page of questions generating itself, like a sales receipt spitting from a cash register. 1) Should he fear for his life, 2) Should he run, 3) Had he unwittingly committed a crime already, 4) How many years did you get for aiding an escaped convict, 5) Was Flush, in fact, even dangerous, and, 6) Was it better to confront him or pretend ignorance?

His instinct was to get up and pace, but there was no place to do that right now. He suddenly flashed on a memory of his father, walking back and forth on the worn pine floor of his office; it was what he did whenever he needed to solve a difficult mental problem or couldn't face dealing with a situation. For the first time in months he felt homesick and thought he might trade all of the unknown adventures that lay ahead in his life just to curl up on the sofa with his dad and watch a detective show on television.

"So what about a can opener? Did we forget the most important thing?"

"What?" His anxious train of thought interrupted, Tucker's whole body went rigid as he tried to focus on what was actually going on at the moment. Nothing scary was happening – Flush had a can of chili in one hand and a spoon in the other.

"Any ideas how to get into this?"

"Oh." Tucker dug in his pocket for his Swiss Army knife and then hesitated. "Pass it here. I'll open it for you." He turned his body slightly so Flush couldn't see the trembling in his fingers.

"Do you need more light? Where's that inflatable solar lantern..."

"I'm fine." Tucker took a couple of deep breaths to calm himself. There was probably nothing to worry about. He tried to convince himself that he was overthinking this situation. "Here you go." He slid the can across the bench and quickly put the knife away.

"Well, cold chili is better than no chili." Flush chewed slowly. "So I know how you ended up here, but where you from, Stoney?"

It was just conversation. Two people spending a long night on a boat deck after a natural disaster. "Vermont. I grew up in northern Vermont. And my earliest years were spent in the Grenadines. And you?"

"A safe and happy childhood in rural Kansas, a bad marriage in Iowa that eventually led me to a sketchy and unreliable life in Key West, and then onto a much better existence in the Caribbean. Until recently." Flush took another hit from the bottle and cleared his throat. "So a small town boy then?"

"Couldn't be much smaller. Juggled back and forth between my parents who never lived together and somehow managed to fight all the time anyway." A mental picture of his mother came to mind. She'd been so angry with him for not properly finishing high school, for choosing to live with Chloe in a treehouse in his father's yard, and for abandoning all her careful plans for his college-bound future by opting to vagabond around the world instead. Hating all the guilt associated with thinking about his parents, he quickly changed the topic.

"So what do you do for work here, Flush? Or what did you do before... Irma?"

"A little bit of everything. All-around tradesman, you might say. Carpentry, painting, wiring, gambling. Although I've been a bit waylaid and laid up lately."

I bet you have, Tucker thought grimly.

Flush straightened up suddenly. "What's the date today?"

Tucker looked at him blankly. In his mind's post-hurricane blur, he could not even figure out what day of the week it was, let alone the actual date. "I don't know, September something. Twelfth? Fourteenth?"

Flush relaxed back against his fiberglass seat. "Okay, okay. There's still plenty of time." He was speaking more to himself than Tucker.

"Why, you have an appointment you've got to keep? Because chances are, it's not going to happen." He waved a hand demonstratively in the direction of the island.

"So here's the real question. Do you think you're a good enough sailor to handle a small boat for a couple of days with the help of an old guy with a bum leg?"

Tucker wasn't sure if the laughter that bubbled out of him was despite his nerves or because of them. "Why – because of the unlikely event that you just happen to own a sailboat on this island that is still in working condition?"

"Well, jury's still out on that one. Let's start here – in this mass of floating flotsam, do you think there is a dinghy that we can use to get out to the West End?"

"Not that's ours."

"That we can borrow, for Christ's sakes. Don't get so righteous with me – this is a time of crisis. It could be months before a regular guy like you without a life-threatening medical condition can actually get off Tortola. Or maybe you'd rather stay here and fight other people for the next day's ration of MREs while the mosquitos are fighting over you." Flush realized that his voice had risen and he lowered his tone to almost a whisper. "Can you sail a boat or not? Because if you can, there is a substantial amount of money in it for you."

Tucker was silent for a few minutes, weighing his options. Why would he even consider the offer – it sounded like an opportunity that had more probability of going wrong than right. The boat rocked a bit with a passing swell and the empty can of chili rolled across the deck to land at his feet.

"I heard the West End took the storm really hard." He didn't have to look in his wallet to know that he had only forty-five dollars cash and a debit card that was useless on an island without electricity.

15

"Well, we ought to go see it for ourselves tomorrow. I have some gear stashed out there as well."

He should bring the subject up now, before he got too involved. Instead he asked, "So what island is it you're trying to get to that you think might be in better shape than here?"

"Culebra. Off the coast of Puerto Rico. You know it?"

Tucker clapped his hand to his forehead in a classic gesture of disbelief. "Yeah, as a matter of fact, I do."

Flush perked up noticeably. "Really? You've sailed into there then?"

"Well, not exactly. It was a long time ago."

"How many years could that be in your life history? And what does 'not exactly' mean?"

Tucker ignored the questions. "So what's between here and there and how many miles?"

"Just St. John and St. Thomas. And it'd be easy because we'd be sailing with the wind." Flush let out a quiet whoop of happiness and took another belt of the Macallan. He began to ramble softly, more to himself than to Tucker. "Lucky at cards, lucky at life. Mr. Royal is gettin' off this pisshole of a rock just in time. Mr. T-Ron, your white shark ass is grass..."

He banged something hard onto the bench next to him and Tucker realized it was the small box of red and white Bicycle playing cards. "Just in time," he murmured again, and with what was clearly a practiced one-handed action, he had the deck out of the carton and shuffled.

"Yeah, I don't know if I want to go to Culebra..." Beyond the fact that he had serious reservations about what it meant to partner up with Flush, he had his own reasons for not particularly wanting the island as a destination.

"Ohhh, you got some history there? An old girlfriend you don't want to run into maybe? Or a poker debt you forgot to pay? I'm sure I can help you out in that department."

Tucker closed his eyes, as if not seeing Flush would make the sound of him go away. And despite how well he had managed to not think about his situation for the last year, he could not keep himself from remembering the circumstances that had led him to be spending a night on a deck of some random speedboat with this man who was clearly an escaped inmate from Balsam Ghut, Her Majesty's prison on Tortola.

"It was the best of times, it was the worst of times..." *He didn't remember a lot about the year he and Chloe had spent cramming for their GEDs in the treehouse in West Jordan. Maybe it was because they'd smoked so much of the pot his best friend, Myles, had supplied them with, or maybe it was because he worked so hard at not recalling it. But he could still remember that opening line from A Tale of Two Cities because they had spent a whole night laughing about how well it described the time they had spent together on Culebra.*

It was embarrassing to recollect how innocent he'd been, a sixteen-year-old virgin seduced by a worldly seventeen-year-old while on a camping holiday with his father. The adventures that ensued had been way more than harmless, and entailed murder, drugs, international intrigue, and a really crazy woman who was actually Chloe's mom. His own perpetually angry mother was nothing compared to Elle. They'd almost gotten killed on Flamenco Beach – it still ranked in the top three scariest incidents he'd ever experienced.

He'd fallen in love on Culebra and that "falling" had irrevocably changed the course of his life. From then on he'd wanted nothing to do with the safe conventional future towards which he'd been headed; all the "college prep" and "career planning" seemed meaningless in comparison to what he had with Chloe. Which in retrospect was mostly sex. Lots and lots of it. When he had refused to be separated from her, and because her own life needed some

17

refocusing, Chloe had moved back to Vermont with him and his father.

For a while it had been an idyllic existence, living and working together towards their shared goals: 1) Study for their equivalency exams, 2) Make as much money as possible in a short amount of time and then, 3) Go backpacking around the world. It had been simple, direct and achievable. He remembered feeling insanely happy and happily sane.

They'd shared everything – until it turned out he wasn't that good at sharing. There'd been the full moon beach party in Thailand when Chloe had been seriously high on something chemical...he'd never known real jealousy before that night. Afterwards, when they'd made up, he'd suggested they should get married, really declare a commitment to each other. Knee-deep in lagoon water at sunset with the entire hostel full of backpackers as their witnesses, they'd exchanged vows. He thought it would make him trust her more – but it didn't. A few months later, when Myles met them in Istanbul, Chloe initiated what turned out to be a fateful three-way, it had been against Tucker's better judgment and undermined whatever tenuous bond they had re-established.

Their relationship had been all downhill from there. When he'd found the sailing gig on Skyros, he'd been happy to take some space and finally pursue something he'd was really interested in, leaving Chloe alone on the island for weeks at a time. He thought maybe it would make her appreciate him more on his short visits back home, but it seemed to have the opposite effect. Each time he returned, he felt she was drifting father away and he had no idea what to do to make it all go back to what it had been. She started modeling for a woman artist, earning her own money, enjoying her life without him in the tiny Greek village where they had settled.

The pregnancy had been the last thing he'd ever expected and a responsibility he didn't want. Instead of bringing them together, it had irrevocably split them apart.

18

He could not understand how a free spirit like Chloe could possibly want to be tied down by a baby and he absolutely didn't want his wings clipped now that he had finally found his passion. Being on the water, propelled by wind, was the place he felt most alive, and he could not be forced to come ashore. Besides, he wasn't mature enough to be a parent.

The last time they'd been together all they'd done was fight. She wanted the baby, he wanted her to get rid of it. When he returned home again two weeks later and found every trace of her gone, he sank into a depression deeper than he'd ever known was possible. Even though Chloe had left him without any means of communication, having taken their phone and ipad with her, he kept waiting for her to contact him in some way. Winter in the Greek islands was colder and damper than he'd ever imagined. Without Chloe, it seemed much longer and darker than the short season it actually was. After a few weeks he thought he might be going crazy; after a couple of months he was sure of it. He could not stop making lists in his head of what he should have or shouldn't have done. Every action, large or small, became a multiple choice quiz in which he was sure he had chosen the wrong answer. From whether to walk to the store or even get out of bed, he could not keep himself from looking at each situation from all angles. What had once been a talent for logistics now had become a cursed and obsessive disorder that he could not make his mind stop doing.

By spring he was ready to jump at any opportunity to get away from the mental misery that had become his life.

He actually had to fill out an employment application form to work on *Second Wind*. When he'd ripped the paper off the clipboard to hand it over to Gus, the left hand corner had ripped clean off the page, taking the first half of his name with it.

"So you are...Stone Mackenzie?" The loose-limbed string-bean of a man who owned the yacht grinned wryly at him.

"Works for me." Tucker had liked the idea of a new identity to go with his new job. Gus and Melania had thought the name suited him, since by then he kept most of his emotions stoically to himself, having learned to suppress anything resembling extreme happiness or sadness over the long lonely winter. Heart of Stone, was what he secretly thought of himself as.

The Kronenbergs were old-school when it came to entertainment – no computers or DVD players, although they did enjoy music. They read books, played cards and worked crosswords, and for a really rollicking night's fun, they unrolled the felt puzzle mat and did a jigsaw puzzle. In the endless weeks at sea that followed, Tucker found these simple diversions were exactly what he needed to calm his anxiety and keep his brain occupied during the quiet evenings aboard Second Wind.

Melania especially worked at trying to get him to open up and relax and laugh. But after a few sessions that ended with tickling or massage, Tucker suspected her interests might be more than motherly and he avoided any alone time with her. Mostly he was thankful to be well-fed and busy, happy to retire to the privacy of his narrow berth with a battered John D. MacDonald paperback, and glad that his father wasn't around to gloat over his enjoyment of classic mystery novels.

"Stone! Stoney! We ought to get going."

Trying to remember where he was, Tucker opened his eyes to the pearl pink and gray light of dawn. The comforting memory of his tiny cabin faded away into the unforgiving hardness of a fiberglass bench and an excruciating pain in his neck.

"You kids can sleep anywhere. I've been watching you dream all night."

Tortola. Irma. Flush. "Ouch." He pushed himself to a sitting position. He felt damp and cranky, but Flush looked way more miserable than him. "What are we doing again?"

"Looking for a dinghy in working order. To borrow. To get us to the West End."

Tucker sank back down, unready to move on yet to whatever this next unknown phase of his life was.

Two hours later he was steering a stolen Sun Dolphin inflatable through the wreckage of the harbor on the far western end of the island.

CHAPTER TWO

September 2017
Tortola, British Virgin Islands

"There it is. Still standing. At least some of it."

Tucker looked dubiously in the direction Flush pointed. Above the harbor, the remains of a bright yellow cottage clung to the steep hillside; it was the only shining spot of color in the defoliated landscape.

"You think your friend is there? She must have evacuated." He wondered how they would even get to shore, let alone up to the house.

"Well, we're going there whether she's home or not. Head towards that inlet."

Tying the dinghy off to the one remaining post of what had once been a private dock, Tucker and Flush waded ashore just as the morning sun crested the top of the ridge. Almost immediately, beads of perspiration appeared on Flush's forehead.

"Feels like it's gonna be a hot one. Let's go. Maybe Maggie will give us breakfast."

A vision of bacon and eggs made Tucker's taste buds tingle even though he doubted the reality of a post-Irma breakfast would include actual cooked food.

Tucker followed Flush along what must have once been a path until they emerged onto a crumbling asphalt road. "This way." They turned right, going uphill, stopping almost immediately to negotiate an electric line that hung across their route, suspended at a crazy angle from a splintered pole. As the incline grew steeper, Flush began breathing heavily and motioned that he needed to rest. While he waited, Tucker gazed back in the direction from which they'd come.

The view out over the Caribbean Sea was breathtaking and expansive, turquoise waters, sapphire sky... in the distance he could see St. John and what he thought was probably St. Thomas. On a normal morning it would have been a vista worth hiking for, but right now he was A) hungry and B) itchy, and C) totally annoyed that he had no idea what the future held for him and that he was letting it be decided by some criminal buffoon.

Relax, he told himself, closing his eyes and tuning into the sounds around him. Somewhere in the near vicinity a generator was running, echoed by another one farther away, and maybe even another down by the harbor. In its current mutation, life was still going on.

"Ready." Flush's abrupt gasp did not sound like he was prepared to continue climbing but he seemed determined to reach their goal.

"You sure?"

"Of course. Just out of shape from a few months of no exercise. Not far now."

The corner of the yellow house came into view; as they approached, the extent of the devastation became clearer. Although the main frame of the structure seemed sound, the metal roof had collapsed on one side over a porch which hung precariously from the edge of the building. Broken beams, shingles and decking all seemed like an avalanche waiting to happen. On the opposite side of the cottage, the outside door had blown off its hinges and was now wedged against a bare tree trunk. The open frame was covered with a piece of black plastic, making the façade appear as ominous as a Halloween mask. A pair of brown chickens pecked in the dirt below the steps.

"Look at the door. And the chickens. Those are good signs," Flush declared before cupping his hands around his mouth and calling, "Maggie! Magsters! Hello? Anybody home?"

A few seconds later a woman's face peered cautiously out from behind the plastic curtain. "Flush Royal? What the hell – I've been worried sick about you!" As she flew at them, wrapping herself around Flush, Tucker saw only a flash image of her – bobbing corn-rowed pigtails in a stark mix of salt and pepper shades, large round black glasses, oversized denim overalls a red tank top, bouncing beads and jangling earrings. A small black dog ran enthusiastically in a circle around her legs. "I thought you might drown or starve to death in that place. How'd you get out? Is it legit? And how'd you get here?"

She stepped back, noticing Tucker for the first time. "And who's this sweet young thing? Don't tell me he was in there with you!" Without waiting for any answers, Maggie enfolded Tucker in a hug. His senses felt immediately dazzled by her soft warmth and the faint smell of sweat mixed with patchouli oil.

"Uh, no, not exactly." Flush looked around, suddenly nervous. "Anybody else here?"

"Just Boo and Betts." She patted the dog's head and waved a hand. "Betts is probably hiding under the house. She's been pretty spooked since the storm. And I managed to save half a dozen of my girls. The garden's gone but at least I've got fresh eggs."

"You rode it out up here by yourself?" Flush's amazement echoed Tucker's thoughts.

"I wasn't going to lose everything I had to some breezy girl named Irma. I put my soul into this place. And now just fixing it back up will take the rest of my lifetime. Sweet Jesus, I'm so glad to see you alive and well. You two must be ravenous. Let me cook you up some omelets while you tell me your survival story. I'm so happy you boys are here!"

She'd actually said the word "cook." At that moment Tucker would have followed Maggie anywhere on earth.

Per Maggie's instruction, they carried chairs and a small wooden table out onto the cleared path in front of the doorway, while she prepared the food on her propane-fueled kitchen range. With the door and a few of the windows covered with black plastic, the interior of the bungalow was damp and dark and beginning to smell like mold. She gave

Tucker a bucket and sent him up to an old cement cistern set into the hillside above the house to get some water, half of which she poured into a pot on the stove before giving the remainder back to him.

"That's for you to wash up with." She pointed him towards an outside showering area where he found a bar of soap and a not very clean towel and promptly stripped off his clothes. After months of living on a sailboat, it was easy for him to bathe with a gallon of water; he'd made do with much less at times.

They finally all sat down together in the shade of the house to eat, using real forks and china plates. Tucker thought it was the most civilized meal he'd eaten in weeks, even if it was just eggs and pancakes. He tried not to wolf it down, wanting this unreal instant in time to last longer than a few mouthfuls.

"Now explain it all to me," Maggie prompted as she leaned back in her chair and sipped a mug of black coffee. "How you got away."

Flush glanced at Tucker who shrugged and grinned shyly. "You think I hadn't figured it out by now? It was the biggest news on the island yesterday. You're kind of a celebrity."

Flush actually appeared briefly embarrassed. "Just so you know, I was framed. Apparently it's guilty until proven innocent in this uncivilized backwater. Who knows if I would have rotted in that cell block waiting for a fair trial? I'm sure that shithead Tiburon bribed some official to keep me there for at least a month to get me out of the way." The redness of his face morphed into anger as he turned to Maggie. "Where is that fucker, anyway?"

"No one has seen him since the day he turned you in. You didn't think I would let him stay here after that, did you?"

"Well, he has a way with women... Fucking asshole Casanova..."

"Give me some credit, Flush. I hadn't spoken to him for months before that even. And I don't want anything to do with that business of his. We're finished."

Tucker didn't want this almost normal moment to dissolve into what now sounded, improbably, like a lover's quarrel. He held his breath as the two of them stared each other down until Flush leaned forward, suddenly all business.

"Okay, okay. Let's not talk about that. So, Magsters...what about the boat? Did it survive?"

"My boat, you mean? The one he left me after he took mine in exchange for my poker debt?" Maggie's expression was inscrutable and Tucker couldn't tell if she was kidding or not.

"It can still be yours – I just need to borrow it back for a while. Stoney here is going to sail me to Culebra and then he can bring it home to you." He reached across the table and grabbed her hand. "Come on, Maggie, don't be like that. These are trying times and unique circumstances. "

When she still did not respond, he stroked the top of her forefinger in a small gesture so intimate that Tucker felt he had to avert his eyes. He stood up awkwardly, and began collecting the dishes. Without breaking her gaze with Flush, Maggie said, "Let me show you how we do the washing up now, Stoney. And I think you boys have some work to do around here if you want to use my boat."

"So it made it through the storm?" Flush closed his eyes. "Please say yes."

Whoever's sailboat it was, Nico Tico II had weathered Irma way better than most of the others they'd seen. At only twenty-seven feet long, it was a compact craft designed for one person or a very cozy couple. Tucker was sure he could handle it alone, with minimal help from Flush. The engine started hard and sputtered for a while and some water had to be bailed out of the cockpit, but there was no serious damage. Tucker would have opted for spending the night on board if Maggie hadn't promised dinner when they returned.

"It wouldn't be a bad idea if you slept here. Keep the thieves and pirates at bay."

Tucker bit his tongue to not say what he was really thinking. He knew that A) Flush himself had done the very same thing to the boats in Paraquito Bay, B) Flush really just wanted some time alone with Maggie, and C) he was sure there was something else Flush wanted to do without him being around.

"Not sure I could negotiate the way after dark. And besides, I promised Maggie I would haul water for her."

"That your boat?"

Simultaneously they whirled around, startled by the unexpected company. "Shit. See what I mean?" Flush murmured.

A grizzled sailor stood on the shore watching them, an astonishingly clean white captain's cap pulled down low over his eyes, a week's worth of beard covering the rest of his features.

"Yeah, what of it?" Tucker assumed a defiant stance.

"Well, you have heard about Maria, right?"

"Maria?" Flush scrunched up his cheeks, apparently trying to put a face to the name.

"The next hurricane. Building up steam right now in the Atlantic, could hit us next week. Just thought you ought to know."

The idea of another storm sweeping across the already ravaged island seemed so implausible that Tucker snorted aloud. "Right. And you know this how?"

"Heard it on the radio. Gotta be prepared, don't'cha know..."

Tucker now recognized his accent as something strong and New England-ish, probably Maine or Boston. "So what do you think we should do?"

"Listen to the news if you can. Stay informed. Bring her in tight and tie her down good."

"Batten down the hatches, yeah, yeah. Thanks, buddy." Flush turned away dismissively. "We'll keep our ears peeled."

But Tucker felt his chest tighten as he watched the man amble slowly away. He couldn't go through another hurricane. He just couldn't.

Maggie took the batteries out of her big flashlight so that Tucker could put them in the old portable radio. "You know how to use this, right?" she asked, pulling up the rusted metal antenna.

He wouldn't admit that he'd never actually seen one before. Flicking the power switch and turning the knobs, he was rewarded with the sound of static and then the scratchy sound of someone singing a Spanish pop song.

"Music to my ears!" Flush grabbed Maggie around the waist and made a grinding hip motion that he apparently thought was a sexy dance move.

"Flush, quit that. We're doing something important here." She swatted at him. "Go to the bottom of the dial, Stoney, you might find some news there."

When he finally tuned in the weather report, they all gathered around the radio, like a family during a wartime newscast. The prospect of another hurricane heading in their direction replaced the party atmosphere with an impending sense of doom and gloom.

"Oh my god, what am I going to do. I don't even have a door." Maggie's shoulders sagged as she surveyed the yard.

"We can put it back on and nail some boards over it, can't we? Secure it in place. I'll help you." Tucker's offer sounded feeble despite its sincerity.

"It could change course, don't make any assumptions yet." Flush forced the cheer back into his voice. "You know how these storms can veer at the last minute. But in the meantime, we need to get our show on the road, so to speak, kid. We've got to sail out of here as soon as possible."

It was not a choice that Tucker had ever imagined he would have to make in his life. Part of him would much rather stay here working for Maggie, keeping busy with all that needed to be done. In the last few years, he'd learned that throwing himself into hard labor and staying occupied was the best thing he could do to keep from thinking. Much as he loved sailing, there were long hours when there was nothing to keep his mind occupied or to stop his memory from remembering.

Flush switched the radio back to the music and the three of them sat silently listening to the repetitive beat and unintelligible lyrics. Finally Maggie leaped up. "We've got to have dinner soon – it's too hard to clean up after dark. Stoney, can you get a couple of buckets of water, and Flush, I need you to make a bed for Stoney on the couch – you know where the sheets are."

Tucker started to protest that he didn't need sheets, but decided against it. He would take what he could get – it might help him make a better decision.

Dark clouds had been gathering overhead and by the time he finished the second water run, a sudden rainsquall soaked him through as he ran towards the house. Stripping off his T-shirt, he used it to dry his face and hair and peered around the dim interior. He could see Maggie stirring a pot on the stove, some open cans on the counter, the whole kitchen lit by a single kerosene lantern. The couch still had a pile of old magazines covering one end of it; he knew by now that Flush was not very good at following instructions. As Tucker started to clear away the clutter, he heard Flush clumsily making his way down a narrow wooden staircase that led to the second floor.

"Here. In case you were thinking that staying looked better than going." He was holding out a wrinkled white envelope.

"What's this?" But as soon as Tucker held it in his hand he knew.

"Half of what I promised you. Other half on delivering me safely to Culebra."

"Ummm, I'm not ..."

"That's five thousand dollars there, boy. And don't act like you don't need it – I've seen what's in your wallet. Yes, while you were sleeping last night." Flush dropped an armload of pillows and bedding onto the coffee table. "And don't worry, you won't be that comfortable. That couch is a pisser on your back."

When the headboard started to bang against the wall upstairs, Tucker undid a corner of the black plastic and slid outside into the night. He didn't want to listen to some old people having sex. A) It made him think of his mother and the lumberjack boyfriend she had when he was younger, B) it reminded him of what he missed most about being with Chloe and C) it didn't seem fair that Flush was getting some when he himself hadn't been with anyone for almost a year.

Since Chloe had abandoned him in Greece, he had not had another relationship. First there was the low self-esteem thing and then there was the depression, which led to lack of desire and a decreased confidence in his social abilities. Chloe had been the leader, strong and sure of herself, the instigator of everything. After the debacle had happened with Myles in Istanbul and Tucker had finally chosen to strike out on his own with the sailing gig, it had seized up the engine of their lovemaking. He knew he was losing her, and his attempts as the initiator always seemed clumsy and wrong. She'd been his first and only girlfriend, and the devastation had been so extreme that he had not wanted to do it again. Since then he had been more terrified by than attracted to the handful of women who had come on to him.

The idea of being on Culebra again, where it had all started, nauseated him. But then he felt the bulky wad of bills in his pocket. He didn't have to stay. He could just drop Flush off and come back; it wouldn't take more than three or four days. And if necessary he could arrange a date to sail back and pick him up.

30

The night air was heavy and humid. Tucker tilted his head back towards the house, straining to hear if there was still a racket going on. Satisfied by the silence, he slipped quietly back to his bed on the couch. Which felt perfectly fine to him.

The next couple of days were the best in a long time for Tucker. They were a dysfunctional family unit, thrown together by a unique set of circumstances – working and living, sharing the challenges and triumphs of a brave new existence.

On the second morning, when Flush questioned what had happened to Maggie's car, she pointed down the driveway to where not just one, but two palm trees had fallen on the rag-top four-wheel drive Suzuki Tracker, crushing it and virtually obscuring it from view. On closer observation, the frame and the engine appeared to be intact and amazingly all four tires still had air in them.

"It might run if we can get those suckers off. You still got that chain saw?"

Turned out that Flush knew a little about making funky equipment run, although, as always, he seemed to get distracted and run out of steam pretty quickly. However, with Tucker's youthful strength and stamina, they managed to get the saw operating.

"Do you think this is even worth it?" he asked.

"Only one way to find out. Soon enough Maggie's going to need a way to get to town – especially now that she's feeding and provisioning us."

"How far is the store from here?"

"Far enough that you don't want to have to walk back hauling all kinds of stuff unless there's no other option." As usual, Flush was sweating profusely in the relentless sun. "Now I hope you know how to run that thing. Because I've got to take a break."

Tucker actually had learned to use a chain saw when he was in high school; cutting and stacking firewood had been one of his teenage chores when he stayed at his father's house. But sawing up fallen palm trees resting on dented metal was not exactly the same as bucking up a cord of maple.

An hour later he'd managed to get into the driver's seat and was pleased to see the key was in the ignition. Clearing the debris away from the gas pedal, he said a prayer and gingerly turned the engine over. Against all odds it started right up. As he gave it some gas, he could hear cheers erupting from the house.

It was only a partial success. There was still the rest of the driveway to clear.

For the next two nights he was too tired to think about anything or hear what else went on in the little bungalow. But it was a good kind of exhaustion; every accomplishment was a small celebration. When eventually the wreckage of the Suzuki actually made it down to the road, Flush collapsed onto the pile of palm trunk wood as Maggie and Tucker drove off, one of the back fenders clanging noisily. There had only been room for one passenger; the back was unusable and any available space was needed to pile up whatever she was able to buy. It had also been determined unsafe for Flush to venture out into the world at large.

They returned shortly before dark with several gallon jugs of drinking water and a strange assortment of groceries, mostly the kind of food that nobody wanted like jalapeno-flavored tuna and cream of celery soup. Nearly a week after Irma, there was virtually nothing available in the store that was worth eating. Maggie had managed to score a government surplus bag of rice and Tucker had collected several of the barely edible MREs that other people were giving away. Then he had waited in line for two hours for a two gallon can of gasoline for the Nico Tico II, paying a scalper's price, while Maggie scored a couple of blue tarps that were being given out to all residents. There was definitely no alcohol to be had anywhere on the island. Hot and sweaty, Tucker was happy to be back in their isolated perch on the hillside, away from the dismal insanity that had become daily island life. He was looking forward to stripping off his clothes and dumping a bucket of well water over his head.

"And there are two pieces of big news. One of them is you, Mr. Royal." Maggie poked a finger into Flush's hairy chest before handing him a heavy sack to carry to the house. "Nearly all the other escapees have been recaptured. With the noted exception of a few."

Flush bowed low, like a celebrity. "And the other news?"

"Maria. She's headed this way. And she might be bigger than Irma."

The next day was all about the boat. Half a dozen times, Tucker tried to convince Flush that they shouldn't go, but he was a man on a mission. By nightfall, he had doubled and then tripled Tucker's commission.

"So who really owns this boat?" Tucker asked after his final equipment check. The only thing that was a total loss was the rubber Zodiac so, against Tucker's better instincts, they were bringing the "borrowed" dingy with them.

"I'll tell you that after you tell me about your marriage." Flush could be incredibly juvenile at times.

"There's not much to tell. You know I haven't lived that long."

"So why'd she leave a catch like you?"

"She..." He'd never said it aloud. No one had ever asked him before.

"Come on, I gotta know your secrets if you know mine."

It was such stupid reasoning and yet Tucker found himself blurting the truth. "She was pregnant."

"What?! That doesn't make any sense."

"I didn't want her to have it. We weren't ready for that. I wasn't." He didn't realize he was crying until a big snorting sob came out of his nose, surprising both of them. Flush had clearly not been expecting or wanting a confession of this level and quickly suggested that they head back to Maggie's before the sun went down.

"You're going to need a good night's rest so that we can get out of here by daybreak." Neither of them spoke on the dinghy ride back to the non-existent dock or on the climb up the path.

"Now you boys just head directly to Puerto Rico, okay? They say that St. John is as bad as here. And that there is rioting and looting on St. Thomas." Maggie folded Tucker into a big motherly hug.

"You're just telling us this now? At five o'clock in the morning?" Flush demanded nervously.

"I didn't want you to worry. And Tucker, don't even think of coming back until after Maria has passed. Apparently Puerto Rico survived Irma way better than we did, you'll be fine on Culebra. I believe you are going to a better place. Oh, and if you can, bring me back some vodka."

Tucker hesitated, still ready to ditch the whole adventure. The reports they were hearing about Hurricane Maria said it could possibly reach a Category 5 and it was traveling directly towards the Virgins.

"A better place, you heard the lady. Let's go before I start singing hymns. Maggie..." Flush grazed her lips with his. "I'll be in touch. Thanks for this."

Loaded down with heavy backpacks and tote bags, Flush and Tucker walked down the path under the gathering light of dawn.

The sun rose over a placid sea as they moved slowly away from Tortola and approached the narrow strait between the British and American Virgin Islands. The air was so still that it was difficult to catch a decent wind and hard to imagine that any kind of major weather event was on its way.

"Calm before the storm."

Tucker did not respond to Flush's comment. Flush seemed way too relaxed for the unknown endings of what lay ahead of them. Instead he gazed out at the ruined landscape of St. John, less than a kilometer away, close enough to make out the broken buildings and missing foliage of what Tucker knew had been a cherished national park island.

As he became familiar with how the small sailboat handled, he was able to settle back and almost enjoy the journey. If there had not been the impending urgency of the approaching hurricane, it could have been the perfect day in paradise.

Their progress was slower than expected and by midday they were just passing south of Charlotte Amalie, the capitol of St. Thomas. From their distant vantage point, they were unable to see much of the destruction, but Tucker was suddenly struck by a vivid memory of what the port had looked like when he and Chloe had been there a few years ago.

"The cruise ships..."

"What cruise ships?" asked Flush, peering in the same direction.

"There are none. When I was here before there were like twenty." He remembered how they dominated the skyline, like floating skyscrapers, and how visible they had been from miles away.

"So you've been here before then?"

"Yeah. So?"

"Listen, we got hours ahead of us, kid. You gotta lose the attitude. AND learn to make some conversation. Why? Because I'm bored and gonna bug the shit out of you if you don't. Seriously, you know by now I can hold a lethal dialogue with myself."

Tucker had to laugh. "True dat. And I'm sick of hearing you talk to yourself. So what do you want to know?"

"I don't know. Tell me about when you were here before. Start the story anywhere." Flush leaned back against the outside of the cabin and tipped a half empty water bottle up to his mouth. "I'm pretending this is whiskey..."

"Chloe and I were hitchhiking our way to Mustique. On boats. We were here with a Norwegian couple. It was my first time sailing." He hadn't let himself think about that adventure in the last year and now he had to stop, overcome with emotion.

Flush's posture straightened and he lowered his sunglasses to stare at Tucker with interest. "Well, don't stop now, boy. My curiosity is piqued."

"It's a long story."

"And we've got hours to kill."

So Tucker talked.

Despite his best efforts, it became obvious they weren't going to make Culebra by nightfall. "I'm going to bring us into Tortuga Bay on Culebrita. It's a good quiet anchorage for the night."

" Wait – didn't you just tell me a tale about this place? Isn't this the island where you hit up the Norwegians for a ride with a fake sob story about being abandoned by a snorkeling tour?"

"You're pretty sharp for an old guy, Flush. Now get off your ass and get the anchor ready to drop when I say so," Tucker commanded with more authority than he felt.

"Aye, aye, captain."

Between the anxiety of safely mooring the boat and the overwhelming flood of memories, Tucker could not enjoy the beauty of his surroundings for several moments. The pristine crescent of white sand and turquoise waters of the popular daytripping destination were as exquisite as they had been on his first visit – the only difference was the absence of foliage in the trees and bushes on the hillside leading up to the ancient lighthouse.

"Playa Tortuga – Turtle Beach. How appropriate." For a moment something dark passed across Flush's face, but then he quickly returned to his usual nonchalance. Yeah, I can see that this would be the perfect place to get romantic with a lady friend. Too bad we don't have any women with us." As usual, Flush's inappropriate comment broke the spell. "So what are we doing for dinner and our evening entertainment? More cooked rice and a few hands of Truth-or-Dare Texas Hold'em?"

Despite the sparseness of the rations and the sunburn on their arms, it almost felt like an enjoyable night on a pleasure cruise. "Shit, you're either damn good or fuckin' lucky. What do you want to know?"

"Your whole story, man. Like what'd you do to piss off this Tiburon guy so bad that he got you locked up. Where'd all that money at Maggie's come from, and what we're really going to Culebra for."

"Hey, hey, hey. You only get one question per win. Pick one."

"What about Tiburon?" Tucker shuffled the cards and dealt a new hand.

"He's an asshole who wanted me out of the way for multiple reasons. For a while we were, uh, business partners." Flush picked up his cards.

"In what business?"

"Uh uh uh! You have to win another hand to learn that one."

Over the next hour, Tucker attempted to piece together the puzzle that was Flush's history. The only thing that was certain was that he was a master at evasion. There was a lot about winning money at poker, and some about losing it as well. There were some shady enterprises, a few that had ended with untimely deaths of associates, and a number that involved "treasure hunting."

"Treasure? Like deep sea or the buried kind?"

"Treasure is a matter of opinion, Stoney. Means something different to everybody," was the unsatisfactory cryptic reply.

The only thing he was definitive about was "that asshole Tiburon," who was not only scooping him on the deal of a lifetime but somehow figured in Maggie's past life and who thought that Flush and Maggie were an item (which, to Tucker's surprise and disbelief, apparently they were not). At a card game a few months earlier, Tiburon had gotten Flush totally wasted on some "super killer weed and other shit" and then proceeded to fleece him of everything he owned. When Flush threatened to expose Tiburon's illegal business as retribution, he dumped Flush's passed-out body on the steps of the customs house with a backpack full of illegal substances ("That I'd never seen before in my life!") and then called the police to tell them.

"Yeah, okay. So I get this part." By now they'd abandoned all pretenses of playing cards. "But what does Culebra have to do with any of this?"

"Better if I don't tell you the details. The less you know, the better, and all that. I already told you before how much it's worth. And now I'm going to bed." Flush staggered to his feet and moved unsteadily to the back of the boat to relieve himself.

"You need to tell me. You've made me an accomplice now."

Flush snorted and coughed. "Accomplice? Hardly. You're my well-paid chauffeur." The boat rocked gently and he lurched toward the hatchway. "Now this not-drunken-at-all sailor is turning in for the night."

"Come on, I'm more to you now than an employee," Tucker called after him. "In fact, I'm in control, I'm your captain."

He grinned to himself in the silence that followed. He felt almost normal – he hadn't made a list in his head all night.

Neither of them complained about having to share the double bed in the fore part of the cabin; for Tucker it was the most comfortable place he'd slept in weeks, even if he had to endure Flush's snoring.

But the momentary security ended when he was awakened in the early morning hours by a loud clanging of chains and the thudding slap of waves against the hull. When he sat up in the semi-darkness he could feel immediately that the craft was rolling much more aggressively than it had been when he dozed off and his heart began to pound wildly.

"Flush, wake up. We gotta get ready to go."

"Huh? Isn't it still night?"

"She's coming. Maria. Get up. Now." Tucker began pulling his clothes on with shaking hands, but Flush stayed prone, not moving. "What the fuck are you doing?"

"Well, I was trying to make an inappropriate joke about getting it up because Maria is coming, but I guess I'll save it for another time." He hacked out a rusty cough before heaving himself to a sitting position. "So I guess coffee is out of the question?"

Getting out of the bay was way harder than coming in had been and Tucker did not want to think how close they came to bashing against the coral reefs. Unlike the previous day, the sail pulled taut and the Nico Tico II heeled hard into the wind. In a short amount of time, they covered the remaining few miles that took them along the west coast of Culebra to the mouth of the Ensenada Honda. The seas were seriously rough now and Flush's pallor had become an unhealthy shade of green. Tucker, on the other hand, suddenly felt more alive than he had in months.

As they rapidly approached the familiar harbor, the absence of any other boats became sharply apparent. Tucker had no clue where or how they were going to shelter from the storm. Seemingly out of nowhere, a fishing boat was suddenly bearing down on them and rapidly pulling alongside, the bearded and wild-eyed occupant waving an arm at them and yelling.

"What the hell are you doing out here?" The man's silver hair blew around his head like a rain cloud. "Get your sails down and head for the mangroves now!"

"Where?" Tucker shouted back at him.

"Follow me!" The motor of the sailboat could not keep up with the powerful engine, but Tucker could see where he was leading them. To the east, the skies were beginning to darken ominously, but Tucker kept his eyes on the fishing boat. The stranger pointed to an estuary that looked shallow and not traversable. He waved his arm to indicate that this was where they should enter; then he sped away, leaving them rocking in a wide wake behind him.

Tucker slowed their speed to a crawl and guided the boat into a narrow waterway between the gnarled roots of the leafless mangrove trees, which soon scraped the sides and bottoms of the hull. Ahead, deeper into the landscape, he could see another boat tied off on all sides in preparation for the storm.

"Careful," Flush warned.

"Do you think I'm trying to be reckless?" he snapped back. "We need to get as far inland as possible but not too close to that other boat. And go find all the ropes and lines we've got on board."

When there was no response, Tucker dared a look over his shoulder. Flush was doubled up over the side of the deck, puking into the water below.

With an ominous scratching sound, the Nico Tico came to a halt, unable to float any further. So this was it, he thought, but then realized there was no pausing for reflection. He grabbed a coiled length of yellow nylon rope and headed for the prow. It was time to get ready for Maria.

CHAPTER THREE

July 2018
West Jordan, Vermont

"Lucy's gone missing, you know." Chloe did not look away from the computer screen as she called to Tyler in the next room.

"What does that mean? Were we looking for her?" Tyler poked his head into the office, the usual tone of annoyance coming into his voice when Lucy became the topic of conversation. His long-ago ex-girlfriend was Tucker's mother, and the grandmother of the fifteen-month-old twins, Artemis and Athena. Lucy had basically checked out of their lives when Chloe returned home pregnant, without Tucker, and clearly in love with Tucker's best friend, Myles. Not only had Chloe "stolen her son," but then she had abandoned him on a Greek island; there was generally nothing but bad blood between the two women.

In fact, Lucy had been angry since the moment, more than three years earlier, when Tyler and Tucker had arrived home from Culebra with Chloe in tow. When she had not accepted that her sixteen-year-old son was having a relationship with a girl who was almost eighteen, Tucker refused to have anything more to do with his mother; he'd given up on his college-bound future to move into the treehouse in Tyler's backyard with his new girlfriend. Since then, being furious at all of them seemed to be the main obsession in Lucy's life.

"Well, George stays in touch with her. Sends her photos of the babies, thinks she will eventually warm up to her granddaughters, now that they are starting to look so much like their father. George even stops in to see her sometimes when he goes to Burlington."

"Does he really? Well, he's a better person than we are." Tyler always had guilt about not doing the right thing as a parent and now he wondered if keeping in regular contact with his son's mother was another benchmark he had missed.

"We know George is better at parenting than you — that's why he's our nanny. He's the one who's going to be sad when the girls are off to daycare in a few months." Chloe smacked the Enter key with her pinkie finger. "There. The newspaper is off to the printers." She twirled the desk chair around to face him, tugging at the frayed hem of very short cut-off jeans and extending her long legs, which were now a rich golden tan from afternoons spent with the babies at the riverside in the summer sun.

"So quickly tell me about Lucy. I am trying to pack up here. My flight is tomorrow." He impatiently displayed his armload of washed and folded T-shirts.

"It's not that short a story." She waved a hand at the other chair in the room before tucking a stray lock of dark hair up into the bun on her head.

Reluctantly Tyler perched on the edge of the seat and waited for her to go on.

"George sent Lucy those super-cute pix of Artemis and Athena in those little dresses that Myles brought back for them from New Orleans, I mean how could you not comment on those, I don't care how much of a witch you are." Chloe's language reminded Tyler of how young she really was, despite what she'd been through. "So when she didn't respond to his texts, he tried emailing and even calling."

"And..."

"Nothing. No response. So he stopped at her place when he made the run to Trader Joe's in Burlington this past weekend and one of the neighbors said they hadn't seen her in weeks."

"So? Maybe she's on vacation." Tyler did not even want to think about Lucy. He was preoccupied with the mission he was about to embark on, traveling to the British Virgin

Islands to start tracking down Tucker, his missing son (and Lucy's, for that matter), as well as the father of Chloe's twins. It was just like Lucy to try and grab all the attention for herself.

"Well, George is pretty thorough when it comes to details. He tried calling her office on Monday morning to see if he could contact her there and find out what was up. And so here's the kicker…" she paused dramatically, but then quickly took up the tale again. "Turns out she was *fired* three months ago."

"Fired? But she started the organization. The CEO, or whatever she was, can't be fired." Even as he said it, he knew it probably wasn't true.

"Apparently they can be – that's why there's a board." She tried not to sound too triumphant as she turned back to the computer and typed a few strokes. "So I did a search on it and found a news article from back in April. When I was gone." Her gaze dropped for a moment and Tyler held his breath, hoping she wasn't about to have a flashback.

"I guess we were a little preoccupied at that time. With finding you. What is it with this family and disappearing? Let me see that." The range of vision in his glasses prescription no longer allowed for reading over someone's shoulder so he dragged his chair over next to hers to look at the words on the screen.

"Is that big enough for you to see, grandpa?" Chloe zoomed in on the print.

"Shut the fuck up, girlfriend." Tyler was used to Chloe's teasing him about his aging body parts and their sparring banter was affectionate in a father/daughter-in-law way.

"Shut the fuck up is right – wait till you read this. I guess Lucy was having a torrid affair with one of the directors on her board, he was a Vermont state rep and his wife publicly busted them before she filed for divorce, trying to ruin his future and Lucy's. The board asked Lucy to step down and then when she refused, they had to forcibly dismiss her and even escort her out of the building. Hard to imagine, isn't it?"

"I guess I don't have to read it now. Thanks for the synopsis. Which part can't you picture?"

"Mostly the idea of some political suit getting hot and heavy with the dragon mother-in-law." Chloe made a face.

"Then I guess you don't know Lucy like I do. Or did. " A memory of a bold young woman with long, wild red hair unafraid of dangerous journalism in foreign countries came to mind, one who had left him in her wake to follow a has-been rock star into more perilous adventures than she ever anticipated.

"Yeah but that was when she was young. Now she's an old–"

"Don't say it," he warned. "Look, Lucy was intrepid back in the day. She survived some pretty intense situations. I can't be worried about her right now. I need to concentrate on the son I haven't heard from in more than a year and a half." He knew this was a touchy situation – Chloe was no longer in love with Tucker and didn't want him coming home, and chances were good that Tucker wasn't interested in seeing Chloe either. But no matter how bad a parent he might have ever been, he needed to find his son and know he was all right.

On a trip to Greece the previous fall Tyler had managed to uncover the name of the yacht that Tucker had crewed on; it had left the Mediterranean the previous summer destined for the British Virgin Islands. With the advent of not one but two hurricanes, he had not been able to learn anything else about the Second Wind or his son's current whereabouts. Now that he had finally sold the Jordan Times newspaper business to George and installed Chloe at the administrative helm, Tyler could take off a chunk of time and put his former investigative journalist skills to use pursuing the mystery of Tucker's disappearance.

"Shit, what time is it?" Chloe leaped to her feet. "I have to go get the girls. Myles took them over to the inn this morning so his sisters could babysit. Thank god there are so many people in West Jordan to help us look after them."

With a few fast and furious motions, Chloe was gone in a forcible whirlwind of activity, self-designed to keep her addictions at bay. He hoped she could stay clean while he was away – it was the main thing he worried about these days. George and Myles would be here to support her, but she still had some very fragile moments.

As he walked down the hall towards his bedroom, he caught sight of an old man coming towards him, and was as startled as ever to realize he was seeing himself in the mirror. His gray curls, bifocal glasses and deeply creased features never failed to surprise him; he just felt so much younger on the inside, it was hard to reconcile how the years had caught up with him physically.

There had been a time when he had taken pains to dress smartly, get expensive haircuts and put some care into his appearance, but that had been decades ago, and at one point had even been superseded by a serious bout of self-neglect, shaggy beardedness and ragged clothing. Now he just preferred not to see his reflection so that he could keep up the delusion that he was still the attractive male he once was. These days he only used his charismatic charm when he had to; it was so much easier to just not relate to people unless necessary.

As he packed his suitcase, he found his thoughts kept drifting back to Lucy. Generally he avoided interaction with her because it always ended up in some kind of confrontation, but he still felt bad for her. Tucker had been her world for years and then she had thrown all her energy into starting a nonprofit that did some kind of work with setting up women in businesses in impoverished Third World villages and then importing their products for sale online. It seemed like selfless work, but somehow Lucy had managed to turn it into a show that headlined her as the star, a five-foot tall dynamo defined by startlingly white curly locks that framed her round face and hung down her back. Most people were enchanted by her looks until they got to know her fiery personality.

Tyler was surprised that they hadn't heard about her downfall sooner, but her ego had probably been so bruised, she didn't want to admit failure. No, more likely she'd just been mad. He wondered where she'd gone off to – maybe back to England to visit her sister. She would land her on feet, she almost always did.

Myles was the one who got up and drove Tyler to the airport at three am. Conversation wasn't necessary at that time of the morning, which was good because the situation was more than a little awkward. The ongoing relationship between Myles and Chloe was indeterminate at present, but what was certain was that adding Tucker back into the mix was not going to make things any easier. The boys, who had grown up best friends, had not spoken since their infamous incident in the Istanbul hostel two summers earlier; it had been the turning point in their lives.

Of the two, Myles was more forgiving; it had been Tucker who cut things off. He was, after all, Lucy's son. Myles was a talented musician who was making waves in New Orleans right now and was anxious to get back to his newfound existence there. Still he had agreed to come home for a few months to help Chloe out with the toddlers while Tyler went off on his search for Tucker.

Myles had plugged his ipod into the radio and was quietly listening to some obscure funky blues, occasionally tapping out a rhythm on the steering wheel. Tyler watched the early sunrise over the Green Mountains, and tried not to think about the gaping void that lay ahead of him in his journey.

"Well, I hope you find him," Myles said as he turned off the interstate at the South Burlington exit. "Not sure I hope he comes back with you, but that doesn't really have to be part of the plan, right?"

"I just want to know he's alive and well, mentally and physically. That's all any parent wants to know." He did not have to add the words "yours included." Myles had left his own mother and father in the dark for more than year as to

46

his state of well-being until Tyler had located him performing in a bar in New Orleans a few months earlier.

Tyler was suddenly exhausted by the role he was playing in all these lives, but he pushed the feeling aside. He had to stay focused on the task at hand.

Twenty-four hours later he found himself hopelessly overwhelmed. Hotel rooms on Tortola were overpriced and Airbnb wasn't much better. He had rented a car to get around and considered that if he had to stay long-term, his best option would be sleeping in the back seat, even though he was too tall for it to be adequately comfortable.

It didn't take long for him to discover that Second Wind, the yacht that Tucker had crewed on, had been destroyed along with dozens of others moored in Paraquita Bay. The marina office had contacted the salvage company for confirmation; they also assured him no bodies had been recovered, which was not a question he had dared to ask.

"A lot of these yachts got pirated in the days after Irma. Stripped clean, some of them were. It was a total loss, that one. Picked bare by the time the owners arrived."

"My son was here working for them. Do you remember him?" Tyler pulled out his cell phone and showed him the most recent photo he had of Tucker, his curls tamed into a hairdo of wild-looking dreadlocks, his expression one of disdainful disinterest.

The man shook his head. "Doesn't look familiar. Their crew boy was a clean-cut loner, name of Stone." He squinted. "I don't know, it could be him. He went ashore before the hurricane and I never saw him again. Things were pretty lawless here afterwards."

"Any way I can get contact info for the owners?"

"Not allowed to give that out." He shrugged. "But like I told that other woman, you might be able to Google them."

"Other woman? What do you mean?" Tyler wiped the sweat from the back of his neck. It had been a long time since he'd experienced the summer humidity of the Caribbean.

"Just saying, you're not the first person to come here asking about the Second Wind and its crew. Sorry I can't help you out more. If I was you, I'd go show that picture around the island, maybe somebody might remember. But most people have been pretty wrapped up in their own recovery since then."

Frustrated, Tyler decided to head over to Cane Garden Bay for a swim. Despite the regrowth of foliage and greenery on Tortola, the destruction caused nine months earlier by the hurricanes was still evident everywhere. Houses stood gaping with blown out windows and missing roofs, roads were rocky and rutted, and many businesses had not reopened. He could easily have been depressed by it all if the natural beauty of the Caribbean sea and sky had not been so stunning. His earlier years of living in the Grenadines had taught him that when all else failed, diving into the water could completely change your mood.

An hour later, dripping wet, sipping an icy Carib beer at the Paradise Beach Bar, he felt infinitely better. He showed Tucker's photo to the bartender, a dark-skinned woman with an hourglass figure encased in a body-conscious, blindingly pink and white striped tank dress. She clucked her tongue sympathetically and shook her head. "Him a fine lookin' boy, I would remember such a boy with dreads like dat if him come here. What he drink?"

Tyler tilted his head quizzically not understanding the question.

"I always remember a person by what they drink. What he drink?"

"I – I don't know. He wasn't old enough to do it legally in the states when he left home to travel. He smoked a lot of pot, if that helps."

"They all do, don't they now. Him a sailor, you say? You should head on down de West End and ask around Soper's Hole. Dis a small place, you know. And smaller still since Irma. If he was here, someone will remember. But chances are he move on to a place less damaged by Irma, maybe south." She gave him a sympathetic smile, large white teeth flashing in bright contrast to the rich darkness of her skin.

They exchanged names – hers was Janice, pronounced like two words "Jan Ice," and he went on his way with a promise to come back at sunset for Happy Hour, to celebrate his successes or failures.

Despite how personal this search was, there was something about being in a strange place and not knowing who he would meet or what was going to happen that made him feel animated. Being slightly out of his comfort zone had actually always been his comfort zone.

He stopped the car by the side of the road to gaze out over the tropical landscape. The brilliance of red hibiscus, bougainvillea and other blooms were bright spots in the greenery and regrowth that now covered much of the countryside. It was hard to imagine how it must have looked after the throes of two hurricanes. He sat for a moment, wishing he was psychic; maybe then he could just sense if Tucker was still somewhere on this island. Instead he drove on to the next marina and bar.

A day became two days and then a week. Jan Ice offered him a place to sleep on her couch, an uncomfortable rattan affair with three worn-out cushions, but it saved him a lot of money and he became her most generous tipper. Her sullen and strapping boyfriend was not as pleased about Tyler's presence, even though he tried to slip in and out quietly and only passed as little time as possible there each night.

His daylight hours were spent canvassing the island, visiting various public establishments, boatyards and even the police station, where he was coldly informed that US citizens were not the priority of the BVI government and that after Irma they had more important matters to look after. "All the prisoners escaped during that time, you know," he was pointedly told. "We had a lot of crime here, yes, mon, a lot of bad tings happen."

Tyler had not heard about the prison breakout. "Did you round up the escaped convicts?" he asked interestedly.

"Not ahll a dem," was the curt reply in a broad West Indian accent.

The dozens of negative responses to Tucker's name or photo became increasingly more daunting each day. The most hopeful event was when someone was able to tell him what English village the owners of the Second Wind had been from and he had actually been able to put a phone call through to them.

"Tucker Mackenzie's father? Is he there with you? We've been trying to get a hold of him for months now." The sibilant hiss of the man's pronunciation sounded clearly upper class.

He could hear a woman's voice in the background shouting something about stones.

"No, I haven't heard from him. I was hoping he might have contacted you."

"What, no, bloody awful, the whole Irma situation. We last spoke with him the day before the hurricane. We were worried sick about him. By the time we finally got to Tortola two months later, the yacht was...well, a total loss is putting it softly, and nobody knew where he had gone."

"I'm so sorry..." Tyler wasn't sure what to say.

"If you do hear from him, Mr. Mackenzie, I'd appreciate him getting in touch with me. We have, er, a few questions for him, shall we say."

Tyler didn't really like the implications in his tone. "How was he, when you last saw him?"

"What do you mean, it's been nine months now..."

"I haven't seen him in almost two years. I'm just wondering how he seemed to you. Was he okay?"

"Yes, yes, fine boy. We were a bit surprised when... Nice, quiet, kept to himself. Did lots of puzzles. Trustworthy sort, no trouble. That's why it was rather a shock when we learned of the pillaging. But I guess, well, I don't know what to think. We've been talking to our solicitors and..." It was clear that Gus Kronenberg wasn't comfortable with this discussion and the call was soon over.

For a few moments Tyler felt some relief, until he realized that he was actually no farther along in his search than before. Not only had the Kronenbergs not seen Tucker since before the hurricane; they seemed to think he might be at some kind of fault.

It was not until two and a half days later that a man in a white sailing cap put down his beer and squinted at the photo on Tyler's phone. "You know there was a woman in here a month or so ago looking for her son also. Maybe the two of them were mates, went off together or something."

It was the second time he'd heard this now. "Really? Where was she from?"

"Don't know. Britain maybe, she was pretty snockered on gin."

Tyler recalled that the owners of Tucker's yacht had been British. "She still around?"

"Don't think so. Haven't seen her since then. A brassy sort, you know the kind, thinks everybody wants to sleep with a drunk old lady." He was still staring at the picture of Tucker, holding the phone with a gnarled, age-spotted hand. "Do feel like I've seen this boy before though. Maggie!" He called to a woman sitting at the other end of the bar, talking to a friend.

She looked up, her corn-rowed gray-streaked locks swinging as she turned her head, to stare with mild interest in their direction. Her gaze ran over Tyler without recognition and settled on the man beside him. "Cap'n Pete. Wassup?"

"Come take a look-see here at this photograph. This fellow is trying to find his missing son."

Maggie rose from her barstool, sturdy legs and Birkenstock sandals carrying her across the room, her body shape indistinguishable beneath a loose lime-green sundress. She took a pair of brightly patterned reading glasses off her head and peered at Tyler's phone. "Oh, I was expecting a small child." Then she gasped and stared up at Tyler's face and back down again. "You're Stoney's father?"

Tyler laughed hesitantly at her unexpected response. "Ummm...what?"

"Oh, my god, you look just like him. Only maybe thirty-some years older!" She seemed to be eyeing him differently now. "So you're the husband too then."

Tyler shook his head. "Sorry, but you've got me seriously confused with someone else. I'm looking for my son, Tucker Mackenzie, who was crewing on the Second Wind, which got destroyed in Hurricane Irma."

Maggie slid onto the stool next to him. "I think we're talking about the same person. I knew him as Stoney, a sweet introverted boy, maybe twenty-something? Showed up at my place after Irma with...a friend of mine. Seemed like he had a lot going on in his head but he was pretty traumatized by the storm. And by a break-up with a girlfriend, or wait – was he married to her?"

Tyler was speechless. "What...when...This guy is who you mean?"

"Well he doesn't have that hair anymore. But he's the spitting image of you." Her pleasant round face darkened slightly. "And, oh, by the way, I'm waiting for him to bring my sailboat back."

Two vodka and sodas later, Maggie had told Tyler everything she knew about "Stoney." There were a few times he was so moved by her description that he wanted to cry. Stunned and puzzled did not begin to describe how he felt when she got to the part where he sailed off to Culebra just ahead of Maria.

"Culebra? You're kidding me, right? I can't believe he would go back to Culebra."

"Well, let's just say my friend is very persuasive and made sure he was well-compensated."

"And you haven't heard from either of them since?"

She nodded grimly. "That's right. And Maria was a bitch over there in Puerto Rico. They went from the frying pan into the fire." She bit her lip. "I'm a little worried about both of them. But for other reasons."

Overcome by a wave of emotion, he found himself blinking back tears. Maggie patted his hand. "How long since you've seen him?"

"A year and nine months. But who's counting. You have any kids?"

"No, not me. Married and divorced once, but never met a man I thought would make a good father. Dogs, cats and chickens are enough to worry about. Taken in a few strays over the years, though, like your boy. Really expected to see him again; he seemed super responsible. Except, of course, for the fact that he kind of stole my boat. Well, it wasn't really my boat." A troubled expression accentuated the lines in her face.

The word "pirate" came to mind and he didn't want to believe that his son had become one. "There has to be a good reason. You didn't try to contact them?"

She snorted. "We didn't have communication services here for months after the storms. And how would I have contacted him – apparently I only knew him by some made-up name."

Tyler felt dazed, not sure how to even go on with this journey now.

"But...did he tell you about our experiences when we went to Culebra?" Images of camping on the beach, congo drumming and a purple houseboat rose to the surface, and some memories he quickly suppressed of incredible dazed and crazed sex with a madwoman.

"No, he's not much of a talker, that one." She upturned her glass and then looked sideways at him. "Unlike your angry ex-wife."

"Who? I've never been married."

"Stoney's mother? About up to here with white hair out to there?" Maggie waved her hands around demonstratively.

His jaw literally gaped open. "You know Lucy?"

53

Maggie's laugh sounded forced as she patted his hand. "Honey, she's come and gone — beat you here by at least a month. And believe me when I say nobody was sorry to see her go. Wouldn't be surprised if they named the next hurricane after that woman."

CHAPTER FOUR

June 2018
Tortola, British Virgin Islands

Lucy felt like she was in a sauna – she couldn't remember the last time she'd been so hot. Or angry. Or uncomfortable. Or as powerless to do anything about the impossible situation she was in. That was the worst part. How had her life devolved into this catastrophe... she had thought she was finally making headway, even if she had been sidetracked by a gin and tonic. Or two. Or three. Or ten.

Her brain felt like it was in a vice grip – even her cheekbones pulsed with the force of the headache she was experiencing, part hangover, part hunger and part pain, which had something to do with the back of her head connecting with the floor in the bar the previous night.

When were they coming back for her? What if she died here? Nobody even knew where she was – she didn't know where she was. Panic settled in around her heart and she tried to breathe slowly. She wouldn't cry again, she couldn't. Just a short while earlier she'd thought she might suffocate from not being able to wipe the tears from her eyes and the snot from her nostrils.

She wished she'd never left the sanctuary of her condo in Burlington. Right now she could still be sitting comfortably on her couch, filling her empty stomach with ice cream and washing it down with gin while she watched a syndicated rerun of *Friends*. Instead she was literally immobilized in tropical hell at the mercy of people she'd never met until yesterday.

She'd thought nothing could be worse than the mess she'd made of her life this past spring. But she'd been so wrong. And now she had endless hours to reflect on it...

Lucy had never known depression before, not even during the gloomier periods in her life. She'd always been able to refocus, find a reason for living, get back on track. But during those dark days in March, after she'd been marched out of her own office with a single box of personal belongings, humiliatingly accompanied by the police, she'd sunk to murky depths she'd never known existed in her own soul.

For a short while anger and hatred fueled her spirit enough to get up in the morning and fume around her apartment, drinking coffee and making plans for revenge. She sent dozens of texts to Albie, expecting a sympathetic and loving response, but she never received any replies. His fucking bitch of a wife had cut him off at the knees, and then worked her way up to his balls, using his political career to castrate and hogtie him, leaving Lucy to sort out her own feelings about the abrupt end of the affair. But as the days passed she found her anger became more directed at Albie than Victoria. They'd been in love, damn it all, they'd shared everything so intimately for months and months, how could he just abandon what they'd had because of his vengeful wife? Lucy's meaningful life had turned into a television soap opera in just a matter of days.

It wasn't fair, it just wasn't. The first night she drank half a bottle of gin and ate a pint of Ben & Jerry's Cherry Garcia. The next night she finished the bottle and ate a pint of Phish Food. From there she'd moved on to consuming a quart, and soon a gallon, of ice cream each evening. She began starting the gin at noon with lunch, which usually consisted of two large bags of sour cream and onion potato chips. She varied her diet from Chunky Monkey to Chocolate Fudge Brownie to Strawberry Cheesecake ice cream and sometimes had ranch or barbecue-flavored chips instead of the usual. The gin never changed, just increased in amounts, the ration of Beefeaters to tonic getting higher.

From behind the sliding glass door that opened out onto her terrace she watched the last of the dirty snow melt and the trees get buds on their branches. Every few days she pulled on a pair of sweat pants (her leggings were too small now) and ventured out to the liquor store and the nearest convenience market. At least she lived in Vermont, where you could get Ben & Jerry's at any corner store. Her signs of success now included thighs that rubbed against each other, a stomach that stuck out farther than her breasts (which no longer fit in her bra) and how much she panted after climbing the one flight of stairs to her condo.

It was bingeing without purging, and she pushed it to the limits. There were no more "meals," it was just eating every hour. Finish one bag, start another. Never let your glass get empty. Keep the spoon in the carton, make sure the ice cream was soft enough to scoop out easily.

After three months, she'd actually managed to put on almost fifty pounds; she hadn't even achieved that when she'd been pregnant with Tucker. Wasn't there some TV show she could go on to be "The Biggest Gainer" or something like that? *"At only 5 feet and one half inch tall, Lucy Brookstone has defied the odds for Body Mass Index by gaining more than half a pound a day. She can also drink any 6 foot tall man under the table."* She took photos of herself in a string bikini, the images fueling her self-loathing, and thought about starting a blog and calling it *"Dumped by Albert Smith, State Representative,"* but that was a lot more trouble than just reaching for the remote and searching for reruns of The Price is Right.

She'd lost everything so quickly – her position, her reputation, her lover, her only son, her willpower, her sobriety, her self-respect. If she could gain nothing else, at least she could gain weight.

But at fifty-one pounds she reached some kind of plateau and that was that, she couldn't even get any fatter. She was now just an overweight, couch-potato drunk, a has-been with no friends, family or future. Outside in the world beautiful spring days were blooming into summer, but Lucy pulled the curtains and sat in the stuffy semi-darkness, wallowing in self-pity. The farthest she went was from her bed to the couch and back again – some nights she didn't even bother to do that.

One day she stubbed her toe on something hard under the coffee table and saw that it was her cell phone. It was dead - she hadn't charged it for two months. She plugged it in and waited to see what came up. Her voice mail box was full but she didn't bother to listen. Several hundred emails came rolling in– she didn't want to read any of them. She clicked on "Check All" and was about to hit the trash can icon when the most recent one automatically opened by itself, displaying a photo of two adorable toddlers with golden curls, their chubby hands waving at the camera.

"We miss you, Grandma Lucy!" read the subject line. The sender was georgethenanny802. The message read, *"Where have you been? Come see us soon! Love, Athena and Artemis."*

Athena and Artemis...her granddaughters. She had grandchildren. They were Tucker's girls. She couldn't remember the last time she'd visited them; their "birth mother" (which was how she mentally referred to Chloe) had been accepted into Tyler's home as a family member, but Lucy had never forgiven that slick bitch for stealing Tucker away from her and then leaving him high and dry and out of touch...

Tucker. Bloody hell, she missed her son so much. Not a word from him in so long. The last they'd been able to find out was that he'd sailed across the Atlantic ahead of the fall hurricane season and no one had heard from him since. Tyler had talked about going to look for Tucker in Tortola which had been the destination of the yacht Tucker had been crewing on. But as far as she knew, before she'd disappeared into her own private nightmare, Tyler had instead been working on finding Myles, Sarah's son, Tucker's best childhood friend, the one who had been there in the hospital room with Chloe, when the grandbabies were born, the one who had run away because he was a suspect in not one, but two, murders, and the one who the "birth mother" had supposedly dumped Tucker for.

58

She stared at the photo of the little girls she barely knew, who looked so much like Tucker at that age. For years it had been just her and her precious boy; they'd been everything to each other. He hadn't been much older than the twins when the two of them had fled from her abusive relationship with a self-centered rock star; they had lived on Bequia in the Grenadines for three years under the aliases of Ruby and T. It had been an idyllic and simple island existence compared to the decadent excessive lifestyle with Kip Kingsley in his gated mansion on Mustique. Her priorities had gone askew during those years when she was with Kip. She'd treated Tyler so badly, leaving him for an egotistical sadist who'd been her teenage idol when she had the chance to do a story on his rebound tour... well, she hadn't behaved much better than Chloe, now had she...

It was the first time that it had ever occurred to her that her "daughter-in-law" actually reminded her of her own younger self, and it was a disturbing realization. But Tyler had been a charismatic opportunist; they had fallen in together as two journalists in the same line of work, without making any commitments to each other. He had known what he was doing. Tucker, on the other hand, had been an innocent, sweet child, unsure of himself but with a keen intellect, easily led, a go-along guy, always eager to please.

What would he think of what she'd become? Angrily she stuffed the phone into the crack of the couch cushion next to her so she wouldn't have to see it anymore. If Tucker cared about her, he would have called or contacted her in the last year and a half. There hadn't been a word for so long, not one word. It wasn't right.

At one time, before Tucker and motherhood and Vermont, before Kip Kingsley and Mustique, she'd been the best investigative reporter in her field. Somewhere inside her was still that brazen girl detective, the one who used to scale spiky iron gates to get into hospital records at night, who impersonated a caterer to scoop a major political event, and who had eventually boldly danced topless on stage covered only by her masses of red curls to attract Kingsley's attention. It had been a dangerous assignment about another shady heavy metal band that had ultimately ended her career; when she had handed that story off to Tyler, it had been his downfall as well. Bloody hell, those had not been good years.

Opening a fresh container of Chocolate Cookie Dough ice cream, she moved to the sliding glass door and pulled back the drapes. It was a sunny afternoon and Lake Champlain shimmered in the distance. For the first time in weeks, she opened the door and stepped out onto her terrace. She needed a shower. Maybe a nice cup of tea; she couldn't remember the last time she'd had anything to drink besides gin.

And then she was going to make a plan. She was going to get her investigating mojo back. And she was going to go find Tucker.

She was far from her best self when she stepped off the little plane at the Terrance B. Lettsome International Airport on Tortola. The customs official squinted at her passport photo, comparing the younger, slimmer picture with the puffier, older reality in front of him. She held her wild, wavy white hair away from her face so he could see she was the same person. "It's been a rough few years."

"Where are you staying?"

She'd been ready for this question. "Sebastian's by the Sea." She had picked the first hotel that had come up in her browser with good reviews. She had enough money not to worry for a week or two. Tortola was a small island. She shouldn't need much more time here than that.

"Sebastian's on the Beach," was the prim correction before she received her entry stamp. It was a small detail, but Lucy knew how important details actually could be.

Within the hour she was drinking a gin and tonic, watching the sunset. At the airport gift shop, she'd purchased a long, loose-fitting sundress; it was a bright, tropical turquoise batik and covered her from neckline to ankles, which made her feel better about her newly acquired bulges. She realized she was actually smiling and could not remember the last time she'd used those muscles. A double order of fish and chips for dinner – she might be the only person who'd ever lost weight on a diet like that.

It took a few days to actually get herself into motion. It was so much easier to just lie in the sun and drink G&T's. By noon it was too hot to do anything but have another and maybe retreat to her room for a nap. In the evening she would get into the car and go over to the beach bar at Cane Garden Bay for more drinks and food. Driving on the left side of the road brought back memories of England, where she'd spent the first two-thirds of her life, when she wasn't traveling off somewhere on assignment.

Her increased appetite for food and liquor meant she was spending money like water, which made her increasingly popular on an island where the tourist economy had suffered a tremendous blow from hurricane devastation. The local regulars were beginning to recognize her, also because getting drunk in public seemed to reawaken a bawdy side of her that she'd suppressed for years. There were a couple of older men who enjoyed matching her drink for drink and who had plenty of advice when she finally brought up her real reason for visiting Tortola.

"You mean your main goal wasn't finishing off all the Beefeaters on the island? You're on an actual mission?" By this time of the evening her memory was so fogged that she did not retain introductions; she had mentally named the companion on her right "Legs" because her eyes kept straying to his tanned thighs covered in thick golden hairs. On her other side was "Captain" because of his jaunty white cap. Legs was some indeterminate middle age, sun-bleached past his prime, with a classic beer belly and a barroom laugh. Captain was a yachting enthusiast and an old proper British drunk, retired military, former sailor and recent widow.

"You don't look old enough to have a twenty year old son," Captain commented obligatorily, although they all knew it wasn't true.

Neither of them knew anything about the Second Wind but gave her an earful about which marinas to try. "You do know how many boats were trashed in Irma, don't you? Never seen anything like it, not in my time." Legs shook his head sadly. "Never going to be the same here."

"You didn't go through Hugo back in '89. Not sure which was worse. More to get destroyed this time." Captain was drinking rum and cokes and seemed to be sinking lower on his bar stool.

When Lucy found herself wondering which one of them might be the least offensive lay, she knew it must be time for her to go to bed. But bloody hell, she was famished. "Is the kitchen still open?" she asked the bartender.

She ended up settling for both a large wedge of coconut cream pie and a slice of gingerbread cake, unable to choose between the two. "You got an appetite on you, girl," said Legs. "And you can hold your liquor too. You're all right, big little mama."

Lucy felt her face burning as she ravenously consumed the desserts and washed them down with a fresh drink. Why should she be embarrassed – he was complementing her. This was who she was now, she might as well own it.

"I'm not bad in bed, either." It was a thing the old Lucy might have said in an empowered way – now it sounded like a sleazy invitation.

And right on cue she felt a hand slide under her dress and squeeze the flesh of her thigh.

When she woke up in her own room the next morning she could not remember driving home or if she had been alone. She had no idea if the sex had been good – or if there had even been any. She thought it might have happened outside the bar, maybe up against the car, but she wasn't sure. She recalled being turned on by the idea of being touched intimately right there in a public place, even if nobody was paying attention to two drunks at the end of a long night. That maybe she had even responded with a little arching motion of her hip and encouraged the fingers to crawl higher, exploring and probing her into primal excitement.

Had she even paid the bill? Did everyone on the island know she had left the bar with Legs's hand inside her underpants? No, no, she was pretty sure they had closed the place down, maybe the Captain had still been there slumped over his drink.

She staggered into the shower, hoping the water would restore her memory, but afraid at the same time. The spray felt like sharp needles attacking her sunburned shoulders and other tender places. She needed to get back on track here, get out to the marinas, look for Tucker. There was no time for more self-loathing.

"That was fun last night, mama." Legs winked at her before turning his back and resuming a conversation with another salty-looking patron.

Once again she felt that flush of embarrassment, not because of his offhand manner but mostly because she had no recollection of what the "fun" had consisted of.

"You two, uh, get it on?" The words sounded ridiculous coming out of Captain's mouth.

Lucy shrugged and resisted the urge to say "I don't know," aloud. Instead she gave the older man her full attention. "How you doing tonight? Can I buy you another?"

An hour later she'd already lost count of her own tab and was gratefully buzzed, when Captain introduced her to the manager of the marina at Paraquita Bay, explaining her plight in his eloquent accent.

"I remember your son. He was minding the ship, so to speak, waiting for parts to come in, before Irma."

Lucy gripped his arm. "You saw Tucker? Was he okay?" Her hearty party voice disappeared into a strangled whisper.

"Well, no, sorry, I don't think that was his name, but I knew that yacht and the owners. Damn shame what happened to that boat. AND to this whole island." He waved his hand demonstratively. He was a good-looking man with a serious tan and chiseled features defined by deep dimples and crow's feet. Maybe the most attractive male she'd met yet, but sexuality had just dropped out of first place on her priorities list.

"What are you drinking? Let me buy you one." Lucy caught the bartender's eye. "What's your name?" She was going to try hard not to forget this time.

Mac gave her the first hard core leads she'd had. He broke the bad news about the fate of the Second Wind and that the owners had declared her a total loss before it had been towed away on a barge full of wrecks. He had not seen their crew boy, who for some reason he called "Stone," since the storm. Lucy vowed to change her lackadaisical style and get down to some real investigating. First thing tomorrow.

Captain was suddenly up in her face, looking perplexed and thoughtful, as though he was trying to recall something. "You got a picture of your boy?"

Lucy fumbled around in her bag, looking for her phone. As usual, she'd let the battery run down again. By the time she'd dug out the charging cord and found an outlet to plug it into, the conversation had moved on to cricket scores and global warming. Nobody would notice if she ordered a large plate of chips to take the edge off her appetite until she could boot up her phone.

"Having a little snack, mama?" Legs leered rudely at her and helped himself to a few of the French fries on his way to the men's room. Lucy cursed herself for having a go last night with an ass like him and tried hard not to let this most recent fiasco get under her skin. Another drink dulled her growing irritation with his disrespectful behavior and by then she was able to turn on her cell and access a few of the photos she had of Tucker.

"That's him," Mac confirmed. "Except minus that crazy hair."

Captain frowned at the image. "I think I saw this lad a few times. But there's one person who can confirm it. Unfortunately she doesn't have cell service since the storm; she only recently got her electric back. But I'll go up to her place in the morning and see if she can come down to meet with you tomorrow night. Maggie enjoys a drink or two now and then."

He bristled a little when Lucy impulsively threw her arms around him.

Throughout the day, her mood swung dramatically from excited to depressed to nervous to overly calm. She could not believe she was meeting someone who might have current information on Tucker. He could even still be here on the island, maybe just a few miles away.

So she'd already had more than her usual number of drinks by the time she was introduced to Maggie, who seemed instantly put off by Lucy's effusive state of inebriation. Maggie's intense attitude didn't jive with her casual island woman appearance, which included a bouncy hairdo of tiny beaded braids, embroidered linen overalls and numerous bracelets.

"This is who you wanted me to meet?" she asked Captain, regarding Lucy with obvious disapproval. She leaned to speak quietly but distinctly in his ear. "You do know I make a point of avoiding tourists like her."

Even though she was beyond the stage of feeling much pain, Lucy's hackles went up. They were barely through the initial exchange before her trembling fingers dropped the phone as she held it up for the other woman to observe. Maggie's swift reaction of disgust triggered the kind of rage that had defined Lucy in her red-haired youth.

"Don't you fuckin' judge me, bitch. You don't know the pain I'm going through here." As Lucy held up the phone,

Maggie flinched and took a step back as if she was afraid Lucy was about to punch her. "This is my son who I haven't seen or heard from in nineteen months."

She could hear Maggie muttering under her breath and then stopping with a gasp. "Oh, my god. You're his mother?" Then she could not keep herself adding in a sarcastic whisper, "The poor thing."

Lucy didn't realize she'd taken a swing until she was being restrained on both sides and snarling like a lioness. The bartender was all up in her face and being stern. "Behave or you are out of here!" he hissed.

Bloody hell, she needed to pull it together. The whole room had gone silent as they watched the drama unfolding. "Sorry, sorry," she apologized to everybody. "Maggie, I think we got off on the wrong foot here."

Maggie visibly curbed whatever retort she had been about to make and pursed her lips. "Okay, let's just get this over with. Yes, I met your son. He stayed with me for a few days after Irma. I thought he was a wonderful boy. But..." she looked around, apparently weighing her words.

"But what?" Suddenly Lucy's vision blurred and she wondered if she was about to black out. Then she realized her eyes were full of tears. "You haven't seen him since then?"

"He took something that he never returned. I'm still waiting for him to come back from Culebra with it."

Lucy heard the words "come back from Culebra" but before she could even ask what the hell Maggie meant, she was consumed with fury again, but now it was fueled by a bit of jealousy. "Are you calling my boy a thief?! You bloody cunt, you..." But this time the onlookers were ready for her; at the first sign that she was about to jettison herself towards Maggie, she was suddenly on the floor, the wind knocked out of her and her arms and legs thrashing against the strong hands holding her down.

The room spun crazily around her and she struggled to fill her lungs with air. She heard derisive laughter and someone saying, "Like flipping an old turtle onto its back

66

and watching it try to get up," and a round of hilarious hooting. Her blood pressure soared so high with the humiliation that everything around her began to vibrate with red electricity.

"What do you want us to do with her, Maggie?"

Do with her? She tried to lift her head but someone grabbed her roughly by a handful of hair. As she pulled against the grip, the back of her skull slammed into the wooden planks of the floor.

She did not know how long she had been sleeping or where she was. Instead of the red aura of anger that had suffused her vision earlier, now all she could see was blue. Blue ceiling, blue walls, blue floor – it all seemed suffocatingly close. Her tongue felt huge and dry in her mouth and her cranium was pounding like a parade drum. But when she tried to sit up she found that all she could move was her head. Her wrists and ankles were tightly restrained in a way that scared her more than anything she could remember.

Fearfully she struggled to lift the upper part of her torso and managed to arch her back enough to see more of herself. She was on a sturdy canvas cot, firmly duct taped to the frame. She felt a small amount of relief at the fact that she still had her dress on, although it was dirt-streaked and torn and had ridden up above the cellulose of her thighs to expose her leopard print knickers.

She could also see now that she was in a tent, the windows and doors zipped shut, the outdoor light filtering through the nylon fabric of the walls. Did that mean it was morning? Where the fuck was she? What was happening? Why was she here?

"Hey! Hey! Help! Somebody!" Her voice was hoarse but audible. Almost instantly she heard scuffling outside and the sound of a zipper opening. Unfamiliar bloodshot eyes in a dark face peered in at her for a second before closing the tent back up again.

"Get Maggie. De bitch wake." The gruff command sent a ripple of terror through her constrained limbs and Lucy whimpered a little, too dehydrated for real tears. She licked her dry lips, for once actually wishing for water rather than gin. She swallowed hard and tried unsuccessfully to wipe her nose on her shoulder.

A few minutes later the flap was unzipped again and Maggie ducked through the opening. The peak of the tent ceiling was just barely high enough for her to stand upright in the middle. She stood at the foot of the cot, in the few remaining inches between Lucy's feet and the door, staring down at her disapprovingly. Lucy angrily held her gaze for a second before looking away.

"What goes around, comes around, you know," she croaked.

"Exactly." Maggie produced a bottle of water from the pocket of her overalls. "You're lucky I liked your son so much." With surprising gentleness, she lifted Lucy's head and held the bottle up to her lips. "Not too fast. We don't want any vomiting."

She couldn't blink back the tears as she took long slow gulps. "Why am I taped to this fucking bed?" she said at last.

"You were out of control. We thought you were going to hurt someone or even hurt yourself." Maggie sat down cross-legged on the floor of the tent. "According to your newfound BVI pals, you get so blotto on gin every day that you have no idea what you are doing sometimes. Plus it means you have to listen to me. And I need you to sober up a bit so that I know you can manage what I am going to ask you to do."

"I can manage anything!" Lucy started to argue but realized she did not have the energy. "Do you even know who I am and what I used to do?"

"I don't really care." Maggie's pleasant features had hardened again. "Right now you can't scratch an itch unless I let you." She turned her head away. "Shit. I sound like a goddam gangster. I'm not." With an almost unconsciously

68

protective gesture, she reached over to tug the hem of Lucy's dress down to cover her legs. "But you were a stark raving lunatic last night and I don't trust you not to snap on me."

"So you're pulling some kind of mafia detox number on me here? If I were you, I wouldn't get between a serious drunk and her drink." The thought of how much she wanted a gin right now made her chest start to sweat.

Maggie didn't reply, just sat and watched her for a while, observing her growing discomfort. Lucy's headache had exploded to migraine proportions and her stomach growled audibly. "This is a criminal offense, you know."

The response was a loud guffaw. "This is the Wild West End of Tortola. And just so you know, this is a way better alternative to you being locked up in our infamous prison for drunk and disorderly behavior." She hopped to her feet. "I'll let you think about that for a while. See you in a bit. Oh, I better unzip the windows – it's going to get hot in here when the sun gets a little higher."

"Kidnapping and torture are international crimes!" Lucy shouted desperately after her. "Fucking fuck fuck fuck!"

"Nobody can hear you but me!" came the faint answer from the direction of Maggie's fading footsteps.

Lucy knew she had to stay calm and play along if she wanted to get out of this catastrophic situation as soon as possible. She'd dealt with professional criminals in her past and this was clearly an amateur stunt, although that didn't make it any less dangerous. They had no idea what they were doing – what if she was diabetic, epileptic or asthmatic?

Her whole body ached – her back hurt so much, her head was killing her and she needed to pee. She couldn't cry. She wouldn't.

It felt like forever before Maggie returned, but it probably wasn't more than an hour. Lucy was now drenched with sweat, perspiration dripped from her brow into her eyes and the back of her dress was soaked through where it met the woven canvas beneath her. She wasn't sure if it was nerves, heat or her need for alcohol, but she could see that Maggie was definitely disturbed by her physical condition, averting her eyes as she held a bowl of oatmeal and a cup of coffee above Lucy's head.

"I brought you breakfast but we have to come to an agreement first." She placed the dishes on the tent floor and knelt down beside her. Lucy usually never touched either of those foods, but she wanted them right now more than she'd ever wanted anything; still she tried not to show her vulnerability. "Although I am guessing you could last for quite a while without eating."

She would not say what she was thinking about Maggie. She wouldn't. She would rise above this humiliation. She *could* rise above this. "And what exactly are your terms?" she asked with as much dignity as she could muster.

Maggie leaned forward and gripped Lucy by the chin so she was forced to meet her gaze. "We both need to find your son. But you are going to do the work and I am going to give you some information that may help you locate him."

She controlled the urge to spit in Maggie's face and replied through clenched teeth. "And you need to find him because..."

As quickly as she had grabbed Lucy, she released her and looked away. "He sailed away from this island to deliver a friend of mine to Culebra in a boat that I had... been given. He was paid a large sum of money to take him there and return the boat to me. He never came back."

Despite the emptiness of her stomach, Lucy thought she might throw up. "When was this?"

"Last September, just before Maria did to Puerto Rico what Irma did to us. I never heard a thing again from either of them. I don't know what happened and it scares the fucking shit out of me." For a brief second Maggie let her guard down and Lucy saw how vulnerable she too was, and then she was all business again. "I tend to be pretty out

70

of touch up here on my hill and that's how I like it. I truly expected to see Stoney again, we had a great connection. But more importantly, I want to know what happened to my friend and my sailboat. And its contents."

Lucy had no idea who Stoney was, but that didn't really matter. "So basically you just want your boat back. Fine, I'm all in." Mentally she added, now throw out that coffee and bring on the gin, but she knew it would be foolish; she was on a roll. "Now can you untape me? Otherwise I am going to wee-wee all over your tent."

"Just squeeze your legs together for another few minutes. You think you're just going to waltz out of here and blow me off?" Maggie stuck her head out of the door flap and shouted, "Buzz! I need you, now!"

The interior of the tent was suddenly dominated by the intimidating and overpowering size, shape and smell of an enormous black man.

"This is my good friend, Buzzard. He'll do whatever I pay him to do."

"Of course, of course. I get it." She would agree to anything Maggie bullied her into at this point. All she wanted was to relieve her bladder. And then a hot shower and a double shot.

"Why is it I don't trust you, Lucy?" Maggie got to her feet. "Maybe because I think you love Beefeaters more than your son?" With a violent motion she ripped the duct tape from one of Lucy's ankles.

"Ow, son of a bitch!" she howled but Maggie ignored her and tore the tape from the other ankle just as roughly. "What the fuck!"

"Here's what going to happen. Buzz is going to take you outside – I hope you know how to squat in the bushes because that's all you're getting. And then you're coming back in here to dry out for a day or two."

Lucy couldn't hold back the sob in her throat. "But, why? I'll do what you want, I promise."

"Because I don't like your attitude. And I've dealt with enough alcoholics in my life to know how unreliable they

71

can be. And I want to know that you can follow my instructions so that we... Shit. Buzz, do you have your knife? This tape has melted."

Lucy could barely hold herself together as the blade slid between her skin and the bonds that restrained her wrists. She stumbled blindly out into the hot sun, Buzz's large hand grasping the straps of her dress as tightly as a harness on a wild horse. Numbly she allowed herself to be led a few feet away to lift her dress and squat, crying noisily all the while. Then he hauled her back to the tent, where Maggie stood holding the dishes and watching the process.

"Please don't make me go back in there!" Lucy begged. "I'll do whatever you ask."

She realized with a start that tears were running down Maggie's cheeks as she answered. "I don't believe you. This is for everybody's benefit, but especially yours. I want to know you are going to succeed at what I am going to ask you to do. I'll see you again in a few hours." Maggie took off her glasses and wiped her eyes. "Damn it, I'm acting just like them. I want to be better than that."

Lucy didn't have a clue who "they" were, but she knew a soft spot when she saw one. "Then do the right thing. Let me go."

Maggie turned away and sniffled a few times. "It's too late for that." She handed Buzz a roll of silver tape. "Just wrists and ankles. Leave her a bottle of water and come up to the house when you're done," she said to him. "Breakfast will be waiting."

Maggie didn't return again with Buzz until nearly dusk and by then Lucy was numb with the exhaustion of the experience.

This time she was commanded to sit; her wrists were still bound together in front of her, but her legs were left free. Her muscles were so stiff and sore she could barely keep herself erect and her fingers twitched uncontrollably as Maggie held out what looked like a jam sandwich on white bread.

"Eat something." When Lucy was unable to grasp the sandwich, Maggie held it away from her. "Or don't. But you will listen to what I have to say."

Lucy worked to control her trembling and reached out in what she knew was a pitiful gesture. "Please."

Instead Maggie broke off a small piece and put it up to her mouth. "One bite at a time. And chew it well." There was something perversely nurturing about the way she fed Lucy bits of the sandwich, as though she was a mother bird feeding a chick. Even with this torturous method, the meal was over in moments and Lucy was hungrier than ever.

"Buzz! Buzzard! Take her to the bush." This time she had to manage the act with her wrists still taped together.

When she was unceremoniously shoved back into the tent, the cot was gone, replaced by a quilt on the floor and a small pillow. "You'll be more comfortable this way tonight." With a small penknife Maggie sliced the wristbands apart. "Now take off your dress and give it to me."

Lucy shrank as far away from Maggie as she could inside the cramped space, unprepared for whatever this new indignity was.

"It's disgusting. I want to wash it. You can put this on." She held out a faded sarong.

She could feel Maggie's eyes on her body as the dress dropped in a crumpled heap at her feet. "Don't judge me. I haven't always been like this."

"Your problem, not mine, sister. Might as well give me your underwear too."

Lucy wrapped the printed rayon cloth around her girth like a towel and tied it tightly under one arm. It was better than nothing. "Thank you," she mumbled.

"It's for my sake as much as yours. Now hold out your arms."

A few moments later she was left alone in the dark, wrists and ankles bound together with tape, but infinitely better than being attached to the cot frame. She could bend and stretch. And scratch the mosquito bites that were accumulating on her skin. She had been warned that Buzz

73

was on guard on the other side of the zippered door and not to try anything funny.

That night the hours seemed endless. She couldn't sleep – every time she began to nod off, she jerked awake, sweating, trembling, starving and desperate for a drink. She tried to think clearly, to work out a plan for what she was going to do next, but there was no reality in her current world. At dawn she finally dozed off and when she opened her eyes, Maggie was sitting on the floor next to her, holding a sheet of notebook paper. She look well-rested and freshly showered and Lucy felt a weak stab of pure resentment. If she ever got out of here...no, *when* she got out of here...

"So, Lucy Brookstone, apparently you have your own Wikipedia page, whatever that is. A friend of mine looked you up last night." She waved the handwritten sheet of paper at her. "You were apparently Kip Kingsley's main squeeze a couple of decades ago. Before he faded into obscurity as a one of the most has-been rock stars in history. You got an award for a magazine piece on life in Northern Ireland. You started a nonprofit in Burlington, Vermont to help poor women in Third World countries – would that include me, I wonder – and you most recently made the news in Vermont for your affair with Albert Smith, whoever that is, destroying his career and your own." Maggie crumpled the page in her hand and tossed it aside. "And now here you are."

Lucy licked her dry lips and closed her eyes again.

"So let's make one thing perfectly clear." Maggie moved her face so close that Lucy could smell the coffee on her breath. "I don't ever, and I mean EVER, want to see this event or what I am about to tell you or anything that comes of it in your web biography. And you are never going to mention my name to anybody you meet. You understand me, girlfriend?"

It was after dark when Lucy was blindfolded and led barefoot down an uneven path and shoved into the back seat of what apparently was her own rental car. After a short drive, the car pulled off the road and the door opened. Her pulse raced as her arms were roughly grasped, but then the cool metal of the knife slid between her wrists again, and the scarf was removed from her eyes.

"'Get back in de cah." Buzzard slammed the door shut behind her and slid back behind the wheel. When they arrived at Sebastian's By the Beach, he passed her handbag to her but stayed in the driver's seat. "I will be here. To take you to airport in de mahning and see you get on dat San Juan plane."

Lucy stumbled blindly past the reception desk, keeping her face down, not having a clue as to what she looked like after her forty-eight hour ordeal. "Enjoying your island stay, Miss Brookstone?" the clerk called cheerfully after her.

Twelve hours later she was on a Seabourne flight to Puerto Rico, changing planes in San Juan for a connection to Culebra.

CHAPTER FIVE

September/October 2017
Culebra, Puerto Rico

There were only so many hands of Truth or Dare poker they could play before they could no longer hear their own voices. Eventually the wind and rain became so violent that the little boat shook like it was going to break into pieces. The pelting of drops from all directions sounded like nails being hammered into metal. At times the pressure in their ears became almost so intense it was frightening. And then came a cracking noise and a crash so loud that they actually grasped each other and screamed.

"What do you think that was?" Flush shouted.

"I don't know!" Tucker tightened the straps of his life jacket. He could not picture what the future would be like if they actually had to abandon ship in the middle of Hurricane Maria. For a while there were scraping and banging sounds along with the howling of the storm, and then the craft tipped a little and seemed to lodge hard against something in the mangroves. Despite the angle, it felt oddly steadier and more anchored than before.

When water did not begin to accumulate around their feet, they adjusted their cushions to accommodate to the new position and relaxed a little, if any moment of waiting out a hurricane could be called relaxing. Tucker calmed himself with lists of what he would do when Maria finally passed. 1) Get the dinghy into the water and the engine running (this was a big IF), 2) Go into town and buy Maggie some vodka, 3) Get himself a money belt to carry all his cash around in, 4) Repair any damage to the boat and sail back to Tortola (there were several IFS here), 5) Eat a really big meal. After a while, he rearranged the list and put the food as the first priority.

Flush was not looking that good; his face went from red to purple at one point and he seemed to have trouble breathing. Tucker knew nothing about emergency medical training, he didn't even know how to administer CPR. "You okay?" he asked tentatively.

"Yes, yes, just a few heart palps, I'll be fine. Give me a minute or two. I'm all out of my meds." Flush's complexion paled until he was almost colorless and then finally settled into an unhealthy shade of gray.

Another blast of wind made conversation impossible for a few minutes and then Flush handed Tucker the cards, saying, "Deal another round, Stoney. I got a few more things I need to tell you. Just in case."

"Don't even fuckin' say that kind of thing, Flush." Tucker tried not to show his nervousness as he shuffled.

"Just win and listen to me, kid." Flush deliberately lost the next hand and then leaned back against a pillow, closing his eyes. "I ain't got no offspring – you're as much of a son to me as anybody has ever been, more really, even if I have only known you for, what, a little more than a week?"

Tucker didn't like where this admission sounded like it was heading.

"So what I am about to tell you, only a few people in the world know about it."

"Flush- "

"Shut up and pay attention now. First thing, go find a flat head screwdriver. And then help me get into the bedroom, or whatever the fuck we call that closet with the substandard mattress that we sleep on."

"You're going to feel worse cooped up in there than out here."

"I know that. I just need to show you something."

At least the request of a screwdriver meant that whatever he was going to reveal was probably not some deadly body ailment. Flush sat on the edge of the bunk and touched a wooden panel above his head, running his finger along the edge of it until he found the spot he was looking for.

"Right here. Put the tip in there and pry this piece of wood off."

"What's in here – a secret map to buried treasure?" The panel was swollen and stiff with humidity and Tucker had to work the screwdriver back and forth to loosen it.

"Don't go spoiling my surprise now."

"Look out, here it comes." Flush ducked as the teak board fell onto the sheet beside him, followed by a long plastic box and a heavy garbage bag.

He knew Flush well enough now to be able to guess what was probably in the bag.

"Turn your back while I count it. If we both survive, you don't need to know how much there is!" Flush yelled over the pounding of the rain.

"Asshole!" Tucker shouted at him, before stretching out on the damp mattress and turning on his side.

"And when I'm done, I'm going to tell you a story. You can decide if it's true or not, but I suggest you file away the particulars, especially about Louie P, in that absurdly organized brain of yours."

"I don't care about your fucking friend named Louie!"

By morning the wind had died down and the storm diminished to a mere steady downpour. Flush was snoring loudly after rambling on for hours, spinning what he referred to as "a tale of the U.S. Navy. treasure, treason, treachery and..." There were a few other "T" words that Tucker couldn't recall now. He only believed a portion of it was actually true; he knew the history of the military taking over Culebra for target practice and bomb testing; he recalled the tanks that still remained at Flamenco Beach, as well as a terrifying night there he could never forget. There were probably still buried grenades and bunkers in existence, but the rest of Flush's bizarre story sounded farfetched, like some island legend or jail house fantasy. At least it had made the endless afternoon go by faster.

With post-adolescent boredom, he repeated place names and instructions to prove to Flush that he had memorized them. When they had finally replaced the booty back in the ceiling compartment, Flush had literally sagged in exhaustion and dropped off into the dreamless sleep of the unburdened.

Although rough waters still slapped hard against the hull, Tucker decided it was definitely safe enough to venture a look outside and assess the damage.

"Holy fuck." He had to steady himself on the edge of the hatchway, not because of the roll of the deck, but because of what he was seeing.

All that remained of the boat's mast was a jagged shard pointing skyward towards the retreating cloud mass of Hurricane Maria.

Two days later, under the merciless glare of the sun, Tucker was waiting again in line with local islanders for ready-to-eat meals and potable water that been dropped by military helicopters. Although Maria had been classified as a Category 5, Culebra had managed to survive wind speeds of 165 miles an hour without the visible wake of destruction left by Irma in the BVIs. But apparently this was not the case on the main island of Puerto Rico, where all the utilities, communications and services originated. This left the small island that was twelve miles off its east coast without power, water, or cell service and only as much petrol as was left in the tanks of the two tiny gas stations. Culebra was essentially cut off from the world – a few sketchy reports were circulating that all of Puerto Rico was without electricity. Entire communities had been destroyed and the neighboring island of Vieques, visible on the horizon, was in much worse shape than Culebra.

Tucker could not believe that this survival mode was his life again, although it felt different here than it had on Tortola. It was a smaller community and it seemed they were all very supportive of each other. People were getting cranky and tired, but with no end in sight they were having to learn how to bathe with as little water as possible and do chores in daylight. And just as it had been after Irma, the folks around him were actually talking to each other rather than looking at cell phone screens. They complained that a "dry law" had gone into effect – no liquor could be sold on Culebra until the law was lifted – and that the bank had quite literally run out of money. With massive devastation and millions of people at risk on the big island, the eyes of the world were not on this tiny desert isle that was only four miles at its widest and seven miles at its longest.

For Tucker, it was just a new side to the tropical frontier living that had become his existence. The shock of losing the boat's mast had been slightly offset by the fact that the dinghy had weathered Maria with just a few chips and scratches. But getting Flush into the dinghy had been harder than launching the boat itself. The older man seemed more rattled and unsteady than before the storm, although he insisted he was fine.

The water was still choppy and murky with all kinds of debris; on a normal day Tucker would not have taken a boat out on the water, but these were not normal times. As he carefully steered the dinghy across the bay towards town, Tucker was flooded with memories from the last time he'd motored across the Ensenada Honda years earlier, Chloe at the helm. He had been an inexperienced sixteen-year-old impressed by her navigational skills as they'd fled a crime scene. He'd lost his virginity that night in an abandoned purple houseboat...

He remembered the place they'd met, a popular bar on the water where dinghies could tie up and big fish swam close to the wooden dock. There'd been drumming and a lot of dancing. It had been right before the big orange bridge.

"Shit. Holy shit. The Dinghy Dock got hit bad." Flush was staring in the direction of the same landmark restaurant that Tucker had been thinking about. "Looks like the sea washed up and the fucking roof caved in. Guess we can't tie up there."

So much for memories, he thought unsentimentally. Makes it easier to move on. But he didn't say this aloud to Flush who was sitting dazed and dejectedly across from him. Instead he steered the boat into the concrete public dock and, grabbing the mooring line, leaped onto the rough cement wharf.

For the next week, it was about merely surviving. Besides the fact that all their straightforward plans had gone completely awry, there was nothing usual or easy about daily life on Culebra. Helicopters continued to arrive with emergency supplies of food and water. Milka's, the small grocery store in town opened and soon had to give local people credit to buy food because many people were unable to access their money and credit card machines were unusable.

This was not the case for Flush and Tucker, who had plenty of available cash and were lucky enough to stock up on items they hadn't seen in weeks. But after the first nerve-wracking trip to town, Flush did not accompany him again. When he had realized they were in a large public community space, he'd suddenly freaked out, letting Tucker wait in line, while he hid in the shade of a building in the shadow of a doorway, sunglasses on and hat pulled down, so that he wouldn't be recognized by anybody he knew. Now he was "laying low," as he called it, which Tucker interpreted as being afraid to be recognized by "that fuckwad Tiburon or any coast guard officer bent on extradition."

Because of the lack of fuel on the island, Tucker tried not to use the dinghy much except for the short trip to the public dock. Instead he explored the small island on foot, alleviating his stir-craziness by walking the neighborhoods and roads, little of which he recalled, having spent most of his previous visit to Culebra at the Flamenco Beach campground, much of which was destroyed and unusable now. Just to get away, he hiked to a few of the beaches and swam, enjoying the distraction of the now tranquil waters but unable to escape the leafless desolation of the strangely quiet shores.

When the municipality managed to fire up the old public generator, daily living took on a new aspect for the

81

locals. There was electricity now, but only from 6 pm to 6 am, so some people altered their routines to staying awake at night to take advantage of having power for appliances, tools and electronics. Phone signals could sometimes be picked up on a couple of high hillsides outside of town, where folks flocked to send whatever short messages they could to the outside world.

Most of this meant nothing to Tucker and Flush, who were still sorting out the trauma of the Nico Tico. Tucker had wanted to motor out of the mangroves to a better anchorage in the harbor, but Flush did not want to call any attention to their presence, especially not with the eyesore of the broken mast. "Remember the plan was for you to just drop me off; the Nico was not supposed to spend any time here."

Obtaining a new mast and sail was more than Tucker was equipped to manage. In the post-hurricane climate, it would definitely take months. "But I promised Maggie..."

Flush spat over the edge into the water. "Don't be worrying about Maggie. She only *thinks* this is her property. It was never really hers."

Even after Flush's "talk" during the hurricane, Tucker didn't really understand the complexities of the dispute in which Flush and his so-called friends were involved. "So where were you going to stay if I had been able to drop you off?"

Flush had laughed in a nasty way Tucker had not heard before. "Hotel Kokomo was the plan, but that really was never going to happen, kid. The boat was staying with me."

Tucker's gaze narrowed as he tried to comprehend the meaning of what Flush was saying. "Oh, really. Why, because you're such a good sailor?"

"You know why. It was always intended to be my floating quarters on Culebra until the rendezvous at Dinghy Dock. Fuck. And now that's all gone to hell. Tiburon is somewhere on this island, but he can't know I'm here. For now, I just gotta stay with the Nico."

Tucker was getting sick of all of Flush's covert activities and he was tired of sharing the tiny space of the boat's cabin with him. He thought halfheartedly about seeing if there was some place on the island he could camp, but he abandoned that idea after realizing he had zero camping equipment.

"You ever swim with the turtles at Tamarindo?"

The question came out of nowhere one night as Tucker was shuffling the cards.

"No, why?" Tamarindo Beach was more of a hike from town than Tucker had wanted to attempt and there were so few vehicles traveling around on the island that he had not attempted to hitchhike.

"We should go. We can go in the dinghy."

"I don't want to waste the gas." These days he didn't trust Flush's intentions; he was sure there was an ulterior motive somewhere there. But he recalled now that Tamarindo had been one of the the places Flush had talked about during the hurricane. In fact it was one of the "T" words he'd forgotten, probably because he didn't know what it was at the time. And in fact, perhaps the other had been "turtles." A little bit intrigued, he decided to play along. "Plus we only have one set of snorkeling gear."

"We can take turns. Look, I'll pay you to take me there."

"I don't need any more of your money."

"Of course, you do. It's not going to last forever. And there's bound to be more gas on this island soon."

"Well you're not the one who's going to stand in line for hours."

"Then take me out of the goodness of your fucking heart. Let's go tomorrow."

The old man would probably be easier to live with if he had a change of scene for a few hours. And Tucker wouldn't mind one also. "Okay. I'll take you for a thousand dollars," he announced, knowing this would entertain them for the next fifteen minutes."

"You're worse than a taxi driver in New Delhi. Two fifty and not a penny more."

"Seven fifty or no deal..."

The weather was perfect, the water a calm, clear Caribbean blue, the sky a nearly cloudless azure backdrop. "Excellent snorkeling day," Flush declared as they motored under the orange bridge and slowly made their way out of the canal to the open sea.

Heading north, they passed Melones Beach, where Tucker had walked to a few times. They went by two more coves before Flush announced they had arrived at Tamarindo. Unsurprisingly, the shadeless beach appeared deserted. The only sign of life was a lone orange kayak that was dragged onto the sand, but there was no paddler in sight. "You're not supposed to motor close to shore here, but obviously there is no one out here now to tell us that."

From past experience, Tucker knew it would be easy to get Flush out of the dinghy into the water, but getting him back in would be a trial. There was a mooring ball bobbing several hundred feet from shore, indicating where boats should tie up. He slowly steered in as near to the beach as he dared, trying to avoid the already damaged reefs. "This is as far as we go," he finally announced. "You've got your life vest on, I think you'll make it to shore."

"Believe it or not, I do know how to swim." Indignantly Flush climbed clumsily over the side of the boat and dropped into the water. The inflated air vest took the brunt of his weight. Tucker tossed him the mask and fins.

"Can you manage the cooler too? It floats."

"I'm fine. I feel great." A moment later he was bobbing his way to the sand with their gear. Tucker took the dinghy back out to one of the mooring balls and tied it up, and then dove in and swam the distance across the bay to where Flush was waiting on shore. If he didn't think about the strange circumstances of his current situation, he could almost pretend that this was just a normal island day trip, albeit with an unlikely companion.

Flush was leaning against the cooler, already looking exhausted. "Why don't you go first? The turtles are usually hanging out off to the left and there is a pretty good reef out that way, if it didn't get destroyed."

Tucker shaded his eyes and gazed intently in the direction Flush was pointing. "Looks like there might be someone out there actually. I think I see a snorkel."

Instantly Flush went into alarm mode. "Shit. Really? I can't see that far."

"Relax. It must be the owner of that kayak."

Moving faster than usual, Flush walked quickly across the beach to peer inside the molded plastic craft. "It's a girl!" he yelled triumphantly, holding up a pair of flip flops and what appeared to be a purple dress.

"Don't steal anything!" Tucker called back, muttering under his breath, "You fuckin' weirdo."

Backing into the water, he pulled on fins, adjusted the mask and swam off.

Almost immediately his mood changed. His new reality, that sometimes felt so small, always became infinitely larger with the addition of the underwater world. He knew none of the names of the fish he encountered, but he was determined that at some point he would learn what those amazing electric blue and iridescent yellow species were, as well as the black and white striped ones that looked like their eyes were in the wrong place. He saw a few spotted rays and a starfish, and some large spiny sea urchins that he knew enough to avoid. Most of the time he was clueless but awed.

He swam around a small rocky coral area, observing the ecosystem of the undersea creatures, watching the small fish interacting with larger ones and steering clear of a ferocious-looking red and white variety that had dangerous looking spines. The name "lionfish" popped into his brain, but he had no idea if he was right.

But where were the turtles... Popping his head above the surface for a moment, he spotted the other snorkeler's spout and headed in that direction. She must be hovering over something worth seeing.

And then suddenly there they were, almost prehistoric in appearance, large oval shell-covered bodies with flipper-like legs that should have been awkward, gliding with the grace of dancers just a few feet beneath him. He watched in wonder as a turtle swam within inches of his face. It kept a calm black eye on him as it surfaced for just a second to get a mouthful of air before diving to join its two companions in the seagrass below. He marveled at the patterns on their shells and legs, at the ancient expression of their classic faces and at how effortlessly they moved through their natural environment.

Lingering in the company of the sea turtles, Tucker contentedly lost all track of time and he was appropriately startled when, in his peripheral vision, he saw a large shadow swimming towards him. He began backing away until he realized he was looking at long human legs ending in yellow rubber fins. A hand waved at him and pointed upwards.

He broke the surface at the same time she did, water dripping from their hair, two sea monsters breathing through tubes and staring at each other with big eyes behind plastic masks. She pulled hers off, exposing the deep red mark where it had suctioned itself to her face around a pair of tilted jade green eyes and an upturned nose.

"Hey. They're incredible, right?"

His mask was fogging up and he quickly took it off, wanting to get a better look at her. Mermaid was the first thought that popped into his mind. The wet hair plastered to her head looked like dark auburn waves; her skin was tanned but at the same time translucently delicate. And from what he could see, only a small percentage of it was covered by a tiny black bikini.

"Yes, really." His tongue didn't want to work. He hadn't expected to speak to anyone, let alone a beautiful girl like this one.

"This your first time seeing them?"

He nodded speechlessly as he tread water beside her.

"Want to see a whole bunch more? Follow me." Without waiting for a reply, her mask and snorkel were in place again and she was swimming away from him. Tucker couldn't get his equipment on fast enough.

The next hour was like the best dream ever, and absolutely the most pleasant adventure of the all the tumultuous events he had endured in the last few months. His companion led him to the most excellent underwater show he'd seen in his limited experience, a large group of turtles all swimming together, a reef with schools of amazing fish, eagle rays, barracudas and an octopus.

"There's one old turtle in particular I'm trying to find," she told him. "Let me know if you see one that is bigger and patterned more intricately than the rest. I'm worried because I haven't seen him since the hurricane."

Suddenly he remembered Flush, waiting for him on the shore for his turn with the snorkeling gear. "Sorry, I have to go back. I have a friend who wants to use this equipment. He's an old guy and I kind of have to look out for him."

"That's okay. I'll come with you, I've been out here for hours." With swift agile strokes, the pair of them swam back towards the shore. Tucker was relieved to see Flush submerged in the shallow water near the edge, wearing his hat and sunglasses, staying cool.

"Well, look what you caught, kid," he commented admiringly, and using a gesture that Tucker found embarrassingly dated and sexist, he lowered his sunglasses to watch the girl as she emerged from the water, carrying her fins.

"Don't be an ass." He handed over the snorkeling gear. "Sorry I took so long. There are tons of turtles out that way. It was fantastic."

"What's her name?" Flush asked, his eyes still following the girl as she moved swiftly across the hot rocks on the beach to retrieve her flip flops and a sarong from the kayak. "She's a hottie."

"Stop it! Just go now. I'll get your vest."

But she was already approaching them, her hand extended towards Flush. "Hi, I'm Fiona." She turned to Tucker. "We didn't properly introduce ourselves out there."

Flush squeezed her fingers like an intimate old friend, holding on for what Tucker considered a few seconds too long. "I'm John Royal, but call me Flush. And this is Stoney."

"Flush. Go. Now." Tucker rummaged in the cooler for a bottle of water and realized he was starving. They had brought a bag of pickle-flavored potato chips and a can of olives, and even these odd snacks looked appetizing at the moment. He held out the chips to Fiona, who now sat crosslegged on the faded sarong patting the space next to her as an invitation to him.

"Thanks, I'm famished." With long freckled fingers she reached into the bag, inspecting it as she munched. "Unusual flavor. Where'd you get these?"

"The best Milka's Grocery had to offer."

She tilted her head and gave him a long sideways look. "So how come I've never seen you around Culebra before?"

Tucker shrugged. "Only got here a couple weeks ago. Rode in on Maria. You live here?"

"Since last winter. I was camping out on Playa Blanca but had to evacuate for the storms. Now I'm down at Datiles."

He had no idea what places she was talking about, but he nodded like he understood. "By yourself or with other people?"

"I was totally solo out at Blanca. But now it's me and another guy - in our own tents. He was there first. So what – you're on a boat?"

Time flew by in a way he could not remember. They talked about everything – how Fiona had come to Culebra on a camping vacation with friends and ended up staying on alone, working at any occupation she could. She had cleaned houses and waitressed, but her favorite job was when she'd been hired as a guide with the kayaking adventure company that gave daily tours and snorkeling trips out of Tamarindo. All of her positions had been suspended since the hurricane.

"No wonder you knew so much!" Tucker was as fascinated by her slim tanned feet and ankle bracelets as he was by her story. Before he knew it, he was telling her the details of his own life – from his previous trip to Culebra, through his tumultuous vagabonding escapades with Chloe, to their fateful marriage and subsequent breakup, and on through his year of sailing adventures.

When Flush dragged himself out of the water, he gave Tucker a knowing wink. After an impassioned exchange with Fiona about how the biggest and oldest turtle had not been seen since the hurricane, he flopped down in the sand several feet away, in the partial shade of some tree trunks, for his afternoon nap.

"I should go soon, it takes me a while to get back because I have to paddle against the current."

"You came here in the kayak?" Tucker was more and more awed by Fiona's gutsy spirit. "I can take you back if you want. I'd like to see where you're camping – I'm looking for a new place to live. Well, I don't have any gear, but if I could get some..."

"I actually have a spare tent you could use. I've kind of just been using it as my closet. What? People give me stuff!" She laughed defensively. "That's how it is here."

Tucker barely heard her words – he had disappeared into the beauty of her smile.

Flush could hardly be roused; he shooed Tucker away, saying he was happy to sleep on the beach until they came back for him. With the kayak secured to the back of the dinghy, Tucker set off with Fiona perched in the prow like an ancient carved figurehead, face to the wind, her springy curls spread out in the breeze behind her.

"Can we stop in town?" she shouted back to him. "I need to pick up a few things."

Tucker hadn't brought any money so he sat at the picnic table outside the store while Fiona shopped. He watched the small stream of customers go in and out during what normally would have been the busiest time of day. They included an obese woman wearing orange pants, a tall man wearing a straw cowboy hat, and an old guy sporting a long white beard and red reading glasses. After a while, the cowboy hat wearer came swiftly out of the store and gave him a long hard stare, before striding off to a rusty Suzuki 4x4 parked on the side of the road. As he drove away, he looked directly at Tucker again, his piercing gaze cold enough to cause shivers in the stifling afternoon heat.

Fiona emerged, zipping up her backpack and frowning.

"What's the matter?" he asked her.

"I'm almost out of money. No income streams and not much in the bank."

"Do you need some cash? I can lend you some. No, seriously," he assured her when she gave him a doubtful look. I happen to have plenty at the moment."

"Don't tempt me. I don't want to start owing people money. I'll figure out something."

As he helped her into the dinghy, he found himself worrying about her – she seemed so lightweight and fragile, although he knew already that this was an illusion.

It was a short hop around a point to the tranquil bay she directed him into. "Datiles Beach is actually over there, but it's too shallow to really swim." She pointed to the next cove that was even bluer and more serene. "It's a bit of a hike from town, up a really steep hill. It's much easier to come in this way. And especially with a motor."

He helped her carry the kayak across the rocky shore and up onto the sand, stopping in front of a damaged wooden picnic table on the edge of a clearing. On one side of the space was a large tan tent with an array of rusty camp chairs and assorted equipment; on the opposite side was a tidy campsite around a green tent under a blue government-issue tarp. A clothesline running to a nearby tree branch displayed another bikini and a tee shirt so tiny it could have been sized for a child. It was probably her alternate set of clothing – Tucker knew that when you had to haul water for washing, you wore as little as possible. For some reason he couldn't explain, he found her laundry endearing.

"Welcome." Fiona unzipped the front flaps and pulled them back. "It's too hot to go inside now. But it's super pleasant at night. And if you decide you want to stay..." She held up a bundle of nylon that was apparently the spare tent.

They sat at the table, sharing a bottle of ice tea and a few more life stories. Tucker didn't want to leave, but he knew he had to return to Tamarindo and retrieve Flush.

"I have to go back and get Flush. But yeah, I am totally ready to come live here with– " He didn't finish the sentence, realizing this was a weird thing to say to someone he had met only a few hours ago. "I'd move in tonight if I could." Shit, everything that was coming out of his mouth was wrong. "I mean, yeah, I would like to stay out here. How about I come out late tomorrow morning with my stuff? Or are you not around during the day?"

She grinned. "Really? Awesome." Then the sunshine of her smile was gone as suddenly as it had appeared. "But just so you know, I am kind of a loner. I'm not always great company. I need my space."

"Well, that makes two of us."

They stood up and there was an awkward second before she threw her arms around him for a quick hug. It was exactly what anyone would have done, but Tucker wanted it to mean way more than that.

"See you tomorrow then."

As he motored back around the point, his mind was filled with images of Fiona and her halo of carrot-colored curls. Off to the west he could see dark storm clouds gathering over the little island of Luis Peña and his idyllic mood faded. He resisted the urge to gun the engine, knowing he needed to conserve his gas, having already used extra to take Fiona home.

The wind was starting to pick up a little as Tamarindo Bay came into view. He steered in towards the shore, more careful this time of the reefs and turtle habitat, swearing to himself that he would never violate the mooring rules again. Shading his eyes, he searched for Flush on the beach; he could see the red and white cooler and the grayish towel they had brought along for something to sit on, but no other sign of life.

A flash of neon yellow caught his eye a short distance away, bobbing in the water. For a few seconds he wondered what it could be and then realized with relief that it was Flush's life vest. He must have gone for one more round of snorkeling while he waited for Tucker, probably hoping to spot the oldest turtle in Culebra's undersea world. He cut the engine down to a soft putter and pulled up beside him, waiting for Flush to lift his head out of the water.

Immediately he could see that something wasn't right. Flush floated towards him, his body grazing the boat in a dangerous way. He wasn't kicking his legs or even moving his arms to hold his place while he looked at something below the surface.

"Flush! Hey! Flush!" he called loudly.

And then with a sickening wave of dizziness, Tucker realized the thing that was most wrong with the picture. Flush was face down in the water wearing his inflatable life jacket, with fins and mask on. But no snorkel.

He was too heavy, there was no way Tucker could drag him into the dinghy. Sobbing and cursing, he dove into the water and started to swim ashore, trying to pull Flush along by the straps of his life vest. But halfway there, he stopped short, breathing hard. What was the point – he would have to leave him there and go to town for help anyway.

He was still swearing and weeping as he motored slowly into the canal, Flush's lifeless body secured by a rope and trailing behind the dingy, just like Fiona's kayak had been just a few short hours earlier.

CHAPTER SIX

June 2018
Culebra, Puerto Rico

Lucy groaned and opened her eyes. She did not recognize the ceiling overhead, or the dirty light fixture full of dead bugs. She peered cautiously around without moving; she knew instinctively that her hangover was going to be massive.

The sound of unfamiliar snoring beside her brought a momentary panic. Then she looked down at the tanned forearm thrown across the soft cushion that was now her belly, saw the shark tattooed along the length of the tender underskin from elbow to wrist, and it all came back to her.

What had she done – she wasn't supposed to end up in bed with this guy. She was supposed to be watching him, following him. Had she just been an easy target after all those G&T's or had there actually been that electric sizzle of attraction she seemed to vaguely recall? The last thing she could bring to mind was standing outside the Chinese bar near the pizza place, trying to talk to the tall man in the straw cowboy hat about her search for Tucker without actually telling him anything...how had she ended up in his bed? Had there been sparks between them or was her self-esteem just that low now...

Her heart started pounding rapidly. She didn't even know where she was or what part of the island he lived on. Where had she left her golf cart? How was she going to get out of here?

Abruptly sitting up, the room reeled around her and the stale reek of sex, sweat and alcohol made her stomach lurch. Her bed partner shifted in his sleep and tightened his hold around her abdomen. She glanced furtively at his face, fearful of what she might see. With relief she released the breath she hadn't realized she'd been holding.

He was age-appropriate, she could be thankful for that much; at least he wasn't some local teenager. His sharp features were accentuated by thin lips, a small trimmed beard and long brown hair, streaked with gray. In the pale daylight streaming in through the frosted louvers of the window, she could now see he was quite a bit bald on top, she hadn't noticed this when he removed his hat the night before; apparently she had been too caught up in the moment to notice much of anything. An intricately carved jade turtle hung from a knotted leather thong around his neck and a heavy gold hoop pierced the lobe of the ear she could see.

Something about that turtle...then it all came back to her in a sickening flash– they'd been flirting hard before she put it together that Tommy Ron McCowen from Iowa City was actually T-Ron. She'd had a hard time believing that the charming joker buying her drinks had been the infamous "Tiburon," the modern day pirate she'd been sent to stalk. And shit – she knew her standards were at an all time low, but from what she could now recall, the sex had actually been unexpectedly amazing. Hopefully she hadn't blown her cover in any post-coital chit-chat.

She needed to get out before he woke up so she could figure out whether she'd jeopardized anything by following her carnal instincts. Bloody hell, she was so paranoid since the incident on Tortola, that she felt like there were spies everywhere, observing her every move, ready to report any misstep to Mafia Maggie.

Trying to disturb T-Ron as little as possible, she slid out from beneath the weight of his arm and scanned the room for her clothes. Her dress was in a heap just inside the door, her underpants and bra hung from a dresser knob. What about her purse, her keys, oh shit. A moment later she found them too, in the next room, tossed in a heap on a plastic chair with her flip-flops. Silently, she pulled on her clothes and slipped out the door.

Where was she? High up on a hill in a neighborhood; she could see the airport strip below. If she made her way down to that, she could find her way back to her guesthouse. She was probably not that far away. The golf cart had to still be in the main part of town somewhere; she'd find it later.

Across the street a man sitting in a hammock on his porch raised his hand to her in greeting.

"Buen dia." She used the local greeting, trying not to reveal the pounding in her forehead and how much she needed a cup of coffee and probably a really big breakfast as well. She wished she had her sunglasses or her hat, but those had not been essentials when she went out after sunset the previous evening.

She needed to get focused. Since arriving here a week earlier, she'd been drowning her sorrows and humiliation in her current unproductive style and had totally lost sight of the singular goal in her miserable life – finding Tucker.

Despite her resolve, by the end of the afternoon Lucy found herself once again at the Dinghy Dock for Happy Hour, nursing a gin and tonic at the bar, staring studiously out to sea, trying not to catch anyone's eye. She wondered how many people had seen her leave with T-Ron. The bartender definitely had known what was going on, but there was a different woman making drinks tonight, young and blonde, maybe the right age to have noticed Tucker.

Lucy scrolled through the downloaded photos on her phone for the most recent one she had of her son. It was originally a shot of Tucker and Chloe in Thailand, from over a year ago; she had cropped Chloe out of the picture (along with the distraction of the crocheted bikini top that she might as well not have been wearing for how much it covered her prominent, well-oiled and very tan breasts). The remainder was a fuzzy enlargement of her beautiful boy's face, which was not entirely familiar to her with its stoned expression and cynical grin beneath unkempt blonde dreadlocks. Around his neck he wore a string of puka shells and some kind of carved amulet on a leather cord; and was that really a turquoise-studded silver feather hanging from his ear? How had she never noticed that before – the jewelry had to be Chloe's influence.

She leaned forward to get the girl's attention, holding out the screen. It seemed like a futile effort; the bar was so busy in this pre-sunset hour, the bartenders had no time for casual conversation.

Something warm and wet touched her shoulder and she turned to find T-Ron's face inches from her, a mischievous look lighting up his tiger-like eyes. Separately his features were not that appealing, but somehow together they had a quirky attractiveness. Even now, not drunk and in the light of day, she found the total sum of his bad boyness to be smokingly sexy. She understood why she had been so easily led astray the previous night.

"Did you just lick my shoulder?" she asked in mock outrage, trying not to acknowledge how that simple overt gesture was making her feel.

The creases in his cheeks deepened and she caught the flash of a gold tooth as he smiled and leaned forward. "I like your taste, lady," he murmured into her ear before boldly running his tongue around the lobe.

She gasped responsively, just as he had intended her to, and she hated herself for not being able to be control her emotions.

"Who's that?" He nodded towards the photo on her phone that she was still holding out in front of her.

"My son. The one I am trying to find. I told you about him last night. I think." His presence was already confusing her – who was the predator here? Wasn't she supposed to be entrapping him? "Do you know him?"

She looked sideways and pulled back, watching his expression harden for a moment into something almost malevolent before he carefully rearranged it into a nonchalant smile. "Know him? I don't think so." As he spoke, his fingers slipped around her waist in an intimate, possessive gesture, playing with the roll of soft flesh she had tried to conceal with the most recent voluminous dress. The one she'd bought to replace the favorite dress ruined on Tortola. "Seen him around? Probably. Don't really recall." His breath was hot against her neck. "There's only one thing I can seem to remember right now."

His debauchery was so bold, she could only laugh, partly because it was so blatantly cliché, but also partly because it was actually turning her on. "Sorry to say I don't remember that much about last night."

"You don't? Well, let me remind you." Putting his drink down on the bar, without any other preamble, he placed his other hand in her lap and squeezed suggestively. Any resistance she might have been trying to display disappeared with the bolt of excitement that shot up from her crotch to her abdomen.

Embarrassed, she looked around, but nobody was paying any attention to what was going on between the two of them. She slid her own hand down to rest on top of his and he leaned in, pressing his chest against her back.

"Does that mean stop or don't stop?" he teased.

"It means I need another drink."

"I've got a whole bottle of gin at my place."

This time she wasn't that drunk at all and the sex was electrifying, even inspirational. For all the narcissistic tendencies he seemed to display, T-Ron was incredibly attentive to and in tune with her needs, making sure she was as satisfied with the results as he was. In the fading daylight that streamed through the open window, she felt exposed and vulnerable, self-conscious of someone else's eyes and hands on her new body type, yet blissfully aware that she couldn't recall the last time she'd felt such acute physical pleasure.

"Oh, I think you enjoyed that, didn't you?" T-Ron propped himself up on one elbow, an almost smug smile playing on his lips. "Your nipples are just about the prettiest pink I have ever seen." She gave a little involuntary sigh at his touch. "Why, I bet I could get you going again, couldn't I? T-Ron's got the power, baby."

She didn't like that arrogant tone of voice. But she did like what he was doing to her. Her resentment could wait until later.

They sat propped up in bed with the pillows behind their backs, drinking gin straight out of a bottle that they passed back and forth. It was a crude way to have cocktails, but the rawness of it seemed right after the primal passion they had just shared. The harshness going down her throat made Lucy cough and the liquor seemed to go right to her brain.

She'd wanted to stay clearheaded, hoping he'd be one of those guys that passed out after sex, giving her a chance to snoop around. But instead he seemed energized and hyper. Maybe the alcohol would help him relax.

They'd dropped their clothes on the floor – she thought her underpants might actually still be in his truck – but he'd carefully hung his straw hat on the bed post. She reached up now and placed it on top of her tangled and wild hair, and then, laughing, struck a pose with the bottle. It had been a long time since she'd felt this uninhibited.

"Whoever said big girls weren't hot and cute never saw you and your luscious naked boobies." Before she realized what he was doing, he had grabbed his phone off the nightstand and snapped a photo of her.

"Hey! No pictures!" She tried to swipe the phone out of his hand but he pulled her down on top of him, hugging her until she squealed for him to let go.

"You feel that? You see the effect you have on me, cowgirl? I think you're going to have to take this old stallion out for another ride. Oh, yeah. Ohhh, yeahhh."

"Excuse me but that should be cow-woman," she managed to gasp.

This time he seemed down for the count. "You rode the bucking bronco and kept the hat on, rodeo gal. Now let me have a hit off the gin before I take a little nap here on that soft belly pillow of yours. And you know I mean that in the nicest way, right?"

Even if he was complimenting her, it was hard to accept the way he talked about her body. Would he have even considered saying those kind of things if she had still been slim?

As he tipped the bottle up to his lips, she removed the hat, inspecting the diverse collection of decorations that adorned its narrow band. "What are all these things?"

"Hunting trophies." He hooted at the expression on her face. "You know, like scalps, or deer horns or animal heads. Some men collect those kinds of artifacts, these are my mementos." He held up the nearly empty bottle. "Speaking of killing things... we did a good job on this. You better have the last of it."

She barely caught the gin as he fell over onto her, his check against her stomach, his face nearly in her crotch. "Best view on Culebra," he murmured before he began snoring.

She finished the rest of the alcohol before maneuvering out from under him. As she stood up, a wave of dizziness nearly knocked her back into bed. She'd had way too much to drink without eating. The first place she needed to scope out was the refrigerator. Hanging over the bedroom doorknob was a red silk kimono with a dragon embroidered on the back; she put it on and was disturbed to find that that the fabric didn't quite come together in the front. She tied the belt around her waist anyway. It was better than getting dressed.

She was disappointed to see only a few crusty looking condiments and a Styrofoam takeout box. Apparently Mr. Tiburon didn't eat at home often. Gingerly flicking open the container, she inspected some forgotten leftovers of gelatinous looking chicken and a scoop of dried-out rice and beans. Well, nothing a microwave couldn't fix; he clearly wouldn't miss the meal.

As she waited for the food to heat up, she poked around the small kitchen, quietly opening and closing cupboards and drawers. Nothing enlightening, but she hadn't really expected anything. Perching on a plastic stool next to the counter, she wolfed down the barely edible remains of his previous dinner, and then hesitantly moved on to a bag of something awesomely crunchy that she'd found on a shelf and that she thought might actually be pork rinds.

Slipping back into the bedroom, she stood still for a moment, assessing the depth of T-Ron's sleep by the volume of his snoring and the evenness of his breathing. Then she quietly slid open the nightstand drawer and peered inside. She was rewarded by the sight of one of the largest and sharpest knives she had ever seen resting on a stack of cash. Although she was appropriately disturbed, it was not that surprising and didn't tell her much except that his weapon of choice was a fairly primitive one. She tried not to think of the plunging and slicing he might have used it for. She shivered, remembering his comment about scalps. There was nothing else there except a small flashlight and a six-pack of batteries.

Disappointed she moved across the room to what passed for a closet, which meant a wooden shelf with a rod suspended beneath it, where a few pieces of clothing hung on hangers. Lucy frowned, not sure where to spend these few stealthy moments or what she was even looking for. She pulled on the handles of the top drawer of a small painted dresser but it did not give easily, apparently swollen by weather and age and she was afraid of the noise it might make. On top of the dresser was a decorative driftwood branch that served as a holder for assorted necklaces, bracelets and earrings – the man seemed to like his jewelry. Lots of nautical cording, seaglass and shells, she recognized a pendant that was similar to the one that she'd seen around Tucker's neck in the photo she had in her phone, but among these typical island baubles, she could see some real gold and maybe even some gemstones.

Under the bed, perhaps? She leaned over to pick up the straw hat from where it had landed, upside down on the floor and examined it again. The random assortment of "trophies" as T-Ron had referred to them were strangely diverse, ranging from a South African war medal to a delicate silver earring in the shape of a feather studded with turquoise.

She caught her breath. Was it just a coincidence? Where had she left her phone... her purse was where she had dropped it by the outside door. When she opened up her "photo gallery" the picture was still up on the screen, the last thing she had looked at before they left the bar. There was no question that this unique handcrafted charm pinned to T-Ron's hatband was the same one dangling from Tucker's ear.

Swiftly she moved back to the dresser, searching through the pendants hanging there and then zooming in on the already pixilated photo. Hard to tell if the one in her hand was identical, but it didn't matter. She was almost certain they were.

Her heart was racing now and she tried to calm herself down. This meant she was on the right track, that their paths had crossed, and that possibly Maggie's boat was involved. But T-Ron had blatantly lied to her when she asked if he knew Tucker. She tried to recall his words. *"Know him? I don't think so. Seen him? Perhaps."*

Who was on to who here? And what the fuck did "hunting trophy" actually mean?

"Whatcha doin', honey?"

She was startled to realize that although he hadn't moved a muscle, T-Ron's eyes were open and watching her.

"Just checking my messages. I thought I heard my phone chime." She closed out of the photo and dropped her cell back into her bag.

He held out a hand to her and pulled her back onto the bed next to him. "You're shivering." He rubbed his hand over the goose bumps on her leg.

She forced a laugh. "Must just be a reaction to all that heat we generated a little while ago." Reflexively she reached for the gin bottle on the nightstand. "Oh, damn. Forgot we finished this off."

101

"I like the way you look in my robe." He ran a finger down the strip of bare skin that was exposed between the front panels, and then closed his eyes again. "Shit, I'm kind of intoxicated."

Lucy was relieved; she needed to take some space and think about what to do next. "Probably I should go."

"No, don't," he mumbled and his fingers tightened their grip on the soft underside of her belly.

"What are you doing tomorrow? Maybe we can go out on your boat. I'd like to get out on the water." She gently pried his hand away and squeezed it between her own.

"My boat? Did I tell you about my boat? Yeah, sure. I'll take you out on my boat. Sounds like fun."

That was too easy, she thought, sliding out of his grasp. As she got dressed, she wondered if he was really drunk or if he was just pretending.

Speeding across the water the next afternoon, Lucy felt exhilarated. T-Ron took the waves hard and fast, grinning at her as she bounced up and down, grasping the edge of the seat to steady herself. This boat, The Great White, was not the one called Nico something that she'd been hoping for, but it was progress of a sort.

"I like that you're enjoying this!" he shouted. "Some women don't."

She found herself wishing that this excursion could just have been a normal date, not the cat and mouse game she knew they were playing.

"Where are we going?"

"Do we have to have a destination?"

Lucy struggled to keep her balance as he veered suddenly, steering the craft in a wide circle until they were facing the way they'd come, and then abruptly cutting the engine. Unsteadily she righted herself, trying to regain her composure and her bearings. As far she could tell, they were just bobbing in the open sea west of town.

T-Ron pulled a beer out of a cooler and popped it open. "Nice, isn't it? So close and yet so far."

102

His philosophical observation made her feel uneasy. "It's beautiful. And it's just us."

"Exactly. No one can see what we do. Or don't do. You want one of these?"

She made a face. "I'd rather have the gin. We've got ice, right?"

He pushed the cooler towards her with his bare foot. "Help yourself. I'm a little off the hard stuff after yesterday."

She sipped her drink and looked around. "So is this just a pleasure boat?"

"Well, now, that depends on who I bring with me." He ran the cold can across her shoulders. "Today, yes, it's a pleasure."

"But sometimes business? I'm just curious, that's all."

"Well, here's what I have to say about business." He moved closer, wrapping his legs around her ankles. "It's none of yours."

"Cheeky monkey." He was way too slick to be easily tripped up. She might as well just play along with him and enjoy what she could.

"You got a bathing suit on under this thing?" He lifted the skirt of her voluminous dress.

"What if I said no?" she teased; she would not admit that she'd had no intention of sitting on this boat with him wearing her matronly plus-sized swim attire.

"Then I'd say you just made my job a lot easier."

"Job? I thought we weren't talking business here." She was almost carried away by the flirtatiousness of the moment until the blinding sparkle of a rhinestone star on his straw hat flashed a warning at her. Tucker. This was about finding Tucker.

As he leaned towards her, she reached out to touch the carved turtle that hung from a braided cord around his neck. "So tell me about this. What's it about?"

His microsecond of hesitation did not go unnoticed. "It's just memorabilia. We have a lot of turtles on this island."

103

She gulped down a hefty swig of gin. "You say that like you own a piece of it."

"Interesting way to put it. I do actually own a house here." He tugged on the rubber band that she had used to keep her thick mane of curls in check during their ride. "You have amazing hair, Miss Lucy. I find it such a turn on."

"You men are all alike," she laughed, shaking her head to release the snowfall of wild locks. Mindless idiots, she added silently. So easily manipulated. She wondered why he lived in such a crappy little apartment if he actually had a real house. "So do you ever rent your property? I'm looking for a place to stay for a few weeks."

"Really?" His steely gaze locked on her own as he thoughtfully rubbed the end of a curl between his fingers. "It's kind of remote."

"Meaning?"

"Like almost as far away as you can get from town. In the countryside. You'd be very alone." She tried not to tremble as he massaged the back of her neck.

"I'm okay with alone. Is anyone staying there now?"

"Not at the moment. There's a little bit of unsavory history associated with the place."

"Like what?" Enjoying the sensation of his touch, her eyelids grew heavy, but when he didn't answer, she peered sideways for a covert look at him. He was staring out across the surface of the sea, towards a small offshore island, a harsh expression hardening on his features, belying the softness of his caress.

"Like what?" she asked again.

"Maybe piracy." He grabbed a hank of her hair suddenly and wrapped it around her neck like a rope. "Maybe extortion." His face was up against hers now, his breath hot against her cheek. She knew she should be terrified, but she felt more electrified than frightened. "Maybe even murder."

"Maybe? Why maybe?" He pulled the hair tighter around her neck for just a second before letting it go and she gasped a little, not because he'd been choking her but because she'd unconsciously been holding her breath. Hell, he was making her feel so sexy, she hated that she didn't trust him.

"Because nobody ever found evidence that it really happened?" Still watching her expression, he reached out and began undoing the buttons of her dress.

"Are you seducing me?" She laughed aloud, mentally trying to process what he'd just said.

"It's a little late for that question, don't you think?" He ran a finger provocatively under the strap of her now open dress, his gaze still locked on her own. "So do you want to be my tenant, Lucy Brookstone? Because I think I'd like that."

CHAPTER SEVEN

October/November 2017
Culebra, Puerto Rico

The sun had already been up over the bay for at least an hour by the time Tucker trudged wearily down the steep hill from the clinic and made his way back to the public dock. The night in the emergency room had been exhausting, both mentally and physically.

After he'd frantically aroused some help on the street to get Flush's body onto the public pier, he'd considered just jumping in the dinghy and fleeing. He didn't understand the fast slangy Spanish of the men who'd assisted him, but it became obvious that it would be more suspicious if he just ran off than if he went along with the process as the concerned rescuer of a drowned man.

But as it turned out, he'd had plenty of time, slumped on a hard plastic chair in the waiting room, to come up with an appropriate story regarding how he'd come across Flush floating lifelessly in Tamarindo Bay.

"Is this man a friend of yours?" the intake clerk asked him in heavily accented English, her tired face an expressionless mask.

"An acquaintance. I only met him after the hurricane." So far nothing that was really a lie.

"What is his name?"

"John something." That was true too.

"Age?"

He could truthfully say he had no idea.

"Address?"

He had hardly had to lie at all.

The police were only slightly more inquisitive. It seemed that nobody questioned his lack of knowledge; they just wanted somebody else to take on the responsibilities associated with death so they could get on with their business. They literally did not want to have to dispose of the body, especially without the contact info of a family member.

He had to repeat his story a few times and he kept it as vague as possible. "John" had asked him for a boat ride to the beach to swim with the turtles; Tucker had left him there with his gear. When he'd come back to pick him up he'd found him floating face down in the bay. "He had a life vest. I thought he would be fine."

A doctor had been called, but there was no one on Culebra to do any kind of forensic examination. The preliminary medical conclusion was that Flush might actually have died of a heart attack and that the water in his lungs could be a result of the fact that he had lost consciousness after his heart failed. Tucker wanted to believe it was true, that even if he'd still been there on the beach, that he might not have been able to save him. He tried not to think of the fact that Flush might have been able to call for help if there had been someone within earshot. How long had he been gone – maybe an hour and a half?

There were only a few people out on the street as he walked back through town towards the dock. He hoped that some place might be open to get something to eat, but in post-hurricane Culebra that was wishful thinking. There was food on the boat – he just had to get himself there. Then he could eat. Sleep. Figure out what to do next.

The wind had picked up in the night and there were white caps forming on the rolling surface of the Ensenada Honda as he steered out across the bay. Bleary-eyed from lack of rest, he didn't notice the motorboat tied up beside the Nico Tico II until he was almost upon it.

"What the fuck..." Angrily he turned off the outboard engine and floated silently forward. There was no one in sight, on deck or in the other boat. Expertly he guided the dinghy in as quietly as possible and tied it off to the railing.

He stood up and peered over the edge of the uninvited craft. Tucker sucked in his breath. There was a black garbage bag tossed into the hull and he suspected it wasn't trash that bulged inside.

"What the fuck..." he repeated in a fearful whisper. The Nico was not just being randomly plundered, it was being strategically robbed by someone who knew what they were looking for. He fought his instinct to run; everything he owned and more was onboard.

Gingerly he threw himself over the railing and landed lightly on the side deck, steadying himself as the boat rolled a little bit under his weight. He could hear someone inside the cabin, tossing things around. He crawled towards the hatchway and peered around the edge.

The galley had been ransacked; contents of the cupboards dumped out unceremoniously onto any available surface from table to floor. The jigsaw puzzle was upside down, pieces strewn everywhere. A couple of empty beer cans had been added to the mix, tossed into the mess on the counter as if it was a garbage dump. A tall silhouette filled the doorway to the sleeping quarters; he could see a yellow T-shirt and a pair of grubby cargo shorts. A low voice was singing softly some repetitive line from an old drinking song.

"Why don't we get drunk and screw? I just bought a waterbed and it's filled up for me and you, so why don't we get drunk..." Between lyrics the man was talking to himself. "Where is it, you motherfucker? Not under the mattress. Not under the bed. There's gotta be more than this freakin' little stash – this is your spending money."

Terrified, Tucker looked around for something to defend himself. His fingers closed around the handle of a dented metal tea kettle, still heavy with boiled water from the previous day's breakfast.

The body blocking the door moved to one side and Tucker could see a heap of assorted belongings of random value piled haphazardly in the middle of the bed. Cash, passports, pocketknives, the solar lantern, a water filter pitcher. His vision focused in on the passports, a few thoughts crossing his mind. First, he hadn't realized that Flush even had any identification; it must have been with his stash at Maggie's while he was in jail. And second, this thief was about to steal his own passport – and he was not about to let that happen.

As he swung the kettle high above his head, the man whipped around suddenly, brandishing a sharp knife; its long curved shape made Tucker think of marauding desert nomads on camels. It clanged against the teapot's trajectory, knocking it neatly to one side and nicking Tucker's thumb in the process.

He was too worked up to pay attention to the stream of blood that gushed down his wrist and forearm. "What the hell do you think you're doing?"

Framed by a graying handlebar moustache and a sparse goatee, a smirk formed on his opponent's lips. With the tip of his knife he hooked the edge of Tucker's passport and deftly flipped it into the air, catching it with his other hand. "So you must be...Tucker Brookstone Mackenzie? My, my, not even twenty years old. Just a... let's see... small town Vermont boy, all alone on a boat in the Caribbean."

"Get off my boat." He did not sound anywhere near as tough as he felt.

"Your boat?" The smirk became a sneer. "Somebody die and leave you in charge?"

In any other circumstances his question would just have been a smartass remark, but given the events of the last twenty-four hours it shook Tucker to his core. He felt something wet fall on his bare foot; glancing down he saw the blood from his thumb wound dripping off his elbow onto the floor. Angrily holding it to his mouth, he glared at the interloper in front of him, his mind racing.

This was a dangerous situation; the man was after something specific – this was no random act of piracy. He should probably just get in his dinghy and go to the police, but he sensed that he was already implicated in something way bigger than just post-hurricane thievery.

"So if this is *your* boat, then where is it?"

Tucker willed himself not to look up at the panel in the cabin ceiling, keeping his eyes on the threatening blade. "Where is what?"

The movement was so swift, he didn't even see the knife move before he felt it against his throat. He held his breath, wishing his parents might have taken him to church so that he would now have a god to pray to. "He never told you?"

"Told me what?"

"How'd he get you to sail him here then? He didn't cut you in?" On the word 'cut' the man snickered a little and then neatly slashed through the braided hemp strands of Tucker's necklace. He held the carved pendant aloft, letting it dangle above their heads.

Tucker understood now why this was the moment in movies when victims peed their pants. "He - he paid me."

Time stood still in the brief hesitation that followed his answer. Then, in another lightning fast action, the man had pocketed the pendant and had a grip on Tucker's silver earring. The blade felt like ice as it pressed against his earlobe and he struggled to keep his legs from buckling beneath him.

"You sure about that now?"

He didn't dare nod. "Yes."

"Hmm. Okay, then." Tucker could feel the tug of the feather-shaped earring as the man twisted it between his fingers. "I fancy this little trophy here. You want to remove it or should I just slice it off?"

A few minutes later, Tucker stumbled off the deck into the dinghy. He knew he should feel lucky to be escaping with his life and without his passport, but at the same time he was angrier than he'd ever been. He had no doubt who the man was who had just terrorized him – and he was not going to be beaten by him. He would fight on his own behalf, and Flush's. And he would return to retrieve the hidden stash as he soon he could manage to get back.

Fiona wasn't around when he finally arrived at the campsite. Unzipping the "guest tent," he crawled in and flopped miserably onto the thin nylon floor, his aching body aware of every rock and root beneath it. Too exhausted to sleep, he lay there, sweating, trying to relax, and attempting to process everything that had happened in the last twenty four hours.

He had not realized that he'd drifted off until he jerked suddenly into consciousness when something wet passed across his forehead and eyes. Involuntarily he flung an arm out, and felt a soft thud as it made contact with whatever was hovering above him.

"Ouch! Chill. It's only me." Fiona's voice had a musicality to it even when irritated. "Just trying to cool you off. And wipe the dried blood away. You look like you were in a fight."

"I was." Tucker's tension drained away like rainwater in a downhill gutter. Through half-opened eyes he watched her wring a cloth out in a plastic bowl and gently wash the battle stains from his dirty hands. He couldn't remember the last time anyone had touched him so tenderly; he was afraid to move, he did not want her to stop.

"You were? With who? And what happened to your thumb? That's a nasty cut."

He didn't know how much he should tell her. "A pirate who was robbing the boat when I got back from the clinic."

"What?" Against his best hopes, the washing ceased. "That opens up a whole lot of new questions. But answer the one about where all your stuff is."

Finally he propped himself up on his elbows and looked at her. Her wild hair was pulled up into a high ponytail that showed off the pleasant contours of her face. His gaze drifted unconsciously down to the freckles covering the sunburned expanse of flesh exposed between the tiny black triangles of her bikini. He barely knew Fiona, he'd not even had time to fantasize about getting closer to her, but now

111

she was pretty much the only friend he had on the island. Although he did seem to have an enemy.

He sank back onto the ground and sighed. "Flush is dead. And I think he was murdered."

They sat outside at the broken wooden picnic table, eating dry sandwiches of stale white bread and soggy sliced cheese, washed down with warm water, while Tucker told Fiona about everything that had happened since he'd last seen her. Her chewing slowed and then came to an abrupt halt as he described the thief on the boat.

"You know who he is?" It was clearly a rhetorical question.

She swallowed and took a sip from the water bottle before answering. "Yeah. It's a small island. Especially now."

"And..."

"Trust me. You don't want to fuck with him."

"Yeah, well, as far as I'm concerned that's not an option anymore."

She touched his arm in a gesture that was meant to be restraining. Instead he found it electrifying, a hot current that was given more voltage by his growing sense of violation. When he placed his hand on top of hers, she grasped it and stood up.

"How about a swim." She was not asking; it was a command.

Leading him to the water's edge, she slid out of her shorts and waded in, turning to him. He realized he still had his swim trunks on under his own shorts; he hadn't changed clothes since long before the trip to Tamarindo Beach, which seemed like ancient history. He was suddenly aware of how gross he smelled and how unclean he must actually be. What he wouldn't give for a real bath right now; he didn't want Fiona to find him disgusting.

The shallow water in Datiles Bay was actually warmer than any shower he'd had in weeks. He sat on the sandy bottom and scrubbed at the dirt on his body and watched

Fiona float on her back. The sun was low; he must have slept away more of the day than he realized. Cotton ball clouds drifted carelessly across the crystalline sky. If he stayed completely in the present, and didn't think about the horrors of the past or the uncertainty of the future, his life couldn't have been better.

His mind wandered to other times that he'd felt like this; there'd almost always been weed involved. He hadn't smoked in months and suddenly he wished he had some. He wondered if Fiona had any pot and then quickly suppressed the thought. She seemed so wholesome and natural — maybe she didn't even drink.

He looked in her direction and she grinned. "What are you thinking about?"

"How awesome this is place is." He laughed. "And how I don't have a clue what happens next."

A faint but persistent buzzing made Tucker wonder if he had water in his ear or if perhaps he was actually starting to lose his mind. As the sound grew louder, he thought maybe a swarm of bees was headed for them, perhaps set off course from some migratory pattern because of the hurricane. Then something passed nearly overhead, like an alien flying spider, marring the perfection of the view. Instinctively they both ducked and then stared open-mouthed at the creature hovering above.

"What the fuck is that?" Tucker shaded his eyes with a hand.

"I think it's a drone." Fiona whispered the words, as though maybe someone might overhear her. "We see them sometimes. Maybe it's the government assessing the damage."

"So, what – like there's a camera in it? Looking at us?"

The boy in him was instantly attracted to the idea of a big electronic remote control toy that could fly. But as the drone circled around and then lingered over them, he began to feel uncomfortable.

"Usually it's just rich tourists, but a few people on the island have them. Don't know why they'd be wasting their electricity charging one now, though." Fiona turned her face skyward and stuck out her tongue. "Fuck you, buddy!" she yelled.

In the spirit of the moment, Tucker jumped up and down, waving his fists and then leaned over and pulled down his shorts, mooning whatever little lens was looking at them. A minute later, the drone pulled up to a higher elevation and moved off, disappearing over the hillside.

"That was weird." Fiona frowned. "It seemed like it was spying on us."

"Different than other times?"

"Yes." The spell felt broken now. "I don't like it. Feels like my privacy is being invaded." She began wading towards shore. In the distance they could hear the sound of the drone engine approaching again. "Let's go up under the trees where we're not so obvious."

Tucker followed, although he knew that the leafless branches would provide little camouflage protection in any way other than psychologically. "Why don't we just go inside one of the tents? It'll be dark in like an hour anyway and then we can come back out."

Fiona pulled her pink sarong and a small green hand towel off the clothesline. "Okay, but dry yourself off." She handed him the towel; if he hadn't lived on a boat it would seem like ridiculously ineffective equipment but he knew better.

As the drone crested the ridge, Tucker ducked inside with Fiona right behind him. He stopped short and she bumped into him, wet skin against wet skin as they fell over into a pile of limbs on the tent floor.

"Sorry–" she began to apologize. But then it seemed like just the most natural thing in the world to wrap his arms around her and put his lips to her lips.

For a second she melted into him, sighing, but then suddenly she was wide-eyed and pulled away, catching her breath. "We shouldn't do this."

"Why not?" He felt dizzy with the reawakened sensations of human closeness.

"It will just wreck things. It always does."

"Always?" He kissed her again, as he tried to consider whether her warning was wise or wary. She tasted sweet and salty at the same time. Like ice cream and pretzels. Hell, why did it everything always come back to food for him. He was hungry for this too.

"Pretty much, for me." She did not move away this time, the breathiness of her words warm against his mouth.

"Mmm, how so?" He was only half-listening, more interested in running his hands along the smooth skin of her narrow waistline and lower back.

"I've only had a few boyfriends. I don't get close to people easily."

"You're pretty close to me now." He pressed against her, joining any remaining gaps between their bodies, savoring the moment, hoping she would relax.

She didn't reply, instead putting her head against his shoulder and lightly grazing her fingers along his arm. He buried his nose in her damp curls, smelling the scent of the sea along with faint remnants of shampoo.

"I haven't been with anyone for almost a year," she murmured. "I'm a little rusty at this."

"Well, I haven't either."

"What? No way. You're just saying that because I did."

"Yes way." Chloe was in his past life now; he would not allow her memory to spoil this experience for him. Squeezing Fiona to him, he said, "So let's just agree this is all new for both us."

"Okay. But...can we just talk for a while? Like this?"

"Sure." He was pretty certain she could tell how aroused he was, but he was also just as certain that he still would be whenever she was ready to move forward.

"Wow. That was amazing." Fiona moved slowly away from him so that they could let the air dry the sweat from their bodies. "You are quite...accomplished." She laughed. "Where did you learn all that stuff?"

Tucker was surprised that he could feel embarrassed after the hours of intimacy they had just shared. "Let's just say I was a good student. My teacher was rather demanding." It was the first time he'd ever allowed himself to make a joke about his failed relationship and it felt really good.

He had never imagined how different it could be making love to another woman. Chloe had been an electric guitar, lusty and raucous. Fiona was more of a delicate musical instrument, a fine violin. With Chloe he had never felt like he could give her as much as she needed; with Fiona he was afraid he might not be gentle enough. Everything about her seemed softer and more fragile, from her small round breasts and raspberry nipples to the fluff of peach-colored curls between her legs. Her orgasms were full of surprise and delight, with the appreciation of someone receiving an unexpected gift.

"Do you think it's the middle of the night? I've lost all sense of time."

"Does it matter?" With his forefinger he idly traced the circle of her bellybutton.

"I'm just wondering how soon till I can make breakfast. I'm starving."

"Why can't we just have it now? Whatever time it is."

Raising her head to rest on one elbow, she gazed at him questioningly. He could see that she was struggling with the idea of breaking her daily routine even further than she already had today, and it endeared her to him even more.

"Okay then. You hold the light while I cook the eggs."

"Wait." He leaned over and let his tongue run lightly over one of her already stimulated nipples. "First I want to do this again. And again."

Fiona fed him a forkful of scrambled eggs from the one plate she owned and then said, "I do need to get some sleep. I have to work in the morning."

116

"Really?" He felt so relaxed and in the moment, he could barely comprehend what world she was speaking about. "Where? How?"

"Cleaning a house out in Zoni. The owners are paying us to get rid of the hurricane's legacy of mold and mildew before it takes over."

"Zoni!" It was the other side of the island, not easily accessible without a car, and not really reachable by boat either. "How will you get there?"

"A woman I work with picks me up at the public dock in town. I usually leave as soon as it gets light." She shivered a little and ducked back into the tent, returning wearing a T-shirt and looking at a watch with a broken band. "Wow. It's almost 3 am."

"I'll take you over there in the dinghy." Her mention of real life made him think about his own. "I'd like to get back over to the Nico Tico and see if I can salvage anything without running into anyone with a big knife."

"Be careful! Your life is more important than your possessions."

He liked that she was concerned about his well-being. "Don't worry. But there is something important I need to retrieve. Believe me when I say it's worth it."

When he helped her tie the kayak to the dock a few hours later, the smile she gave him was a mixture of exhaustion and contentment. "Promise you'll go back to the campsite as soon as you're done, right?"

"Yes. Promise." A battered blue SUV was coming down the street towards them and she waved and moved towards it. When she opened the passenger door, a little brown dog hopped out to greet her, its fluffy tail wagging like a welcome flag, and then hopped back in on her lap. Tucker averted his face as the dark-haired driver gazed at him with amused interest while she lit a cigarette before turning the car around.

He sighed and gunned the motor as quietly as possible. It was hard to be stealthy in a motorized dinghy. Even at this early hour there were signs of life on the few boats in the harbor. He could see a man having coffee on the deck of a beautiful wooden schooner that had somehow escaped the hurricane unscathed. He would love to sail a boat like that someday. Across the bay, a shaggy slim sailor was climbing off his small sloop into a rowboat which he pointed in the direction of town.

Low clouds in the eastern sky kept the sun from making its usual brilliant display as it breached the horizon, extending a facade of predawn protection. But as he approached the mooring in the mangroves, any false sense of well-being he was experiencing slipped quickly away.

The Nico Tico was resting at a precarious angle, the aft deck underwater, the hatchway flooded to at least knee level. The wreckage of the interior furnishings floated around the half-submerged craft, cushions, containers and clothing bobbing and sinking in the shallow sea water.

Tucker heard a low growl and realized it had come from his own throat. With a blood-curdling war cry, he leaped onto the slanted deck and clawed his way over the cabin to peer in the open doorway. Through the water-logged galley he could see that the bedroom in the fore section was still mostly dry, although the mattress had been slashed to ribbons and their possessions had been trashed. Cautiously, he lowered himself into the murky mess, literally climbing his way upward to what was now the highest part of the cabin. Hanging onto the clothing rod in the empty narrow closet to steady himself, he looked up at the ceiling.

The panel was still intact.

Fifteen minutes later he was on his way back to town, two black garbage bags tucked securely under his seat, a small stack of wet clothing and a sopping backpack at his feet, a soaking crossword puzzle book drying in the wind.

By the time Fiona returned that afternoon, he was passed out from the exhaustion of his exertions. He'd tried to dig a hole in the hillside, but the hard-packed dirt and coral were almost impossible to penetrate without proper tools. He had eventually resorted to rocks and dead branches as camouflage cover and protection. After sucking down a can of soup that he'd managed to retrieve, he'd collapsed onto the air mattress, unconscious for several hours.

Equally tired, Fiona unpacked a backpack full of groceries and curled up next to him. When Tucker finally awoke it was almost dark and she was wrapped tightly around him, sleeping so soundly he could barely detach himself from her grasp to go outside to take a leak.

It took another minute or two for him to register the monotonous tone of the buzzing overhead. He looked up to once again see the drone, moving slowly across the sky above the campsite clearing to hover above him.

"Fucking perverts," he muttered. "Get away from my day."

In the next forty-eight hours Tucker felt more content than he had in years. It was the circle of life in its most primal perfection – make love, talk, sleep, make love, talk, eat, make love, talk, swim, and repeat. The only dark cloud in the landscape was the return appearance of the drone. Once in the late morning and then again, just before dusk, the remote control device appeared out of nowhere, watching and waiting. They had gone out in the dinghy just beyond the reefs to see if they could catch something fresh for dinner with Fiona's fishing line, when they saw it coming through the sky towards them. There was no doubt in either of their minds now that it was watching them, and out on the open water they felt exposed and vulnerable.

Later, when they were cleaning and cooking the catch of the day over a small barbecue pit, Fiona was strangely quiet, not in her usual introspective way, but in a distant, brooding manner that made Tucker a little nervous. He knew everything couldn't stay perfect forever, but he was hoping.

They sat on the bench eating off the new red plastic plates using the cheap metal forks that Fiona had picked up on her last trip to town when she'd returned from the cleaning excursion.

"This is incredibly civilized. And delicious," Tucker declared. "Props to us."

"Mmm." Fiona's reply indicated she didn't really feel like talking and he'd learned to respect that, but there was something different about this silence.

"You okay? What's up?"

She put down her fork and looked seaward at the lingering sunset glow that defined the horizon.

"I don't think it's safe for you to stay here."

Staring at her, he swallowed the mouthful of food. "What? Why?"

She poked at the meal, not meeting his gaze. "Well, for starters there's Phil."

"Who's Phil?" His appetite was suddenly gone. "I thought you didn't have a boyfriend."

"The guy who lives in the tent across the clearing. I told you that was his name."

Tucker had only seen the lean, ragged, and rather savage-looking camper a few times during his stay and had tried to stay out of his way. For the last few days he had left early in the morning, a small dirty white dog at his heels, and had staggered in after dark more than a little inebriated. He had paid no attention to Fiona's side of the clearing other than to tell the dog to stop barking.

"Is he a problem? He doesn't seem to give a shit about what you do."

"He's a gossip. He talks to the other local drunks about any little thing that's new and different on this island."

Tucker considered this, not sure what she was getting at.

"And then there's the drone," she went on. "Someone is watching you, I'm sure it's not me they're interested in."

He could feel reality beginning to seep into the cracks of what he had hoped was an airtight fantasy life with Fiona. "So...what are saying? You want me to leave?" He couldn't believe he had even voiced that unthinkable question.

"No." She reached out to grasp his hand. "But I'm afraid for you. I think you should stay somewhere else."

He started to protest that he had no place else to stay on Culebra, but then he sensed that she had a plan. "Like where? And more importantly, will you be there too?"

The buzzing noise came to him through his early morning dreams and he swatted at the air, assuming it was a mosquito disturbing his pleasant reverie. He had been diving beneath the surface of crystal blue waters with Fiona by his side in the company of half a dozen turtles and then he was rising swiftly to consciousness to kill some annoying bug that had disturbed his fantasy.

He reached out, expecting to come in contact with Fiona's soft skin and instead felt only the warm indentation on the mattress of where she had been. "Fi?" He said her name aloud, without opening his eyes, not ready to break into the reality of daytime yet, hoping she had not already abandoned him for her morning routines. His body was telling him that the best way to start his day would be with a little predawn sex play.

When she did not respond, he pushed himself up onto his elbows and looked around. The buzzing was getting louder now and he realized that it was not the sound of a hungry insect at all – it was the sound of the drone.

"What the fuck." As he came to a sitting position, he heard a strange whistling rush of air followed by a muffled thump. Then the whirring of the motor hovering above abruptly stopped; the ensuing silence was broken by what sounded like a large animal crashing through the underbrush.

"What the fuck," he repeated, reaching for his shorts and scrambling for the screened opening of the tent. "Fiona! Are you all right?"

He stepped out into the clearing, panicking when he did not see her anywhere. "Fiona!" he called again.

121

"Over here."

He turned to see her emerging from beneath a large broken branch of a leafless tree. She was naked except for a pair of flipflops and a crocheted bag that she wore slung across her scratched and mud-streaked body. In one hand she held what appeared to be a primitive slingshot; in the other was a black contraption that she grasped by a broken wing as though it were a freshly killed bird that she was bringing home for dinner.

"Got it." With a triumphant grin she held up the drone, a huntress proudly displaying her quarry. At that moment, he thought he'd never seen anyone so beautiful. "Now – do you want to do the honors?" She laid it at his feet like a mother cat delivering a rat to her young.

Gleefully Tucker lifted a large rock and smashed the offensive object into a heap of small plastic pieces. Then he folded Fiona into his arms for a massive kiss.

"You are amazing."

"Mmm, maybe. But I probably just put you into more danger than you were before. Whoever owns it is definitely going to come looking for it. And soon."

A day later Tucker was living in a gecko-infested cottage behind a multi-million dollar mansion overlooking Zoni Beach.

CHAPTER EIGHT

July 2018
Culebra, Puerto Rico

Tyler had forgotten all the things he liked about Culebra. Sitting now at the Dinghy Dock bar with a cold beer, watching the sky turn sunset colors over the bay, he felt himself unwinding into what he considered a "Caribbean state of consciousness," relaxed and in the moment. For the next hour, he vowed to let go of his reasons for returning here and just enjoy the island scene.

From what he could gather, this popular watering hole and eatery had only reopened a few months earlier, after being closed for more than half a year for reconstruction due to the ravaging of Hurricane Maria. Reinforced to withstand the rages of future storms and rebuilt with a bigger bar and a wider deck, it still had the same open, airy atmosphere and the sense of being the central place where seafarers and landlubbers converged and merged. There were only a handful of yachts in the harbor, way fewer than he recalled, and just a couple of dinghies tied up to the restaurant's mooring cleats.

An assortment of tanned and tattered regulars populated the bar stools, some staring fixedly at their cell phones, others chatting intently, sharing the island news and/or their own views. He remembered a few of the more distinctive characters – a bald man with wire-rimmed glasses and a fuzzy white waist-length beard drinking a Margarita, a very bronzed woman with a small brown dog sitting in her lap, a patrician-looking sailor in a faded red T-shirt, and a looming lunk of a man with eyes as wild as his silver hair.

"Hey, haven't you been here before?" The large fellow had a gravelly voice that matched his size. "I kinda remember seeing you a few years ago."

Only a few moments on the island and he was already busted. "Good memory."

"Yeah, yeah, you were involved with that chick who turned out to be a lunatic murderer, right? What was her name?" He snapped his brown fingers as he tried to recall the incident and a few nearby patrons looked up with interest at his comment.

Tyler bent his head low and took a swig of beer. "Elle," he said quietly. "Her name was Elle."

"Yeah, yeah, Elle. The big bust down at the campground, right? That was a pretty major story around here for a while. Before the hurricanes." The guy laughed. "So what, you came back for more excitement?"

He'd wanted one night just to chill before he jumped into the work of continuing his search for missing family members. But apparently the question had been rhetorical, because the man went on. "Elle – now there was a perfect example of the aggressive female predators that Culebra seems to breed. Blonde and dangerous, is what I call them. A local species you don't want to talk about."

"I resent that remark, Barry." A big-boned woman with well-defined shoulders and strong arms edged her way into the bar between them. Her sun-bleached hair was pulled up in a messy ponytail; the rest hung in heavy bangs above a well-weathered face. "On behalf of all the empowered females on this island, let me welcome you to Culebra." With a defiant sideways smile at Barry, she leaned over and kissed Tyler on the cheek. "I'm Kay. What's your name and where are you from?"

Above her head, Barry mouthed the words, "See what I mean?"

Tyler had to laugh. Throughout his life he had made the same mistakes over and over again, but there was no way he was going to be romantically or sexually entrapped in the Caribbean again. Ever.

Kay was more than helpful. When she heard Tyler's story, she clucked her tongue sympathetically while she sipped the glass of red wine he'd bought her. After sharing her own photos of grown children and grandbabies with him, she took Tyler's phone and moved around the bar, showing the photo of Tucker to the various customers, all of whom she seemed to know. He noticed a few of them scanning him with odd expressions on their faces that ranged from curious to suspicious, and a couple of times Kay glanced in his direction with raised eyebrows as she listened to their comments.

Tyler watched her as she worked the room. She'd told him she'd been living on a boat in the harbor since February, keeping an eye on it for some friends. Her can-do attitude was definitely her defining feature, more than any physical prowess. The faded yellow tank top and khaki shorts she wore were baggy enough to hide a shape which spoke to an athletic youth that had evolved to a more sedentary middle-age. First impression was that she was probably a good ally to have on this island, but he knew from a lifetime of experience that he was a notoriously bad judge of character.

"Well, Tyler Mackenzie, there seems to be some island buzz around this photo of your son. Is there a bounty on his head or something?"

He felt his stomach grow a little queasy. "Why would you ask me that?" He had no idea if Tucker might be wanted for some island crime.

"Because apparently a few of these good people here say they've seen a picture of him before. Recently, in fact." She slid his phone across the bar and cocked her head quizzically, waiting for his reaction.

He called on all his acting abilities to keep his face expressionless. "Really. And where did they see it?" He hoped she wouldn't say on the eleven o'clock news.

"Apparently someone else was in here a couple of weeks ago doing the same thing as you."

125

He took a large swig of his beer before replying. "You mean showing his photo around on a phone."

"Exactly that."

"And? Anybody recognize him?"

"Perry thought he remembered seeing him, but like months ago. And Mo thinks he might be a friend of a young girl who works with the kayak operation out at Tamarindo." Kay leaned her elbows on the back of his barstool and smirked a little. "So you act like maybe you know who the other person looking for him was."

"I have a pretty good idea. She still on the island?"

"Your ex-wife, you mean?"

He nearly spit his beer out on the counter. "Hardly. I've never been married. But she is the mother of my son."

"Well, from what I hear she's a real piece of work."

He had a strange sense of deja-vu back to his conversation with Maggie on Tortola. "Whatever. I'm not looking for her. She can take care of herself."

"I wouldn't be so sure of that. Shit." In a surprisingly un-islandlike gesture, Kay glanced at her watch. "Here comes Mirabel. I'm going to have to leave in a minute."

A dark wiry woman in a short black dress was approaching them. Thick chin-length gray hair swung in a sharp arc as she shook her head in exasperation when she saw Kay. "If we don't go over to Zacos now, we may not get served quickly enough to make it to the game on time."

Kay turned to Tyler. "Do you play poker?"

Before he could respond, Mirabel spoke up. "Just so you know, we play for money."

He had no idea what he was actually agreeing to, but it seemed like an offer he couldn't refuse. With unforeseen opportunities for information gathering. "If you're inviting me, I'd love to join."

Mirabel shrugged. "Then let's go. I've got to eat something or I won't be able to think straight."

The two women walked up the stairs in front of him, heads together, laughing and talking in an exclusive girlfriend-like way that made Tyler briefly question his decision.

"You sure it's okay for me to play?" he asked as the three of them crossed a metal bridge under an arch of sturdy industrial steel beams painted bright orange. The structure seemed overbuilt and out of place on an island where nearly every street was a maze of potholes and crumbling asphalt. "I know how insular these games can be."

"It's an open game. In the summer we especially welcome new blood, when there are fewer of us playing on a regular basis." Mirabel's attitude made it pretty clear to Tyler that she was not much interested in adding some tourist gringo to her Culebra social circle.

"It's fine," Kay assured him. "It's mostly a bunch of pot-smoking old hippies from Vermont anyway. You'll fit right in."

"Hey – I don't actually fit that profile," he started to protest, but neither of them was listening as they stared in dismay at the "Closed" sign on the door of Zaco's Tacos.

"Damn, I can never keep up with their current days of operation," muttered Mirabel. "What's our alternative?"

Forty-five minutes later, they sat in Mirabel's rusted Jeep Cherokee outside a blue house in a neighborhood Tyler was unfamiliar with, finishing up pizza slices washed down with plastic cups of red wine.

"So when's the best time for me to find this girl who works for the kayak tours?" Tyler had a feeling that as the night progressed, he might lose his investigative edge into the distraction of the game.

"You probably know better than me, Mirabel. I haven't been out to Tamarindo that much."

"What are we talking about?" Mirabel took a hit of a carved wooden pipe and passed it to Kay.

"Oh, I guess you missed that part of the conversation." Kay held the pipe out to Tyler but he waved it away. Pot was a vice he rarely indulged in anymore. "We think the kayak girl might know something about Tyler's missing son."

"That one with the curly red hair? She's cute, I don't know her. Only seen her. They usually take people out around mid-day. I would just go hang out at Tamarindo, you'll see her. Or ask someone out there."

"You guys coming in or what?" A deep voice bellowed at them through a louvered screen door. "It's time to buy in."

"Rules, rules. There're more enforced rules for Thursday night poker than there are for anything else on this island." Maribel kicked open the car door. "Unless you want to climb over the seat, you'll have to reach through the window and use the outside handle," she told Tyler. "We're coming, Simon!" she called.

Maribel had not been joking – there was nothing laid back about Culebra poker. Tyler was surprised to see how a group composed primarily of pot-smoking retirees and sailors could be so serious about a weekly card game. But as he settled into the rhythm and got to know their personalities, he realized how shallow his first impressions had been.

Besides Kay, Maribel and himself, the current evening's players included a local farmer, two former lawyers, a mystery writer, a retired carpenter, a restaurant owner and a sailor who had apparently just inherited a family fortune. The most interesting and disturbing character was the one who arrived late, a tall man wearing a straw cowboy hat festooned with trinkets and an expression of superior smugness.

"Shit, I was hoping he wasn't coming," Maribel muttered under her breath to Kay.

"What's up with him?" Tyler whispered in Kay's other ear.

"He's an erratic player who bluffs a lot and raises the stakes too high. You'll see." Then she greeted him in a louder voice. "Hey T-Ron! What's happening, dude?"

The hawk-faced man gave obligatory cheek kisses to the women, nodded at the men, and made a sharp scrutiny of Tyler.

"Fresh meat?" he asked Kay.

"Don't be a dickhead," was her response. "Or at least try to be less of one."

The newcomer accepted his dressing down silently as he counted out his chips amid an amused round of chuckles and exclamations. There were no chairs left so he squeezed in at the corner of the table and perched high on a stool. Regular conversation dissipated into terse poker talk as the game commenced, but Tyler could sense the shift away from comfortable neighborhood banter.

Pretending to study the two of hearts and king of spades in his hand, Tyler observed "T-Ron," as he'd heard him called. Although not particularly handsome, there was something compelling about his appearance in a dangerously unconventional way. He could imagine that a certain kind of woman would find him incredibly attractive. There were three things that immediately caught his eye: the ridiculous hat, (which he had not removed even though it was night and he was indoors), his oversized moustache that hovered somewhere between dashing and sinister, and an ostentatious studded belt with a distastefully ornate buckle. But as Tyler's eyes traveled lower, he realized he had missed the most defining feature of all. From a tooled leather holster on the belt, emerged the gracefully curved handle of a large knife, its long wide blade concealed within the sheath. When he looked up, the man was watching him with a troubled gaze, as if trying to work something out.

"Tyler, your call."

"Check."

When the betting came around to T-Ron, he calmly pushed twenty chips into the center of the table, still keeping his eyes on Tyler. "See you and raise you."

A murmur bristled around the table and Tyler heard Mirabel mutter, "Stupid bluffing fuck."

One by one each of the other players folded and T-Ron raked the pot into his own pile. As the next round was being dealt, he nodded at Tyler. "I've forgotten your name."

"Maybe because we've never met before?" There was something about this guy that rubbed him the wrong way, and apparently he was not alone in that feeling.

"Tyler, Tiburon. Better known as T-Ron." Kay made the formal introduction with a flippant wave. "There. Happy?"

In a just a few seconds, the tension around the table had escalated to an acutely uncomfortable level. A bearded man named Ben lit a vaping pipe and sucked on it vigorously as the farmer named Wilson shuffled the cards. On the following hand, T-Ron again started the betting with an outsized raise, forcing everyone to fold. "So Tyler, is this your first time to Culebra? Because I feel like I've seen you somewhere."

Tyler stared at his cards and didn't answer right away, trying to keep his annoyance under control. A pair of aces...what were the chances... He was going to see this hand through. "Actually I was here a few years ago. Were you here when those murders took place?"

"Which ones would those be?" someone else asked. "We've had more murders than you might imagine for a four-by-seven-mile island."

"Remember a woman named Elle?" Tyler watched as T-Ron once again pushed a large pile of chips to the center of the table while the other players sighed in disgust. Tyler held up a hand. "Hold on. I see you and I raise you ten."

A hush settled over the room. "Crazy Elle?" asked Ben.

"Not now." Ben was quickly shushed by the others as everyone concentrated on the dynamics unfolding between Tyler and T-Ron.

"Okay, then. Now we've got a game." T-Ron matched Tyler's bet. "Pot's right."

The current dealer laid out the cards – one face down and three up. A four, a jack, an ace. A flurry of oohs and aahs and then a silence descended. "To you, Tyler."

"Raise ten."

"How much you got left, I'm putting you all in."

Tyler pushed the remainder of his chips to the center. Even if he lost this hand, it was worth twenty bucks to give this jerk a run for his money.

The next card turned over was a nine. The last card, another nine.

"Okay, let's see 'em, boys."

Tyler laid down his aces and the group went wild. "A full house, a freakin' boat, way to go!"

"Show your cards, shark man," Mirabel demanded.

After a brief dramatic hesitation and the ghost of a smirk, T-Ron put his hand out on the table. "Guess you got me."

The man had nothing – a five and a six. It was a pure bluff and Tyler assumed that probably most of his playing was that and everyone here knew it and disliked him for it.

"Thank you," Kay whispered, patting his thigh.

After a few more rounds of T-Ron's same playing style, Ben stood up abruptly. "If this is what our poker night has become, I am not in this game anymore."

"I'm with you." The player to his right rose as well.

"Hold on." Simon, the owner of the house put up a hand. "This is an open game, but it has to be for people who play fair."

"Are you saying that I'm cheating?" There was no ignoring T-Ron's threatening tone.

"I'm going to just say it straight up." Behind his wire-rimmed glasses, Ben's pale blue eyes had gone from merry to piercing. "You're turning something very enjoyable into an unpleasant competitive experience. This is not how we do it here in this community."

"And what makes you more part of 'this community' than me?" T-Ron was as still as an ocelot watching its prey, but Tyler noticed that he now had one hand resting on the shaft of his knife.

"My attitude, for starters."

131

For a few seconds it seemed like nobody at the table was even breathing, and then Simon stood up forcefully. Pulling a twenty dollar bill from the till, he smacked it down on the table in front of T-Ron. "There's your buy-in. As the host, I'm telling you that you are purposefully acting like an asshole, and I'm asking you to leave."

T-Ron gripped his knife intimidatingly and looked around the table. All sense of island relaxation had disappeared from the faces that stared him down in solidarity. The intensity of the moment would have seemed beyond belief if Tyler had not witnessed a similar situation the last time he was on Culebra.

"Please go." Mirabel's command was soft but firm.

In a gesture that was dramatic enough to seem absurd, T-Ron's knife flashed through the air and stabbed the twenty, piercing it like a pork shish-kabob and then raising it in the air. Plucking the bill off the point, he replaced the weapon in its sheath. "Okay, then. See y'all later."

Nobody spoke until they heard the sound of a car spinning its wheels on gravel. Then a buzz of relieved chatter erupted. "Well done. All of you."

"I doubt we've seen the last of him."

"And we're going to have to watch our backs."

"Sorry you had to witness that," Kay apologized to Tyler. "This isn't the norm."

As the cards were shuffled and dealt, Tyler asked, "So what's the deal with that guy?"

"What isn't?" Mirabel sniffed. "He's one of the shadiest characters I've seen here in a while. He's got too much money and it doesn't seem legit."

"It's hard to understand what the appeal of this low-key little island is for someone like that. Why do you guys think he's hanging around?" Kay asked the group.

"Been here since Maria," Simon commented. "Don't know his story. I call and raise four."

"He's also been hanging with some crazy-ass woman for the last month. Short with wild white hair out to here..." Mirabel waved her hands around her head.

Kay glanced meaningfully at Tyler, who felt his heart pound a little faster. "Is that unusual for him?" He had no idea how to ask any questions about this new topic that wouldn't seem suspicious.

"Only because he's such a narcissistic dickhead I can't imagine how any woman would find him attractive, even a manic one. What?" she looked questioningly at Kay, in an intuitive girlfriend way.

"Later," Kay spoke in a low voice and then announced, "I bet sixteen." She pushed a couple of stacks of chips forward.

It was a diversionary tactic and although Mirabel understood the gesture, Tyler was left wondering who was protecting whom.

"Where can we drop you?" It was late by any standard, but especially by island time, judging from the darkened neighborhood they were driving through. The game had lasted longer than Tyler would have expected for a group that probably went to bed by nine and were up with the sun.

"I'm staying at a little guesthouse not far from the airport, you can just leave me at the corner." As he opened the outside door handle through the window, Kay touched his arm.

"Give me your cell number; I'll text you if anything comes up." There was more than a little suggestiveness in her remark, but Tyler played along, sending her a message so she would have his contact info. Kay had already proven to be a good local connection.

"Nice meeting you, Tyler," Mirabel called over her shoulder in a perfunctory and impatient way. "How long you staying with us?"

"As long as it takes." He stepped away from the car. "Thanks, it was a great night. See you again."

His room was small and cozy, but warm and airless in a way most northerners would find uncomfortable. Tyler turned on the floor fan and took off his clothes, enjoying the feel of the humid air on his skin. There was something about being in the Caribbean that always felt like coming home. Although these days his home in Vermont was nowhere near as relaxing as this.

Despite his exhaustion, his thoughts were too troubling for easily drifting off to sleep. It seemed like Tucker had gone underground and Lucy...whatever the hell she was doing here, it wasn't good.

Unsurprisingly the guesthouse owners were as easygoing and welcoming as the environment they maintained. They were a grandparently couple (Tyler always had to remind himself that he was this age now), who had once worked the carnival circuit and kept a colorful pet macaw in an upstairs room. In the morning, after he'd feasted on homemade banana bread with his coffee, they offered to drive him out to Tamarindo Bay and even lent him some snorkeling gear.

"The kayak tour may happen or it might not," he was advised. "Depends on how many come on the ferry who want it. But you can swim with the turtles regardless."

Despite the warning, he was disappointed as the hours went by and no curly-haired redhead showed. The sun was hot, the water was calm and the snorkeling was amazing. It had been years since he'd indulged in the sport; he saw rays and turtles, squid and octopus, and countless kinds of colorful tropical fish. But by mid-afternoon he gave up and caught a ride back into town with some other beach-goers.

"*What are you doing? Come down for a drink,*" a text from Kay urged him. Freshly showered and feeling somewhat sunburned, he could come up with no better late day activity.

"*See you soon.*"

The breeze had picked up a little and it was a pleasant walk along the bay into town. He wondered if there was some place to rent a bicycle; he would have to ask his landlords when he got back. He needed transportation if he was going to work efficiently here, but the high cost of

134

renting a car or golf cart on this island was daunting and absurd.

As he came down the steps to the Dinghy Dock, he could see out into the harbor where he recognized Kay coming ashore in a small outboard. As he joined the crowd of usual suspects, he did a quick assessment of the patrons at the bar. Primarily the same as last night with the addition of a very intoxicated-looking couple with skin the color of cooked lobster and a pair of businessmen speaking in rapid Puerto Rican slang. At a high table along the water's edge sat a tall silhouette facing away from him, wearing a now familiar straw cowboy hat. Tyler tensed a little at the idea of a public confrontation with T-Ron, but the apprehension of that event faded as his gaze moved to the short white-haired figure sitting across from him, sipping from a tall icy glass.

Although Tyler had been anticipating this moment, Lucy clearly had not. Her eyes widened in alarm and she stood up abruptly. Her drink teetered dangerously but was saved in the nick of time by her quick-fingered companion. As she moved towards him, Tyler was embarrassed to admit that the first thing he noticed was how much weight she had gained in the months since he'd last seen her. Despite a healthy tan, she appeared dangerously bloated and unfit, barely recognizable as the razor sharp, athletic female investigator she had been in her younger days.

"What the hell are you doing here?" she hissed, nodding imperceptibly in the direction of the rest rooms as she walked past him. For a second he was flooded with half a dozen memories from decades earlier, when he and Lucy had worked a few stories together, undercover and totally in sync. It had been years since they'd done anything as a team; even conceiving a baby had been her secret agenda – he hadn't even been let in on that one until his son was nearly six.

He waited a few beats and then followed her across the restaurant, glancing covertly over his shoulder before slipping behind her into the door that had a picture of a mermaid over it.

"What the fuck?!" she demanded angrily, leaning back against the paper towel dispenser.

Her visible anxiety made him over-react with blatant composure. "Nice to see you too, Lucy. Believe it or not, there are actually a handful of people in Vermont who are anxious to know that you are alive and well."

"I have this. I am going to find him. You need to... to not be here. To not screw this up." Her face had become such a dark shade of red, he thought she might be about to have some sort of seizure. He had seen a lot of different Lucys over the years, and plenty of them angry, but nothing like this madwoman.

"How-"

"How what?" she interrupted before he could he even form the question. "How will you screw this up? Just with your presence. I've got a delicate balance going on here, watching someone who thinks he's watching me..." Her voice trailed off as she seemed to take in his persona for the first time. "Damn it, Tyler, why do you look so good? It isn't fair. You're as old as I am."

Despite her weepy voice, he did not think her comment warranted a sympathetic response. "This is not about us, Lucy. How are you working on finding Tucker? Do you have any actual leads?"

She gave him a deep, thoughtful glare, at the same time defiantly crossing her soft plump arms across her chest. "You think I'm going to give this to you? Let you be the hero again, like you always are, finding the missing, reuniting them with their loved ones, getting the glory." Her misplaced resentment made him uncomfortable. "No, I'm doing this, Tyler. I'm finding my son, and then I am pulling my life back together. Maybe not in that order. But probably, damn it."

"Why does it always center around you, you freakin' narcissist?" He hadn't realized she'd pushed him to the edge until he was already over it. "OUR son is a deadbeat dad with two beautiful daughters who don't even know him, who look at ME as their father figure. And YOU, you were so wrapped up in your own pity party, you didn't even come around when your grandchildren's mother disappeared for almost two months. And you know what's worse? We noticed your absence, but we didn't even care."

Ignoring her puzzled expression, he went on with his tirade. "So, FINE. You look for Tucker and I'll look for Tucker. Let it be a contest in your warped competitive mind. And we can have two prizes – one for whoever finds him first, and one for whoever gets more fucked over in the process."

A loud pounding interrupted whatever fiery comeback was coming next. "What the hell's going on in there? People out here need to pee!"

As Tyler flung the door open, Lucy shouted after him. "FINE! Game on, asshole!"

Two angry women in short skirts and bright tank tops stared openmouthed as Tyler strode by. "Sorry for the inconvenience. All yours, ladies."

CHAPTER NINE

July 2018
Culebra, Puerto Rico

Shortly before midday, Tyler saw her arrive. Even from a distance of a hundred yards, hidden behind the branches of a fallen tree, he knew she was the one he was looking for. Slight but strong, with a mass of red curls secured behind her head, she reminded him of a young Lucy. If Lucy had been an outdoorsy type, which she had never been or even aspired to be. It was hard to get the image of the current Lucy out of his mind; he'd been barely able to sleep after their heated confrontation the previous evening. He hated himself for allowing her to bring him to the boiling point. He forced the memory out of his mind so he could focus on his present task.

He watched as the girl unlocked a storage container and began tossing red lifejackets out onto the beach. These were soon followed by snorkeling gear and then kayak paddles. As she stood back taking inventory, Tyler approached her casually, moving slowly as though she were a wild animal that he did not want to scare. At close range he could see how youthful she was and it reminded him of Tucker's actual age, so much younger than most of the people he had met on this island.

When she looked up at him with a clear gaze and a questioning smile, he was instantly disarmed by the appeal of her innocence. "Hey," he said, almost forgetting what his goal was here. "Somebody told me you might be able to help me."

"Do you want to go out on the kayak tour? We leave in about half an hour." He could see her doing a quick assessment of his physical condition.

"Actually that's not what I'm here for."

She tilted her head, waiting for him to continue.

"I'm looking for someone you might be friends with." He could sense her defenses immediately rising and he hastily went on. "It's my son. He's been missing for a while now."

He could see her almost freeze into place and then force herself to relax. "What's his name? I might know him."

He hated taking advantage of her uneasiness, but it was part of how the game was played. "I'm sorry, I haven't introduced myself. I'm Tyler." He held out a hand. "And you are?"

She hesitated, and he wondered if she was running him through her dirty-old-man filter. "Fiona." Her eyes darted across the sparkling blue waters of the bay and back again to the road. "Sorry, Tyler, but I've got people coming in a few minutes so I don't have much time to chat."

"Sure. Thanks for your time. So my son's name is Tucker. And this is what he looks like." He could tell she was surprised by the lightning speed with which he whipped out his phone and held it in front of her face. "Apparently he might also go by the name of Stone."

Fiona deserved extra credit for her attempt to control her facial expressions. Her pale eyelashes flickered several times as she squinted at the picture and her cheek muscles tightened as she tried to hide the emotions that seemed to be galloping across her features. "So you're his father?" Her voice came out as little more than a whisper before she cleared her throat and straightened her shoulders in a gesture that he recognized as post-adolescent defiance.

"Yes. Do you know him?"

"He was around after the hurricanes." She was still staring at the photo, avoiding meeting Tyler's steady gaze. "Kind of disappeared after that."

"'Kind of disappeared'? What does that mean?" He tried not to sound like he was reprimanding a misbehaving teenager.

She managed to give him the required eye-roll of exasperation. "Like he hasn't been seen around since then." Her eyes strayed out across the bay and then quickly back to the equipment at her feet. "Maybe he caught a boat going somewhere. Or went to the big island. So what, he never calls you or anything?"

Fiona definitely knew more than she was saying but Tyler wasn't sure how he was going to get it out of her. "No, I haven't talked to him in a year and a half. I miss him. Did you get to know him at all?"

"Yeah, I did. He seemed fine. Not interested in being around other people much." She was busying herself moving lifejackets from one place to another, clearly trying to ditch him now. She glanced up again at the water as though she might be gauging the wind speed or the current, but her eyes seemed fixed on a spot father away, on the horizon of the little island across the channel.

"Sorry to bug you, but I really need to find him. Do you think there is anybody else who knew him?"

"Yeah, I don't really know. Look, I have to get to work now. The bus will be here any minute."

Okay, just one thing. If you ever happen to run into him again, will you tell him that Artemis and Athena are waiting to meet him."

"Who?" The expected puzzlement crossed her face.

He held up his phone again so she could see the photo he had quickly brought to the screen. "His daughters."

Tyler realized that if he was going to follow Fiona in any discreet way, he was going to need a vehicle. He figured he had enough time to hitch into town, rent a golf cart and drive back before she returned from her stint as a kayak tour guide.

He pulled off onto the side of the road along Tamarindo Bay and then settled himself into the shade of a tree along the beach to watch for the incoming group of boats. It was not long before he saw them paddling in from the point, like a small naval invasion with matching red life vests as their uniforms.

Keeping one eye on the activity down the beach and the other on the road, he tried to gauge when the equipment was all packed up again and what was happening next. The busload of tourists came rumbling by and then all was quiet. It took him a few minutes to realize that Fiona was gone too.

"Shit." He leaped into the golf cart and headed back towards town, frustrated with his inability to make the vehicle go more than twenty miles an hour. He knew he had to find Fiona and follow her; the expression on her face when she had seen the photo of the twin girls had revealed all. His investigative skills told him that if she knew where Tucker was keeping himself, she would be deadheading directly to him as soon as possible.

He was only a car behind the battered bus when it slowed down near the crossroads by the airport where traffic became a single lane because of a giant pothole on the opposite side of the road. He had a good view of the bus as they bumped along to turn onto the main street of the tiny downtown, where it stopped for only a brief second to eject a single passenger who darted across the one way street before heading in the other direction.

Tyler swore again as he watched Fiona move swiftly to the next corner and turn right. He wasn't sure what the traffic pattern was and whether he was going against it as he made a quick left and then another right. He relaxed a little when he caught a brief glimpse of her as she turned off the orange bridge towards the grocery store. She was probably doing a little food shopping before going home.

He was so positive of this that he parked across the road from "Colmado Milka" and pulled his hat low over his eyes as he watched the door. Sure enough, several minutes later she walked out of the door and headed to the right across a hot empty lot. He knew the road dead-ended a few hundred yards in that direction, at the gas station, so he thought he might be less conspicuous if he followed her on foot.

A moment later he stopped in frustration, looking frantically around. Although there were no buildings to duck into, somehow she had disappeared. Then the sound of an engine starting reached his ears and he realized that the manmade canal that connected the bay to the open sea was just a few feet away. He got to the wooden wharf that ran along the edge of it just in time to see Fiona maneuvering a dinghy through the green water and mangroves.

"Double shit!" he swore loudly. He watched until she reached the end of the waterway by the ferry dock; he could see her steer the boat to the left.

He wondered where she was heading – as far as he knew there were not many anchorages or boats moored in that particular part of the island. Inspired, he raced back to his golf cart and drove it as far as he dared, creeping up to the top of a hill that was nearly seventy-degrees steep before coming to a halt where the pavement ended and the road forked into three rutted and rocky options that he didn't dare drive down. From that vantage point he had a good view to the west towards Vieques, which stretched low across the horizon at the other side of the white-capped waves of the Caribbean.

The noise of the outboard motor carried easily over the stillness of the afternoon and he was able to identify Fiona's location as somewhere just out of sight, beyond the nearest hillside, the wake of her boat still showing in the water below. Unsure of his next move, he stood there listening, trying to tell how far she might be traveling. He was surprised that within a few moments, the motor suddenly shut off; she could not be that far away and yet he had no idea how to navigate by land to where she might have gone by sea.

As he made his way back down the precipitous slope to town, he tried not to feel discouraged. He'd actually made progress today; now he could make a plan how to continue it tomorrow.

Late the next morning he was camped out again at Tamarindo awaiting Fiona's arrival. Although he had been expecting her by the road, there she was suddenly, tying up the dinghy to one of the mooring balls in the water. With a

142

dry bag secured across her chest and shoulder, she slipped gracefully over the edge and swam in to shore. He contemplated whether it made sense to approach her again and decided that it would look less suspicious than not approaching her.

Grabbing his own mask and fins, he began walking down the beach as though his intention was merely another swim with the turtles. "Hey, hi. Fiona, right?"

One glance at her face told him his suspicions from the day before had been correct. Her serious expression and the puffiness around her eyes gave away the fact that she had probably spent some part of the night or morning crying.

"Oh. Hi." She turned her back, making it obvious she did not want to speak with him, but he persisted anyway.

"I wondered if you might have come up with any ideas about where my son might be. I'm leaving the island in a few days and it would be great if I could connect with him before then." Did he sound like a concerned father or a used cars salesman?

"Yeah, sorry, no." She did not even look up, but he was almost certain he saw a tear fall on one of the life jackets she was tossing onto the sand. For a fleeting second he felt compassion for her, whatever it was that she had experienced as a result of the information he'd imparted; maybe she'd been a victim of Tucker's irresponsibility, just like Chloe, and the twins, and even he himself had been. But then the emotion evaporated. He already had his own feelings that were enough to deal with.

"Okay, well, if you hear anything..."

"I probably won't." This time she met his gaze and her message couldn't have been clearer.

"Okay, but I'm staying at Las Palomas Guesthouse if you do. They'll pass the message on to me." Had he totally blown it here? He didn't think he could have gauged her reaction so poorly but it was possible.

In the meantime, he needed to get back up the hill and see if he could figure out which road led down to the bay

143

where she had brought her boat in last night. He probably had about three hours.

Thirty minutes later he found his way down to the large clearing at Playa Datiles, which was itself a narrow crescent of white sand around a shallow and placid turquoise bay. On opposite sides of the open space were two tents; one very clearly lived in by a disorderly masculine presence; the other so neatly organized as to not be occupied at all. As he poked around a bit further, he decided that this was very much the case; it did not appear that anyone had actually stayed in the latter campsite for a long time.

"Hey!"

Tyler turned to see a scruffy middle-aged male standing on the beach waving a spear gun at him threateningly.

"Get away from my camp!"

Tyler held up his hands in the classic gesture of surrender. "Sorry, I was just looking for Fiona. I thought she told me she lived here."

The man sneered and wiped one hand on a dirty T-shirt that was more holes than fabric. "Not very likely. In all the time I've known her, she's never directed anyone to come here. Besides the fact, that she hasn't slept in that tent in months. Now get off this property."

"I'm guessing you don't own this place." Tyler didn't like standing his ground against a madman.

"Squatter's rights are as good as any on Culebra. That's how it works here. So you better go before I harpoon you like a big snapper." He made a grand display of aiming his weapon at Tyler.

Going against his basic survival instincts, Tyler sat down in a ripped blue canvas camp chair outside of what was now apparently Fiona's former tent. "Well I think I'll just wait here. She should be back from work soon enough."

The bravado disappeared as quickly as it had shown itself, spear gun lowering, thin shoulders shrugging. "Suit yourself. But get ready for a long wait. And don't touch any

144

of my shit." Without a backward glance, the squatter waded out to a wooden rowboat and began oaring out of the bay.

After a few minutes alone, Tyler unzipped the tent and peered inside. It was so impersonally neat, that it could well have been a camping rental on Airbnb. The single air mattress on the floor had a patterned sheet tucked around it, a red plastic milk crate served as a nightstand, a gallon jug of water rested in the corner and a small torn straw doormat sat at the entrance. There was something incredibly suspicious about the whole set up, but he was damned if he could put his finger on it.

He wandered back outside and down to the strip of sand along the water's edge, squinting at the landscape in both directions. If Fiona hadn't been coming here, then where had she been going? He walked along the beach, ducking under branches and wading in a few spots, until he came to the rocky promontory that defined the end of the cove. Although it appeared treacherous at first, there was definitely a traversable way over the jagged coral and rocks.

Within a few minutes he had come down the other side into a wide open bay. What appeared to be white sand from a distance was actually broken bits of bleached coral, which made the surface difficult to walk upon. Halfway down the beach, as it were, was a corroded concrete tower of some sort with large cables hanging from it. The sea was much choppier here, aquamarine depths breaking against dark irregular reefs. But after going a few hundred yards, he stopped short as he caught a glimpse of something in the low trees along the shore.

A blue tarp strung between the branches offered shade and protection to an outdoor living area. Behind it, under cover of the overhanging foliage was a dark green nylon tent. More heartening than the sight of the camp itself was what hung on one of the lines that secured the tent fly to a nearby tree trunk.

Slung over the line was a tiny purple tank top; next to it was a pair of men's khaki-colored swim trunks.

The shorts seemed to be as much of a decoy as the encampment on Datiles was. Although there were clear signs of Fiona's occupancy here, there was no other indication of a male presence. Still, he sat down in the shade of an almond tree on a flat log that served as a crude bench to await her return.

An hour of sitting, another of strolling the waterfront, another on the log. He discovered that there was actually a very rough road that made its way out to this beach and no doubt connected up with the one he had walked in on. As the sun got lower in the sky and he began to get hungry and thirsty, he had to admit to the real possibility that Fiona wasn't coming home tonight. He could not wait until after dark to negotiate the rocks back to where he had left his golf cart near the town water tower or to wander up a dirt track he was unfamiliar with.

He decided to take the road so he would know how to get back here more easily. He was surprised how quickly it met up with the trail that diverged down to Datiles and he was back at his car in less than twenty minutes, just in time to witness an awesome sunset from this high vantage point over the sea. There were some constants in life that he never grew tired of and watching a glowing red orb disappear into sparkling water was one of them.

Back in town, he wandered around looking for some place to eat and drink and be alone with his thoughts other than the Dinghy Dock. He found a small outdoor café open across from the ferry dock where a kindly but weary blonde woman brought him a satisfying fish burrito while he got a cold beer from the bar next door. He recalled sitting in this same location several years earlier on a hot afternoon, beginning another long and sinuous search for his son over cocktails with a different blonde, a seductive and ultimately lethal one...

As he settled into his meal, the wild-haired man he had met a few days earlier at the bar appeared with a guitar and began a set of old-school rock and roll songs sung with off-key enthusiasm. Elsewhere in the world it might have seemed amateur and inappropriate; here on a steamy Culebra evening it was just right. A few locals appeared and sang along; there was some random dancing by wiry women in sundresses and some percussion played by a serious bearded fellow with thick glasses.

It was so easy to get distracted from his mission here. Tyler found himself wondering about Lucy and what she was actually doing on the island. She'd seemed like such a hot mess the night they'd run into each other - maybe he should be caring more about her welfare. The thought was exhausting – it seemed like an added burden to his already impossible job.

"Barry, right?" Tyler considered it a minor miracle that he had remembered the name of the singer, who had now sat down next to him to consume a plate of food, the apparent payment for his performance.

Barry nodded, his mouth too full to respond. "How's it goin' man?" he managed finally. "You find your son yet?"

"No, but I found Fiona. You know her?"

"Fiona, yeah, she's a sweet young thang, isn't she."

"What's the name of that beach where she lives, out there by where the cable hangs in the water..."

"Electric. She camping out there now? I thought I saw her riding out to Zoni the other day with a bag of groceries. But maybe she's housesitting for someone."

Tyler perked up. "Zoni? The other side of the island you mean?"

"In every way, man." Barry laughed, his teeth flashing white against the darkness of his tanned face.

"How could I find out exactly where?" He was eager to pursue this new lead; he had a good feeling about it.

Barry shrugged and picked some spinach out of his teeth as he kicked back his chair. "Ask around. Get online. Eventually someone will know."

Back in his room, he felt less hopeful as he enlarged the image of Culebra on Google maps, zooming in on the eastern part of the island called "Zoni." It was a sprawling mostly undefined area that appeared to consist of expensive homes with multiple buildings grouped around pools. Clearly the best way to get a handle on it would be to go there – in the morning.

He jumped a little as his phone dinged in his hand. *"Haven't seen you for a few days. What have you been up to?"* He barely knew Kay, but instant friendship seemed to be the way of the islands sometimes. And a resourceful woman like Kay was an acquaintanceship worth cultivating.

"Keeping busy. What are you doing tomorrow morning? Want to do some exploring with me?"

She was waiting when he pulled the golf cart up to the city dock. He had the odd thought of how 'normal' she looked compared to most people he knew and was not even really sure what he meant by that. Dressed simply in a green tank-top, blue shorts and flip-flops, she could have been ready for gardening, sailing, or her kid's soccer game. Her blonde ponytail was pulled through the back opening of a faded canvas cap and a well-worn backpack was slung over one shoulder.

"Perfect timing," she said cheerily as she swung herself up into the passenger seat. "Where's the seat belt in this death machine?"

They headed out towards the west end of the island, skirting a pothole by the cemetery that looked like it could swallow the entire vehicle and fording a washed-out place in the road where Kay hopped out to rescue a pair of land turtles that were swimming across. The landscape was different, more rustic – steep dry hills, scrubby trees and occasional glimpses of the sea in the near distance.

"Do you know where we're going?" she asked.

"Not a clue," he admitted.

"So what's the game plan?"

"We'll pretend we're a couple looking for a house to buy." It was off the top of his head but made perfect sense.

148

"We've fallen in love with the island and want to retire here. Money is no object."

"Not bad. As long as we don't run into anybody I know. Then we'll have to modify it." Kay clearly liked a well-laid out strategy and began fleshing out the details. "How'd you make your money? There are no fixer-uppers in Zoni."

"Trust fund?" They laughed together and suddenly Tyler felt lighter than he had in months.

"We could just tell them the truth – that you're looking for your son who might be housesitting out here."

"Or squatting. Or something worse." He was not sure what might be worse, but anything was possible. "Let's play it this way first and see what pans out."

It was harder than he expected to even get a look at many of the Zoni residences. In most places they were greeted by locked gates, iron fences, and shuttered houses tightly buttoned-up against impending storms. There was a strong breeze blowing from the east that was not felt on most other parts of the island that Tyler could easily imagine becoming gale force winds during weather events. Many houses had spectacular views over the Zoni Beach shoreline, where a wide strip of white sand ran for a mile north to a rocky point. In the distance, beyond Culebrita and its iconic lighthouse, St. Thomas could be seen, a mere twelve miles away, under a canopy of dark rain clouds.

"Most of these places are owned by gringos who don't come in the summer," Kay commented. "They go to their other homes in Martha's Vineyard or the Hamptons."

"Look, there's a jeep parked outside that one. Let's try it."

They got out and stretched and looked around. Kay had a pair of binoculars hung around her neck ("You never know when you're going to need field glasses.") and Tyler held up a map and his phone. "We look authentic."

"We are authentic. Sort of."

The door to a house opened and a deeply tanned woman wearing a stained dress and a scarf tied around her head stepped out to shake a rug. A small copper-colored dog ran out to the edge of the walkway and began barking furiously at them.

"Suki, stop that! What can I do for you – are you lost?" she asked in a guarded but not unfriendly way.

"Hi. Tyler and Kay. We're house-hunting, can't get enough of this island, decided we want to retire here." Tyler was already gushing their story out before he realized Kay had put a restraining hand out on his arm.

"Let it go. We know each other. Hi, Janet. Haven't seen you out in a while." The two women air-kissed and Janet tilted her head quizzically.

"Yeah, I've just been cleaning houses, laying low. So what's up with this..." she waved her hand in a circular gesture between Tyler and Kay.

Kay turned her back on Janet and said softly to Tyler, "Why don't you take a little walk and let me handle this?"

He strolled slowly away, trying not to show his exasperation with the way the scenario was playing out. From a safe distance he turned to watch the exchange, trying to guess what they might be saying. Janet pointed first in one direction and then in the other, her hands still gesticulating wildly as she spoke like she was in a silent movie. Kay stood motionless, occasionally nodding. When his frustration finally got the best of him and he walked back to join them, they were not talking about Tucker at all, but discussing the last movie that had shown at Cine Culebra, the tiny, twenty-seven seat movie theater next to the library.

Kay extracted herself from the conversation as soon as she saw Tyler's impatient stance. "Sorry, we should get going. Let's have a drink some night, Janet, or maybe go to the movies!"

"So did you learn anything? And why the hell couldn't I be there?" Tyler got into the golf cart, unsure of what to do next. He frowned again as he looked at the bank of dark gray clouds closing in from the west. Driving around in an open vehicle was a bitch in a heavy rainstorm.

"Turns out that Janet and Fiona used to work together as a cleaning team until they had a falling out around Christmas time, when she discovered that Fiona was letting a friend of hers sleep in a cottage behind one of the houses they cleaned."

"And?"

"So now Janet cleans by herself. Fiona can't manage getting to Zoni on her own, because she doesn't have a car. So they split out some of the work. Fiona cleans a couple of places close to town, up on the hill overlooking Melones." Kay beamed a little. "I did good work, don't you think?"

"Stellar." Tyler had to admit that he probably would not have been able to get such key information out of Janet as fast as Kay had. "Any chance you found out which houses Fiona kept?"

She nodded and then glanced at the ominous sky. "I got a couple of names, we'll be able to find out. But I think we better head back now, so maybe we can beat the storm. It might not even be raining on the other side of the island."

When the sudden downpour became so hard that he could no longer see, Tyler pulled off into the parking lot of the tiny Culebra museum and they huddled together with a towel wrapped around them. The rain whipped in on all sides, over the top of the useless half windshield and sideways through the golf cart, soaking everything in its path. Then as suddenly as it had arrived, it was gone.

"And we were just getting cozy!" Kay commented jokingly as Tyler used the already damp towel to dry off the steering wheel and dashboard. "That could have been a very romantic moment."

He started to say something and then thought better of it. It was more important not to alienate Kay than not to lead her on. He could do that later. "All set?" he asked instead as he turned the key.

The potholes were full of water now, making them easier to spot as he navigated the roadway back into town and out again. When they had nearly reached the narrow rocky beach known as Melones, Kay pointed at a turnoff that went sharply up to the right. "Up that way."

It was new territory to him, another of those vertical hills that you would not normally explore unless you had a reason and the golf cart just barely made its way to the crest. When Tyler dared to take his eyes off the road, he could see that the water view to the west was spectacular. "I think this is one of the houses, up here on the left," Kay directed.

Stretching his limbs, Tyler surveyed the sprawling multi-million dollar home that perched on the cliff before him. It seemed designed to fit into its surroundings better than the Zoni houses, although it still baffled him why anybody on a Caribbean island with as many beaches as Culebra would need a swimming pool. As they followed a fieldstone walkway to the house, a large white Great Dane appeared, followed by a willowy woman in a lacy white beach cover-up waving a leash. At the sight of strangers, the dog froze and began growling while its lead was swiftly attached to its collar.

"Same story?" Kay murmured at the exact moment that the woman called, "Can I help you?"

After Tyler's hasty introduction, they quickly learned that she was only a renter who was surprised at being told that the house was potentially for sale. "Well, it's a beautiful place. I'm happy to show you around," she said, with clearly no thought to the possibility that she was being conned.

The comprehensive tour given by their gushing guide made it clear that there was little chance that any vagabond could be crashing on the property undetected. Tyler's questions about crime were answered by a detailed discussion of the security system features that Kay managed to divert by asking about housekeeping. "How often does a cleaning person come in?"

"Oh, there's a young girl who came up a couple of times to change the sheets and towels. We're only here for two weeks, leaving tomorrow. I guess she must do a thorough cleaning before the next guests come."

Kay and Tyler exchanged a meaningful look before they said their goodbyes and Tyler purposefully patted the ferocious-looking canine on the head. "Does he come with the place?" He forced a laugh.

"Oh, no, Rex is ours. He travels in a big crate."

The next house on the road was tightly shuttered against burglars and hurricanes and did not look as though it had been used for several months. A cursory survey was all it took to determine there were no signs of current life. This was followed by a modern boxlike edifice of cement and glass where they were able to peer into all the windows at the tidy, sterile interior and marvel at its lack of color and character. There were no outbuildings of any sort and it seemed virtually impossible that trespassing would go unnoticed in a glass house like this.

The last place they came to seemed to have all kinds of possibilities. Located at the highest point of the dead end road, it was a low rambling structure with the look of a Spanish hacienda. There were several buildings and the gardens were thriving but somewhat overgrown. Two vehicles were parked in the driveway – a new truck and an expensive silver SUV.

By the time they had stepped out of the golf cart, a very fit elderly gentleman was already approaching them. "You must be lost," he stated matter-of-factly. "This is private property."

"Oh, sorry, we've been house-hunting and thought there was something for sale up this way. Your place is beautiful." Kay gave him a bright smile. "We'd love a place like this."

"Yes, it's been a great place to retire. And it made it through the hurricane with only minimal damage. It's quite well built."

"Are you here year 'round?"

"We go away for a couple of months in the fall, till the season is over. But pretty much, yes."

There was no point in pursuing the real estate angle so Tyler pushed the conversation desperately onward. "How hard is it to get cleaning and landscaping help here? We've heard resources are limited."

"Oh, it's not easy, but after a time you figure it out. We have a lovely young woman who comes in a couple times a week to take care of the house. And her boyfriend did our yardwork until he fell sick a while back. Haven't been able to find anybody since." The man kicked ruefully at a clump of long grass.

"Is that the little red-haired one? We've heard about her from a few people." When Kay put on her chatty rich person's voice, her body assumed a different stance; she seemed a bit taller and haughtier as though she could actually look down her nose at whomever she was speaking with. Tyler would have found it amusing if he wasn't so intent on his purpose here. "I didn't know she came as a package with a landscaper!"

"Oh, I wouldn't call him that – he was just a boy with a weed whacker and a pair of clippers." He chuckled. "Luckily he took instruction well, or I might have lost these hibiscus totally. Well. Good luck with your search. It can be discouraging – there's not a lot available."

Before they could ask any more questions the man tottered unsteadily off into an open archway that connected two of the buildings.

"Damn. Should we run after him?" Kay asked.

Tyler frowned. It had all sounded promising until the part where 'the boy' got sick and couldn't come to work. Did that mean Tucker had left the island? "No. I wish there was a way to ask how long since he'd last been here without sounding seriously suspicious."

Kay looked down at the ragged lawn covering the ground at their feet. "Oh, I'd say judging from the length of the grass, at least two months, maybe three."

Depressed and discouraged, Tyler had trouble falling asleep. He was reading a lot into the few clues he had

154

uncovered today, but it was all he had to go on. What if Tucker was no longer on Culebra? How would even find out where he had gone? But then again, what had kept him here in the first place...He guessed the answer was Fiona. Somehow he had to win her trust.

Why wouldn't Tucker have just hopped on a sailboat and left? It probably wasn't as easy as that sounded. But if he loved sailing as much as he claimed he did...And what had ever happened to the boat Maggie had told him about, the one Tucker had supposedly made off with. Tomorrow he would have to get Kay to take him around the bay to talk to some of the sailors. He smiled to himself, he knew she would be more than happy to do that. As well as happy to do more than that.

CHAPTER TEN

July 2018
Culebra, Puerto Rico

"Damn it." Lucy retrieved the key ring from the dirt and fumbled once again with the padlock on the iron gate. She hated having to do this in the darkness, but on the nights when she went out, she rarely made it home before sunset. T-Ron, or whoever the owner of this property really was, should install a frickin' solar light out here or something. She didn't understand why the driveway to Casa Laguna had to be secured every time she left; the house had its own lock on it and it was not like there was anything of value to steal in the yard.

She drove the golf cart through the opening and parked it next to the house. Sighing, she blindly made her way back up the driveway to sling the heavy rusted chain around the spikes of the gate and click the lock through it. By the time she had climbed the steep stairs to the veranda and flung herself into a padded wooden chair, she was breathing more' heavily than the short back-and-forth jaunt should have warranted. In a minute she would get up and make herself a drink, even though she had promised herself that she would cut back. But there was nothing else to do out here in the quiet rural eastern side of Culebra where there was no cell service and the wifi had been taken out by the hurricane.

It was a ridiculous place to build a house. Far from town, not near a beach, and it was hotter than blazes in the noontime heat. There was no view of anything except for a scummy , mosquito-breeding pond in the backyard. It had been dark the first time T-Ron had brought her here and she had been thrilled at the idea of a comfortable living room and a kitchen with a dishwasher and the oversized open-concept tiled shower. The bed had been sturdy enough to hold up under their celebratory gymnastics and afterwards there had been utter quiet rather than the off-key singing and bad guitar-playing broadcast over the loudspeaker of the local Pentacostal church back in town.

But when she awoke that first morning, alone and hung over, with only an inch of gin left in the bottom of the bottle, she didn't really appreciate the birds, whose names she didn't know, swooping low over the murky waters of the pond, or the rustling of the almond trees in the faint morning breeze. She was a city girl at heart, London-born and bred. When she'd ended up in Vermont, she'd never enjoyed its small town intimacy; eventually she moved to Burlington, the only place that distantly replicated the urban life she enjoyed. Being alone in a house on a Caribbean island reminded her of the terrifying years she had spent on Mustique, basically captive with her baby son on the luxury estate of a sadistic and egotistic rock star, a time she tried not to dwell on.

Over the next week, as she struggled to come to terms with the place, she reminded herself that it was free, a "housesitting" job supposedly, that came with a no-strings-attached relationship with a man whose badness she was perversely attracted to. Unfortunately it seemed to lessen her opportunities to snoop around in his apartment, now that they spent most of their together time out here at Casa Laguna. The few chances she'd had to stop by his place, he had been out and the door had been locked.

One afternoon when she was standing outside the gate fussing with the chain, a passing car had slowed and the gray-haired woman behind the wheel had given her a piercing stare before calling out, "Are you living here?"

Lucy had felt immediately affronted and had responded defensively, "Do you have a problem with that?"

She then saw that there were two women in the car and that the passenger was speaking furtively to the driver, her eyes riveted on Lucy. She heard the words, "You ought to tell her," and her hackles went up.

"What? Tell me what?"

"She's keeping the gate locked. She'll be fine, let's go."

"Why wouldn't I be fine? What do I need to know?"

There was a silence and then the passenger leaned over and spoke directly to Lucy. "Did you get this place for very cheap?"

Lucy snorted inwardly. "You might say that. Why do you ask?"

The two exchanged a glance and finally the driver spoke. "Well, okay. Because after the last resident was found dead, nobody has been willing to stay out here."

This time Lucy laughed aloud. "You're joking, right?" When neither replied, she continued nervously, "Okay then what was it, natural causes or murder?"

"Have you met the owner?" The driver had neatly dodged the question.

"I don't know." She realized she only had T-Ron's word for it that he actually owned this house. "Should I?"

"Do you notice she answers everything with a question," the companion whispered loudly. "Let's not get involved, Jane." Then she called out to Lucy, "Just be careful. We like our neighborhood to be safe."

"How is this bloody deserted hillside even a neighborhood..." By the time the words were out of her mouth, the car had pulled away.

Shaken by this unlikely confrontation, Lucy had driven her golf cart directly to Tiburon's house, where she had found him getting into his truck parked on the street. He appeared annoyed by her unexpected arrival. "What's up, Miss Lucy? You look agitated."

"What happened to your last tenant, Mr. Landlord?" She climbed into the seat next to him. "And don't give me that 'I have no idea what you're talking about' look." She suddenly felt like she was burning up with anger and anxiety.

"Don't go apoplectic on me now, girl. Your whole body is turning red as a blood sausage. You need to calm down." But in contradiction to his own statement, he reached over and stroked the inside of her thigh in a way he knew excited her. In a single sweeping motion, she tugged her dress down and pushed his hand away. "Oh, come on then, let's go talk about it over a gin and tonic." With an impatient gesture, he started the engine.

"No, tell me now." Lucy leaned forward and turned the key to the off position. "How did she die? Or should I ask why?"

"Why do you care? It has nothing to do with you." He smirked at her openly, clearly aware that his nonchalance was infuriating her further.

"I need to know if I should worry that I might be murdered in my sleep, asshole."

He leaned against the driver's side door and tipped his straw hat down on his forehead, scrutinizing her from beneath half-closed eyelids, chewing lazily on the end of a plastic coffee stirrer as he contemplated his reply. "Lucy Brookstone, girl detective, I should just let you figure this one out. Add it to your list of 'solved mysteries.' But I don't want you going around asking a lot of questions and making more trouble for me."

"More trouble–" she started to complain but he put a finger to her lips and tapped three times.

"Nobody's going to murder you in your bed, Lucy. The last tenant drowned." His smirk was already beginning in anticipation of her reaction.

"Like what – in the bathtub? Don't treat me like I'm stupid; there is only a shower." Then the meaning of his statement became clear. "Bloody hell, you mean in the scuzzy pond? That is so..." She couldn't describe the gorge rising in her throat at the idea of anyone swimming in that murky green water. "Why would she go in there?"

T-Ron shrugged. "You tell me." With a mischievous wink, he leaned forward and started the engine again. "Maybe she tripped and fell. Maybe she was trying to catch a big fish with her bare hands and it pulled her under. Or maybe she had a quarrel with her boyfriend and he thought

159

that was an easy way to end the fight. Endless possibilities, right?"

Her mind reeled out of control as she considered the ways a person could die in an inland salt water lagoon. When she didn't answer, he asked, "So you coming with me to Happy Hour or were you headed somewhere?"

Lucy sat quietly at the bar, staring out at the sailboats bobbing on their moorings in the harbor. T-Ron was busy using the wifi to do "business" online, whatever that meant for him, she thought darkly as she turned away. The man on the barstool next to her was a local with glasses and a long fluffy white beard, whose name she couldn't remember.

"How you doin' today?" he asked her politely.

"Oh, I'm, okay." She glanced over her shoulder to make sure that T-Ron was engrossed in his phone work. "Know anything about people who drowned on this island recently?"

"Well, you mean the woman who drowned out by Zoni last month? Or the guy who they found floating out at Tamarindo last fall?"

"Umm..." she glanced over at T-Ron but he was engrossed in his phone screen. "...the one in the pond."

"The one they say was face down in the water wearing a snorkeling mask covered in green slime?" He grinned at the horrified expression on her face. "Yeah, strange as fuck, that one. Wonder what she was trying to see in that muck."

Lucy swallowed and composed herself. "So I guess she wasn't a local?"

The man took a swig of his beer and laughed. "I'd say probably not. I don't know who she was. But I think it's a little bit of a weird coincidence."

"What is?"

"Well, the guy who died in the bay – he was wearing a mask too when that kid pulled him in. I mean, it's pretty normal to be wearing snorkel gear in the sea. But it just strikes me as kinda fluky that the two drownings we had here this year were oddly similar."

Lucy wanted to ask more questions about the woman in the pond, but T-Ron had put his phone away and had turned towards them now. "So what about the other guy? What was his story?"

"They thought maybe heart attack. But it wasn't long after Maria and nobody was calling in any forensic teams." Her confidant's pleasant smile faded when he noticed that T-Ron's attention was directed at him. Nodding curtly at Lucy, he transferred his interest to the couple sitting on his other side.

"What were you two talking about?" T-Ron's hawk-like eyes belied his lazy tone.

"Just local gossip. Hurricane stuff. Everyone's favorite topic. They never seem to get enough of it." She suddenly realized she hadn't even touched her drink and quickly gulped down half of it. "Will you order me another one of those? I need to use the baño."

Now as she sat on the porch in the darkness, still trying to catch her breath, she was startled by what sounded like a splash in the direction of the pond. Since the conversation a few days earlier with T-Ron and the guy at the bar, she had stared for endless hours at the cloudy surface of the algae-covered water, considering various scenarios associated with death by drowning. There was a white egret that hung out in a nearby tree, she had noticed a few frogs and had even thought she had seen movement beneath the surface, as though some fish and aquatic creatures might actually exist within its depths. Nature had never been her forte and there was more life to the ecosystem in her backyard than she might have expected.

But the loudness of the wet gurgling noise made her feel uneasy. An image of a prehistoric sea serpent came to mind and she tried to dismiss the idea that the Loch Ness monster might be hovering out there, or that an immense iguana was about to crawl out onto the muddy shore and head for the house.

"This is ridiculous," she said loudly to reassure herself and then stood abruptly, feeling along the wall for the outside light switch. As the pale white glow of the LED bulb flooded the porch, her sigh of relief was released in a shrill shriek.

Someone was sitting in the other Adirondack chair just a few feet from where she had been. In a sudden panic all she could think about was that she had nothing to defend herself with and the keys clutched in her hand were useless; she could not even flee in the golf car unless she stopped to unlock and unchain the gate.

"You're slipping up, Lucy. I wondered how long it would take you to realize I was sitting almost next to you." At the sound of the familiar voice, her cold blue fear morphed into flaming red rage.

"You fuckwad! What are you doing here? How did you get in?" Her fury grew at the sight of the insipid grin growing wider on Tyler's face. "You scared the living shit out of me!"

"You gave me a wide window of time to slip through the gate after you unlocked it. I could have marched a whole army in and you wouldn't have noticed." He looked so smug and relaxed, she had to suppress the urge to smack him.

"So – what – you parked your car out on the road and waited for me to come home...how did you even know where I am staying?" She sat down heavily, a hand pressed to the place on her chest where her racing heart threatened to thump its way out of her body. "Why am I even asking that question..."

"I followed you, you fool. Drove past you while you fussed with the padlock, parked my golf cart on the side of the road and had plenty of time to dart inside before you made your way back to lock it up. Just FYI." He leaned forward and patted her arm, which she pulled away in irritation. "Really, Luce, I'm sorry I scared you."

"No, you're not or you wouldn't have been sitting here in the dark like that."

"Okay, you're right. I didn't think you would take it so hard. Now what the hell are you doing all the way out here on the edge of nowhere? This isn't your style." He got up and leaned against the wide arm of the chair, looking down at her with what appeared to actually be concern.

She wasn't going to be fooled by his fake sympathy. "What are you here for, Tyler? Because for some reason I don't think this is just a social call." She wanted to go inside and fix herself a drink but she wasn't going to give him the satisfaction of figuring out her greatest need.

"Well, it kind of is, Lucy. I thought maybe we could lay down the swords and join forces. Share information. Work together as a team to find our son." As always, his calm clarity had the opposite effect on her temperament.

"Really? The way we did last time you were on Culebra? When he was sixteen and disappeared for two weeks and you never even called me until you found him?"

He raised his open hands. "Fair enough. I concede that was not my best behavior. But this situation is a little different, don't you agree?"

The hell with what he thought. She needed a gin to deal with this. She stood up abruptly, ignoring the dizziness that came over her with the sudden movement, and went inside the house.

"You're just going to walk away?" he called after her. Then hearing the sound of ice cubes clinking in a glass, he said, "Oh. Okay."

"I'd offer you one but I know how much you hate the taste of gin." She could make a drink faster than she could do anything, even when she was already snockered.

"Thanks anyway, but I have to drive back to town on that dark road." His manners had always been better than hers. She realized that everything about him infuriated her these days.

"So you want to know what new information I've learned lately? The former tenant died in that lagoon down below. So yes, I am a little bit jumpy."

"There's water out there?" Tyler held up his phone and switched it to flashlight mode. The bright beam illuminated the yard and the edge of the pond but was not strong enough to show much more than that.

"Yes, but not what you're thinking. No glorious view of the Caribbean, just a stagnant pool of scum. Do you think that someone swam in it voluntarily? I doubt it." She took a long sip of her drink. "And to make it just that much more improbable, she was wearing a mask."

"Like for a Halloween party?"

"No, for diving or snorkeling. Whatever it is people use for seeing underwater. As though there might actually be something visible in that murk." Another deep mouthful and she began to feel more relaxed.

"Well, that's bizarre. So what do you think about that?" His tone sounded patronizing but she tried not to let herself rise to the bait.

"It stinks of murder, that's what I think. And it doesn't make me feel very safe here." Well, she had blurted that out faster than she had meant to.

"Do you know her name or anything about her?"

"No, nothing. But there is something else." Suddenly she was glad she had someone familiar to share these details with. "Last fall another person died snorkeling at Tamarindo, found the same way, floating face down with a mask on."

His amused expression made her wish she hadn't said anything. "That's not exactly that much of a coincidence. I mean, that's much more likely to happen there than here." He waved his hand in the direction of the water. "But none of that has anything to do with finding Tucker. Does it?"

Instead of telling him to fuck off, she took a deep breath and another swallow of gin.

"So tell me again, why are you staying all the way out in the boonies of Culebra?"

"Boonies?" she countered. "Is that some quaint American expression that even I am unfamiliar with after more than a decade in the states? But I can guess what it

164

means. It was a free place to stay and it looked good at the time."

"Free? I'm impressed. How'd you manage that?"

"The man I'm seeing owns it. Or something."

"Tiburon. Or T-Ron, as his friends, or I should say acquaintances, call him."

She was startled that he knew the name. "So you already know the answer to these questions you're asking me?"

"No, I just recognized the unsavory character you were with at the bar the other night. I met him at the local poker game. And just in case you're too dazzled by love to see it, he's not well-liked on this island."

"And maybe that's why we get along!" she retorted, disturbed by the truth of his words. She hadn't really paid attention to T-Ron's interactions with other people; she had been too caught up in the complicated electricity of their own relationship. She softened a little, trying not to let Tyler put her on the defensive all the time. "You know I'm always attracted to bad boys."

"I guess I was the exception."

"Yes, you were."

For a few seconds they actually shared a little sentimental reflection, before Tyler broke the spell. "You did do a good job of alienating the folks on Tortola. What happened there?"

Lucy felt an uncontrollable tremor rattle through her body. "Nothing. Why would you even ask that?"

"Really. Because you seemed to have left quite an impression on someone named Maggie. You remember her? The nice woman Tucker stayed with, the one whose boat he sailed here?" His voice had become increasingly louder and harder.

Her outburst of tears surprised her as much as it did Tyler. "You have no idea!" Her blustering turned into more blubbering and eventually she had to put down her drink to bury her face in her hands. When she felt his arms go around her in the universal soothing gesture, she finally calmed down, enjoying the comfort for a minute before reverting to her usual irascible self. "I don't need your sympathy. What that woman did to me was inexcusable and I will not discuss it."

She heaved herself out of the low chair, retrieved a roll of paper towels and proceeded to loudly blow her nose. "I'm gross, I know, but I don't really care what you think of me. Why don't you just leave?"

"I can't actually."

"Yes, you can. Just go, let me be the sad excuse for a mother that I am."

"I can't leave. You locked me in with you."

She choked out a laugh between a new torrent of sobs before she felt him tugging at her arm.

"Lucy, let's go inside and talk before the bugs eat us both alive out here."

Blindly she let him lead her to the living room couch, where she finally managed to get control of her emotions. She drained the rest of her drink, silently vowing that she would not have another.

"You go first," she deferred, since she had made barely any headway in her search for Tucker, and because she wasn't sure how much she dared share with Tyler.

Staring into her empty glass rather make eye contact, she listened while he told her about a girl named Fiona who led tours at Tamarindo and a campsite on a deserted beach, about a bungalow out at Zoni and something about a weed whacker, but she felt angry and exhausted and was having trouble concentrating. "Did you even hear what I just said?" he demanded.

"Don't yell at me," she responded crossly. "I heard you. You think this Fiona knows where Tucker is."

"I believe they may have been seriously involved. I think she's protecting him, if he's still here on Culebra."

Now she looked up at him in confusion. "Where else do you think he might be?"

"Why would he stay – it's been months since the hurricane. Ferry and airplane services are back to normal.

Even some yachters have returned. The boy was into sailing. And as you obviously know, he sailed here in a borrowed sailboat with a man named John Royal, also known as Flush."

A moment earlier she'd felt chilled, now she felt an unpleasant heat radiating over her whole body and up her neck and face. "And how did you learn that?"

"Don't be absurd. The same place you did. Why else would we both be here? What's wrong with you – you look like you're getting hives." Tyler had leaned back to stare at her.

"I might be. I've been pretty stressed lately." Self-consciously she put her hands up to her burning cheeks.

"Let me get you some water. Can you drink it from the tap here?" He was already headed for the sink with her empty glass.

"I don't know. I – I guess so." She didn't want to admit to him that she never drank just plain water.

"Okay, it's your turn. Any promising leads on our son?"

Unwillingly she took a small sip of water and then another to stall for time. She'd been sworn to secrecy under physical threat to her life; what could she share that wouldn't compromise her deal with Maggie? "Have you asked anyone about the boat?" Maybe she could turn this back on him without revealing her ulterior mission.

"I'm going to work on that tomorrow with Kay, my sailor friend. She's got a dinghy and knows everyone in the harbor. How about you?"

"Yes. I have." She thought about the short fruitless conversation she'd had with T-Ron about him owning a sailboat. She hadn't found out anything except that the man was incredibly turned on by the idea of open-air sex on the deck of his motor cruiser in the middle of the sea.

"And?"

"No luck so far." She wanted desperately to tell him what she was up to, how she'd ended up involved with the man she had been sent here to spy on as part of a totally fucked-up scheme in trade for her personal freedom and a slim thread of info about Tucker. That she suspected T-Ron of knowing something about Tucker, but was afraid to ask for fear of blowing her chances to learn more. That she was in way over head now with a guy who was probably a dangerous psychopathic criminal, and that yes, finding Maggie's bloody boat was central to everything here.

"Lucy!" Tyler was shaking her by the shoulders. "What's wrong with you? Pull yourself together, for Chrissake!"

Lucy blinked and then angrily pushed him away. "What's your problem, Tyler? Get your hands off of me."

"I give up. You're a freakin' nutcase these days." He held his hands above his head in surrender and stood up. "First you disappear for months without contacting your family, then you claim you've been looking for your son but you won't help me find him, and all you've really been doing is throwing a self-pity party and fucking and drinking yourself into gin-soaked oblivion!"

He stepped aside as she swung out wildly at him, easily dodging the off-kilter aim of her fists. "Get the fuck out of here, Tyler. Get the fuck out of my life! We'll see who finds him first and who's still standing at the end of all this."

"Fine. But I guarantee it won't be you." He pulled the ring of house keys out of the door lock where she had left them hanging in her shock at seeing him on her porch. "And don't worry, I'll let myself out."

"Wait! I need those keys, you scumbag!"

"They'll be on the ground, just inside the gate. But if I were you, I wouldn't try to negotiate those stairs again until morning."

"I'm not the irresponsible one!" she shouted after him. "I'm not! I never was! You are! You're a horrible parent. The worst. Fuck you, Tyler Mackenzie!"

From somewhere down below the house he shouted back, "Not a chance, Lucy Brookstone!"

She did not know how her life could have gone from bad to worse. But somehow it had. As she made herself another drink, she vowed that tomorrow she would pull herself together. She would not be this Lucy anymore.

Stretching out on the couch, she pressed the icy glass to first one cheek and then the other, trying to cool her burning skin down. When she heard footsteps on the porch a few minutes later, she swore loudly again. "What the bloody hell, you got a few more insults you haven't already hurled at me?"

"Woah, now settle down there, girlfriend. I don't remember fighting with you tonight." Before she realized what was happening, T-Ron had pried the cocktail out of her hand and set it on the coffee table just out of her reach. "You havin' one of your nightmares, darlin'?"

Cold sweat was running down her face now as she stared uncomprehendingly at him. "How...what... when did you get here?"

With surprising strength, he grabbed her by the forearms and pulled her to a standing position. "I think a shower might do you some good right now, Missy."

Did he actually care about her? The thought had her sobbing uncontrollably again as he walked her to the bathroom. Holding her tightly in an upright position, he turned on the water and then pushed her under the tepid stream.

"Wait, my dress..." she protested.

"Forget your frickin' dress. Just stand right there."

He held her forcibly in place, her head directly under the shower until her wet hair was plastered to her shoulders and her dress was soaked through and her crying dissolved into shivering. "Okay, okay. I'm cold. How long do I have to stay here?"

"How about until you're sober?" Although he sounded amused, T-Ron did not loosen his grip, easily pushing her back under the water when she tried to move away.

When her shivers became violent shaking and her legs began to buckle, he finally turned the faucet off and wrapped a towel around her.

"Why'd you do that?" she whispered, leaning against the tiled wall, wiping the water from her face.

"Because I don't want to play with someone who's a quivering fool. I like my women large and in charge."

She covered her eyes with the towel so he wouldn't see if she started crying again.

"Come on now, Lucy. Let's get you out of those wet clothes and into the bedroom." She left a trail of water on the floor as he led her through the doorway; the air from the ceiling fan causing a fresh set of tremors as it hit her skin. "I need a blanket."

He peeled the saturated dress from her body and commented, "Well at least somebody's hard." When he fingered one of her nipples, she flinched as much from his hurtful comment as his rough touch. "I'll get you a blanket. And then we're going to have a talk."

She was confused. She'd thought they were about to have sex. Despite her ragged condition, he was somehow turning her on. "Talk?"

Her head was starting to hurt and she had the unpleasant realization that maybe she was sobering up. She curled into a ball and listened to him banging drawers and closet doors in search of something to cover her. Finally he threw something fleecy on top of her and then grunted as he threw himself down on the bed next to her.

"Too tired to talk," she murmured. She wanted a drink but was afraid to ask. "Let's just screw and go to sleep." Had they ever even had sex when she wasn't drunk?

"Oh, Lucy, Lucy. Horny Lucy." His hand found its way beneath the blanket and she opened her legs a bit so he could find his way, sighing a little in anticipation. But then his fingers rested on her inner thigh as he asked, "So how you doing with the search for your son?"

His change of topic was so extreme, she felt dizzy.

"What?"

"Your missing boy. Wasn't that the reason you came to Culebra to begin with?"

"Yes, but —"

170

"So how you doing with that?"

How was this happening to her, twice in one night. She moved away from him, pulling her knees up into a fetal position. "I've got a headache."

"Oh, come on, now. Don't be like that." T-Ron ran a finger up and down her spine. "I know I've been a distraction, but I want to offer my help."

There was something fishy going on here, but in her current condition she couldn't quite remember why she didn't trust this man who had just taken care of her and put her to bed, albeit in a very twisted way, and was now seductively caressing her.

"Go on. Tell me how."

"I know lots of people here. Tell me a little bit about him and I'll ask around. We haven't really talked about it at all since we first met." He rubbed her shoulders and her neck in a way that warmed her cold flesh and made her feel cozy.

"He's a sweet boy who got misled by a sex-crazed girl when he was too young to know better." Speaking her pent-up feelings actually made her foggy brain clear a little. "When he decided to become a sailor, she left him for his best friend." She knew this was not exactly the truth, but close enough.

"Oh, sassy bitch, huh?" He squeezed the fleshy part of her shoulder blade in a way that made her uncomfortable and brought things into a little clearer focus.

"Yes, but this isn't about her."

"What makes you think he's on Culebra?" His hands were doing such nice things to her now. She closed her eyes, not wanting the feeling to end.

"He did a cross-Atlantic sail and ended up on Tortola right before that big hurricane." Tortola. With a sudden woosh, almost like giving birth, it all came back to her, everything that had happened to lead her here to this time and place. In bed. With a man who carried a very sharp knife. Oh my god, she thought. I need to keep my wits about me, I need to work this moment to my advantage.

She coughed a few times and then rasped, "Anyway, he–" she coughed again making a harsh noise in her throat. "Could you get me something to drink?"

"No. Unless it's water."

"Yes, please," she croaked. "Thank you."

When he went into the kitchen, she sat up but the room spun around her and she sank back down again. She needed to get her bearings, accept his assistance, reel him in. She could do this.

He returned with a glass and a couple of white pills in his hand. "For your headache," he said.

"Thanks. You're actually a sweet guy for a badass."

He sat down on the edge of the bed, leaning one arm across her waist, studying her as she drank and swallowed.

"So tell me again – Tortola?"

"Ever been there?"

"What do you think. Have I?" Dropping the figurative gauntlet, she thought. Here we go.

"I'm guessing that means 'Yes, Lucy, I have.'" She tried to keep her eyes from straying to the mementos on his hat, but seeing the silver feather gave her the confidence to meet his gaze.

He nodded almost imperceptibly, conceding the point. "And the only way most people get from Tortola to Culebra is by sailboat. And how is it you know he landed here..."

"By talking to the right people. Showing his photo around. Like what I was doing when I got derailed by you." It was hopeless to play coy, but she did it anyway.

"By me?" He laughed mockingly. "I think we all know how you derail yourself, Lucy." He patted her hip with a condescending gesture. "Did you find out the name of the sailboat he supposedly arrived on?"

She wasn't going to tell him she knew the name of the boat as well as he did. "Don't you think I would have told you if I did?" she countered.

Well, the place to start is with the sailing community. Tomorrow we'll go out in The Great White and ask around."

For a second she couldn't think what he was referring to and then she remembered that was the absurd name for his own motor cruiser. She hadn't called him on it before, but now she was starting to feel relaxed enough that she couldn't resist. "You know that's kind of a racist thing to call your boat." She thought her words sounded a little slurred.

He gave his habitual smirk. "Wouldn't be the first time I was accused of that."

"That doesn't bother you?"

"What bothers me is that you haven't been making any headway with finding... what's his name again?"

"Tucker." She was suddenly drowsy. Somehow her eyelids had closed and now she forced them open so she could finish the conversation.

"As in all tuckered out?" He laughed at his own bad joke and she thought sleepily that she didn't think she liked him much anymore. "So I'll come get you in the morning then."

"You're not leaving, are you... Because...T-Ron. I have to tell you something."

Her sudden seriousness made the smile go instantly out of his tone. "What?"

"I heard something in the pond tonight. Something big."

After an infinitesimal delay, his response was a resounding round of raucous hooting that included pulling the blanket away and squeezing handfuls of her flesh and making crude comments. "Oooh, something big, like this? Or as big as this? Or these?" he teased, leaning over and licking her sloppily. "Mmm, yum, look how big these lollipops are."

Much as she'd wanted some bedtime foreplay before, she felt more annoyed and offended than turned on by his lascivious sucking. Her vision seemed to be blurring now and she put a hand to her forehead as the pounding in her temples began again. "My hair is still so wet. I need to..." She couldn't remember what she was going to say. "T-Ron, how about a nightcap? Just a little one? A shot maybe?" She cringed at the sound of her own voice so high and pleading against his loud and jovial response as he moved away from her breasts.

"Oh, sure, let's celebrate. Looks like you might need another headache pill too. You're going to need a good night's sleep."

Where was the blanket? She needed the blanket. Still covering her eyes she felt around for it.

"Here you go, Lucy Goosy. Take this." He placed something on her now very thick tongue and wrapped his hand around hers as she held the glass up to her lips. "The hard stuff. Straight up. Just how you like it. Ha, ha, oh, I'm killing it here tonight!"

Lucy coughed as the welcoming harshness of the undiluted gin burned its way down her throat. T-Ron's laughter was the last thing she heard as she sank back onto her damp pillow.

CHAPTER ELEVEN

July 2018
Culebra, Puerto Rico

By mid-morning Tyler was waiting on the public dock, watching Kay motor towards him in a small wooden dinghy. As usual, she had been more than willing to help when he'd messaged her earlier about the latest strategy in his search for Tucker. As she tossed him the mooring line, he had a sense of relief at the prospect of spending a day in her sane company and he realized that his evening visit with Lucy had rattled him more than he'd wanted to admit.

"Hop aboard. I just need to stop back at the boat for a few minutes and then we can be off."

Tyler had only seen the yacht Kay was boat-sitting from a distance and now he found himself more than a little curious as to her Culebra lodging situation. "Wow, it's a small one," he commented as they pulled alongside a fiberglass craft that he estimated at about 26 feet long. "I guess I was picturing something bigger and more luxurious."

"Yeah, it's tiny. But it's enough for me. Come inside and take a look around if you want." With the ease of a much younger woman or perhaps just an experienced sailor, she climbed nimbly up a small metal ladder and onto the deck.

"I can probably see fine from out here. You won't have any space to move if I join you down there." He hovered in the doorway, peering down at the neatly made double bunk, a small polished wooden table and the narrow two burner stove.

"Believe it or not, this boat actually sleeps four. There are two aft berths as well, but some people feel they are more like coffins than sleeping quarters. Come on down and sit on the bed. I'm just making us a couple of sandwiches."

"Oh, you don't have to do that. I'll buy you lunch." He descended the few steps into the interior and brushed past her to perch awkwardly on the edge of the mattress. There was no way to get comfortable without sprawling.

"No, I've got leftover grilled fish that needs to be eaten. I made us some grouper salad that will work well between two pieces of bread." She held up a plastic bag that had clearly seen some previous use. "And we could be gone awhile."

"Resourceful, as always. At least one of us is a strategic thinker. Where are we headed exactly?"

"Well–" Before he realized what was happening, Kay was seated next to him, her body close against his, with a plastic-coated depth-finding map spread across their laps. Distracted by the heat generated by her proximity, he could barely focus on the geography she was pointing out. "According to Steve, there's a wreck out here in the mangroves that is post-Maria. When the salvage team came in February to haul out all the submerged boats, they didn't even bother with this one. I mean they did check it for bodies but then wrote it off."

"Who's Steve?"

"From the schooner over there. He and his boat weathered out both the storms here so he's pretty much the authority on harbor history from that time." As Kay bent over the map, the beads of sweat forming on the back of her neck were only inches from Tyler's face. "I've never been back into the mangroves in this area. Hopefully we won't get stuck."

"Okay, so you know where we're going then?" The heat in the small cabin suddenly felt oppressive and he stood up abruptly, his head colliding with an overhead lantern. "If so, let's get on the road. Or the water. Whatever. My brain seems to be cooking in here."

Kay laughed at his obvious discomfort with what was actually raising the temperature in the atmosphere. He waited on deck until she appeared in the hatchway wearing only a bikini top and shorts with a dry bag in one hand and snorkeling gear in the other. She handed these things up to him and then came up herself, juggling a T-shirt, hat and sunglasses.

"Hold these too, please." She struggled to pull the shirt over her head, giving Tyler ample time to see how tanned and strong her stomach muscles were, despite the obvious thickening of her waist and pull of gravity that came with age. "Did you bring sunscreen? Because we are likely going to fry out there."

It felt good to be speeding along at whatever top speed the little 6 horsepower outboard could achieve. Kay waved at a few of the yachts they passed before they were out in a more open area, heading east to the mouth of the Ensenada before angling left towards the quieter waters of the thickly wooded shore. Kay slowed the engine to a putter as they reached a part of the harbor that reminded Tyler more of the bayou than the tropics.

Kay steered into a narrow canal and then swore as the dinghy scraped bottom. She handed Tyler an oar. "Hopefully just a shallow spot. But you may have to push us through with this."

"It's like we just took a trip to another country." He marveled at the tangled growth of the mangrove roots on both sides of the waterway. Small silver fish darted through the shadows; the prehistoric shape of a pelican fluttered out of a branch, its peaceful hunting grounds momentarily disturbed by their presence.

"Yeah, I think we may have taken a wrong turn. There's no way a sailboat could have gotten through there. Oh, wait. This is deeper up here and probably connects."

They were in a wider channel now, farther from the bay. Kay turned off the motor, and for a short while, they cut silently through the murky brown water, Tyler using the oar like a river pole to help move them along. When they came to another artery, Kay started the outboard again and steered them back in the direction of the harbor.

A sudden chime startled them both and then Kay laughed. "Oh, that's just my cell." Tyler was surprised that she actually dug into her bag to look at it and then deftly texted a one-handed message back.

"Important?"

"Just a reminder about a commitment I made for tonight." She put the phone away as quickly as she'd taken it out. "Now if Steve is correct, the wreck should be just up here on the right."

"Look, what's that? There it is."

About thirty feet ahead, a contoured triangle of dirty white fiberglass rose from the surface at a steep incline. Kay silenced the outboard and they glided slowly closer. "Holy shit."

Submerged beneath the water surface was most of a small sailboat, heeled over onto one side, with the top of the cabin leaning against the mangrove roots, the prow protruding high, the keel apparently sunk in the mud and sand below.

"How do we know if this is actually it?" Tyler felt the need to speak in a hushed whisper, as though they were visiting a graveyard.

"There's one way to find out." Kay held up the diving mask. "Do you want to go down and look at the name on the back or should I?"

He looked down at the cloudy depths and swallowed hard. "This is my deal. I'll do it."

As he started to remove his shoes, Kay stopped him. "Keep your footwear on. You never know what you might step on down there. Besides, it's not deep. You should be able to stand on the bottom to do this deed."

For some reason there was a certain relief in that knowledge. Sure enough, after carefully lowering himself over the side, the water only came to up to his chest. It was hard to imagine how or why a boat would sink in such shallow depths. Removing his eyeglasses, he adjusted the mask and snorkel. Sucking in a deep breath, he dove beneath the surface.

The visibility was as poor as he'd expected and he had to go down a few times before he located the letters painted on the hull. Barnacles and algae had already begun to obscure the words, but he saw enough to confirm what they had expected. When he finally came up for the last time, gasping for breath, he slammed his fist angrily onto the metal side of the dinghy.

"Well?" Kay asked anxiously, reaching out to help him aboard.

Ripping the mask off, he wiped his face on his dry T-shirt before he finally replied, "Nico Tico. Tortola BVI."

"So what now?" Kay was blithely tearing into one of the sandwiches she had made as Tyler stared listlessly at the ruined boat. "Maybe we should look inside the cabin. Although I'm sure it's been plundered." She gave an inappropriate giggle. "Sorry, that's a weird word."

"Yeah, I guess we should. I don't really know what I'm feeling right now."

"Aw." She patted his hand. "If you want, I'll do it. You never know what might be inside that was of no value to anyone else."

"You don't have to. Just knowing that it's the Nico Tico is enough to confirm that what I learned on Tortola was probably the truth."

But Kay had already hoisted herself up onto the upper edge of the wreck and was sliding gingerly down the other side to peer into the cabin. "Ugh, it's gross," she called. "And it looks like it was totally destroyed before it sank. Even the ceiling boards were smashed. Wait, what's this…"

Something flew through the air and landed in the dingy. Tyler lifted it with two fingers and held it up. A few pages rippled out from the front of what appeared to be a paperback book; the rest were permanently sealed together in a waterlogged mass of lost fiction. "A Tan and Sandy Silence by John D. MacDonald," he murmured aloud in wonder. Had Tucker actually been reading a Travis McGee novel? "Must have been the other guy," he concluded for his own benefit. But there was still a part of him that tried to imagine how his son might have entertained himself for days on end as a sailor.

"I say let's go take a real swim somewhere and wash this crappy lagoon water off our bodies," Kay suggested as she dropped unceremoniously back on the other seat of the dinghy. Before Tyler could reply, her phone began dinging annoyingly.

"I better take this. Yes?" she asked in an irritated voice. "Yes, I'll be there. Yes. No, nothing." Unsmilingly, she shoved the phone back into the bottom of her bag.

"Everything okay?"

"Fine. Let's go." But she seemed more serious than usual.

Tyler was deep in thought as they motored back across the harbor; he had no idea where they were headed and didn't really care. He was more concerned with what his next strategy for finding Tucker was going to be and was surprised when Kay pulled up alongside a expensive-looking catamaran, until he saw a man on deck waving her over.

"You know about tonight, right?" he shouted.

Kay gave him a thumbs up and sped away as suddenly as she had slowed. "Mind if we stop at my boat for a minute?"

It seemed like a rhetorical question. As he stretched in the shaded area in the back of the little yacht to wait for her, he felt exhausted from just two hours in the sun and open air. As he dozed off, he thought maybe he was just getting old.

He had no idea how long he'd been asleep when he awoke to the sound of Kay talking on the phone again. "Yeah, it's all set. No problem. 7:30. See you then. No, I've got company right now."

Through half-opened eyes he saw her peek out at him. "You awake? Here, I'm guessing you're dehydrated." She handed him a bottle of water and sat down on the plastic cushion next to him. There was something so companionable and comforting about her presence that it didn't feel wrong in anyway when she casually put one arm across his bare chest and tucked her hand around his body.

"Thanks. I think you're right. I passed out there for a bit. You'd think I'd be used to this heat by now." He drained the bottle and sprinkled the last few drops over his face. "So you got something big going on tonight, or what?"

He sensed her stiffen for just a millisecond before she grinned mischievously. "Why – did you want to do something together?" She squeezed his rib cage.

"No, I mean, I don't know, just sounds like you've been making plans all afternoon." He couldn't believe she could fluster him so easily; he was certainly losing his edge from lack of experience.

"Yeah, actually I'm getting together with some sailors for an... event."

"Sounds interesting. What kind of event?" He'd placed his hand on top of hers with the intention of stopping her, but somehow it wasn't working that way.

"A high stakes game, you might say. And sorry, no, don't ask." She put a finger to his lips. "Because you can't come this time."

As her face grew closer to his, he was surprised to realize he was not ready for where this was headed. Not yet anyway. In the second before she kissed him, he asked, "How about that swim?"

It was way nicer than he had imagined; he didn't know why he felt so resistant.

"What's the matter?" She pulled back a few inches to study his expression.

"I've just been burned a lot that's all."

"I'm assuming that you don't mean by the sun." To his further surprise, she straightened up. "Then let's go for that swim. Probably best to take your cart. We'll get there faster."

"Hey." He gripped her hand as she stood up, pulling him to his feet beside her. "I'm not in a hurry. But thanks."

The second kiss was longer and even better than the first. They broke apart and then purposely did not look at each other again until they were face to face in the dinghy. The heat between them was so tangible now that they both broke out laughing.

"Burned?" she said softly as she started up the outboard. "I don't know about that. I'd say you're still smokin' hot."

For the next few hours they stayed in the water at the far end of Flamenco Beach, in the calm sandy area that Tyler remembered was ironically called "Shark Tank." In the late afternoon as the sun began to set, they pretty much had the beauty all to themselves, sitting in the soft sand, enjoying the way the late day light played on the waves. Kay seemed a bit preoccupied and they didn't talk about much of anything, the unspoken energy between them eclipsing whatever objective they might have been intent upon earlier in the day, studiously avoiding the inevitable outcome.

Eventually Kay said, "It's getting late. I need to go," and they packed up their gear and walked back to the golf cart.

There was an awkward moment when he dropped her at the dock. "I guess I'll go have a beer before I head back. Have a good time tonight."

She started to reply and then changed her mind. "You too. I'll text you in the morning." Before he could answer, she had lowered herself over the edge and into her dinghy.

Tyler decided he could live with salty skin and damp trunks for another hour or two and headed straight to the Dinghy Dock. He hesitated on the stairs and did a quick sweep of the room for any sign of Lucy or T-Ron. Satisfied that neither of them was present, he took an empty seat at the bar and ordered a beer.

"So, did you and Kay have a good day?"

He was a little taken aback but after a momentary memory lapse, he recognized Steve, the owner of the schooner, sitting on the next stool. "Yeah, great, thanks." Unsure exactly what the man was referring to, he added, "She's a nice woman."

"Funny, you're not really her type."

"Is that right? How so?" He was as amused as he was curious.

"For starters you don't have a yacht bigger than fifty feet. Although I suppose you could be a multi-millionaire, and just slumming it. Don't be offended; she's a self-admitted predator. And you know we sailors don't have much else to do when we're tied up except mind each other's business." He grinned.

"Well, if it's my bank account she's after, she's going to be sorry." He suppressed the urge to ask Steve who Kay's last prey had been and tried to convince himself that it didn't matter.

"So did you find what you were looking for today?"

"Yes, thanks for the tip. Unfortunately it doesn't really put me any closer to finding my son."

"Yeah, I feel for you." As Steve started in on the tribulations of his own children, Tyler felt himself mentally fading. There was only so much emotional turmoil he could manage in a day. But when the sailor said, "You know, I remember seeing your boy around," his focus sharpened.

"You do? Recently?"

"No, it was months ago. Last winter, when the salvage teams were here, hauling boats out and declaring them losses or not. Everyone on the island came out to watch; there wasn't much entertainment then." Steve stared off at the harbor, with the pale eyes of a captain who had spent a lot of time staring at the horizon.

"So you actually saw him then?" Tyler hoped his tone wasn't too impatient.

"Yeah, after I talked to Kay this morning, I thought about it some more and it came back to me." Steve upended his beer and Tyler quickly signaled the bartender for another one for him. "There were a few people who came out of the woodwork hoping to get a good deal on a wreck that week."

"Was there anything like that?" Tyler felt suddenly hopeful again.

"Yeah, a couple. One in particular, there was a guy name Ted from Florida who came down to see his ketch get rescued. Sad story – they told him that if they'd come a few weeks sooner they could have saved it but some marauders had stripped it of everything, even the keel. It had a few holes in it as well and was no longer sail-worthy and so he was pretty much giving it away."

"And..."

"Well, I'm not sure but I think your son may have taken it off his hands. Ted showed up at the bar, everybody was going to Zaco's then because this place was under reconstruction, and rumor has it that he was celebrating because somebody had actually paid him a fair amount of cash for what he'd considered a total loss. He drank until he had to go to the airport but swore he would never tell the name of who it was who'd bought his boat. The next morning a few of us went out to Dakity where it had been anchored and it was already gone. And the salvage barge had left early that same morning. Old Pedro the fisherman swore he saw them towing that boat out past the point." More than a few other patrons were listening to Steve's story now.

"Maybe they were just taking it out to sea to sink it," an eavesdropper volunteered.

There was a murmur of agreement.

Steve shrugged. "Pedro didn't think so. He was out there that day and thought they were hugging the shore. And then later that day he saw the barge steaming back towards St. Thomas without it."

"So what makes you think it was Tucker that bought it?" Tyler tried to keep from getting excited.

"See that trawler over there?" Steve pointed at a large ungainly boat not far from the dock. In the same field of vision, Tucker saw Kay in her dinghy, motoring away from town; he tried to see where she was headed but could not keep her in view. He turned his attention back to what Steve was saying. "It had washed ashore during Maria and the owner thought it was a goner and Ricardo bought for a song. The salvage team literally lifted it up with a crane and put it back in the water and now Ricardo has a valuable piece of floating real estate."

Tyler was beginning to think Steve just liked having an audience. "And..."

"Ricardo partied with the salvage workers that night and he says they told him some young guy offered Ted a wad of bills for his wreck. My point is, your son showed up that day and I've never seen him since. I don't know, it's just a thought."

"But..." Tyler was baffled. "Where would he go with a boat that was not sailable?"

"Well, not very far, I'd imagine."

Too many beers and too little to eat combined with the new ideas buzzing in his brain kept Tyler from falling asleep that night. He didn't remember the short drive back to the guesthouse, he was already going over the list of leads he needed to follow up on tomorrow. Find a way to contact Ted, the unlucky boat owner, (Kay would be a great one for that task), find Pedro the fisherman and talk to him, and if necessary, communicate with the salvage company who had come all the way from Jacksonville.

It occurred to him that he ought to get in touch with Maggie on Tortola and tell her he'd found the remains of her boat. She would not be happy. He wondered what had happened to the friend with whom Tucker had supposedly sailed here. He would have to ask Kay about him too. Kay the golddigger. He laughed to himself. Well, maybe he'd broken the mold.

He thought he was still awake until a persistent rapping brought him back to consciousness. His room was small enough that he could pretty much just lean over and turn the door handle without even totally get out of bed. In the narrow crack he could see a familiar silhouette outlined against the dim nightlight of the common room.

"I was hoping you'd still be up."

"I'm not really. But come in." He fell back onto the pillows and adjusted the sheet up to his waist. "It must be late. How'd you get here?"

Kay slipped her backpack off and sat down on the edge of the bed next to him. "I got a ride most of the way. But it's not like I couldn't have walked. Nighttime is the nicest time to walk in Culebra. It's not hot."

Still disoriented he asked, "How'd you know which room was mine?"

"A couple of kids out on the porch directed me. It's still early if you're a backpacker in your twenties."

Tyler yawned and struggled to sit up, reaching for his glasses. "Sorry, I wasn't expecting to see you until morning." As Kay came into focus, he saw that she looked almost as full of energy as she had earlier in the day and that she was dressed in uncharacteristic dark clothes, wearing a tight, long-sleeved black top and a short stretchy skirt that rode up over her thighs as she perched on the edge of the mattress.

"Do you want me to go?" She tilted her head, her blonde ponytail swinging like a question mark that punctuated her words.

"Well, I may not be up for much." They both laughed at the double meaning of his words and he couldn't resist resting his hand on her bare leg. "So how'd that 'high risk' event go? Were you a winner?"

"I could be. The night's not over yet. Maybe I'll come out on top."

"Well, I think you won that round." Tyler fell back onto his pillow and used the corner of the sheet to wipe the sweat out of his eyes.

Kay smiled and sighed contentedly before propping herself up on one elbow. "That was refreshing. How about another?"

"You have too much energy for a woman your age. Go to sleep now."

"Pretty good for a couple of old people, aren't we?"

"Who're you calling old?" As his breathing finally slowed to near normal, he closed his eyes and said, "Remind me to tell you about my evening. In the morning."

"Well, I'm wide awake after all that stimulation. You can tell me now." She bounced up expectantly.

"In the morning."

"Jeez. Okay."

But by the time he finally woke up Kay was already gone. Had he just dreamed that she'd been there? He put on his glasses and reached for his phone. As he'd expected there was a text from her.

"*That was sweet and hot.*" The message was followed by a line of emojis that alternated from hearts to flames.

"*Where'd you go? Hoping you'd still be here.*" He was shocked to see it was nearly noon.

"*You just waking up now? I've been taking care of business for hours. Come down to the dock when you can and give a holler.*"

He wondered what kind of business Kay had to take care of. He realized there were some black holes in the life of this woman he'd had some rowdy intimate sex with in the middle of the night, big gaps he knew nothing about.

"*Do you know a fisherman named Pedro?*"

"*No, why?*"

"*How about a guy named Ricardo who lives on a trawler?*"

"*Him I know. What's this about?*"

187

God, he loved how connected she was. Almost like Lucy when they'd first met twenty-five years earlier. Thinking about Lucy reminded him of how she'd been when he'd seen her a few nights ago. It depressed him to recall how fucked up she'd been. Maybe if he could find Tucker, she'd get out of this slump she was in.

"Tell you when I see you. Probably within the hour."

"Thanks for the warning." Followed by another row of flames.

He had fully expected they would jump immediately into bed again, his mind seemed to drift back to that track every time he tried to focus, but when Kay picked him up to the dock, she seemed to have other ideas. "I saw Ricardo on his deck. Did you need to see him about something?"

"Do you ever sleep?"

"Not much. Yes or no?" Not waiting for his answer, she deadheaded for the trawler.

"Yes. Let me ask you first, were you here back in February?" His eyes seemed to fixate on the well-articulated muscles in her upper arms as she expertly steered the tiller.

"I flew in midway through the month. Why?" He realized he was seriously distracted when he found himself wondering if she was wearing a bra under her blouse rather than listening to her answer.

"Before or after the salvage crew did their thing?"

"Just after. I was sorry I missed all that excitement. And all those hot guys." She grinned and then slowed the dinghy down to a crawl and shouted, "Hola, Ricardo! Podemos ir en tu barco?"

"I didn't know you spoke Spanish." Today he admired everything about her.

"Ha. Barely."

"Si, yes, come aboard." A short, wiry man wearing a red shirt and matching shorts, Ricardo waved and pointed to a ladder and platform at the back of the boat. "Buen dia, amiga. Que tal?" He greeted Kay with a kiss on the cheek as they climbed up next to him.

After Kay introduced Tyler, Ricardo invited them to sit in the shade on folding camp chairs under a canopy covering the back deck. His English was much better than Tyler's Spanish and Tyler was relieved that he wouldn't have to carry on the conversation in the rapid Puerto Rican dialect that he only occasionally understood.

"Si, si, how could I forget that day." Ricardo made a circular gesture with his hand. "All this is because of that day. I gambled all my money on this boat, not knowing if it could be saved or if it would still float." He touched his heart. "It was a risk that changed my life." He looked at Kay and switched back to Spanish. "Pero mi amiga aqui sabe como es ganar, si?"

Kay laughed and shook her head. "No verdad. No ahora." Tyler wished he knew what they were talking about.

Ricardo nodded emphatically when Tyler asked him if he'd heard the story about the boy who paid cash for an unsailable boat. But he looked blankly at the photo of dreadlocked Tucker. He had definitely seen the little red-haired "chica" around but didn't know her boyfriend. However he was able to give them directions to Pedro the fisherman's house. "He won't be there now. But later you will find him. Maybe around four in the afternoon."

Tyler had arisen so late that four was only a few hours from now. As he descended back down into the dinghy, Kay lingered behind for a moment, exchanging a few more words in Spanish with Ricardo.

"What was all that about?" he asked curiously.

"Just boat talk. En español." Her tanned fingers grazed his knee. "Want to go back to my place for a bit?"

"What do you think?"

The sex was even hotter than the air in the cramped, sun-baked cabin. Afterwards he was ready for a nap but as

189

he dozed lazily, Kay was already up, tying on a sarong and downing a bottle of water, checking her phone.

"Hey." He grabbed her around the waist and pulled her down next to him.

"Hey what."

"Tell me again whose boat this is and how you ended up here."

"Why're you interested in that all of sudden?"

"Maybe because I want to know everything about you, okay, even the things you've already told me that I've forgotten." He tried unsuccessfully to loosen the knot of cloth behind her neck. "Or maybe I want to thank the owner. For you being here."

"Aww. My story's boring - why don't you do the talking? So you don't fall back asleep," she teased. "How'd you make all your money?"

He laughed. "ALL?" Then he remembered what Steve had said about Kay being a "gold digger." He wondered if she would lose interest if she knew he was far from wealthy. "I owned a newspaper. Just call me William Randolph Hearst."

"Oh, interesting." She had to realize that he wouldn't be staying in the least expensive guesthouse on the island if he had any money to burn. "Tell me more."

"So I guess you didn't know Ted then?" It was an abrupt change of subject but at least it would divert the attention away from him and his low income.

"What? Who's Ted?"

"The guy whose boat we were talking with Ricardo about today. I'd like to get in touch with him, see what he has to say."

He was annoyed when, instead of answering, she turned her attention back to her phone. But in a few seconds she held it up for Tyler to see. "Here he is. We can send him a message."

A Facebook profile was displayed on her screen; a gray-haired sailor on a sailboat with a familiar-looking hillside in the background. "Wow. I'm impressed. How'd you do that so fast?"

"Oh, we're both part of a sailing group notice board. It was easy to figure out. Why don't you friend him from your own account? That way I can stay out of it."

"Good idea." But he noticed that when he handed her the phone, she clicked the friend request button before closing out of the page.

"We should probably get going if we want to catch Pedro." She tossed him his shorts and he wondered cynically if she had looked in his wallet last night. Nah, if she had then she would have known he had no money.

Pedro's house was small and ramshackle, the peeling turquoise paint on cement walls stood in contrast to his brand new wooden deck. An air-conditioner in the front louvered window rattled noisily and somewhere inside a television was blaring. Tyler wasn't sure anybody would hear them knocking, but the door opened almost immediately.

Unlike Ricardo, Pedro spoke almost no English or at least acted like he didn't. Tyler waited awkwardly as Kay translated slowly, stopping frequently to consult a language translator in her phone.

Not particularly friendly at first, Pedro became quite animated when he finally realized what they were inquiring about. He used his hands to point and visually describe what he had seen that morning.

"He says the barge was going first with a sailboat behind. Pulling it. Very slow. He went by on his way to go fishing. He was out in the channel between Playa Larga and Culebrita when they passed him. With no boat."

Eventually Kay pulled up a map of Culebra on her cell and Pedro showed them the area he was talking about. "Ask him where he thinks the boat might be," Tyler coached excitedly.

"Y donde crees que esta el barco ahora?" Kay dutifully choked out the Spanish words.

Pedro shrugged. "Aqui?" He indicated a large area labeled as Manglar Bay. "No se. Nunca viajo alli. Voy a pescar y voy a mi casa. Estoy muy cansado de trabajar todo los dias para explorar."

He was clearly ready to end the conversation and get back to his TV and the cooler air inside his house. They thanked him graciously as he disappeared into the dark interior.

"Wow. That was amazing. Again you were an incredible help." Tyler could not contain his enthusiasm once they were back sitting in the golf cart.

"Yeah, don't thank me yet. This is not an easy area to get to. By car or dinghy." Kay was studying the map, a dark frown on her face.

"Consider it a challenge. We'll figure it out."

She looked up finally and forced her expression to clear as she patted him reassuringly on the arm. "Oh, we will. We definitely will."

CHAPTER TWELVE

February 2018
Culebra, Puerto Rico

Tucker felt a tug on his line and jerked it hard to set the hook. It felt like a big one this time. Bracing his feet against the nearest rock, he reeled the line hard, hoping the hook wasn't just caught on the reef. He was rewarded by a silvery flash as his fishing pole arced with the fight of something big.

He swung the line through the air and landed his catch on the sand behind him. A large barracuda maybe. He still didn't know his fish very well but whatever it was, there was definitely some eating there. Now came the part he hated almost as much as cleaning out the guts. Picking up a heavy boulder he brought it down on the head. The barracuda flopped a few more times and then lay still.

Fiona was still much better at the whole procedure than he was, but she had taught him well. Too bad she wasn't here today with him on this deserted beach on Luis Peña island. He hoped the seas would calm down soon so that she could manage to get over here from Tamarindo in the next few days. He was running out of everything. Especially patience.

He'd lost track of how many days he'd spent on this little national reserve island half a mile off the west coast of Culebra. After a few weeks, he'd stopped counting time and started making lists again. He thought it was probably more than a month now that he'd been camping here, living like an aborigine, blending into the landscape, camouflaging himself into the bush at any signs of civilized human beings going by on the water, laying low if he heard any voices or noises from the more accessible beaches and coves on the other side of the steep ridge.

At first it had been A) fun, B) almost relaxing, C) different, D) none of the above, finally not having to worry about himself or the trash bags full of money being discovered. The seas had been unusually calm for early January and Fiona had been able to visit regularly, helping make his campsite cozy and well-hidden from view, bringing him A) food, B) water C) news and D) most important of all, companionship. She'd managed to score a new tent for him, a dull olive green that merged with the natural colors of the surrounding terrain and she'd taken away any piece of his clothing that was even remotely bright in color, leaving him with only khakis, tans and browns. But even after his minimalist sailing lifestyle, this Robinson Crusoe existence was getting old. If not for Fiona, and the lack of a passport, he would have left Puerto Rico in his wake ages ago.

Then again, "Louie P" had been his destiny for months now, ever since his do-or-die instructions from Flush on that frightening night during Hurricane Maria. He just hadn't realized it until Fiona had suggested it as a new hideaway after the Zoni fiasco.

The unused back bungalow at the Zoni house had been like a luxury vacation for the two of them. The furniture had been protected by old sheets that were covered in so much gecko shit that they'd had to throw them away and it had taken two days of vigorous scrubbing to get the rest of the sticky droppings off the floors, sinks and other fixtures.

But then...a real bed with real bedding. A couch and a table with two chairs. Running water, even a toilet that flushed. Electric lights.

After months of living outdoors he could not have cared less about the million dollar view of the mile long sandy beach. He was much more excited by the television with a DVD player and a stack of twenty old movies. Even more so by the shelf full of jigsaw puzzles.

Fiona stayed with him for two wonderful days and nights, but then she had to go back. She said it would be too

194

suspicious for her to already be out in Zoni when Janet came to pick her up the next morning for their cleaning jobs. She'd had to walk halfway across the island before she got a ride back to town. When she snuck away from the cleaning job the following afternoon to see him again, she was exhausted and nervous.

"I'll come back in a couple of days," she promised.

Despite the amenities, it had been a lonely forty-eight hours until she returned. "I have a surprise," he told her after she'd enjoyed a long shower and some great reunion sex. "I found these in a shed behind the house."

When Fiona saw the two mountain bicycles, she hugged him with joy.

The bikes gave them both what they needed – for Fiona it was transportation at any time as well as a great excuse not to accept a ride to or from work. For Tucker it was a freedom he hadn't experienced in months. To covertly slip out for an early morning or late afternoon ride and duck down one of the nearby dirt roads that led to Playa Larga or Mosquito Bay and spend a few hours exploring, made him feel almost normal. There was a certain rush in pedaling furiously home under the cover of dusk before complete darkness fell, especially when Fiona managed to join him.

She reported proudly that she had taken down another drone with her slingshot and assured him that the harassment seemed to have stopped now that he was gone. "I'm sure whoever it is came by and checked out my tent while I was out here but I think they may be satisfied that you have left."

"I'm worried about you."

"Don't be. I've been careful to make sure no one is following me here. Trust me?"

It seemed odd that she'd posed it as a question rather than a statement, almost like a dare. "Of course." He didn't add that he had no choice but to trust her.

An undisturbed couple of weeks followed and he was soon lulled into a false sense of security at this quiet, upscale end of Culebra, where a few old people waved at him as they walked their poodles in the morning and the random jeep passed on its way to the beach. As the Christmas holidays approached and some of the empty houses began to be occupied, this bolder recklessness eventually betrayed the safety of the sweet retreat.

"What's the matter? What happened?" He looked up from a thousand-piece color rendering of the Matterhorn when Fiona burst into the cottage sobbing.

"Janet saw you on the bicycle. You have to go now or she's going to call the police and have us both arrested." She wiped her nose on the back of her hand. "And I have to go too. She and I aren't working together anymore."

They walked and hitchhiked and walked some more to get back to her campsite, weighed down by a few cloth shopping bags of food and a couple of jigsaw puzzles that Tucker couldn't resist bringing along.

"You know you don't have to work at that stupid job, I have plenty of money for both of us," he reminded her as they trudged up the last steep hill before the dirt road to Datiles.

"Yes, I do. But I am not going to be dependent on you for income. And besides, I don't like that money."

Her last words sounded so absurd that they both laughed, although he knew what she meant. At the top of the hill they stopped to rest for a minute, but the sun was quickly disappearing behind a band of clouds on the horizon. Tucker realized that being on the east side of the island, he had not realized how much shorter the days had become at this time of the year.

"We better get going. It'll be dark before we know it." He picked up his bag and then reached for hers, but she pulled it away.

"I can do it, thanks, anyway."

"You are such a little toughie. You're allowed to be tired, Fi." The truth was that he was still in awe of her strength and endurance.

As they walked the last few hundred feet, Fiona came to a sudden halt and sucked in her breath. "What the..."

she pointed at a place in the dirt track where a deep rut gleamed with fresh mud. "Somebody drove down here today."

"It is a public beach, it could have been anybody. Remember that it's almost Christmas."

But she had already taken off, running the rest of the way. He hurried to catch up with her, looking hastily around the clearing. Everything looked pretty much the same as it had when he'd left weeks earlier, Fiona's campsite as tidy as ever, Pete's as neglected and derelict as before. A quick detour to the place where he'd half buried the trash bags full of money showed it to be undisturbed and intact.

Fiona had dropped her bags and was unzipping the tent flap. "Shit. Shit. Shit." She sank to her knees.

"What is it?" Tucker was by her side in an instant, peering over her shoulder.

There was no need for her to answer. The inside of the tent had been totally ransacked, belongings flung everywhere, air mattress deflated, bedding tossed.

"Shit is right, Oh, I'm so sorry, sweetie." He hugged her close as she sat there shaking and immobile. "What do you think they were after - money?"

She picked up a little metal box that was upside down on the tent floor and showed him its empty interior. "It wasn't much but they took it all anyway. But it wasn't that hard to find –they didn't have to do all this." She waved her hand. "This is a message."

They spent the next two hours cleaning and packing, finally collapsing on a quilt in the middle of the space.

"Electric Beach." Fiona spoke into the darkness, answering the unanswered question that loomed large. "I've been scoping it out for a while now. It's well protected and nobody goes there because it's not really a beach. Turns out this cove is a favorite of locals and big islanders, because it's safe for non-swimmers and children. And with the holidays coming…"

197

"Can we get there by boat?" Tucker ran his fingers through her thick tangle of curls, his nose against her cheek.

"No, maybe by kayak on a calm day. The reef is like rocky fingers that reach out into the water. There is a path, kind of, that goes around the point or you can get there by the road. It's where the electricity cable and water line come onto the island through a pipe under the sea. Or used to."

She didn't need to explain. Even Tucker, in his sequestered state knew that now, three months after the hurricane, Culebra had three generators run by FEMA that produced twenty-four-hour power. No one had any idea when the destroyed cable would, if ever, be repaired, but the residents were grateful for a reliable source of electricity – many places on the big island were still totally in the dark and in much worse shape.

"Okay, whatever you say." Tucker was so tired he would agree to anything if she would just unwind and go to sleep.

"We'll go at first light. We've got the other tent and a good tarp. We'll leave this one here as a decoy." Even though she was curled around him like she was relaxed and cozy, Fiona's mind was still clicking away.

"A decoy? We're not ducks."

"Sitting ducks. Yeah, we kind of are."

She sat up suddenly. "Hell, I've got tours starting up again day after tomorrow."

"But that's a good thing, right? It means things are getting back to normal and you've got another source of income." He stroked the bare skin of her hip and then slid his hand around to rest on the warmth of her belly. Something about her anxiety attacks always made him get super-calm, like maybe he could save her or protect her from whatever harm was out there. "What are you worried about?"

"Everything. Why aren't you?" She fell back down again, nestling in the crook of his arm.

He didn't know why. But life always felt perfect when he was with Fiona, even just for a few minutes. He didn't want to let go of that.

By the following evening they'd made the new campsite into a comfortable living space. Tucked back under some trees with a protective spread of overhanging branches, the location was several yards back from the sea and not easy to spot unless you were directly in front of it. The bleached coral rocks that covered the rugged shoreline were difficult to traverse and added an element of safety in their lack of appeal for daytrippers and beachgoers.

The newfound solitude seemed to bring some kind of peace to Fiona despite the hectic pace of the holiday season. Whatever harassment she had been experiencing on his behalf seemed to cease and Tucker sensed that there had been a lot more than she had actually been disclosing. They'd set up the old tent site to look like it was occupied, but had left nothing of value there. He'd moved the money to a location in the thicket of bushes behind their new place and was secure in the knowledge that there was way less likelihood of it being discovered.

His days took on a new leisurely rhythm that felt far more natural to him than his time at the Zoni cottage. When Fiona left for work, he would tidy up the tent yard and then wander up the beach past the cable tower to a place where he liked to snorkel. The reef in this area was extreme and fantastical in a way he had never seen before, with unique formations and lots of large bright fish. On calm days it was just plain awesome; on rough ones navigating the coral formations was dangerously exhilarating, watching the underwater life move with the current and trying not to bash his body up on the sharp coral as the waves tossed him around.

Because of her superior kayaking skills, Fiona was soon able to traverse the hidden hazards of Electric Beach and paddle her way to where the dinghy was moored by Datiles or even all the way into town. Although he'd never been much of a cook, Tucker felt the least he could do for her was make dinner after her work day. But after his first failed attempts at real meals, he generally made a pot of rice to supplement whatever she stopped to buy on her way home, usually cheap barbecued chicken or pizza.

But his favorite part of any twenty-four hours was making love to her at night and again at dawn. He was always surprised how easily he could satisfy her needs. The first time Fiona had said, "I'm good," he had been hurt and worried, until she assured him, "I mean I'm great, that was fabulous," and then a few minutes later fell asleep, worn out by the physical intensity of her daily activities.

He had been used to Chloe's insatiable desire to get high in every way – one orgasm had never been enough if there were multiples to be had and sex enhanced by drugs could go on for hours. She got off on doing it anywhere and everywhere, and as their relationship had grown strained, he'd learned to perform in more improbable places, conditions and positions just to keep her happy. And as for getting stoned – her appetite for illegal substances had been even harder to keep pace with and had made him increasingly uncomfortable.

Now, with Fiona, sex was just a delightfully gratifying beginning and end to each day. And there were no drugs and alcohol involved at all. Afterwards he would watch her even breathing while she slept, marveling at the delicate whiteness of the triangles of skin that never saw the sun, gently running his fingertips over the sweet rosiness of her nipples and through the bright unshaven thickness of the curls between her legs. She reminded him of an ancient painting of an angel he'd seen once in an art museum, a vision of delicate beauty and enduring strength.

Since they were alone at Electric most of the day, with only an occasional adventurous tourist or snorkeler appearing for, at maximum, an hour or two midday, Tucker often didn't wear any clothing, having grown comfortable with nudity early on in his time with Chloe. But Fiona was not at ease being totally naked, and he found it amusing that the tiny scraps of cloth she called a swimsuit made her feel dressed. Unlike Chloe, she was not turned on by the idea of an all-over tan or of the heat of the sun on her open crotch.

If he had not been so hopelessly in love with her he would have already left Culebra behind in the dust, passport or no passport.

Christmas Day was pretty much like any other for the two of them. Fiona had to work since there were tourists whose holiday plans included a kayaking adventure tour, but she came home with a bottle of wine that someone had given her and two pieces of chocolate cake. It was Tucker's third Christmas away from home – the first spent in a mountaintop hostel in Sumatra with Chloe, the second alone in Greece – and he was no longer nostalgic for childhood traditions. But by the time the bottle was half empty he was sharing tales about how his father made him use scavenger hunt clues to search the house and yard for his presents and about Boxing Day celebrations with his British-born mother. Fiona told him, a bit mournfully, about her big family and their festivities somewhere in the Midwest, so different from his own. As they watched the sun set into the sea, Tucker thought that, as a stand-alone moment in time, right now was pretty perfect.

A few afternoons later he emerged from the water to find a youngish couple sitting in camp chairs on a small stretch of sand between him and the campsite; they were eating sandwiches and watching him in a relaxed, curious way. There was no way to avoid speaking with them without appearing suspiciously paranoid and he did not want to draw attention to the living area a few hundred yards away.

So for the first time in weeks, Tucker had a conversation with someone other than Fiona. He was surprised by how much he had missed talking with people, just sharing information and socializing. Two hours went by while he sat with them and discussed snorkeling, sailing

201

and places in the world he had traveled. When they finally left, he felt incredibly conflicted – both full and empty, happy yet bereft.

"I think I need a trip to town," he told Fiona that night.

"I don't know, it's really busy right now. There are even some street concerts happening at night for New Year's Eve." Her doubtful tone implied that she didn't want to go anywhere near that many people.

"But that's excellent. We'll just get lost in the crowd. No one will pay any attention to us – there'll be no standing out. Look, no one's bothered us since we moved; it will be fine. Just come with me. We can celebrate the beginning of a new year together."

Fiona was silent for a bit and then squeezed his hand. "Okay. I'll think about it."

Unfortunately a turn in the weather brought in some heavy rain and what Fiona told him were called the "Christmas winds." The seas became too rough to navigate even from the most protected beaches and it was hard to even keep their tent from blowing away. Kayak tours were canceled and even Fiona began to grow a bit stir crazy in the damp camp.

Eventually it wasn't hard for Tucker to convince her to accompany him to town to hear some music, although he doubted it would still be happening. They put on rain jackets, pulled up their hoods, and by the beam of their headlamps, slogged through the mud of the road until they reached the pavement at the top of the hill. From there they could see colored lights and hear loud speakers blasting.

Tucker felt a boyish excitement at the prospect, but Fiona hung back. "I don't know. This is not my kind of scene."

"Come on, Fi. It'll be more fun than sitting in a wet tent."

She had to concede on that point.

Among the throng of people huddling under umbrellas and shielding their eyes from the rain, nobody paid any mind to a pair of young lovers with their hoods low over their eyes, eating empanadillas and watching an electric salsa band play beneath a storm canopy.

When they finally staggered home in their dripping jackets and muddy flip-flops, Tucker was mentally saturated from the overstimulation of the evening yet overwhelmingly happier.

After another day of high wind, he found it easy to convince Fiona to go out again. There was no party in the plaza in town, but they ate pizza at a corner table inside a restaurant and Tucker felt almost normal. A few local people greeted Fiona, expressing surprise at seeing her out. A pair of girls gave Tucker a good once-over with raised eyebrows and then one of them asked Fiona if she wanted to take over a cleaning job. "I gotta go back to Florida for a while. It's a really nice old couple up on the Melones hill."

Back at Electric Beach the wind had died down, the moon had come out and the celebratory sex was the best yet.

In Puerto Rico the holiday season seemed endless, culminating in Kings Day nearly a week after New Year's. By then Fiona was back to daily kayak tours at Tamarindo and although she did not agree with him, Tucker was feeling much more secure with the idea that the demonic party who had been pursuing him since Flush's death must have finally left the island.

While Fiona was at work he began expanding his universe, short excursions that he didn't bother to mention to her so that she wouldn't worry. An afternoon at the library which had only recently reopened, a dinghy trip to the beach at Punta Soldado, another out to the Ensenada to see whether any new boats had arrived in the harbor. The island was still quiet, many tourists having chosen not to visit yet and a good portion of residents having left to seek gainful employment elsewhere. She did agree he could accompany her to help with the cleaning of the new house where the owners eagerly accepted his offer of yard work, since their property had not really been looked after since the hurricane.

As they walked home together one afternoon after several hours of housekeeping and lawn care, with backpacks full of groceries and plans for a great dinner, they were stopped in their tracks by a familiar buzzing sound overhead.

"It can't be. Damn it." Fiona looked at the sky, her fury beginning to build.

"Don't jump to conclusions. Plenty of people have drones now." But Tucker found himself ducking instinctively as the object soared into view and began to hover over them.

Fiona grabbed him by the arm and pushed him into a thorny thicket that had clearly never hosted any large living beings before. "Stay here!" she hissed. "Let me go alone, back to the old campsite."

"Ouch, what the fuck. Don't be ridiculous!"

"I'm serious." She was as grim as he'd ever seen her. "After five minutes you go as fast as you can to Electric, and then stay as close to the tree line as you can. When you get to the tent, wait inside. I'll see you after dark."

"This is insane. You're a paranoid maniac!" he whispered loudly. But he stayed where he was, watching the blood form in the scratches on his arms and legs and listening to the hum of the drone as it moved off in the direction of Datiles Beach. Although he felt he should not desert her, he trusted her instincts more than his own. Incurring a few further scratches as he disentangled himself from the prickers, he traveled as quickly as he could down the deserted road towards home.

It was dark by the time Fiona unzipped the tent flap and slipped inside. By then Tucker had worked himself into a frenzied state of worry. If he thought he would feel better when she finally arrived, he was wrong. She stared at him with red-rimmed eyes, gripping something in one hand, holding it out in front of her at arm's length.

Even in the fading solar lamplight he could see what it was. A page cut from a passport – a black circle drawn around a name with a line drawn through, a small pen knife still sticking out of the slash where it had been jammed through the forehead of the glossy head shot.

Dropping it on the floor, she collapsed on the air mattress beside him.

"Well, now at least we're sure who's stalking me. That fucking pirate." Tucker's tone was way bolder than he actually felt.

"His name's Tiburon. And it's my fault." She covered her face with her hands. "All of this."

Tiburon, the one responsible for Flush's imprisonment and who Maggie hated. How had he not put it together. "You have nothing to do with this. It's a mess I brought with me from Tortola."

"No, really. I led him to you. I had no idea..."

What was she talking about? He froze, waiting for her to go on.

"That first day when you brought me to Milka's. He was in line at the store, flirting with me, asking me who my new boyfriend was. I was just making conversation, I told him your story." She sobbed a little. "I didn't know. And then when you told me about the guy on your boat... I didn't want to believe it was all connected. I'm really sorry. I figured if I could just hide you, he'd stop."

"Shh, it's not your fault." He didn't know what to do with this new information but he did know he didn't want to lose her.

"You have to go."

"I'm not leaving here without you. Come with me." He wrapped his body around hers. She was trembling with every breath.

"It's not safe for either of us if you stay."

"Where can I go? I don't even have a passport." With one hand, he stroked her hair back from her forehead, while tugging at her shorts with the other. "Take off your clothes, you're all sweaty."

"We'll go to the big island on the ferry and you can get a new one." She pulled her T-shirt over her head. "You need to get out of here."

"Come with me. We'll buy a boat and sail around the world. Together. You and me."

"I can't."

"Yes, you can. Give me one good reason." He kissed the back of her neck.

"Because I don't have a passport either."

"What?" His lips stopped their trail down her shoulder.

I've never had one. I didn't need one to come to Puerto Rico." She rolled over to face him.

"Then we'll both get new passports." He was getting more and more aroused by his spur-of-the-moment idea. "Say yes. Because I am going to make you say yes. Yes, yes, yes."

Despite everything, she laughed a little and moved against him. "Okay, yes, yes, yes. But it could take months. Meanwhile, I have a plan."

He could count on her to always have a plan. "Me too. And mine is happening right now. I could do this for months."

"I don't think so. We're leaving here at first light."

And now here he was, weeks later – A) alone, B) dirty and C) feeling nauseous as he whacked a fish on the head with a rock. He didn't feel much like eating at this time of the morning, so he carried his catch back up to his tent to put in it the cooler. Not that he'd had any ice for days, but at least it would keep the ants and flies away until he was ready to cook it later.

He felt kind of weird, like his bones were aching. Maybe he'd take a nap. It was a weird thing to do so early in the day but what did it matter. The smell of fish on his hands was making him feel even sicker so he headed back down to the water to wash up. He didn't even notice the yellow kayak on the beach until he had already waded into the surf and was leaning over.

Fiona's kayak was a faded orange. Or if she brought one of the tour company's boats it would be red.

Tucker looked around and then froze. A hundred feet away, a man in a broad-brimmed straw hat was standing perfectly still, watching him. He was lean and athletic, wearing a long-sleeve T-shirt and a pair of flowered board shorts, and he seemed harmless enough. In one hand he was holding a faded blue and white buoy that Tucker knew had washed ashore a few days earlier.

They stood there for a moment, warily sizing each other up and Tucker realized he must looked as feral as he felt – at least he had shorts on. Then the man held up the buoy. "This isn't yours, is it?" When Tucker shook his head, he continued, "Good, because I could use one of these."

"Feel free."

The man glanced around, as though searching for something before taking a few steps toward him. "This is usually a good scavenging beach. I've found some great stuff here, life jackets, coolers, kayak paddles. Lots of rope. I would have thought there would have been more stuff washed up after the hurricanes. But it's pretty clean right now." As he talked he kept moving in Tucker's direction until he was only a couple of feet away and Tucker understood now that this was a strategy, a careful approach, as one might do when stalking a wild animal.

"Yeah, that's true." He wasn't sure how much to say – should he mention that he had been picking up debris for weeks, that his whole campsite was furnished with ripped boat cushions, wooden boxes and even a beach chair that had floated ashore.

When the stranger tilted his head quizzically to scrutinize him more closely, Tucker could see by the lines in his face and neck that the man was much older than his original assumption. "Been camping out here for a while, have you?"

"A couple of days."

There was a nod and the ghost of a grin. "It's a reserve, you know. But I'm sure you're aware of that. And I'm not the policia." He stooped to pick up a large conch shell, still fully intact. "This a beauty. Mind if I keep it?"

Tucker shrugged. "Suit yourself." He didn't know what to do next; he didn't want to go back to his tent because he didn't want to lead the kayaker to his campsite.

"Guess you weren't expecting any visitors today. Or any day, for that matter. Most folks would be afraid to traverse that reef for fear of flipping over, especially when the water's like it is today." He walked over to his kayak and tossed his treasures into a milk crate that was secured to the sides with bungee cords. "Except for crazy ones like me. Who know where the break is." Then, picking up a soft-sided lunch cooler, he headed for the shade of an almond tree. "Hungry?"

Was he hallucinating or was the man actually holding out a plastic baggie with a sandwich in it? "Uh, sure. I'm always hungry."

"How about a beer to go with it?"

They sat in the sand, leaning against a fallen tree trunk, sharing lunch. Tucker knew he was behaving like a stray dog, but he didn't care. He couldn't recall the last time he'd had ham and cheese on white bread or anything to drink that was as cold as the can of Medalla in his hand.

"So I'm Vance and I'm not going to ask your name. Probably better if I don't know it. That way I won't give it up under torture." He nodded at the empty sandwich bag that Tucker was holding. "So what have you been subsisting on here?"

"Fish. More fish. I have some other supplies." There was no way he was going to tell him about Fiona.

Vance continued to gently probe into Tucker's existence on Luis Peña; he clearly had some experience with extracting information from introverts and semi-crazy people, letting Tucker steer the conversation in whatever direction he wanted. By the time Vance had popped open his second beer, they were discussing the history of Culebra and the impact of the military occupation. It seemed like a safe topic. "Disappointing that the bomb squad has the Flamenco campground all cordoned off for testing these days, isn't it?"

"Um, yeah." Maybe Vance thought that was why he was out here. Tucker only knew a little bit about the government teams that were searching for old bombs to explode. From what Fiona had told him, the "bomb guys" with their expense accounts and per diems had been the main source of income for guesthouses, restaurants and jeep rentals during the past few months.

"And how about that guard stationed at the path to Carlos Rosario? Day and night." Tucker suspected he was fishing now, testing his knowledge. "But I guess they've actually found some undetonated explosives out that way."

"Yeah, I've heard about some old structures that are still around from then." Two could play this game. "A bunker out at the end of Playa Blanca?"

Vance nodded as he sipped from his open can. "I've seen it from the water, but never hiked there. And a couple of old wells on the path to Brava as well."

"I thought I heard that path was pretty much unusable since Maria."

"Yeah, I've heard that too."

The conversation migrated onto sailing and a carefully edited version of Tucker's experiences as well as his dreams of one day buying a boat.

"So you know what they've been doing this week in the Ensenada?"

Maybe it was a trick question, but Tucker had no idea of the answer and he waited for Vance to continue.

"The salvage team from Florida is here on a hurricane recovery mission with their barge and crane. Saving whatever boats they can." Vance described the various rescues that had been accomplished and Tucker could not resist asking about a few specific yachts and power cruisers that he knew of.

"A few were considered total losses and some were just sad cases of reefed boats that had been vandalized." Vance went on to tell him about a guy named Ted who was trying to sell what was left of his ketch. He'd sold the dinghy to a local woman and was hoping that somebody would take his sailboat off his hands before he flew away and permanently relocated back to the States.

"How much does he want for it?" Tucker had trouble concealing his excitement.

"Oh, I'm guessing he'd pretty much take anything. Maybe a few thousand bucks. Why, you interested?" Vance laughed at the improbability of that prospect.

"Yeah, actually, I am." Tucker stood up and wiped the dirt off his shorts. "Will that kayak hold two people?"

"Uh, sure. But for real?"

Tucker was already headed up the path to his tent. "I'll be back in ten minutes!" he called over his shoulder. He made sure Vance was not following him and then he diverted around the campsite and scrambled through the brush on the side of the hill. With one final look back, he moved the palm fronds and branches concealing the remains of a stone foundation before ducking down inside.

When he returned shouldering a heavy backpack, Vance was stretched out in the sand, apparently napping, with his hat shading his face. Tucker coughed discreetly. "Ready when you are."

Vance lifted the hat and looked up at him, taking in the fact that Tucker now wore a shirt and cap and was carrying luggage. "We're really doing this? You do know the ATM machine still doesn't work most of the time and I doubt this guy Ted will honor a credit card."

"Not a problem. I've got...access to cash." The money felt heavy on his back and he hefted the straps up a little.

"Okay, well, I'm not a taxi service that's bringing you back here tonight, so I hope you've got what you need." Vance frowned as he stood up and Tucker hoped he wasn't reconsidering his offer. "Too bad I didn't bring a second paddle. But I wasn't expecting company."

"Hang on." Dropping the pack in the sand, he ducked under some branches that hung over a cluster of rocks and tugged at an object hidden there. "Here we go." He held up a spare paddle that Fiona had left in case of an emergency.

"Well, all right then." Vance grinned and picked up his insulated lunch cooler. "Here we go."

CHAPTER THIRTEEN

July 2018
Culebra, Puerto Rico

Lucy felt like she had been sleeping for days.

Every time she rose to consciousness, sleep just seemed to suck her back down like a vacuum tube to another realm. With the shades drawn and the door closed, she couldn't tell if it was day or night when she woke. All she knew was that it was easier just to stay where she was and drift back off again. Her head was too heavy to lift off the pillow; her limbs were sodden logs that could barely float in the sea of oblivion, and her throat was a sand trail through the Sahara trodden by hundreds of camels.

It was hunger that finally propelled her from the bed, dragging a damp twist of sheets with her. A wave of dizziness sent her reeling into a wall and then the sudden need to empty her bladder had her trying to remember where she was and which way it was to the bathroom.

Daylight blinded her as she staggered out of the room. The refrigerator was so far away, a mirage of an oasis on the horizon. Miraculously there was an untouched pint of ice cream in the freezer, Haagen Daz, not Ben and Jerry's, but it would do and so would the dirty spoon in the sink. Beneath the lid, the contents seemed to have melted and refrozen a few times and tasted a bit off, but flavor hardly mattered in her condition. She stood naked at the counter, enduring how the initial brain freeze added to her pounding headache, until she had consumed the entire container. Only after leaning over the sink and downing multiple glasses of water, did she finally look around.

Where had she left her phone; she felt a desperate need to know the time. As she stumbled from room to room she caught sight of herself in the hall mirror and screamed. She looked like a victim in a horror movie – her hair was a matted tangle that stuck out from the side of her head, a deep red crease marked one cheek where she had been face down on the edge of the mattress. And her body...she hadn't looked at herself below the neck in months. Now she remembered why.

Grabbing a sarong from the floor of the bedroom, she tied it around her chest and continued her search for the phone. She finally found it, sitting right where it usually was on the coffee table, but totally dead. Another frantic hunt turned up the charger still plugged into the wall. When the screen eventually came to life, she was surprised to discover it was only a little after noon. Until she realized it was noon on Wednesday, not Monday.

Had she really slept for two and a half days? Could a person do that? She tried to recall what had happened before she passed out on whatever night it had been. She could remember anger and T-Ron; maybe there'd been great sex before she blacked out, but she could bring nothing to mind. Wait – Tyler had been there, they'd had a fight about something. Her brain was foggy from all that sleep, so much sleep, and yet she still felt tired.

Fighting the urge to go back to bed, she stepped out on the porch and was immediately steamrolled by the thick humidity of the air heated by the midday sun. And before she knew it, she had retreated to the cool darkness of the bedroom.

When she woke again a few hours later, she felt different than she had for weeks. Rested. Aware. Clearer, somehow. As she stood in the shower, feeling her brain and her body coming to life, she realized that she hadn't had a drink in almost three days. Thinking about gin made her crave it, but she felt so good that she actually resisted the urge and made a cup of tea instead. Wrapped in a towel and armed with a wide-tooth comb, she took her tea out onto the porch and began to pick the tangles out of her hair.

Everything seemed sharper, the colors were brighter, the sounds more defined. The pond seemed more still and denser and she remembered her sense of seeing something large emerge and of the plunking sounds at night. Other than a swarm of bugs skittering over the surface, there was no movement now.

As she forced the comb through her curls, she leaned over the railing and looked around the yard. What was she seeing – were those really muddy tire tracks coming up the slope from the water? When and why...Of course, anything could have happened during the time she'd been asleep. Still working on one stubborn knot, she descended the stairs to the ground below.

But her curiosity about the tracks disappeared as she reached the bottom step. Where was her golf cart? Her immediate reaction was indignation at the idea that someone had stolen it, but then that didn't seem possible. She had locked the gate behind her when she'd come in. She walked over to where she usually parked, trying desperately to remember the events that evening, however many nights ago it had been.

Tyler had scared her on the porch. They'd had a fight and he'd taken her keys to get out of the gate, saying he'd toss them through onto the ground inside. That bastard, had he left with her golf cart instead? Why would he do that – he'd come in his own vehicle. She could see that the gate was securely padlocked at the moment, which meant nobody could come in. Or get out. Bloody hell, where were her keys?

Wait, T-Ron had arrived after Tyler had left. He'd let himself in – he had his own set of keys to the property. You'd think he might have mentioned it if he noticed Lucy's cart was gone. Maybe he had and she couldn't remember. Damn. She couldn't keep herself from walking back and forth in the driveway looking for the keys even though she knew that if the golf cart was gone then the keys were too. And how the hell was she going to unlock the gate?

Somebody was fucking with her. Her newfound calm disappeared into the fury and frustration of her current circumstances. She was basically a prisoner at Casa Laguna until T-Ron returned; she couldn't even use her cell phone to call for help – it was useless out here without a signal. "Well, we'll see about this!" she muttered aloud, stomping back up the stairs.

Before she knew it, she was searching the house for her bottle of gin. It didn't take long to discover that not only were her wheels gone, but her alcohol was too. Fuming, she made another cup of tea and took some deep breaths. Had the man left her any food? She opened the fridge – why had she expected there to be anything in it, she never bought any groceries. In the cupboard she found a tin of tuna and a box of rice, apparently left by the previous tenant. Well, she wouldn't starve today anyway.

An hour later she had consumed all the food in the house and was back at the gate assessing whether or not she could scale the spikes or get out some other way. Decades ago she had actually been able to pick door locks; but a padlock was much harder. And she had no tools. Armed with a safety pin, a paper clip and a bent fork, she began working at it, but was saved ten minutes later by the first car to drive by. The occupants immediately hopped out to assess her problem.

Quickly fabricating the story of a fight with a boyfriend who drove off in her vehicle with her keys, which was almost the truth anyway, she was soon the object of the couple's sympathy and assistance. The woman stayed with Lucy while the man drove off in search of a bolt cutter to break the chain. Half an hour later, she was riding in air-conditioned comfort in their back seat, headed towards town.

Not having thought her plan through, she wasn't sure where she even wanted to go, but opted for being dropped at the street corner up to T-Ron's house. Better to surprise him, if that was at all possible, although she assumed he didn't expect her to turn up anytime soon. If ever.

The implausible thought that perhaps he had actually been trying to kill her passed through her mind and she hesitated at the bottom of the steep road that led up to his building. But any trepidation she might have been feeling was replaced by anger at the sight of the red golf cart parked at the end of his driveway.

"You bastard." The increase in her heart rate as she climbed the hill only added fuel to the fire. By the time she got to the top of the stairs she was breathing so hard she could barely speak as she burst through the open door. "Who the fuck do..."

A young woman holding a mop froze into position and stared at her with wide and frightened eyes. Her head was covered by a green silk scarf which held wild auburn hair away from a face that would have made Lucy think of a Botticelli painting if she wasn't wearing a tiny bikini top and a faded cotton print mini-skirt. As her gaze took in Lucy's appearance, her body visibly relaxed and the mop continued its path across the tiles.

"Don't come in. I mean, the floor is wet. I'm almost done here and I don't want to have to do it again."

Her quiet assertiveness left Lucy speechless and floundering. She backed up and waited on the cement landing as the girl finished up her work with a few broad strokes. Then heaving her bucket of water through the doorway, she dropped it a few inches from Lucy's feet, and stepped back to block the entrance to the apartment. Pulling off her headscarf, she used it to wipe her brow and the back of her neck, and then finally gave her attention to Lucy.

"If you're looking for Tiburon, he's not here."

"Well, thanks for stating the obvious." Here she was again, starting off on the wrong foot, butting heads with another female as soon as they met. She had to break this cycle if she was going to get anywhere. "Any idea where he might be?"

She shrugged. "Somewhere off island for a couple of days. Won't be back until tomorrow."

She had a sudden sinking sensation in her stomach – was this beautiful young woman..."I'm sorry, are you living here now?"

"With him, you mean?" The girl gave a wry laugh. "You couldn't pay me enough. I just clean for him when he's away."

"Oh." Lucy couldn't quite absorb what this information meant. "So, he's not on Culebra then." He had actually left her locked in Casa Laguna while he went away for a few days – as if she were a cat or a pet iguana. Feeling infuriated again, she asked impatiently, "Any chance you know where the keys to that golf cart might be?"

"Um, yes. I'm driving it today. He said I could use it till he came back." She looked at Lucy quizzically, waiting for an explanation.

"He what?!" She turned away for a second, blowing a slow stream of air out of her mouth like a hot tea kettle. She was not going to alienate this girl, she was not. "So he actually had no right to do that, I'm the one renting that vehicle and I need the keys back now."

The girl gasped and put her hand to her lips as she glanced in the direction of the street. Like a character in a bloody Disney movie, Lucy thought to herself, some beautiful innocent princess. But as her eyes followed the young woman's gaze, she saw now that the golf cart was piled high with boxes, coolers and equipment. Even the passenger seat was loaded with a five gallon water container.

"Looks like you're moving somewhere?"

The girl's shoulders fell and she leaned against the doorframe, clearly exhausted. Lucy was surprised that she felt momentary sympathy for her; it was the first time in a long while that she'd felt sorry for someone other than herself. "If you're in a bind, I can drop you off if you'd like," she heard herself saying.

"Thanks, but it's not quite that simple. You want to come inside for a minute? Oh, right." She sank down on the steps and Lucy now had a full view through the door. The spare apartment looked neater than Lucy had ever seen it. "How often do you come here to clean? I'm surprised he gives you a key."

"He doesn't. There's a lock box outside and he changes the code as soon as he gets back. Besides, he doesn't keep anything valuable up here. It's all down there." She pointed below to a door in the windowless concrete foundation. "With a combination lock designed to keep safe crackers out."

Lucy had never noticed the lower part of the building before. She'd always arrived totally inebriated and departed in a hangover haze. "That explains so much," she muttered. "So bloody sly."

"Not as sly as he thinks. I take out his trash and wash his sheets. Oh." Once again she covered her mouth. "Are you his..."

"I'm Lucy. And if I was anything to him, it's a former situation now. And you are?"

"Fiona."

The name rang a few alarm bells in her head but she couldn't think of why. "And this is what you do for a living on Culebra?"

"Did. But this is my last cleaning gig for a while." Fiona swallowed like she wished she could take the words back, so Lucy let the topic slide.

"And how did you end up here? That's the question everybody always asks right?"

"I came here with my boyfriend on a camping vacation and we broke up almost immediately. Usual story, except that I loved it so much that I stayed." A little light came back into her eyes.

"Sorry, the mother in me has to ask, you didn't go to university then?"

"Undergraduate in marine biology. Gave me a great resume for taking tourists out on kayak snorkel tours."

With a memory jolt that was almost painful, Lucy remembered that Tyler had told her about someone named

Fiona who had something to do with Tucker. "You broke up with your boyfriend?" Her voice came out squeaky and stiff.

"Almost two years ago. A lot has happened since then. So what about your children?"

"What makes you think I have any?" Two years ago. Tucker hadn't been in the Caribbean then.

"You said 'the mother in you' before."

"I did, yes. I have a son." How should she play this? She had a feeling she'd get more information out of Fiona if she didn't divulge any details. "I miss him, I haven't seen him in a long time." She touched Fiona on the arm. "So I'm interested. How is it to be a woman alone on this island? Is it safe?"

Fiona's expression changed so quickly it was like watching a video in fast forward mode. "Yes. I'm fine. It's fine." She stood up suddenly. "I really have to go before it gets dark. What are we going to do about..." Her eyes flickered to the golf cart laden with baggage.

"Where are you going? I can drop you."

"Well, it's super complicated." Fiona frowned and bit her lip. "What if I drop you off and bring the cart back in a few hours? Would you mind?"

"I live pretty far from here. Out towards Zoni."

"That's actually the way I'm going."

She'd made so many bad choices lately, Lucy wondered why she should even consider trusting Fiona; she was obviously hiding something. But it seemed like an opportunity – and the truth was, she was starving for some companionship and conversation.

They stopped first at a food store, one that Lucy didn't normally go to and then she remembered why – it didn't sell liquor. Just as well, she thought. There was no way she would have passed up a bottle of Beefeater's, or any similar substitute, if it had been staring her in the face.

Fiona offered to ride in the passenger seat with her feet on top of the water container and the three bags of groceries in her lap. Lucy tried to put the twenty minute drive to good use with some heart-to-heart girl chat about men and boyfriends, but Fiona made it clear that she was not about to divulge any details about her own love life and her appearance gave away the fact that she was not interested in fashion or makeup.

"So how about some trash talk then, love. What did you find in that rotter's garbage bins that gave you a clue to what he keeps in his basement? What's he secretly into?"

"Electronics. Devices you wouldn't believe. I don't know what he does with some of them."

"Like what?" She flushed for a moment, thinking maybe Fiona was referring to kinky sex toys, but dismissed that as her own gutter mind.

"You know, drones, web cams, GPS type-things, alarm systems..." She waved a dismissive hand. "And knives. He loves all kinds of knives."

Lucy nodded, shuddering. "That he does. Where does he get his electronics?"

"Big island, maybe. Orders them online. We get a UPS delivery a couple of times a week on this island."

How long have you been cleaning for him?" There were so many questions she wanted to ask, but didn't dare to address directly.

"Every couple of weeks since February." The answer came so quickly that it seemed suspicious. "How long have you been on the island?"

She realized she didn't even know how many days ago she'd arrived. "It's so lovely here, I've lost track."

"How'd you hook up with *him?*" There was no mistaking that the real question was 'why.'

"You know, drunk. At the Dinghy Dock. One of those—"

"This is where you're staying? I've been here."

Lucy noticed Fiona's hands tightened on the shopping bags.

"You have?"

"He brought me out here last month. To clean the place after...the last tenant left. It – it's a nice place." There was so much that she wasn't saying, but Lucy didn't need to ask.

"You think? If you ask me, it's bloody creepy. But it's free." She turned the cart around so it was pointing out towards the road.

"I don't know. I like nice quiet places like this in the country away from people. And the lagoon – you must see all kinds of birds." Fiona handed her the groceries and slid into the driver's seat. "I really need to go before the light disappears. I'll be back in an hour, I promise."

"Do you want to have some dinner with me?" Lucy tried not to sound desperate as she shouted over the putter of the engine, but Fiona was already gone.

She didn't want to be out here alone anymore. Maybe she should pack up and just go stay somewhere in town when she took Fiona back.

Fiona didn't return for more than two hours and Lucy was starting to think she'd made another bad decision when she heard light footsteps coming up the stairs. "Sorry, it took so long. I'm going to wait out here, my feet are filthy." The girl looked more bedraggled than before; dirt streaked her face and sand stuck to her toes and to her ankles.

"I don't care. I'm not the one who cleans this place." She smiled a little awkwardly as Fiona took a moment to get the weak joke. "You can use my shower if you want. It's hot water."

"I shouldn't. But...okay. That would be really nice."

Fiona knew the way and a few minutes later Lucy could hear her sighing with pleasure under the steamy downpour. She'd hoped for a chance to poke through Fiona's bag, but all she'd brought in with her had been the keys. Lucy was going to have to do better; she couldn't blow her chance at finding out if Fiona might know something about Tucker.

When Fiona finally emerged from the bathroom, she was clean but still dressed in the same filthy clothing she'd worn all day. Before she could protest, Lucy handed her a bowl of pasta with tomato sauce and a fork. "Eat something. You look half-starved to me."

Without a word of objection, Fiona sat down at the table and did exactly as commanded, visibly relaxing as the food hit her system. "Your kids are lucky to have a mother like you. Tell me about them."

Just like that and she could lose control of the conversation. Should she lay down all her cards...or just show a few...

"I only have one, a son, whom I haven't seen in a very long time."

"Oh, that's too bad. Where're you from – Australia? Britain?"

Lucy smiled. "I never lost the accent, but I left London a long time ago. I live in New England now."

Fiona nodded. "How old's your son?"

Lucy hated the fact that she had to stop and think for a second. "Twenty. How old are you?"

"Twenty-four. I know – I look like I'm about fourteen."

Although it was true, that wasn't what Lucy'd been thinking.

"What's your son studying?"

"Hmm? Oh, he's not in school. He went traveling instead. Decided he wanted to sail around the world instead of getting a real job."

A troubled expression settled on Fiona's brow.

Sorry, people tell me I'm too judgmental. So..." Knowing she was doing a bad job of sounding casual, she hopped up to get the teapot from the kitchen counter. "With your looks, you must have to fight off the boys."

Fiona actually blushed. "Not exactly. I'm pretty bad at socializing."

"No new boyfriends then?" Lucy poured them each a cup of tea, and then sat back, trying to not look intimidating.

"Yeah, one, but I don't see him that often."

"Oh, does he not live on Culebra?" Lucy couldn't decide if she was disappointed or relieved.

222

"No, not exactly. He likes to sail too." She hopped to her feet suddenly. "I really should be going. I have to get an early start tomorrow. Do you mind running me back?"

"Why don't you just stay here?" Besides needing more time to gain Fiona's trust, the idea of having company for the night was suddenly very appealing. "There's an extra bedroom. But you know that. I can take you as early as you want."

To her surprise, Fiona looked almost pleased at the suggestion. "Could I? I don't really like walking out to my campsite in the dark."

"Your campsite?" Even though Tyler had said something to this effect, the reality of this sweet young woman alone in a tent at night unnerved her. "At Flamenco? All alone?"

"No, the campground isn't really open since the storms. I've got my own set-up." Fiona patted her on the arm. "It's okay, Mom. I do it really well. Let me just go grab my pack from the golf cart."

Lucy breathed deeply and congratulated herself on the progress she was making. She picked up her phone to check the time and realized that, even though there was still no cell service at Casa Laguna, there were some new notifications she hadn't seen before. They must have come into her phone while she was in town.

A missed call and a terse text from Tyler. *We need to talk. Call me.*

Another message from T-Ron. *See you in a few days, Sleeping Beauty. Keep that sweet cooter of yours warm for me.* She couldn't believe how she'd allowed herself to be turned on by his lowlife language; now it just disgusted her.

There was also a voice mail from a number she didn't recognize but she was unable to access that without service. It would have to wait until she drove through town again tomorrow morning.

She scrolled through her photos to find the one of Tucker she had been showing around. Eventually her conversation with Fiona would bring her around to this –

maybe not until morning. Where was that picture...maybe in her downloads? Frantically she ran through the files in her photo gallery; had she accidentally deleted it?

"Everything okay?" Fiona had returned carrying a worn daypack.

"I was just looking for a picture of my son, I wanted to show it you, but I can't seem to find it." Hearing the desperation in her own voice, she suddenly wanted to cry. It was all too much, especially without any gin to absorb the pain. "I'm sure it's there. I'll show you in the morning."

"Okay, if you don't mind, I just want to get out of these clothes and maybe go to sleep? I don't stay up very late. You don't have to do anything – I know where everything is." She disappeared into the unused bedroom and Lucy picked up their dirty dishes. This was the homiest evening she'd spent in months and she tried not to feel so emotional about it.

"Hey, let me do those. It's the least I can offer for your hospitality." Fiona was standing behind her; she'd already shed her skirt and top and was wearing a ragged oversized T-shirt that fell halfway to her knees. Lucy stepped obligingly away and watched from a distance as Fiona washed up.

Her heartbeat raced a little as she stared at the familiar logo on Fiona's back. "What does that say on your shirt? Jordan Jaguars?"

"What, this?" Fiona looked down. "I guess so. I don't even know who that is. It's my boyfriend's."

With trembling hands Lucy smoothed the cotton fabric out so she could confirm what she already knew. A basketball team T-shirt from Jordan Regional High School in Jordan, Vermont – for years she'd washed it week after week.

"Can I ask you something?"

"Yes. Sure." Reluctantly she released her hold on the familiar piece of clothing; she could tell it was making Fiona uncomfortable, she was standing still with her hands in the dishwater.

"How well do you know him?"

"Who? T-Ron? It depends in what sense you mean, I guess." She laughed ruefully. The truth was that, other than physically, she knew almost nothing about him.

"I mean, are you part of the turtle thing."

"The what? Did you say turtle... like... a turtle?"

She turned around, drying her hands on the hem of the shirt. "I thought maybe, because you were staying out here..." She shook her head when she saw Lucy's blank look. "Forget it. I'm tired and don't know what I'm saying. Do you think we can leave here around six in the morning?"

Lucy wasn't sleepy at all. In fact, after three days of nonstop sleeping and a night with no gin, she was as wide awake as she'd been in months. She stretched out on the couch with another cup of black tea, thinking over everything she and Fiona had talked about. Her mind kept coming back to the electronics thing – what had Fiona said? Drones and cams and GPS trackers...the sneaky bastard...like he was a bloody spy or something...

She sat up suddenly and grabbed her phone. Turning on the flashlight app, she made her way outside and through the darkness to where the golf cart was parked. Groaning, she got down on her knees and began crawling around the vehicle, illuminating the underside of the carriage and running her hands along the wheel wells. This had been so much easier in her younger days; she vowed she would get back in shape.

Nothing. Grunting, she heaved herself off the ground and lifted the front seat to inspect the area around the gas tank. Disgusted, she dropped the seat and sank down onto it. She felt under the dashboard and the open compartment on the passenger side and finally slid her hands down below the steering wheel and into the rough housing below. Her hand closed around a little rectangular box; it came loose when she tugged at it and then immediately reaffixed itself. She pried it off more diligently this time, keeping her

225

fingers between the magnet and the metal it was so attracted to.

"You nasty son of a bitch." She trudged back to the house grasping her prize tightly. What other ways had he violated her privacy, she wondered, her eyes sweeping the corners of the ceiling and floors for video cameras and sound bugs.

Finding nothing obvious, she sat down heavily again on the sofa and stared at the offensive object in her palm. Not only had he left her here, locked into the yard with no food or alcohol or vehicle or cell service, but – no, there was something here that didn't make sense. Lucy never went anywhere except to the bar or the store or to his own house or home again.

T-Ron had known exactly where she was, using her own weaknesses against her, had helped render her incapable of doing anything,. He'd taken the golf cart away. And then loaned it to Fiona.

He wasn't following Lucy's movement around the island. He was tracking Fiona.

Lucy was still awake when the sky faded from black to gray to rosy pink. Her head throbbed from trying to figure out why Fiona might be so important to T-Ron. Maybe he just didn't trust her, thought his "maid" might be stealing from him. And maybe she was – Lucy hardly knew anything about the young woman sleeping in the next room. Except that she was wearing her son's T-shirt and that probably meant that following Fiona might eventually lead to Tucker. Did that mean T-Ron was hoping for the same outcome she was? If that was the case, she didn't think his goal was a joyous family reunion.

By dawn she was no closer to the truth but had made a few important decisions. The first of which was pitching the tracking device over the railing and out into the center of the lagoon where it sank instantly. Then she woke Fiona.

"This is good. You can drop me off here." Fiona pointed to a steep road across from the library. "I don't advise driving this thing up there."

"That's where your campsite is?" Lucy knew she would never be able to make it up that hill on foot in her current physical condition and she was worried now about losing touch with Fiona. "I hope we can get together again while I'm still on the island. I enjoyed your company." It was now or never. "Oh, wait. I wanted to show you a photo of my son. Hold on. Where is it? Damn, I'm so bad with this thing."

"Here, maybe I can help." Fiona looked over Lucy's shoulder at the screen as she scrolled rapidly through the few pictures she had on her phone. "Hold on. What's that?"

"Oh, those are my granddaughters. Twins, Athena and Artemis. Cute as buttons, aren't they?"

Fiona's rosy complexion had gone quite pale and she was staring at the photo in disbelief. "Your granddaughters? Yours?"

Lucy laughed, unsure why Fiona was responding in such an extreme manner. "Sweetie, I am quite old enough to be a grandmother. Oh, I know where I can find that photo. Let me just go to my email and do a search." She typed in "Tucker Mackenzie" and up popped the pathetic handful of emails that she had received during Tucker and Chloe's travels. "Here we go. Ignore the girlfriend. I usually crop her out of the picture, although she is the mother of those beautiful babies. He doesn't have the hair anymore. What do you think, cute, right?"

Fiona's suppressed reaction revealed what Lucy already knew. She swallowed hard and backed away, saying, "Cute. I really have to go now. Thanks for everything, Lucy."

"Fiona! Here. Take my contact info." She dug around in her purse until she found a battered business card. "I don't have this job anymore, but the number is still the same. See you soon?"

Much as she wanted to follow Fiona and see where she went, Lucy knew there were a few tasks that were more pressing at the moment. As she pulled up in front of T-Ron's house, she was relieved to see he had not arrived home in the night. She left the golf cart where it had been the day before, and walked down the hill and around the corner to the rental company to get a different vehicle. It was so early that they would not be open for another hour. Well, at least her phone had service in town, she could listen to her voice mail while she waited; she had been wondering who had left her a message.

"Hello, crazy Lucy. Mad Maggie here. I hope you have some news for me because patience is not my greatest virtue. Don't make me go to Plan B. I look forward to hearing from you soon. Girlfriend."

Bloody hell.

CHAPTER FOURTEEN

March –July 2018
Culebra, Puerto Rico

At first he thought it was just an intestinal bug, although he had no idea where he would have caught the flu. For forty-eight hours Tucker barely got out of his berth except to stagger to the head or barf in a bucket. He knew he had to replace his fluids and he drank more water than he'd ever consumed in two days. When he finally stopped blowing his insides out both ends, he thought he would start to feel better. Still his arms and legs felt numb and heavy and ached when he tried to do anything. He barely had the energy to get up and look for bug repellent to keep away the no-see-ums that seemed to be on a nonstop attack of his body.

The itching was driving him crazy. Once he started scratching it seemed like he itched everywhere, even on the most improbable parts of his body like the soles of his feet and the insides of his ears. At times he felt like a swarm of bees was attacking him someplace like his elbow or shoulder blade; other times it was stinging nettles on his chin or abdomen.

Fiona had finally come to visit and was horrified that he'd been so sick, all by himself, alone on the broken boat hidden in a remote anchorage deep in the mangroves along Manglar Bay. She helped him wash up and put on clean clothing and then heated up some fish broth. "You need some sustenance," she insisted.

The soup made him feel better and by the time Fiona left him, she was encouraged that he was on the mend. An hour later he felt sick to his stomach, his intestines let loose again and the itching became so intense that tears ran

229

down his cheeks. When he splashed water on his face it felt like a shower of spikes on his skin.

Eventually he fell asleep only to wake himself up because he was unconsciously scratching the shit out of his shins.

"Anybody home?"

Tucker sat up with a start, trying to remember where he was and why he was sleeping in the middle of the day.

"Hello? Permission to come aboard!" Through his sleep fog, he recognized Vance's voice. Since the day last month he'd brought him to the harbor to purchase Sea Urchin, Vance had taken an ongoing interest in Tucker and his boat project. Tucker never would have found this secret mooring spot if it wasn't for Vance and his knowledge of Culebra's coastline through years of kayaking. Now he visited the boat a few times a week, bringing food, tools, equipment, companionship and carpentry experience.

"In here!" Tucker responded hoarsely. Making his way unsteadily through the cabin, he reached the deck just as Vance was climbing up the ladder.

"Hey, buddy, you look like hell. What's going on?"

"I've been sick but I think I'm getting better now." He scratched his arm with one hand and his head with the other as he answered. "Except that I itch all over."

"Here, I've got some water that's been on ice. Drink this. But not too fast." He handed a bottle to Tucker. The plastic was so cold it felt like his fingers were burning and as he upended the container into his mouth, his tongue suddenly tingled like he'd scorched it while drinking hot tea. It was confusing and not refreshing at all.

"What the fuck – was that some sort of sick trick or something?" he sputtered.

Vance looked puzzled and took a sip of out of the bottle that Tucker thrust back at him. "Nothing wrong with this."

"Except that it's boiling hot instead of freezing cold!" He swatted at whatever invisible bug was stinging his ankle and then scratched the back of his neck.

From beneath the brim of his straw hat, Vance squinted at him keenly and then asked, "What have you been eating lately?"

"Nothing at all for few days, except a cup of broth from some barracuda soup I made last week. Before that, mostly fish that I've been catching."

"Barracuda? Where have you been fishing?"

"The reef out that way. I don't know. Around."

Vance was already on his cell phone, looking something up. "You know, you should use some of that trust fund of yours to get one of these. It could be useful."

"Trust fund?" Tucker wasn't sure what that even was but he was pretty sure it was not what you called the kind of cash he had at his disposal. More like a mistrust fund.

"Yeah, whatever that money is you've been spending to fix this piece of crap up. Okay, that's what I thought. Read this."

"Ciguatera?" He glanced up at Vance's serious expression before reading aloud. "'Ciguatera is a foodborne illness caused by eating reef fish whose flesh is contaminated with certain toxins. Symptoms may include diarrhea, vomiting, numbness, itchiness, sensitivity to hot and cold, dizziness, and weakness. Any reef fish can cause ciguatera poisoning, but species such as barracuda, grouper, red snapper, moray eel, amberjack, parrotfish, hogfish...'"

Tucker felt a wave of dizziness and handed the phone back to Vance, who scrolled down and continued. "It says that gastrointestinal symptoms develop within six to twenty-four hours of eating a reportedly good-tasting reef fish, and usually resolve spontaneously within four days. However, the neurologic symptoms often become prominent after the GI symptoms, particularly with fish obtained in Caribbean waters. Neurologic symptoms vary among patients and include...numbness and tingling in the extremities and oral region, generalized itching, muscle and joint pain and fatigue."

231

"Ciguatera." Tucker repeated the name as if saying it would make him understand it.

"Okay, you could just have the flu, but here's the deal breaker," Vance went on. "'Characteristic of the disease is a distinctive symptom reported by many patients – an alteration or "reversal" of hot/cold temperature perception, in which cold surfaces are perceived as hot to the patient, or produce an unpleasant, abnormal sensation.'" Vance looked up from the screen and grinned. "The good news is that it says it is rarely fatal."

"That's not funny. So what's the cure?"

"Um, well, there is no cure." Vance's smile faded. "I've known other people who've had ciguatera and the neurological symptoms usually last for several weeks to six months. And you have to stay hydrated and not eat fish or you might have a relapse."

"Months?! You're kidding, right?"

"It's going to get better, I promise you. But you should take it easy for the next few days. And do you have anything to eat besides fish soup?"

Tucker hadn't felt so depressed in a long time. He sat on deck in the shade because the sun made his itching worse and closed his eyes, thinking about all the fish he had caught and eaten on the Luis Peña reef. They had seemed so beautiful and life-giving; now they danced like demons on the back of his eyelids, along with images of Flush's dead body floating in the current. Vance had promised to come back in the morning with some kind of antihistamine so at least maybe Tucker would be able to get some sleep without scratching himself awake. Vance said he should drink lots of water even if it felt weird in his mouth.

And what about Fiona? Was she sick too? He thought probably not – when she'd visited him on the island she'd never actually eaten much with him, companionship and sex being his much greater needs. They'd been planning a trip to the big island next week, to get their passports and to buy some boat parts and equipment. He wondered if he'd be able to go now.

Hell, this was slowing his timetable down. He'd hoped to leave Culebra behind in a month or two. Now their status quo would have to continue in its predictable unpredictability, with Fiona still doing kayak tours and cleaning for T-Ron while keeping tabs on his comings and goings, and with Tucker living on the boat in the midst of reconstruction. Now that he was back on the island, so to speak, her brainstorm idea to work for "the enemy" had paid off.

"Keep your friends close and your enemies closer. Somebody said that," Fiona had quipped to explain her strategy, which actually made sense. The previous week when T-Ron was off-island, Tucker had been able to go into town with the dinghy, visit the hardware store, buy food, and spend a night with Fiona at Electric Beach. He hated that the man had him on the run, but short of murder, there was little else he could do now but hide out and then flee.

As the days and weeks passed, he did start to feel better. When he could distract himself, sometimes there were symptomless periods. The hours that he and Vance worked at boat repairs, when he could lose himself into work and conversation, were the best. A couple of times he talked Vance into letting him have a beer, but the itching and tingling definitely worsened afterwards. He didn't dare eat any fish, subsisting instead on eggs and the barbecued chicken that Fiona brought him every few days from the take-out place in town, along with an armload of books from the library. She also brought him the news of the outside world, at least from her perspective. The bomb squad was leaving, Flamenco Beach would be open soon but not the campground, the kayak tour business was picking back up again. But what seemed to overshadow her mood much of the time was the status of the turtles.

233

"They seem to be disappearing. Like maybe ten since January. Some of my favorites are gone." After all these months of swimming with them almost daily, she could identify most of them by sight and they were like family to her. Tucker could only relate a little to why she cared so much for these animals, but he respected her need. He just hoped her passion for wildlife activism didn't impact her desire to leave Culebra with him.

Dates had no meaning in his current lifestyle, marked only by milestones like the arrival of new rigging equipment, the phases of the moon or a symptom-free day. When Fiona showed up late one afternoon to announce that she was there to celebrate the momentous occasion of the second "blue moon" in the first three months of the year, Tucker had to think hard as to which month it must be now. They took the dinghy over to Playa Larga to watch the moonrise over St. Thomas and Tucker decided he felt well enough to celebrate with some fresh fish grilled over an open fire and some spirited sex on the beach. As he admired the sensuous sight of Fiona's silhouette arching above him in the natural light of the night, he tried not to remember another full moon party with Chloe in Thailand, an Ecstasy-enhanced event with electric music, and some very X-rated public sexual activity that embarrassed him to think about in retrospect.

He paid for the Blue Moon mistake with a two week relapse of cramps, fatigue and itching, the soles of his feet especially driving him crazy. Having warned him of the possibilities, Vance had little sympathy for Tucker this time around and abandoned him through the Easter holidays with the excuse that he did not want to risk being run over in his kayak by what he called "the Puerto Rican Navy." After seeing and hearing the flotillas of oversized motor cruisers, some three or four decks high, that moored in Manglar Bay for the long weekend, and after being subjected to the side effects of their competitive racing and loud music, Tucker understood and actually forgave Vance for not coming by.

By mid-April everything had quieted down; the sea became calm and warm, the winter tourists were mostly gone, and Tucker's body actually began to feel almost normal again. He had the energy to work longer, scraping the barnacles off the sides of the hull, as well as sanding, refinishing and painting parts of the interior and exterior of the cabin. But he felt hamstringed by his lack of decent carpentry skills and was pleased when one day he saw the kayak gliding through the passage that led to his mooring.

"Ahoy, captain. How's it hanging." Vance greeted him with his usual sardonic humor.

"Well hung, matey." Tucker unconsciously scratched his ear and then expertly caught the rope that Vance tossed him.

"Still got the itch to travel, I see. I brought you a few things. And your new keel has arrived. If you can figure out a way to transport it here, I'll help you install it before I go."

"That's hella good news!" Tucker leaned over to grab the plastic bags that Vance was holding out. "Where you going?"

"Home. I fly out next week. Been here all winter, I'm itching to go back. Sorry, wrong choice of words. Jesus, I'm getting old. Help me up on deck."

"But..." He had not really considered the fact that Vance would be leaving before he did.

"You do know that us snowbirds fly north this time of year, right?"

Despite the uncommitted nature of their friendship, there was something about his relationship with Vance that had made Tucker feel more secure. There were so many things he could not have accomplished without him, he was indebted to the man. Besides the fact that he was pretty much the most normal person he'd encountered in months. "Here, I brought you something. Old school style, you'll like it. Careful, it's heavy."

The gift was a hardbound atlas of the world. Secondhand, with mildew stains on the cover and pages rippled by wetness, but complete with color plates and descriptions of continents and countries. Tucker thought it was one of the best presents he'd ever received. "Wow, this is amazing, where did you find it? Shit, Vance, what am I going to do when you're gone?"

"Hey, don't go getting sentimental on me now. You're a survivor, you'll be fine." Vance clapped him on the shoulder. "When I think of how you were living when I met you...this is a success story, boy. Soon enough you're going to sail away into the sunset with your girlfriend. It's a happily ever after story, right?"

Tucker's shoulder prickled violently and he tried to not give in to the urge to scratch.

Even though his visits had been erratic and unpredictable, once Vance had left the island Tucker felt very much alone. Although he rarely spotted another boat or human in his safe refuge, he was fearful about leaving the Sea Urchin unattended for more than twenty-four hours at a time. A few nights a week he managed to convince Fiona to stay over with him, during which time he would lavish her with attention but remain respectful of her need for space, afraid that she would protest that his neediness was too much, which it sometimes was and she sometimes did.

"Did you ever see T-Ron's boat?" she asked one morning as they sat on the deck with bowls of cold cereal.

"I didn't even know he had one. Unless you mean the Nico. Which wasn't really his." He shivered a little at the recollection of his unpleasant encounter with the man.

"No, he has one of those snorkeling tour catamarans. You know, two hulls, with a big open cabin between. I've seen him going by in it when I'm out at Tamarindo and sometimes he's way out on the open sea with it when I'm at Electric. He keeps it in the harbor. It's a weird boat for someone to have."

"Well, perfect for a weird whack job like him."

"I think he's got something going on."

"Of course he does. Something illegal, no doubt." Tucker wondered how much Flush might have had to do with whatever scam T-Ron was working.

Fiona seemed suddenly fascinated with the cereal flakes floating in her bowl. "He asked me if I wanted to make some extra money."

"He came on to you? That stupid fuck–" All the skin on his body began to itch intensely at the thought of the pretentious old fart propositioning her.

She put a restraining hand on his forearm. "No, he did not."

"Yeah, well, I'm sure he wants to. I can't wait until we're out of here."

"No, he wanted me to do some underwater photography for him. Of the reef and the marine life at Tamarindo, because I know it so well. When I said, no thanks, he gave me a GoPro to take home and test out. Just told me to think about it."

"Really?" Despite his mistrust of the man, Tucker could not hide his interest. "That's kind of cool. It would be fun to try it out. Do you have it with you?"

"No, it's back at the campsite. Yeah, but why me? He could have asked any one of the other guides." She put down her bowl. "Oh, I completely forgot. I need to get back to town so I can go to the post office before work; I got a card in my box to pick something up at the window. I think our passports are finally here."

Tucker did a fist pump in the air.

The next month passed in a blur of activity. Test sailing, stocking up on supplies, trip planning and maintenance, Tucker thrived on the whirl of activity, staying busy enough to ignore the random bouts of itching and tingling that still plagued him, spending his evenings pouring over nautical charts and studying the maps in the Atlas of the World.

Meanwhile Fiona seemed to have become totally caught up in her own intrigue built around T-Ron.

"I think he wins a lot of money playing poker." This was no surprise to Tucker, but he said nothing. "He tipped me big after a game last week."

"I wouldn't trust him. He must want something from you."

"Of course, I don't trust him. I wouldn't be working for him if I did."

"He's got a girlfriend," she announced one day. "I think she must be in on whatever deal it is he's working."

"Really?" Tucker couldn't even pretend mild interest.

'I've only seen her from a distance but she seems as old as him. Go figure. And they've been tearing the apartment up. Hard to imagine."

"Let it go. How soon will you be ready to leave?"

This unanswered question hung in the air for days. When Fiona failed to show up one night as expected, Tucker began to grow nervous. Why was she dragging her feet about this; did she really not want to travel with him and live their dreams? Was this Chloe all over again?

When she finally arrived late the next afternoon, she appeared exhausted, bedraggled and withdrawn. "What's up? Where have you been? Are you all right?" His questions rained down on her, bullets in a battlefield, revealing all the insecurity he did not want to expose.

She looked at him with a wounded expression and he could not imagine what he had done. "Athena and Artemis."

Puzzled now, he waited for her to go on.

"Do those names mean anything to you?"

"Uh...they were Greek goddesses? Do I win some kind of prize? What's this about?"

Arms crossed, she glared defensively, until finally her face softened as she realized he actually had no idea what she was referring to. "You really don't know?"

"Of course, I do. I spent nearly a year in Greece. I've seen the ruins of their temples." She was scaring him now. "What's going on with you, Fi? You're freaking me out."

238

She shook herself as though waking up from a bad dream. "Nothing. Forget it. I brought chicken burritos. Let's eat."

But he could not forget it. Their relationship had never felt so strained before. They shared the Mexican food in silence. They had spent a lot of time together not talking, but this was different. Every now and then, he touched her foot with his, stroking her instep with his toes, hoping for a response, but she stared out at the water, not speaking.

When he returned from carrying their trash inside, Fiona was standing in the stern, shooting rocks into the water with her slingshot. Tucker hung back for a minute, awed by the skill she had acquired with this most simple of weapons. He watched as each pebble arced through the air to splash down hundreds of feet away, until she had used up all the ammunition in the worn crocheted shoulder sack she kept it stored in.

Something was so wrong and he had no idea how to make it right.

"Tell me about your family. You never talk about them." These were the first words she'd spoken in hours. His body was curled around hers in their usual post-coital spooning position, after an intense, almost fierce, session of lovemaking. He realized he was gripping her more tightly than usual, as though she might slip away from him in the night.

He did not want to think about his former home life, but right now he would do anything to keep her engaged. "I've told you some. My dad was an investigative journalist but now he runs a small local newspaper in northern Vermont. My mom was was the same – that was how they met I think – until she ran off with a rock star."

"Really – that's kind of a romantic story."

"Yeah, but it was kind of weird because she was old. Like almost forty. And he turned out to be a nasty guy."

"But then your parents got back together and had you?"

"No, not really. I don't know exactly. They've never lived together. It was like one night or something while she was still with Kip, the musician. I never even met my father until I was six. The truth is they can barely stand each other. You see? It's a sad story and that's why I don't talk about it. Not like your big happy farm family." He squeezed her playfully and managed to make her squeal a little.

"Tell me what your dad looks like."

"Why do you care? I haven't even seen him for almost two years. He might not even look the same anymore."

"I don't know. Maybe I want to know if you'll be fat and sloppy when you're old and gray."

"Why? Would you leave me if you thought I would be?" he teased. "Well, it's too bad I don't have a photo to show you then, because I do take after him. He looks okay, still has all his hair, it's kind of bushy, not as curly as mine but it used to be. He wears glasses. He's still tall and if anything he's too thin."

Despite his playful caresses, she'd gone quite still. "Okay, I can kind of picture him. What's his name?"

"Tyler. My mom, on the other hand, is quite short. She used to have red hair like yours, freckles too." The similarity between his mother and Fiona suddenly made him uncomfortable and he immediately looked for the differences. "But she's not like you, she hates camping, she wants her good bed with fancy sheets and lots of pillows. Doesn't like being alone in the woods, she's more comfortable in the city."

"But the first time you came here was with Tyler, your dad, right? When you met – what's her name – Chloe?"

"Yes. But please don't make me think about her. Let's talk about you now." He buried his face in the curve of her neck.

"When Chloe left you in Greece, do you know where she went?"

"No, I don't, and I don't care. That's ancient history. Like ancient Greece."

"But – you are still married, right?"

"Is that what's bothering you?" He sat up and tugged at the ring on his finger. "A bullshit wedding on a beach in a foreign country. It was never real. Where's that slingshot of yours?"

Before she could stop him he had her crocheted bag and was outside on deck, loading the offensive gold ring into the leather sling and then catapulting it into the night sky. The tiny splash it made was the most satisfying sound he'd heard in a while.

He was dozing on deck a few days later when he heard the sound of an unfamiliar outboard motor approaching. Immediately on guard, he slid down the hatchway and into the cabin, grabbing a pair of scavenged field glasses that Vance had left him. More of a monocular than binocular, since one lens was cracked and cloudy, but it still gave him a view of what he couldn't see with the naked eye.

A small fishing boat was moving slowly into the inlet towards his yacht, an unfamiliar blonde woman at the helm. There was nothing threatening about her, she had the appearance of a classic sailor, tanned and toughened by the sun, a worn cap pulled low over her eyes, a rod and a bucket of bait at her feet. He could also see that she knew how to maneuver a small craft as she cut the engine and glided up silently beside the Sea Urchin.

He waited for her to call out but instead she seemed to be searching through a dry bag. When she finally held up a cell phone as though she was about to take a photo, he decided to make the first move.

"Buenos dias!" he called, even though he was pretty sure she wasn't Puerto Rican. "What can I do for you?"

"Oh! You startled me. I didn't think anybody was here." The phone disappeared quickly into her pocket. "I fish around here quite often and don't usually see any boats moored out this way."

He resisted the urge to blurt out that he'd been in the location for more than four months and had never seen her before. "Yeah, it's quite peaceful," he said carefully.

"Do you own her?" As she talked, her eyes roved up and down, scrutinizing all aspects of the ketch from stern to prow.

"Yeah. You got a problem with that?"

"Not at all. I just don't usually meet yacht owners as young as you." She laughed pleasantly and although the sound should have put him at ease, it made him feel warier. "So how'd you get this mooring? Do you know the people that own the shore property?" She was looking through her bag again as she talked.

"I don't ever go ashore. There's no access to land from here. And the water isn't owned by anybody." He nodded towards her fishing gear. "If it was, you wouldn't be allowed to do that here."

"True enough. Hey, can I ask you a favor?" She held up an empty plastic bottle. "I hate to ask you this because I know you have to haul all your water, but would you mind filling this for me? I realized I totally spaced this out when I planned my day and I can't be out here all day without water or I will get seriously dehydrated. And then I'll leave you alone, I promise."

"Sure." As he reached out to take the container from her, she hopped nimbly onto the deck. Surprisingly agile for an older woman, he thought. He couldn't imagine his mother executing a move like that.

"Sorry, just thought it would be easier for you this way. So you're from Florida?" she called after him as he went into the cabin. She was friendly, but way too nosy for his taste.

"No, the guy I bought the boat from was from there. I just haven't painted over it yet." He did not want to have this conversation. When he came back up, she was sitting comfortably on one of the deck cushions, like she was an invited guest or something, one arm thrown over the pillow behind her back. "Here you go. Have a great day."

"Thanks so much. You have no idea what this means to me." She held out a hand. "I'm Dee, by the way."

Why did he think she'd just made that up. "Tim," he said. "Pleasure to meet you. And the fishing is better out in the deeper water, you know. Nothing but sardinas around here."

He had a bad feeling as he watched her motor away. Other than Vance and Fiona, nobody had ever visited him out here before. It was definitely time to move on.

Fiona was resistant to the idea of leaving immediately. "I think he's got something going on in the next couple of days." The 'he' being T-Ron, of course. "He's getting the big boat ready for something and I want to follow him when he goes out."

His initial reaction of "You're insane," did not deter her from her plan. "Well, you're not doing that alone. I'm going with you. But before next weekend, I am moving this boat. And by next week we will be sailing southeast away from here."

"You'll go with me? I love you." Those words and the physical gratification she demonstrated were enough to convince him that however crazy her plan was, it was worth it for him to go along. "I'm glad you're coming because I'm going to need someone to hold the light. All right, I'll hold the light – you can steer the dinghy."

"Wait – this is a night excursion? You are seriously out of your mind." But even though it seemed foolhardy, the idea that she'd been ready to do something so outrageous excited him in a way he hadn't experienced in a long time. "Where are we going in the dark?"

"Playa Larga. It's not far. And I know a place just beyond it where there is a sand channel to the shore where we can pull the dinghy up on the beach."

"I know that place. And we can't do it at night, it's too dangerous."

In the end they went early, before sunset, armed with a sleeping bag, mosquito net, bug spray and Fiona's good binoculars. After dark, they hiked the narrow stretch of sand and waited in the blackness of the night for what was definitely hours. Tucker fell asleep, eventually awakened by Fiona's violent shaking of his arm.

"Look. I don't know what's going on, but it's happening."

Simultaneously a boat on the water and a truck on land were both backing up to the dock. There was some shouting and the harsh noise of some kind of cargo sliding across metal and wood. More shouting and then it was over. The faint lights of the boat's cabin could be seen as it chugged away in the direction of St. Thomas. Truck wheels could be heard spinning out on the steep incline of the road back up the hill.

"Drugs," Tucker declared. "Gotta be. Really we're no wiser than before. Can we go now?"

"Yes. But I'm sure it's something other than drugs. He's flying off island tomorrow and I'm positive he's going the same place that boat is."

"Okay, but this is over now, right? Please tell me that it's out of your system. You don't want to get involved. This is the time for us to go. In the morning you start packing up the campsite."

Fiona said nothing as they trudged back up the beach to where they'd left the dinghy.

Tucker was surprised when she showed up at noon the next day in the dinghy. "He's letting me use a golf cart he has for a couple days while he's gone. It'll be so much easier to move stuff than with the boat."

"You didn't tell him what you wanted it for, did you?" He was already nervous, but her strange behavior was making him itchy again.

"Don't be ridiculous. He thinks I'm just using it to get to Tamarindo and his house and back home. I can drop stuff off at the Manglar dock and you can ferry it out in the dinghy. It'll be much more efficient."

He was so relieved that she was still on board with going that he just agreed to the new plan even if it didn't make much sense.

"I'll do a load tonight, one in the morning before work and then one at night and we'll be done. Give me the empty water jugs. Just moving those alone will be so much easier, it will be worth it."

He had to admit she was right.

"Anyway, you need to take me back to town now. They're expecting me to do the afternoon kayak tour."

"You haven't quit yet?"

"Today. I didn't want anyone to get suspicious."

They didn't speak as they sped back to town and it was not their usual companionable silence. The tension of the upcoming events was overriding everything now.

He was over-the-top with anticipation by the time he met her for the last pick-up at dusk the next day. It was finally happening. In the morning they would be off.

The light was almost gone from the sky when she arrived half an hour late with their final load of gear. "It's almost dark. Hurry," he complained.

"There's a problem." She wiped the sweat from her neck with a dirt-streaked hand and leaned back against the frame of the golf cart, clearly exhausted.

Instead of asking the obvious question, he waited impatiently for her to go on.

"Turns out the cart belongs to his 'girlfriend.' She showed up this afternoon looking for it. I dropped her off on the way here, the place isn't far, but I need to bring the cart back to her tonight."

Tucker dropped the box he was holding and crossed his arms. "So I don't get it. How does this change things?"

"Well, I'm not going to ask her to bring me down here, that would be pretty strange, right? So I'll just have her drop me in town and I'll sleep at the Datiles tent. We were leaving that one anyway. You can pick me up there in the morning. What's the big deal, I was going to have to take the cart back early anyway."

He was silent for a few seconds. Pick your battles, he reminded himself. Plans change, it's just a small hitch.

"Okay, fine. Just – be careful. And be ready. I should get there by seven."

She laughed. "I'm always careful. I spend a lot of time on my own, you know."

Tucker had wanted it to be a romantic and celebratory night. Now it was just him alone, again, entertaining himself, and he tried not to let his disappointment bring him down. The bottle of champagne could wait until tomorrow, when they were safely harbored in Lana's Cove on the other side of Luis Peña. It was backtracking from his planned route, but the stop was necessary. There was still unfinished business to attend to on the little island.

Before dawn he was up, getting ready to set sail at first light. The Sea Urchin's engine coughed and sputtered to life. As he motored out of his protective inlet and across the quiet bay, a few pelicans rose slowly from the water, like prehistoric creatures and settled in the mangrove branches to watch him. Beneath the surface he could see a spotted ray swimming swiftly beside the hull before veering off on its own aquatic mission.

There was so little wind at this time of day and time of year that he had to motorsail quite a distance until he finally caught a breeze near the mouth of the Ensenada. Unlike smaller motorboats, he could not take a shortcut across the harbor and through the manmade canal to the east side of the island. His mast would not fit under the orange steel bridge, so he would have to navigate all the way around the perimeter of the island to get to the calm waters of Datiles Bay.

He passed a lone fishing vessel heading the other direction but there were no other signs of life on this early midweek morning. He felt exhilarated by the freedom that he felt, at last almost underway on his journey. This was his destiny, as he'd known since the first time he set sail in waters not far from here.

As he went by the rocky shoals of Electric Beach, he was almost nostalgic. Fucked up as the existence had been, they'd had such a fine campsite there and some beautiful times. But when he skirted around the reef that protected Datiles, his sense of liberation faded. There was no sign of Fiona. He took down the sail and put the engine on so he could navigate into the deeper cut next to the shallow bay. He calmed his anxiety by reminding himself that, few as they were, all her belongings were on board. He could see her kayak still there on the beach, awaiting her arrival, and its presence reassured him.

The tension in his stomach reminded him that he hadn't eaten breakfast, or, for that matter, dinner the night before. He ducked below for something to munch on, returning with a bruised grapefruit and a bag of tortilla chips. The fruit on Culebra generally sucked; it all came from somewhere else, sometimes thousands of miles, and much of it did not survive the trip well. As he tossed the peels into the water, out of the corner of his eye he spied some movement on shore.

Fiona appeared suddenly on the beach, her chest heaving as though she'd been running. When she reached the kayak, she knelt in the sand, apparently trying to catch her breath, leaning her head against the molded plastic, her shoulders heaving.

"Fiona! Over here!"

Her head flew up and she saw him waving but she didn't respond. Moving more slowly now, she dragged the kayak out into the water and climbed in. As she paddled towards him, he could see now that she did not look well, her eyes puffy and swollen, her nose running.

"Do you have a cold? Are you having an allergic reaction to something? What's wrong?" He caught the rope of the kayak as she tossed it to him. Without a word she came aboard, trailing wet footprints behind her as she made her way down to the galley.

He tied the kayak off to the railing; he would need her help to haul it up on deck, but for now he needed to find out what was going on.

She was standing at the counter finishing off a bottle of water and when she saw him her eyes filled with tears. He wrapped his arms around her but she did not respond in any way other than a couple of choked-back sobs. "Oh, I know it's hard for you, babe. I'm sorry. I promise you it's all going to be all right."

She mumbled something into his shoulder and then pulled back. "Athena and Artemis," she cried accusingly. "Why have you been lying to me?"

"What are you talking about – I haven't been lying to you! And why are you so obsessed with these Greek goddesses?"

The mystified look in his eyes made her shake her head. "Lucy is your mom, right?"

His puzzlement grew. "That's her name. What does she have to do with this?"

"Because apparently I spent last night with her."

It was such an absurd statement that he burst out laughing. "You dreamed about my mother? I'm sorry for your pain."

"Tucker."

She'd caught his attention now. She never called him that, always referring to him with the ridiculous "Stoney" moniker that Flush had given him.

"Both of your parents are on Culebra. I met your father last week. They're looking for you."

"What? Together?" The outlandishness of what she was telling him was beyond belief.

"Separately, together, I don't know. But I believe they want to take you back to Vermont."

248

CHAPTER FIFTEEN

July 2018
Culebra, Puerto Rico

Every time Tyler thought that he should probably get up, the gentle rocking of Kay's boat lulled him back into sleep. She'd been up before the sun and told him not to worry, to stay in bed as long as he wanted, there was coffee on the stove, and she'd be back to take him to shore in a few hours.

The woman was more hyper than any he'd ever been with; usually he was the one in high gear. Maybe he was just getting lazy in his old age, but whatever. It felt good to be more relaxed than the way he'd spent most of his life.

Lethargically he opened his eyes and looked around. It was such a small space, he couldn't imagine living with someone here for weeks, let alone for months. Square footage like this made the crowded cottage in Vermont seem expansive. At least it had bedrooms with doors.

It had been Kay's idea for them to spend the night here. He'd gone with her to the local poker game again, feeling like an old regular on his second go-round. When the subject of his missing son came up, this time he had concrete information to share and ask about. Yes, most of them knew Fiona the red-haired kayak tour girl by sight, but didn't know much about her. A few players had been on Culebra when the salvage team had come and knew of the yacht that Tucker had supposedly acquired, but nobody had any idea where it ended up.

For some reason Kay had cut that conversation short. "We're on top of it," she had assured the others, with a smile at Tyler. "A friend is lending me a boat in a couple of days so we can go exploring. For now I see you and I raise you, Simon." The large pile of chips she pushed towards the center of the table diverted the interest away from Tucker.

Spending time with Kay made it easy for him to put Tucker on the back burner; what was a few more days in light of the whole picture? Once they found him, Tyler would have to leave and take him back to whatever god-awful reunion scenario might ensue at home in West Jordan.

Wondering what time it was, he searched for his phone, finally finding it in a little net pocket on the wall above his head. He had no recollection of putting it in this safe and convenient place, but these days that meant nothing. He was surprised to see that it was after ten; his recently active sex life combined with the motion of the boat had made him sleep like a teenager.

Sitting on deck with a cup of reheated coffee, feasting on a stale cinnamon roll and a view of Caribbean blue waters under cloudless skies, he couldn't think of a better way to jumpstart his day. A handful of yachts, mostly unoccupied during the quiet summer sailing season, bobbed in the harbor nearby. It all felt impossibly perfect, except for needing a shower and not wanting to use up Kay's water. And the fact that, unless he wanted to swim to the public dock where he had left his golf cart, he was actually a virtual prisoner on this boat.

It was a disturbing thought, so he tried not to think about it. He wasn't really captive; he had his phone, although he had no idea whom he would call if he had to, and if he really could swim to town if it came down to it. Which it wouldn't.

He sent Kay a text message. *"Good morning! How soon are you coming back?"*

He was relieved when her answer came back instantaneously. *"See you in an hour or so. Everything okay?"*

He was a paranoid idiot. Impatient and a little bored. Maybe she had something good to read.

All he could find were a couple of very worn paperback novels, *Shogun* and *The Far Pavilions*, both of which he had read decades earlier. Clearly Kay wasn't a reader; she was too busy being... busy. The more he thought about it, he realized that he didn't really know that much about her. Had she gone to college or studied something specific? How was it that they had not even talked about that? Sexual attraction could be very blinding. He was embarrassed to realize that most of the time they talked about him.

His fundamental curiosity was getting the better of him now; he was here alone on her boat and he had spent a good part of his life as a professional self-employed snoop. He should be able to learn plenty about Kay in the next hour before she returned.

Where to start... There was no bedside table with a ubiquitous drawer, but she had to store her passport and important documents somewhere. He opened the one narrow closet; it was tightly packed with clothing on hangers and shelves, almost impossible to search through. There were two larger compartments beneath the sleeping space that contained a wide variety of everything from equipment to food. Stuffed along one edge was a soft-sided duffel bag with an airport luggage tag on the handle.

Short of looking up where the flight had originated, he could see she'd transferred through Chicago to San Juan, as you would from any small Midwestern city. He looked for some sort of personal identification on the bag and finally found it in a clear built-in slot on the side. The duffel belonged to a Kelley Hoffhauser from Dubuque, Iowa. Was that Kay? It had not occurred to him that maybe "Kay" was an initial rather than a name. He unzipped it and looked inside; there were some zipper pockets concealed in the sides and he quickly explored these.

Without having to even look, he knew that the first pocket was filled with cash, lots and lots of it. Okay, that wasn't so weird, the post-hurricane economy had been strictly cash and plenty of people were still working that way. In the second pocket his fingers closed around a

251

passport, in fact two passports. He carefully extracted them, trying not to dislodge the order of anything else.

Opening one of them he saw Kay's photo and that she was indeed Kelley McCowen Hoffhauser, but the address was listed as Lake Okechobee, Florida. She was also older than he'd thought, but kudos to her on that. There weren't that many stamps on the pages; she'd been to the usual – British Virgin Islands, Bahamas, St. Martin, as well as Panama, which he found interesting.

He picked up the other passport, wondering who it belonged to. Here was Kay's photo again but the name was Delia Kelley McCowen from Iowa City. That was weird. Similar but different. Maybe she'd gotten married or divorced; it was confusing and he didn't have time to puzzle it out. He pulled out his phone and took photos of the two passport identity pages and then quickly flipped through the rest of the second one. Well this was more intriguing – Hong Kong, Dubai, Johannesburg, and a couple of trips to Taiwan.

What else was in there? From the second pocket emerged a soft velvet drawstring pouch. Dumping its contents on to the bed, he saw a couple of gold wedding bands, a ring with a large sparkly diamond and oddly, a pendant that appeared to be intricately carved from tortoise shell. There were also some heavy gold chains that he could only guess the value of, and he assumed it was a lot.

Swiftly replacing all the objects in their appropriate secret places, he attempted to stuff the duffel bag back under the bed where it had been, hoping he was successful in making the compartment appear undisturbed. Did all the rest of this gear belong to the owner of the yacht... now he found himself wondering who exactly it was that Kay was "boat-sitting" for and how he could figure that out in the next few minutes.

There had to be a license or registration or certificate of ownership somewhere. Unless this vessel was completely hot, which was unlikely if it was moored in a public place. Tyler stood in the center of the cabin and made a slow circle around, his eyes finally coming to rest on the shelf with the battered paperbacks. Beneath the books, a clear plastic sleeve protruded slightly. He had to pry it off the surface to which it had stuck, half-melted in the tropical heat and humidity.

It was all here, Bill of Sale, Certificate of Ownership. Registered in the British Virgin Islands, the boat was owned by a Margaret Onorato. For some reason he hadn't pictured the friend as a woman. He laid the documents out on the table to photograph them and saw one more sheet of paper in the protector, yellow-lined and folded in half. He gingerly opened it up and spread it out on top of the others to read the scrawled handwriting. *"I, Margaret M. Onorato, being of sound mind and body, sign over title and ownership of Blue Heaven to Thomas Ronald McCowen as payment for my debt of $50,730."* It was dated a little over a year earlier, just a few months before the hurricanes and actually had an embossed stamp on it with an unreadable signature by a public notary.

That was interesting. Did that mean the current owner was actually family? He had no problem with that, except why would Kay tell everybody on Culebra otherwise. Well, that was Kay who was in reality Kelley. Or Delia. None of which was his business anyway.

A fast photo and the documents were all returned to the spot where they had clearly been for several months now. Jesus, was it just his suspicious mind or what kind of hornet's nest was he sitting on here?

Pouring himself the last dregs that remained in the coffee pot, Tyler flopped down on the bed and propped the pillows up against the wall. He was not going to get involved. In any way. He didn't need any more drama in his life. He was going to find his son and get off this island. Something was poking uncomfortably into the back of one hip; he turned around to adjust the pillows and saw that an object of some sort had fallen between the mattress and side of the cabin.

His fingers closed around a metal handle designed to be held and then a long knife slid effortlessly out of the crevice between bed and wall. The blade was sharp enough to leave a little test line of blood on his palm.

"I see you found my means of defense against rapists and thieves." Kay was standing on deck peering through the open hatchway. How had he not been aware of her approaching?

"Well, hello there." He forced himself to be calm. "I didn't hear you coming." He brandished the knife. "This would terrify anyone. In fact, it terrifies me that I was sleeping next to it."

"Actually it's usually under my pillow. I moved it so we wouldn't hurt ourselves." She descended the few steps into the cabin and came towards him. Even for a sailor she appeared hot and sunburned, sweaty-necked and pink-nosed, her hair in two short braids like a young girl.

"Well, thank you for that." Carefully he put the knife down and with eyes still on her, touched his tongue to the tiny spots of blood on his lifeline. "Now I understand why you're not afraid to be out here alone."

"Here, let me do that." Without breaking their gaze, she took his hand and licked at the scratch on his palm. The raw sensuality of the gesture was as scary as it was exciting, the fear factor keeping his testosterone from going into overdrive.

"So where'd you run off to?" He was still trying to process what he'd discovered in the last hour and overlay it on the person in front of him.

"I do have a life here, you know. I had plans to go fishing with a friend."

"Catch anything?" He could not stay out of the way of his racing thoughts now.

"No. Nothing we could keep anyway. How about you – catch anything? Like extra z's?" She squeezed his leg and then moved away. "But I did stop to buy a few groceries and some ice." When she realized he was still just lying there, she tossed the heavy bag of ice onto the bed. "You gonna just watch me work? Help me out here before this melts."

Reluctantly his feet found the floor and he hauled the bag of cubes over to the cooler box that passed for a fridge. "How about we ditch this classy cruise ship and I take you out to lunch?" he suggested, suddenly feeling a bit claustrophobic.

She frowned and looked at her watch. "Okay, but I have some work to do so I'll have to be back in a few hours." Her serious expression became playful again. "No nookie tonight, I'm afraid. I have other plans."

Tyler was curious what she was doing but thought it was better not to ask. As he collected his belongings he realized that he'd left his phone up on the shelf with the books. He guessed it was not that suspicious, any place safe and out of the way was fair territory.

As he reemerged on deck for only the second time that morning, the glare of the sunlight seemed harsh and too bright. It was hard to recall the rosy glow of satisfaction he'd felt just a few hours earlier.

The golf cart was where he'd left it the night before, on the side of the street leading down to the public dock. He must have been a little drunk; he thought he'd done a better job of parking, but the back wheels were almost in somebody's driveway.

There was also a heavy splatter of reddish-brown dirt across the passenger side. He didn't remember Simon's yard being that muddy but it must have been. He hadn't been able to see it that well in the dark and recalled almost side-swiping a car that had parked quite close to his vehicle. He wondered where he could find a hose to rinse it off.

After a quick lunch at Zaco's Tacos, Kay kissed him goodbye and told him she would walk the short distance back. "Call me later, let me know what you're up to. We'll try to get out on the water tomorrow and look for your son's boat."

As he drove back to his guesthouse, the island seemed strangely quiet in the early afternoon heat, the only sign of life being a large hairy black pig that ambled slowly and steadily along the sidewalk as though he was boss of the neighborhood. Dark clouds were moving in on the eastern horizon and Tyler made a hasty decision to go for a swim before he went back and showered and started his online research project on Kelley Hoffhauser. Besides he wanted to see if he could run into Fiona again.

During a leisurely snorkeling reconnaissance mission on Tamarindo Bay he saw a handful of kayaks out by the reef but no sign of Fiona. He decided he had nothing to lose by asking the other tour guides if she was around.

"No, we're not that busy and she's having a few days off," he was told. "Maybe catch her on the weekend."

A few hours later he sat on the back porch with his laptop and beer, scouring Facebook and Instagram for various combinations of Kay's collection of names. He could actually find no one with the name Hoffhauser, there was a Hoff Hauser in the improbably named, but real, town of Manly, Iowa, but no one with the run-on version that was in Kay/Kelley's passport. There were plenty of McCowens in the world, but none seemed to be called Delia although there was a Kelley who was way younger than the woman he was looking for. Well, all it meant was that Kay, by whatever alias, didn't go in much for social media.

He found a few dead Delia McCowens in findagrave.com and that made him a little uncomfortable. The only Hoffhausers he found were in Hungary and some of those were not living either. He supposed people who traveled the world by boat could fall off the radar, the way Tucker had, but it seemed unusual that a social networker like Kay would not be connecting with other people online. Perhaps she had a third identity that he hadn't even discovered yet – it was definitely a real possibility.

He was surprised when the sky turned pink and the light faded around him. The internet was certainly a black hole in which he could lose himself. Speaking of black holes, he hadn't seen Lucy in days, not since they'd had their falling out at her place. She had not responded to the message he'd sent her the day he'd learned about Tucker buying the boat. There was a part of him that still worried about her – but it was just a tiny part. He was no one to judge her current drinking jag; years ago he'd spent a lot longer on a bender, the main difference being he had wasted away to a beanpole from lack of eating rather than blimping up from bingeing.

Damn, why did Kay have to turn out to be another sketchy partner choice; how did this always happen to him? He'd vowed he was not going to get involved on this trip and how long had that promise lasted. No, he was no one to judge Lucy and her vices. Discouraged and depressed, he swatted at a mosquito that was chewing on his leg. It was not the first time his blood had been tasted today.

When Kay did not contact him or respond to his texts the following morning, he could add disappointment to his emotional woes. He drove down to the dock and looked out to where her little boat was moored, the dinghy cheerfully bobbing at the end of its tow line. Did that mean she was home and just ignoring him? Frustration and failure could go on the growing list of the feelings that were plaguing him.

As he turned to walk back to his vehicle, his phone dinged. *"Sorry, I ended up having to go over to the big island on some errands. Will be back on the evening ferry. Good news is have water transportation lined up for us tomorrow."*

So much for wallowing in self-pity. He thought about suggesting that he meet her when she got off the ferry tonight but decided not to push his luck. Another day in paradise wasn't going to kill him.

He sat in the shade, enjoying the view of Flamenco Beach and puzzling over the mystery of Kay and her

257

multiple identities. When he responded to the chime of another text message, he expected it to be from her and was startled to see it was from @georgethenanny. *"A couple of young chicks are here in your bedroom looking for you."* There was a picture of Artemis and Athena jumping on the quilt covering his Vermont bed. *"We haven't heard from you for a while. Everything okay?"*

Tyler couldn't remember the last time he'd called home. He'd give it a try, at least until the connected failed, which it routinely did.

Chloe answered in a breathy voice, as though she'd been running. "Hey, Grandpa. Your ears must be burning. We were just talking about you."

He assumed she meant with the twins, but a deeper voice in the background reminded him that Myles had been staying there with her. What was wrong with him, he'd been so focused on his current situation, he hadn't been thinking at all about what he'd left behind, even though essentially that was what this trip was about.

For a while they chatted about small stuff and what the girls were doing. He wasn't surprised that Chloe didn't ask him if he was making any progress on finding Tucker; he knew she was secretly hoping he failed in his mission. "Sooo..." she said eventually.

That was never a good sign. "Uh oh. What."

"Myles and I have been talking about me and the twins maybe moving to New Orleans in the fall. I mean, he'd have to find a place for us first, I'm not going to just vagabond around with little kids. I can't do that anymore."

As much as this was not an unexpected twist of fate, Tyler found himself feeling suddenly empty and nostalgic, as well as a bit worried about the future of his dysfunctional extended family. Then the call dropped while he was advising Chloe about not doing anything rash and he was suddenly in a dead zone with no bars and a 1X rating where there should have been 4G. After weeks on Culebra he knew this meant texting only and he swore aloud at being brought back to the reality of Third World communications.

He had to stop playing around here, letting himself get so distracted. He hadn't planned on actually getting back home any time soon, he didn't even have a return ticket, but now he felt like he needed to get back and do damage control, do whatever he could to keep Artemis and Athena in his life. He didn't want to lose them too.

No longer feeling relaxed, he got up and paced along the water's edge, trying to figure out what to do next. Thinking back over the trip so far, he wondered how Maggie was doing. He'd been putting off making the call about finding the Nico Tico sunk and ransacked. And he learned nothing about her friend, Flush Royal, who had accompanied Tucker on the sail from Tortola. Perhaps that was an avenue he could explore today.

Back in town at the Dinghy Dock happy hour, he asked a few of the regulars if they'd ever known a man called Flush. "Not exactly a name you'd forget, is it?" commented Steve the schooner captain. "Must be a poker player, am I right?"

Tyler wished he'd thought about asking the group a few nights earlier. Kay would probably know him.

Barry always seemed to have the best memory for characters in local Culebra lore. "Yeah, yeah, I remember that guy a few years back, I used to call him Flesh because he was kind of flabby. Guess we all get that way eventually. And a friend of mine used to call him Toilet." Barry laughed. "Juvenile, but it was hard to resist."

Tyler resisted bringing up the topic of bullying. "Do you recall who he might have hung around with?"

"Nah, he wasn't here that long. I just remember the name." He closed his eyes for a minute. "I can see him sitting over there on the other side of the bar. Drinking whiskey. Little ponytail and a matching goatee. Piece of work, that guy. Who the hell did he hang with..." He shrugged. "I don't know, maybe it will come to me. I'll let you know."

"Wait – so he wasn't here last fall or winter after the hurricane?"

"Nah, I'd remember that. So few folks stuck around, we pretty much knew who was on island or wasn't. Of course, whiskey was hard to come by then too."

Tyler told himself it wasn't much, but at least it was something.

The next morning, despite his resolve, Kay didn't have to work very hard to convince him to come out to her boat before their excursion.

"Another waylay with Kay," he joked, as she once again totally sidetracked him from his goals for the day.

"You're so easy, Tyler." She was sitting naked on the edge of the mattress, apparently scrolling through messages that had come in while they'd been otherwise preoccupied. With a sudden sense of urgency, she stood up and pulled on his ankle. "We should get going. The boat we are using is on borrowed time and we need to drive to where it is docked."

It didn't matter how small an island this was, nothing on Culebra was simple. They went back to the public dock in her dinghy, took his golf cart out to a private dock where they then got into a small fishing vessel with double outboards for speed. They motored through the bay, passing immobile yachts on their moorings, most of them tightly closed up and unoccupied. Out on the horizon beyond the channel, a sailboat was visible as it headed west.

"You're so impressive." He meant the compliment, even as he wondered who she really was. "Not only can you handle a motor, but I suppose you have an idea of where we're headed as well."

"We're headed east out of the Ensenada and then we are slowly going to explore the coastline. There are not that many potential places that a boat could hide without being spied, but we'll be looking at them all."

As usual, the storm clouds began to build up with the heat of the day and Tyler hoped they wouldn't get rained out. He'd waited too long for this.

"So this is Mosquito Bay, obviously there's not much hiding out available here." Kay slowed down so that he could take in the view of the rocky reefs and deserted beach. "And the next is Manzanilla. Pretty much too shallow to even anchor there."

Mosquito, Manzanilla... They were all sounding alike now. "Manglar. Manglar Bay is where Steve said, right?"

"Right. Soon come, mon." She flashed him a 'trust me' smile. "I have a good idea of where it is we're headed."

Tyler was beginning to feel nervous. If everything went according to plan, in a few minutes he might actually be reunited with his son.

"Do me a favor," she asked as she kept her eyes glued to the surface of the water, watching for color changes of depth and telltale signs of reefs, "and pull up Google Maps on your phone and zoom in on this area. And then go to the satellite image. That should give us a pretty accurate view of what we want."

He did as she asked, blowing up the colorful image until the foliage of the trees was visible against the brown of the island, and the reefs appeared as turquoise jewels against the darkness of the sea. "Wow, this is great. I can even see the boats in the Ensenada. I wonder how up to date this image is."

"Probably within the last six months. Now move it over to where we are right now."

"Bahia de Almodovar? And that little island is called Pela. Okay, I'm oriented." He came over next to her and held the phone up so she could see the screen.

"So this is where we are headed into this area." She pointed at a white spot on the map. "And there, what is that? Make it bigger. Looks like a boat to me!"

She was right – an oblong silhouette was clearly visible nestled into a little estuary along the coast.

"Not only is she handy, but she's a genius too." He kissed her on the cheek as she begrudgingly grinned.

"We're not far from there, so keep your eyes peeled." Kay slowed the engines to a putter as they glided towards a narrow channel between the mangroves. "Should be right up here." Suddenly she seemed as tense as him, her hands gripping the wheel. "See anything?"

"Hmmm. No." Tyler looked back at the map and then at the landscape. It was hard to transpose the aerial view to three-dimensional reality. He stared intently at the dense mangrove roots that defined the shoreline, creating a treacherous network in the shallow waters and kept them from getting too close to land. A pair of pelicans flapped their wings and moved from one perch to another, keeping wary eyes on the environmental intrusion that was disturbing their ecosystem. "This should be it, but..."

Kay nosed the boat into a calm and empty inlet and tightly circled around. "A perfect hideaway," she murmured. "But nothing here. Well, we could be wrong. Let's keep going. The satellite shot was not taken yesterday."

"Wow, this really seems like the place we're seeing..." Tyler's voice trailed off in disappointment and Kay squeezed his arm reassuringly.

"Don't give up. We've got at least another mile or two of coastline to explore here."

When the sky opened up an hour later it seemed like a fitting statement. For a few minutes the rain was so heavy it obscured their view of everything. Tyler and Kay huddled under the inadequate shade canopy, with a large towel wrapped around them to shield themselves from the sideways shower of pelting drops.

"Aww, I'm so sorry, sweetie." Kay put her head on his shoulder sympathetically. "It would have been so great to see your reunion with your son. But we'll keep searching. I'll put the word out on some Facebook sailing pages. He's probably just on another island not far from here."

"Thanks for your optimism. I just feel like I've hit a dead end." More like smack into a brick wall, he thought darkly. He had pinned too many hopes on finding Tucker safely ensconced on a tidy little boat in a hidden refuge and then welcoming him with open arms. He had totally pushed aside the fact that the boy hadn't made contact with anyone in his family in almost two years, not even to let them know he had survived two hurricanes. "I probably should just let it go."

"No, not yet. Look, I can probably keep the boat for another day or two. How about we go on a snorkeling adventure tomorrow? I know a great place that will bring your spirits back up."

He gave her a weak smile. "Okay, Miss Positivity. I'll let you take me somewhere special tomorrow. But I think I just want to go back and be alone for a bit now. Figure out what's next for me."

"Honeymoon Beach it is then." As if on cue, a patch of blue sky opened up above their heads.

"Honeymoon?" He laughed. "Did you make that up?"

"No, it's real. It'll help you forget about finding Tim for a few hours."

"Who?"

"Your son."

"Tucker."

"Oops. Right." She giggled and moved away, using the end of the towel to dry off the steering wheel. "Sorry. I don't know who I was thinking about."

When he dropped her at the dock, he saw the black pig again, snuffling around a garbage can that had fallen over. Nothing had really changed on Culebra except his mood.

His phone rang suddenly and keeping one eye on the potholes, he glanced to see who the caller was. Lucy.

"Where the hell have you been all week?" he answered irritably. Last time he'd seen her, she'd been drowning her sorrows in a veritable bathtub of gin. A lot had happened since then.

"I'm afraid it's a long story. But the main thing is this – Fiona stayed with me last night."

He was so startled he almost dropped the phone. He pulled off the road in front of the big yellow school and said, "Fiona from Tamarindo?"

"Yes, there's so much to tell, but… she's gone." Lucy did not sound wasted, but she wasn't making any sense.

"What do you mean, not at your place anymore? Did she talk about Tucker?"

"Tyler, she was wearing his shirt. The Jordan Jaguars one. Sorry, it keeps making me want to cry when I think about it. Hold on." He heard her blow her nose. "But no, I mean she's really gone. I'm at the beach right now where the cable tower is."

"Electric Beach?" In a swift motion, he turned his golf cart around and headed back towards town.

"Yes, I bribed the guy at the other beach to tell me where she was really staying."

Lucy was actually doing something productive to find Tucker. He repressed his urge to comment on this fact and said, "She's probably at work."

"You still never listen to me when I talk, do you? I'm saying she's gone. Like left the island gone. The campsite is empty, nothing left, but a couple of broken chairs in a clearing and a fire pit."

"Lucy, stay where you are." Hell, he could not drive that road in this vehicle, he would have to hike in. "I'll be there in half an hour."

CHAPTER SIXTEEN

July 2018
Culebra, Puerto Rico

"You met my father last week and you never said anything?" Tucker stared at Fiona, a cold sweat sweeping over him despite the humidity of the morning.

"Yes. And–" She had been glaring at him defiantly, but now she averted her eyes back to the shoreline. "Look, let's get underway and then we can talk about this."

"But..." The whole idea of both his parents being on Culebra together was still beyond belief, especially the part about his mother. "My mom is here? Not really, right? She's got white hair and she's small–" He stuck a hand out at shoulder height.

"Well, she's short but I wouldn't exactly call her small." She shook his arm, trying to spur him into action. "Come on, help me get the kayak up."

"And she's got a British accent," he added triumphantly, sure this would be the deal breaker.

"Yes, strangely she does." Fiona turned away, suddenly weepy again. "There's so much you apparently don't know. But I think we better get to Luis Peña first."

It was not the romantic crossing he had imagined; the silence between them was tauter than the sail and his agitation and emotion were so great, he could barely manage to hold the wheel steady. Of everything he was feeling, it was guilt that overcame him most of all. For the first six months he hadn't called home because he'd been such a depressed mess after Chloe left him on Skyros. Then he'd been at sea and by the time the hurricanes and all the aftermath had occurred, Vermont was just a distant memory of the place he'd grown up. He'd been happy to leave it that way.

But the fact that Tyler and Lucy had both come to Culebra looking for him had him shaken to his core. Had someone in the family died? He could not imagine who would be important enough that they would show up together. But most of all, how had they tracked him here in the first place, when all those months ago he had virtually disappeared over the horizon with Flush by his side and Maria on his tail.

For most of the journey, Fiona sat still as a stone, staring out to sea, her face strangely pale, her posture stiff. He wasn't quite sure why all of this would be so upsetting to her, unless she was worried that they were intent on taking him back to Vermont and out of her life. The thought that maybe she actually loved him that much touched him more deeply than his hereditary bonds. She was his family now and more than anything, he was most distressed by the idea that she might desert him; he couldn't deal with another abandonment.

By the time they dropped anchor on the opposite side of Luis Peña in Lana's Cove, Tucker was so stressed that he found himself scratching again, his nervous system triggering the itching on his elbows, shoulders and the soles of his feet. But as soon as they were safely moored, Fiona dove over the edge and swam away in the direction of the perfect crescent of white sand that lined the quiet little bay.

"Oh, no you don't," he murmured and, stripping off all of his clothes, he was in the water, catching up with her as she emerged onto shore.

She did not seem surprised that he had followed her. "You could've left something on. We'll have to sit up there so you don't get sand in your butt crack." She waved towards a wooden picnic table in the shade of an almond tree, a testament to the fact that Lana's Cove might not always be as secluded as it was this afternoon.

Once they were seated, she still seemed as distant as she'd been all day and finally Tucker reached over and squeezed her hand. "Okay, tell me what the fuck is going

266

on. And also, just so you know, I am not going back to Vermont. Or for that matter, anywhere without you."

Fiona sighed and finally looked at him. "Where to start... Your father came looking for me at Tamarindo a bunch of days ago. Wanted to know if I knew you. I told him the truth, sort of. That you had basically disappeared a while back, that you hadn't been seen in public for some time."

"I don't get it. Why didn't you just tell me he was here?" Tucker tried to think how he would have reacted to that information.

"Well, I probably would have if he hadn't told me that Athena and Artemis were waiting for you in Vermont. And then he showed me a picture of them."

He still couldn't fathom what she was talking about but he remembered the conversation they'd had in bed last week. "Is that why you asked me... so who are they, his new cats or something?"

Fiona made a noise that sounded like half of a laugh. "Oh my god. No, my clueless dear. They are little girls. YOUR little girls."

Tucker snorted. "Don't be ridiculous. I don't have any..." He stopped mid-sentence, feeling suddenly nauseous. "That's impossible. He was just trying to trick you."

She nodded. "That's what I thought the first time I asked you about Athena and Artemis and you clearly had no idea what I was talking about. But this morning Lucy showed me the same photo."

"What?!" He was the one who pulled away now in speechless disbelief.

"Right before she showed me the one of you and Chloe with your dreadlocks."

"You saw a picture of Chloe." This conversation couldn't be happening. "My mother hates Chloe."

"She did say that she usually crops the girlfriend out of the picture." Fiona looked at him sideways." Even though she is the mother of 'her two beautiful granddaughters.'"

267

"What?!" he repeated, leaping to his feet, obviously giving her the reaction she was expecting. "But..." A memory of the last time he and Chloe had ever spoken came suddenly to mind. They'd still been arguing about her getting rid of 'the baby' when he'd walked out of their dank little apartment under Niko's house in Skyros. When he'd returned from sea ten days later, she and all her possessions were gone and he'd never heard from her again.

"I don't believe it. It's some kind of trap."

"Don't believe it or can't believe it?" Fiona's voice was gentle now.

"How old are these... girls?" He couldn't be a father. Or wouldn't be a father. Or didn't know how to be a father. Suddenly everything was multiple choice again.

"I don't know. Maybe a year, year and a half. Stoney, Tucker..." she paused, seemingly as confused about his identity as he was now. "They look like you. It's not your fault. You didn't know."

He stumbled back towards the water, not wanting to hear any more about these twins with Greek names, but then turned back with one more question. "How did you meet my mother?"

Now it was Fiona's turn to look uncomfortable. She squirmed a little as she answered, "At T-Ron's house. This is the part that gets really dicey."

"What the hell was she doing with that dirtbag?"

"Um, I don't know, I guessed they hooked up somehow. Turns out she's been 'the girlfriend' I've been seeing evidence of."

"Like she's sleeping with him? Oh my freakin' god." He shook his head. How had this situation gone from bad to absolutely horrible. "What else can you tell me – that she's coming for me with a big knife too? To cut my balls off and tow me home?"

He walked as far away from her as he could get on the little beach, about a three minute stride. Just like that, bam, his whole life had been undermined again. When he was finally about to get out from under all the shit that had been dragging him down for the last year.

None of it made sense. Why would Chloe have gone back to Vermont? He knew instantly that it was because she really had nowhere else to go. For a brief second, he had a lusty pang for the adventurous innocence of how it had been for the first half of their relationship, before it got all weird and stressful between them. He pushed the desire away – what he had with Fiona was so much better than any of that.

Except that Chloe had his babies. Not one but two. The thought of twins and all the responsibility that went with that made him literally double over with pain and his limbs began to itch violently as though he'd just come down with ciguatera all over again. By the time Fiona reached him and pried away his fingers, his legs had big red track marks from the trail of his nails.

"Come on, let's swim back out to the boat. And eat something. I'm starving."

How could she act so normal; Tucker wasn't sure if he'd ever feel like eating again.

"I still don't get it. Tell me again why you didn't tell me you'd met my father." Tucker was face down on the bed where he had immediately thrown himself as soon as they were back on the boat. Fiona had been silently chopping vegetables in the galley and they had not spoken since climbing aboard.

"I thought you had been lying to me. That you were..." she seemed to be searching for the words, "a deadbeat dad."

"Maybe I am. Whatever that means." Dead and beat were exactly how he felt right now.

"It's someone who skips out on supporting his kids. Doesn't take any responsibility for them." He could hear oil sizzling in the frying pan. Both the smell and the conversation made him feel like vomiting. "I don't think it counts if you never knew about them."

"Well, thanks for that."

269

"You know you do really look like him."

"Yeah, I know." He could hear the sound of a large insect buzzing around in the cabin, something big like a giant fly or a hornet.

"That's not a bad thing."

"So what were you going to do – leave me? I mean if I had been lying."

The buzzing seemed to be getting louder and then suddenly Fiona was shouting and swearing. Before he could lift his head to see what was happening, she had abandoned the garlic and onions and was on deck yelling.

Tucker leaped up so quickly that the room spun dizzily around him from the swift change of angle. Finding his balance, he moved as fast as he could towards Fiona's voice outside.

He saw it immediately, black and shiny with four robotic landing legs and a powerful little propeller whapping rapidly to keep it hovering only a few feet above the boat. "What the fuck…"

But Fiona the huntress was already on her mark, slingshot in hand. The drone was so close that she hit it easily on the first try; the jagged piece of coral she used for ammunition ripped squarely into the bottom of the body, taking off one of the legs, before the rock ricocheted straight down, landing with an unpleasant thud that left a large ding in the boat's fiberglass surface. With only the briefest glance down, she reloaded and aimed again at the now sputtering aircraft, which this time fell to the deck with a satisfying crash.

"Fucking piece of shit. How the hell did he find us here." Tucker leaned over to retrieve the broken drone, noticing that the red light of the camera was still flashing. "Fuck you, asshole," he yelled into the little lens. "Come on, bring it. Whatever you've got, we are ready for you." Realizing that he was still buck naked, he moved closer and made an obscene gesture.

Fiona shook her head in disgust and then with one graceful yet powerful motion, kicked the offensive piece of

270

machinery overboard. "That was immature of you." She sank down onto one of the outdoor cushions and held up a hand as he started to protest. "But entirely appropriate." Then desperation crept into her tone. "Oh, my god, what are we going to do? Is he going to track us everywhere we go?"

But Tucker was relieved to have something else at which to channel his anger and frustration, a satisfying alternative to hating himself as the devil of his own undoing.

"I've had it with that old fucker. Let him follow us. We'll be ready for him and we'll crush him." His boyish bravado sounded absurd even to his own bruised ego and when Fiona rolled her eyes at him, he added hastily, "Okay, we'll take the kayak around to the other side first thing tomorrow, go to the bunker, get the money, and get out of here."

"I don't understand it. How could he know we left? He wasn't even on the island this morning." An unpleasant burning smell brought her back to her feet. "Shit. I left the stove on."

"Do me a favor." Lucy leaned forward and spoke quietly to the Dinghy Dock bartender. "I want a club soda with lime and a shot of your cheapest gin on the side."

He tilted his head to one side and looked at her with a questioning grin. "Ohhhkayyy. That's different for you."

"Yes, it is. And don't think for a minute that I'm drinking that bloody swill. Because I'm not."

"Just so you know, you have in the past." He put the two glasses in front of her.

"Yes, well, not straight up, anyway. Or at least not that I can recall." She held the gin up to her nose and sniffed it. For a few seconds she desired it as much as a lover in the throes of passion and thought she might just throw it back. Instead she tossed a little on each of her shoulders and dabbed it on her neck and behind her ears.

"A little juniper berry perfume?" The man with the glasses and long beard whose name she could never recall was watching her with amusement.

She held up a hand. "No questions." The last few drops she rubbed on her lips and and then closing her eyes, tenderly licked the inside of the shot glass. She pushed it back across to the bartender and winked. "And now it's business as usual. Except this is what I'm drinking tonight." She squeezed the lime into the soda water and sighed.

"Here comes your date with a couple of San Juan tourists." The bearded man nodded towards the stairs where T-Ron was descending, laughing and flirting with a pair of voluptuous girls with big hair and bigger breasts, wearing lacy beach cover-ups over neon orange bikinis that left little to the imagination. "Looks like they got dressed up for dinner."

"Yeah, I don't think he was expecting me to be here." Though T-Ron's eyes were hidden behind mirrored sunglasses, Lucy could tell the very second that his gaze fell on her, although nothing changed in his expression. He knew she was aware that she was watching him as for the next few minutes he continued his exchange with the two young women, which finally ended when one of them handed him her phone so that he could take a few beauty shots of the two posing seductively, lacy tops tucked up to display one pair of hefty bronzed thighs pressed closed to another as they squeezed into the pic together.

"And a selfie of all three of us," T-Ron said, making a big show of an intimate embrace with him in the middle. "Gracias, chicas. Now don't miss your ferry." Clearly pleased with himself, he sauntered over to Lucy and pulled down his sunglasses to peer over them at her. "Well, well, well." He leaned over to give her a kiss, inhaling the scent of gin and nodding. "Feeling a little better than the last time I saw you?"

"It's been days," she said petulantly. "Where have you been?"

"Working. Off island. Just got back." He cocked his head slightly. "So how'd you get here, babe?"

She took a big gulp of her nonalcoholic drink and smiled at him genially. "You bastard."

He ran a finger down the inside of her arm. "Now, now. Play nice. I take good care of you, don't I?" He put his mouth up to her ear. "Let me tell you what I can do to take care of you tonight."

On cue, Lucy's cell phone chimed in her purse and she pulled away. "Excuse me." She held it up so he couldn't see the screen.

"Did he get there? Everything okay?"

She hit the thumbs up emoji and turned back to T-Ron. He was giving her that scary, slit-eyed look, hat tipped down low, cheekbones hard and taut. She had to play this right. "Actually I have plans."

"Well, break them. We've got some catching up to do." With his customary blatant sexuality, he put his hand on the lap of her dress and stroked suggestively.

Damn, he knew just what she wanted. Maybe she could just – no, she couldn't. "Hey, you abandoned me. You're still a bastard."

"Well, I'm back now." He leaned over again, this time biting her earlobe and whispering, "Feisty bitch."

She knew a good fight turned him on, but something about his possessive manner scared her tonight. "Well, I'll tell you what."

"I'll tell you what." He squeezed her crotch as he called out, "Julio, over here, another one for mi mujer, por favor."

Lucy caught the bartender's eye and he nodded knowingly. "I think you owe me more than a drink." She put her fingers over his and tried to pry his hand away, but he tightened his grip and pressed his body against hers.

"How about we go back to my apartment so I can pay you back. With interest. In fact, I can make it really interesting." He finally released his hold on her so he could pick up his beer. The place where his fingers had been felt seared as though by a pulsating electric current and Lucy

273

hated herself for the physical chemistry between them. Or maybe she hated the fact that she was going to have to give it up.

He was close enough to her that she could feel his phone vibrating in his pocket. He glanced at it. "I gotta take this. Don't go anywhere." As he stepped away, he pointed with one finger and mouthed the words, "You. Me. Fuck. Tonight."

Hell, it was the only way she was going to get back inside his apartment. What Tyler didn't know, wouldn't hurt him. And why should he care anyway.

She could see right away that T-Ron's demeanor was different as he moved back towards her. There was nothing playful or even seductive about the hard set of his jaw or the way his nostrils flared a little as he contemplated her.

"So something has come up." Normally he would add a sexual innuendo to words like that, but now he just studied her in a way that frightened her more than a little.

Be brave, you got this, girl, she reassured herself. "Something not good?"

"Well, it cuts into our time together because I'm going to have to take my boat out really early." He nodded then and pursed his lips. "How about you come over to my place tonight and then I take you on a little sea cruise tomorrow morning, Miss Lucy?" His face lit up with self-satisfaction at the brilliance of his own solution.

Should she play along or fight it... Truthfully, the man's devious scheme had saved her from herself. She should be thanking him for giving her self-worth back, even if he was unaware of it. "I don't know. I'm still really pissed at you. Is this a work trip? Am I just going to be bored?"

He twisted his smirk into a smile and seemed to force a laugh. "I can promise you an exciting ride. Starting tonight. What do you say, old cowgirl?" He leaned closer and said with his usual audacity, "My horse is ready for you to mount it."

"Hmmm. And what am I getting up for at the crack of dawn?" She tried not to giggle, anticipating the smartass double entendre to come. "Where are we going?"

"A snorkeling expedition to Honeymoon Beach. On Luis Peña. See how much I love you – how romantic is that?"

"I don't know, I haven't been snorkeling in almost twenty years," she said aloud, while internally she congratulated herself for everything going better than expected. "But I'm game," she added brightly, sliding off her barstool. "Let me make a call right now and break my date for tonight."

She could see the surprise that crossed his face. "You really..."

"Oh, you thought I was fooling, didn't you? Yes, I was moving on, but I'm willing to give you a second chance. Baby. Be right back."

It was her turn to walk up the stairs with a phone pressed to her ear.

"How's it going? You all right?" Tyler did not bother to say hello.

"Yes, we've made up and he's taking me out on his boat tomorrow. I'll be sticking to him like glue till I find out what I need to know."

"Excellent. Stay in touch then."

"Tuna tacos and Margaritas, remember? You coming?"

"Sorry, just getting the boat ready for tomorrow. See you in 10."

Tyler had no idea what she meant about preparing the boat, but as long as Kay was showing up at Zaco's, all was cool. He swallowed a mouthful of his drink and studied the display of tequilas lit up on the shelves behind the bar. Tequila had never been his alcohol of choice, but Sarah, his longtime friend in West Jordan was an aficionado. Now, rum... that was a different story. He'd had a love affair with rum once that he chose not to remember.

Contemplating tequila brands helped him keep his mind off the plan at hand. After spending his afternoon with Lucy, sharing information and comparing notes, they had come to some disturbing conclusions and he was feeling a little unnerved. The connections and related events had to be more than coincidental. The only thing he felt certain about was that, for whatever reason, all paths converged on Tucker, no matter the consequences. Although given the players, the outcomes could be dangerous and extreme. As evidenced by what had happened to Lucy after their fight several evenings ago.

When Tyler had expressed his concern about what could have taken a seriously deadly turn, Lucy had snapped, "Well, it didn't. Despite how deviant it might sound, we actually have enjoyed each other's company, and in some perverted way he cares about me," to which Tyler had retorted, "Well, the devil always fools his disciples, especially the ones who fuck him," and then they agreed to let it drop before they descended into an even more heated and juvenile exchange.

At least Lucy had cleaned up her act as a result of all this. She definitely seemed determined and back on her game after last weekend's crescendo of bingeing. He did not understand her disconcerting attraction to the unsavory character at the center of all this drama, but he'd never understood why Lucy chose the partners she had throughout her life. Except for him; their relationship had made sense. Until it didn't.

"Hey, stranger." Kay slid onto the next barstool. "And my drink is waiting. You are just the most thoughtful guy."

With her blonde ponytail, washed canvas baseball cap and short denim skirt, she could have been the most normal soccer mom in all of suburbia. It was hard for him to accept that there was some seriously gray areas to Kay that he didn't understand.

"You good?" she asked, sensing instantly that things were not entirely as they had been earlier in the day.

"Yeah, fine." Would he ever fall in love with a woman who was just what she appeared to be? If the past was any kind of barometer, he figured the odds were unlikely.

"So here's the new wrinkle to our outing tomorrow." She smiled up at him coyly. "We're going to sail over to Honeymoon Beach in my boat. I mean, the one I'm housesitting."

"Really?" He wasn't sure what to make of this news. "That's…interesting. And very cool."

"So the best thing is if you sleep over tonight so we can get an early start."

"You know what you're doing, right? Because I haven't done much sailing." This was not entirely true, but he wanted to put it out there.

"I've got my captain's license, of course I know what I'm doing. You're in good hands, honey." The arrival of their food caused all conversation to cease for a bit, but then Kay swallowed and went on. "You know, we could stay out there for a night or two. Let's stop at your house so you can pack a few things."

"Really. Maybe just one night. I kind of have to be back." There was something strange about 'busy Kay' ready to take a vacation that seemed suspicious. "Some stuff is going on at home that I have to be on call for."

"Well, let's just plan for an overnight then." She punched him playfully in the arm. "It'll be fun. Especially at night when any daytrippers go home. And I can show you some awesome snorkeling spots."

"I'm thinking about the South Pacific." Tucker opened the atlas to a bookmarked page. "Raratonga. Vanuatu. Huahine." He pronounced the strange place names slowly and carefully. Now those are exotic islands."

"That's really far." Fiona gazed blankly at the map of the Pacific Ocean. "How long will it take to get there?" Pulling the sheet up to her waist, she leaned against Tucker's shoulder, closing her eyes.

"I don't know. A couple of years? We should be really good sailors by then." Most nights this bedtime ritual of studying the atlas brought him intense satisfaction. But today's traumas had left both of them feeling too emotionally crippled to enjoy much of anything.

"What are you going to do?" Fiona's voice sounded tiny and faint. She didn't have to elaborate on what she was referring to; it had never left either of their minds all night.

"I don't know." He let the heavy book fall into his lap. If it hadn't been for the news she'd brought him today, he would have been savoring these first moments of the journey with her.

"Will you at least get in touch with one of your parents? Talk to them about...at least acknowledge that you know..." She seemed afraid to even say their names again.

If it would make her happy, he would do that. But he was not going home to – to do whatever you did with babies. Change their diapers, give them bottles. But if they really were his twins, which he was pretty sure they were, then would he be expected to support them? How could he...

Suddenly he laughed loudly and Fiona sat up in astonishment to stare at him.

"Yes. Yes, I will. And I don't have to be a – what's it called – deadbeat dad? Because after tomorrow morning, we'll have enough to open up a lifetime bank account for those little godforsaken goddesses."

Her eyes widened. "Is it that much?"

"I don't know, but probably. We'll, you know, invest it or something." He didn't care what he said now since it seemed to be dramatically lightening the mood. "I think you are going to be surprised."

Fiona snuggled up against him and, a few seconds later, began lightly snoring. So much for sex; at least she didn't seem to be mad at him anymore.

In the morning he didn't wake her as he prepared for their departure, not until the sunrise was moments away and it was time to haul up the anchor.

"Remind me of the plan," she yawned, pulling on a bikini bottom and a sweatshirt. "I thought we were taking the kayak."

"It makes more sense to motor sail around to the north side of the island and moor at Honeymoon Beach. It will save us a lot of time to have the boat closer. We'll take the kayak around the point from there and it will probably take us a few trips to get everything."

She nodded, glancing at the horizon. "Looks like some rain might be coming."

He didn't mention that his decision was largely due to the fact that he didn't want to be that far away from the Sea Urchin after last night's drone incident. "Watch for shallows and rocks for me."

"We should be fine until we're fairly close to the bay. Then it's a bit tricky." Fiona pulled on her brimmed cap and walked carefully along the deck to sit up on the bowsprit. "Oh, look there."

A blinding strip of sunlight was just breaking over the top of the Culebra hills. It was not the fresh rosy pink of dawn rising above the sea, but already a blazing ball of yellow in the sky. After an all too brief interval, it disappeared into an ominous strip of black clouds that ran the length of the island and then some.

"We'll wait it out if we have to!" Tucker called to her as the first heavy drops began to hit the deck. Rain had not been part of his strategy for a quick and easy departure.

Too much tea and not any alcohol... Lucy had hardly slept at all for the last few days and overstimulation combined with stress made this particular night a standout.

Without the usual comfort of a gin-induced haze, she had a much harder time giving herself up completely to the joy of sex with T-Ron. Although he performed as expertly as always, she was aware that he seemed preoccupied, his mind miles away from what his body was doing. Meanwhile she concentrated on acting as sotted and besotted as usual, realizing what a drunk ditz she had been during the last months of her life and vowing never to be so extreme again.

Unfortunately, despite her best efforts, he seemed as restless as she was and whenever she tried to slither out of his embrace, he awoke and readjusted his grip on her. "I've missed this," he growled in her ear. "Don't go slipping away on me now. I'd like to get you worked up again, baby, you're already so wet and wild."

Only once did she manage to reach for his phone as he snored only to find it was password protected, of course. After a night of accomplishing nothing, she had just barely fallen asleep when she felt his fingers searching between her thighs and heard the sound of an alarm dinging someplace nearby. "Time to get going. And feel how fast I'm waking up. Oh, my. I think we've got time for a quickie, Miss Lucy. Wake up now, that's it. Move that thing against me. Let's see how fast I can make you come."

Feeling the nearly instantaneous crescendo radiating through her body, she had to admit his skill at eliciting her response was impressive and would be hard to replace. How could a man be so bad and so good... When he exploded inside her a few minutes later, she thought maybe she could steal some extra minutes of sleep. But after a couple of deep, gasping breaths, he was on his feet and then tugging provocatively on her nipples. "Okay, get up now. Let's see you stand up like these girls are."

"Ouch. It's still dark out. Don't make me." She drifted off for a few blissful seconds before she felt him grasp her by both wrists and wrench her upwards.

"Shower's on. Come on."

"Stop it. You're hurting me. Okay, I'm coming."

"You're a big grouch this time of morning. Don't worry, I'll never ask you to do this again."

She shrieked as the cold water shower rained down on her skin. And then she was wide awake and cursing.

She bounced beside him on the seat of the truck as they painfully made their way over the potholes on the journey to the dock where he kept his boat. "This isn't as much fun as I thought it would be," she muttered to him, pretending be nursing a hangover. "I don't get why we have to go so early."

"Oh, sourpuss. I've got a bottle of gin in the cooler that'll set you straight again. Dawn is the best time, the seas are calmest and the fish are feeding. Besides, you're going to love it. It's going to be the ultimate orgasm of your life, you'll see." He pulled off onto a dirt track that ended at a wooden wharf.

"What – snorkeling? I doubt it," she scoffed.

His mocking laughter sounded harsher than usual to her overly alert ears. "Oh, I'm going to miss your biting sarcasm when you're gone, Miss Lucy." He slammed the door of the truck. "Now shake a chunky leg and let's get on board."

She'd hoped for a minute of alone time to send a text to Tyler. "Just a sec. I need to take a pee in those bushes there."

"You can always hang your big moon over the railing, I won't let you fall."

She was tired of his fat jokes at her expense. "I won't be a minute," she called moving behind a mangrove tree and squatting.

A message from Tyler popped up. *"App on her phone tracking something west of Luis Peña."* Shit, it was from hours ago. She felt a momentary wave of competitive anger that he'd been more on the ball than she was.

"Leaving on boat trip now. Text me when you can."

She heard an engine roaring to life and stood quickly, groaning. She was getting too old for this cloak-and-dagger lifestyle. Maybe she was ready to sit down in a rocking chair and learn to knit.

"How long since you've sailed this boat anywhere?" As always, Tyler was impressed with Kay's skills at captaining. They had motored out of the Ensenada at first light, and after reaching the open water had hoisted the sail to catch the wind from the east.

"Since never. This is the first time it's moved since I've been living on it."

"Really? You make me feel special."

She threw back her head and laughed in that self-confident manner he found so engaging and now so threatening. "Yes, this is definitely a relationship like none other I've ever had."

It was as good a lead-in as any. "Ever been married?"

"Me? A couple of times. Those were lost decades. To say marriage didn't work for me would be an understatement." A bitter expression flitted briefly across the lower half of her face.

How had he not learned this before... wait, he vaguely remembered her showing him pictures of grandchildren the first time they'd met. "Any kids?"

"Unlike you, no." Apparently she'd forgotten the tale she'd originally fabricated to enchant him. As she glanced uneasily at the sky, he wondered where she'd downloaded those photos of cute children. "Looks like some weather moving through. Did you bring a rain slicker?"

"Nothing but my birthday suit." Although he actually was starting to feel a bit chilly and the idea of being naked in a storm was not really that appealing.

"Well you better put that on unless you want to be soaked. And would you grab me my jacket? It's in the clothes closet by the bed."

"You mean that cupboard just wide enough for a broom handle?" He swung himself down into the cabin. "Any chance you've got a long sleeve shirt that would fit me?"

"Take anything you can find if you think you can get that skinny body of yours into it. I mean that totally hot body of yours."

Any smart retort he was going to toss back disappeared as he was thrown against the galley counter as the boat heeled hard in a sudden gust of wind and lurched across a swell.

"Sorry!" she called. "This is the roughest part. It gets better once we're on the west side of the island. And this storm will pass soon."

If this kept up it was not going to be much of a day for snorkeling. But as he came back up on deck, he could see

282

she was right; behind the ominous gray clouds releasing sheets of rain, a band of blue sky could be seen on the horizon.

"Glad I'm in the safe care of such an experienced sailor." As he helped her on with her rain gear, she gave him an odd look that verged on melancholy. "I know, it's a little short in the arms, right? But I think the color looks good on me. What do you call this, melon?"

"You're funny." But she wasn't smiling anymore. "So what's your next strategy in your search for your son?"

It was a joltingly serious response to his joking remark and seemed to change the holiday mood of their outing. "I don't know. Probably start checking in with those online sailing message boards like you suggested. Might have to go back to Vermont soon for some household intervention." The last thing he wanted to think about this morning was what might be happening to the home and business he had left in Chloe's hands and her flighty plans to move with the twins to New Orleans. "But right now I want to concentrate on my good-time adventure with you today."

"Right. Yes. How do you think you might be with making some coffee while we're underway? I would surely love a cup right now."

"Anything you say, captain."

When he emerged onto the deck again to hand her a steaming mug, she was studying the screen of her cell phone. She quickly pocketed it to take the hot cup from him. "Just checking our depth coordinates. We're good."

He said nothing about this suspicious comment, but he wondered what she had really been looking at it, as the navigation to their nearby destination was based on visual landmarks that she knew well. Even he knew where they were, just past the ferry dock and heading towards the point by Melones Beach. "Watch out for this guy coming up fast on our, uh, starboard side?" He hesitated for a second, hoping for some reassuring approval of his nautical wordage. "He's leaving a big wake."

They both turned their heads to view the speedboat vaulting hard across the waves as it raced past them. "Bastard," Kay muttered as she tightened her grip on the wheel.

Tyler could just make out the shapes of a tall man and a short woman behind the protective glass of the open cockpit. The woman was holding her bushy white hair behind her neck with one hand while hanging desperately onto the frame of the bouncing boat with the other. The man seemed focused on the horizon, determinedly pushing the engine to its limits, taking the bumps fast and hard as though he were galloping on a favorite horse. Tyler felt sick to his stomach; why did Lucy always play so close to the edge of the cliff? He needed to check his phone to see if she'd sent him a message.

"What a jerk." He glanced sideways at Kay to see if she showed any signs of recognition but all her attention was now on keeping upright and on course.

"Steady yourself while we ride this out," was all she said. "The wake will be past us in a minute."

Tyler knew the adrenalin rush he was experiencing was not about the anticipated bout of rough seas but more about the potential showdown in the near future.

A few minutes later, when the sailing was calm again and the sun was breaking through the clouds, he ventured a weak smile and a reassuring pat on her arm.

"Well done. Are we having fun yet?"

"We will be soon. Can you make me some more of this? I'm afraid it spilled during that little episode." She handed him her empty mug.

When he peeked through the porthole at her, she was looking at her phone again, but this time she was furiously texting a message. Not to be trusted, he reminded himself. You know this. He looked at his own phone and saw that Lucy had contacted him some time after they'd set sail. *"Leaving on boat trip now. Text me when you can."* Well, that told him nothing.

"Damn, looks like we're not the only ones with the idea of an early morning snorkel today." They had made a wide tack to the north of Luis Peña and now had a good view of Honeymoon Beach with its calm aquamarine waters and picture-perfect curve of white sand. Even from a distance they could see not one but two other boats were already moored there. Just outside the protective reef, a white sailboat was visible, its mast bobbing lightly. And improbably close to shore, the offensive motorized craft that had passed them had thrown its anchor down. Off towards the point he could see the silhouette of two swimmers snorkeling.

Shit, Lucy and T-Ron were here?

"Should we stay?" He threw out the question, already knowing the answer.

"What do you think? Now help me get the sail down." It was an order, not a request and something in her tone made him wish he'd checked to see if the big knife was still in its hiding place between the mattress and the wall.

CHAPTER SEVENTEEN

July 2018
Culebra, Puerto Rico

Lucy was glad she hadn't eaten any breakfast before the white-knuckle boat ride to Honeymoon Beach. Although visibility had been almost nil during the cloudburst of heavy rain, T-Ron had barely slackened their speed. By the time he slowed down to enter the bay, she wasn't sure whether she was shivering from dampness or fear.

"How much fun was that?" he asked impudently as he cut the motor, clearly aware of how tightly she was still gripping the side rail and how pale she had grown. "Oh, come on, that little ride couldn't scare the pants off you, because I know you're not wearing any." As always, he laughed loudly at his own bad joke, but Lucy had trouble even pretending she was enjoying his humor right now.

Ignoring her lack of response, he hummed softly to himself as he heaved an anchor overboard into the soft sand below the crystal waters. Shading his eyes, he peered over at the only other occupant of the bay, a white sailboat that appeared uninhabited at the moment. "Perfect. Seems like we've got it all to ourselves for the time being."

Lucy took deep breaths, trying to regain her equilibrium. "I'm not sure I can do this yet," she protested as T-Ron opened a compartment and began tossing out snorkeling equipment. "I think I need to just sit for a few minutes."

Whether exhilarated by the journey or for some other reason, T-Ron seemed to be running at a faster pace than his usual carefully-modulated, cooler-than-cool, cruise control. "Well, how about some of this then?" He produced an icy bottle of gin from an insulated bag. "Nothing like a little sunrise G & T to steady those nerves of yours."

A belt of Beefeaters sounded like pure heaven and Lucy knew it would calm her down like little else. "I – I should put my swimsuit on." She dug in her bag and, out of some false sense of modesty, turned away to slip the unflattering garment up under her dress. The spandex fabric did not fit as snugly as usual and it occurred to her that she might actually have lost some weight in the past week. Either that or her one bathing suit was wearing out from overuse. "You do have a life jacket I can use, right? I'm not that confident of a swimmer."

"Oh, there's no way you would sink with those built-in flotation devices of yours." He hooted and slapped his knee. "I know, I'm so corny. Yes, I have a special inflatable I brought just for you, darlin'."

Why was she subjecting herself to this abuse... oh, right. This was a stop on a way to 'doing business' of some sort. She was going to be a fly on the wall and find out what he actually did for work. "And where are we going after this?" she asked, pulling her hair back into a braid to get it out of her face.

"What?" He looked at her blankly as he reached out to run a finger over one of her diamond stud earrings. "Oh, big island. Fajardo."

"Can we go a little slower on the next leg maybe?"

He chuckled as he began to unscrew the back of the earring. "You don't need to worry about that, darlin'. But we do need to take your shark bait off. Don't want to go snorkeling with anything as sparkly as these on."

"But I never take them off. They're family heirlooms."

"All the more reason for safe keeping." The earrings twinkled in his palm before he deposited them in a flap pocket of his shorts. "We'll leave them on the boat."

"I'm always afraid my holes will close up." She touched one of her empty earlobes.

"Oh, you walked right into that one!" He could not contain his mirth as he grabbed her around the waist and pulled her back against him, slipping a hand inside the leg of her swimsuit. "I can always get at least one hole of yours to open wide." He probed roughly between her thighs until he elicited a gasp and she pushed him angrily away.

"Admit it, you love it when I talk dirty about you." He grabbed at the top of her bathing suit and pulled it down until her breasts spilled out over the stretchy fabric.

"What are you doing? Stop it."

"Just checking to make sure your other family heirlooms don't have any sparkly nipples rings that might attract the barracuda. Oh, that's right, I know they don't. I play with these treasures all the time. Why, I've even slept with them in my mouth." With his eyes on hers, his fingers played a swift caressing tweak that his experience told him was guaranteed to arouse her. "I would know if they had any... shiny spikes."

His sense of humor was getting on her nerves. When she didn't give him the sexual response he had anticipated, he tucked the cups back up again over her soft flesh while he went on talking. "I once knew a woman with a diamond stud in her tongue. Now she could give some serious head. She also had a pussy ring – maybe I better check you for that? Because I know that's a place you do like to be... shall we say... pierced?" Before she could move out of his grasp he had pulled the crotch of her suit to one side and was tugging at her pubic hair in gleeful exploration.

"You're such a pervert!" She couldn't keep from hissing her thoughts as she sat down heavily on the passenger seat and stared at him angrily.

He held up his hands and put a sheepish look on his face. "Okay, okay. Just messing with you. Crossing the line maybe. I thought you loved that sort of thing; I've certainly enjoyed it during our times together. Here, peace offering." He took off his hat and unpinned something from the band. "I know you've always admired this. Why don't I let you wear it while we swim?"

Between his forefinger and thumb was a silver feather dangling from a turquoise bead. What did this mean... Lucy tried not to tremble as he slipped it through the hole in her right ear. "Thank you." She gulp hard knowing that some kind of corner had just been turned and that there was no going back.

"A quick toast before we dive in?" He brandished the gin bottle.

"I – I should probably have something to eat first." Her dissent sounded feeble.

"What? The Lucy I know always enjoys a liquid breakfast." He tipped it up to her lips the way he had that night at Casa Laguna. "Fortification, yes?"

Her resolved melted away with the first swallow. The buzz burned its way into every extremity with that warmth she loved so much. She coughed at the harshness and then took the bottle from him, drinking deeply until her fears slipped away and she felt courageous again.

Swaying a little she stood up and shoved the gin back at him. "Take that shit-eating grin off your face. Okay, I'm ready. Suit me up for snorkeling."

"Oh, yes." He slid the life vest over her head and buckled it around her waist. "Wait there's a strap that goes between your legs too – please let me." He snugged it up high enough to make her wince and she could feel his body shaking with laughter behind her.

"Not funny, you bastard." She turned to swat at him and fell sideways, bruising her hip as she landed on the deck. Wow, the gin had gone straight to her head. She should never have given in to it.

"No more for you, lady. Okay, maybe just a little." He offered her the bottle again as he knelt down to help her get the fins on. "Drink up. Once the mask is on, you won't be able to have any more, unless I pour it down your snorkel. Hmm, now that's something I never thought of before."

She glared at him. "I can hold my bloody liquor. See?" She giggled as she held out the bottle for a second before taking one more long swig. "Okay, let's go before I don't want to." Jesus, how could she have gotten drunk so fast.

Hopefully a dip in the sea would clear her mind out for the rest of the day. She had work to do.

Standing up unsteadily she took a dizzying glance at the moving surface of the water and looked back to see if T-Ron was ready. When her vision finally focused on him, she saw he was already wearing a neoprene wetsuit jacket and something that looked like a camera hanging from a cord around his neck.

"Why are you bringing that?" she asked curiously as he clipped his buck knife sheath onto a belt at his waist.

"To protect you in case we see a shark." His mask was perched on his forehead now and his flippers were in one hand.

"We're not really going to see any sharks, are we?" She started to back up, but he grasped her firmly by the elbow and pressed her against the railing.

"Jump now, Lucy. Or am I going to have to push you overboard?"

She sputtered as her body sunk into the sea but after a brief second of panic she bounced to the surface, her arms flailing. Beside her T-Ron was bobbing gracefully, his mouthpiece in place, his eyes watching her behind the lens of his mask.

"Relax," he said removing his snorkel so she could hear him speak. "Let me help you." Much more gently than his previous sparring play, he adjusted her equipment until she felt comfortable breathing through a tube. "Follow me. We need to swim out to the reef to see any fish."

Again she found herself wishing she hadn't given in to the gin. The world below the surface beckoned with colorful fish and waving coral fans, but even the slight motion of the waves made her feel like she was going to be seasick. And tired. She was having a hard time keeping up with him, she didn't know why he didn't stop so they could observe the awesome array of sea life swirling around them.

She was relieved when he swam back to her and grasped her hand, tugging her along with him. The inflated vest was keeping her afloat; maybe she could just close her eyes and rest until they got there. Wherever it was they were going...

"This is crazy. We don't need all this money." Fiona paused to wipe the sweat from her brow as they emerged onto the beach again, each of them with two black garbage bags slung over their shoulders.

"Somebody can use it. We'll give it away. I promised Flush that I would do this so you-know-who would never get his hands on it." His nightmares of Flush's dead body drifting in the bay floated ominously through his mind again.

"Hell, what is in your backpack? Feels like lead." Her biceps strained as she heaved it into the kayak. Their eyes met and Tucker said, "Don't ask. It's worth it."

"I don't know about this. Is it okay to do good stuff with bad money? Does this make us... pirates?" She straightened up, hand resting momentarily on hips, but her small blue and black striped bikini did little to hide the tension coursing through her slim muscular body.

As appealing as she looked to him right now and however endearing her 'pirate' comment was, Tucker could feel the heat of the rising sun and knew they had to keep moving. "How about we start a turtle research center with some of it and make a big donation to preserving the coral reefs, too. How does that sound?"

Fiona's mood brightened significantly and Tucker was glad he'd come up with an idea that sparked her imagination. "I love it. But we're going to have to make another trip. This is as much as we can take in the kayak right now and still have the strength to paddle it. We're going to be sitting really low in the water as it is."

As usual she was spot on in her calculations; Tucker waded out onto the reef towing the heavily laden craft while Fiona pushed from behind before leaping aboard. "Get in now or you won't be able to!" she shouted and he tumbled into the front of the kayak as she used her paddle to navigate them through the tricky narrows.

This second load was bigger than the first had been and Tucker's arms were beginning to ache as they rounded the point. Suddenly he stopped paddling and held up a hand. "Shit. Look."

A motorboat was anchored on the other side of the bay from the Sea Urchin.

"Oh, no. And what's that?" Fiona pointed out to sea where a small yacht was reefing its sail as it headed towards Honeymoon Beach.

"Fuck. Okay. Just act cool. We could have anything in these bags. Coconuts. Conch shells. Maybe we're good citizens who have been picking up garbage." Tucker took a deep breath to stop his racing heart. "We'll tie up to the far side of the boat to unload this cargo. Out of view, where they can't see us."

He dipped his paddle back in the water and they continued their slow progress through the choppy waters, where the strong currents of the open sea to the north met the crosswinds around the island. Tucker tried to keep his mind on the task at hand, which was the difficult maneuvering of the overburdened kayak, but he could sense that Fiona's nervous energy was interfering with her ability to concentrate.

"Do you see any people on that motor cruiser?" she called forward to him.

"I think they're snorkeling." He could see someone floating towards them in the fast stream of the current. "One of them is right over there..." He squinted until he could see another form making swift strokes towards the bay. "And the other is going back."

"This is an intense place to snorkel, you have to be careful in this swift water."

Tucker could sense that Fiona's instinct was to check on the swimmer making his or her way in their direction. "We can't stop to help anyone, Fi. It's too dangerous with this load."

"That's not how it works, Tucker." She was steering them nearer to what now appeared to be a white-haired woman wearing a yellow life vest. "Something doesn't look right. Help me get closer."

Tucker froze as a vision of Flush's lifeless body seared once again through his brain like a hot iron rod. "Please don't say she has no breathing tube." This was no coincidence.

"I'm going in. Stay near me." There was a splash behind him and by the time he turned his head, Fiona was already out of the kayak and into the water.

"No, no, no..." He did not want to relive that awful moment again. Why did this have to be happening right now when so much was at stake?

Fiona had already reached the woman and her shriek carried clearly to his ears. "Oh, my god, her snorkel is missing! And her vest has been slashed. Tucker, help me, she's bleeding."

With the skillful ease of someone more at home in the sea than on land, Fiona grabbed a handful of the wet hair to pull the woman's head out of the water and rip her mask off. When she screamed again there was way more than just terror in her shrill voice.

"Oh, my god! Oh, my god! It can't be! No!"

Somehow, through whatever horror she was experiencing, her automatic responses were still performing a rescue, her fingers feeling for a pulse in the neck as she kept the face above the surface. Tucker put all his strength behind his paddling to keep the kayak from drifting further away but getting closer only by inches.

"She's still alive!" Fiona seemed to be bawling as she looked around desperately, trying to figure out what to do next. "Throw me one of our life jackets. I'm going to drag her to shore."

"Fiona! That's insane! You'll get ripped to shreds on the rocks." The coast was not far but the jagged coral and rough waters were a recipe for physical disaster.

"Throw me the fucking life jacket, Tucker! Don't you see who this is?" His angry bewilderment as he heaved the cushioned flotation vest at her forced her to answer her own question. "It's Lucy. It's your mother!"

Tyler gazed at the tranquil scene into which they were sailing. Turquoise water bordered by a half circle of pearly sand that rose up to sage green foliage of late summer under a now cloudless azure sky. Off to the right, a white sailboat rocked gently on its mooring, a dinghy tied to the stern, the occupants still seemingly asleep on this beautiful morning. To the left, anchored way too close to the beach was T-Ron's motorized fishing cruiser that had sped past them, the one Lucy had been on.

He told himself it was a common model, he'd seen plenty of Puerto Ricans cruising around in similar boats. But even at a distance he could see Lucy's blue dress hanging over the back of the passenger seat. Hell, this was an unanticipated wrinkle in his planned romantic interlude with Kay.

"Looks like that jerk who sped past us is here, too. Hope that doesn't cramp our style." When Kay didn't respond, he glanced over at her and was unnerved by the stony and unemotional expression on her face as she intently scanned the surrounding waters.

"Plenty of room for everybody to do what they need to." Realizing that he was staring at her, she smiled stiffly. "Would you be a love and get me the field glasses? They're just inside, right by the sink."

Be a love? When did Kay ever talk like that? The atmosphere had changed and he wasn't sure why. Tyler suddenly felt the need to be cautious and defensive. When he leaned over to give her a kiss on his way down to the galley, she actually dodged aside and added, "Why don't you bring up the snorkeling gear too? The sooner we get out there, the better."

Hanging the binoculars around his neck, he retrieved the net bag with fins and masks from under the narrow table and then, with a covert peek up the hatchway, decided to quickly check his phone. Nothing, in fact, no bars and no

294

service out here at all. As he slipped it back into the mesh wall pocket by the bed, his eyes strayed to the place behind the pillows where Kay kept the big knife. Before he even realized what he was doing, he had slipped his hand between the mattress and wall. A hasty but thorough search came up empty.

It meant nothing, he told himself. Maybe she felt no need for a weapon with a companion on board and had put it away in a safer place.

Kay was calling him. "Tyler? I need your help throwing the anchor down!"

"Coming." He tossed the snorkeling equipment up onto the deck and climbed up after it. "Just tell me what to do."

Her hand was out and he realized she was waiting for the binoculars, which she instantly put to her eyes. Following her gaze, he could see someone swimming towards the motorboat and reaching for the ladder. Too tall and svelte to be Lucy; he wondered where she was.

"What do you see?"

"Not much. Just another snorkeler." She put the glasses down. "Let's do this."

Under her proficient guidance, he opened a compartment in the prow and dragged out a heavy chain and steel-pronged anchor to lower into the sea as she slowly reversed the boat to firmly set it. Over the sound of their own motor, he heard a louder engine start up and was startled to see the cruiser moving across the bay in front of them.

"Well, maybe we are going to get some privacy." Kay frowned as they both watched the progress of the other boat. The captain did not look up or acknowledge them in any way and he wondered if she'd recognized T-Ron yet and what her reaction would be when she did.

"Oh, that's weird." The motorboat had circled around the other yacht and maneuvered to a mooring position on the far side of it, out of their view. "Can I have the binoculars?"

295

Instead Kay handed him a set of flippers. "These are bigger, they will fit you better. And use this mask; it leaks a little but you should be fine if you tighten the strap. I'm keeping my T-shirt on so my back doesn't burn. Might be a good idea for you too." When he continued to stare at the other boat, she grabbed his chin and turned his face towards her. "None of our business, right?"

His curiosity still burning, he followed her lead instead. "I need a safe place to leave my glasses." He started to go down into the cabin again but she carefully took the folded pair from him and disappeared below. "They'll be on the shelf down here. You can still see well enough without these, can't you? The water acts like a magnifier, you should be able to see fine under the sea."

Tyler didn't like to admit how blurry the world was now without his eyeglasses, although he knew she was right about his underwater vision. "Hey." He grabbed her hand as she came back up, and pulled her towards him. "Happy Honeymoon Beach Day."

Disappointingly, her kiss seemed more obligatory than heartfelt. She waited for him to dive off the ladder first before plunging into the water herself. He paddled in place, waiting for her to take the lead and with a thumbs-up signal, she swam off to the rocky shoals at the left of the cove. He started to follow and then a sudden brainstorm swept over him. If his theory was correct…

Veering right, he swam as fast as he could in the opposite direction, away from Kay and towards the other sailboat.

"That's crazy! You're wrong!" Tucker shouted. "That can't be my mom. What would she be doing out here?"

"I don't know, maybe looking for *you*?!" Somehow Fiona managed to inject a twinge of youthful sarcasm into her frantic yelling as she tried to strap the life jacket around Lucy's limp form. A small wave put both of them under water for a second and the sight of Fiona sputtering as she tried to keep Lucy afloat tore through Tucker's heart.

Before he could think any more about it, he dove over the side and tied the tow rope around his waist so that he would not be separated from the kayak and began maneuvering towards her.

As he got closer he felt a vise tighten around his already torn up insides. The woman did look a lot like his mother, shit, it was her. Somehow Fiona had managed to buckle the flotation vest around Lucy's neck in a way that kept her head above the surface and she was now attempting to swim toward shore with one arm looped through the heavy weight of an unconscious body.

"Fiona! Let me do it! You take the kayak back and get help from one of those other boats." Somehow she had already made it to a shallow spot where there was a possibility of standing but a more likely chance of brutally cutting your feet and limbs on sharp coral or sea urchins.

"No, you don't know what you're doing. I need to do CPR on her. Right now." With the amazing strength that seems to manifest in emergency situations, Fiona was now dragging Lucy up onto a small spit of pebbly shore between two jagged rocky outcrops. For a second he again questioned if this soft round little person who Fiona was muscling back to life could possibly be the petite angry dynamo he'd known as his mother. He hadn't seen her in almost two years and a lot had certainly happened to him in that time, he had just never expected his mom would change so much, at least physically. She was bleeding profusely from a deep slice down the back of one thigh that was too straight and clean to have happened accidentally.

Then quite suddenly Lucy was coughing up water and spewing a foul stream of vomit. Fiona fell back, exhausted from her efforts and called out to Tucker, "Get something to tie around her leg. We have to stop the bleeding." When he didn't move, still frozen in horror by the scene unfolding before him, she yelled again. "Tucker! Now!"

By the time he reached them, still dragging the kayak, he was covered with bloody scratches from scraping against the reef. Too overcome to speak, he knelt beside Lucy's body as Fiona used a webbed strap as a tourniquet and a T-shirt as a bandage. "Tilt her head up, make sure she doesn't choke."

Numbly he did as he was commanded, and as he gently placed her cheek against his thigh, he saw what was hanging from her ear. "What the fuck...how did she..." He lifted the little feather, remembering the last time he'd seen it, when he'd given it up at knifepoint.

"There isn't time to be sentimental. Use that life jacket as a pillow and then you need to go get help from whoever is on those other boats. We have to get her to the hospital."

"I'll stay here. You go. What? She's my mother and you're a faster paddler than I am anyway."

It took her only a second to agree, but then she shook her head as she looked at the kayak. "We've got to jettison the money. It's too heavy."

Legs shaking unsteadily, he scrambled back to the kayak and with trembling hands began tossing the black garbage bags towards shore. "Are you trying to save it? Tucker, really?"

As he slung the heavy backpack over one shoulder, he finally spied his sandals tucked into a corner and put them on his scarred feet. Fiona had been wearing her water shoes all along; as always, every move she made was smarter than anything he did. He staggered back to shore, guiding a couple of the black bags in with him.

"Go. It's empty now. I'll wait here." He grabbed her hand and pulled her towards him. "Fi, be careful. Please." As his eyes filled with tears, so did hers. They cried together for about five seconds before she pulled away and floundered towards the slowly drifting kayak.

He had a fearful change of heart as he watched her go, small and fierce, a girl and a paddle taking on the world.

Tyler swam underwater as much as he could, trying to keep Kay from easily tracking him. He had never told her he'd spent five years in Grenada; true, much of it was in a drunken stupor, but when not imbibing rum or working as a chef, the rest of his time was spent in the water. Like riding a bicycle, another thing he'd been better at when he was younger and fitter. But he was still very at home in the sea and could swim nearly as fast as twenty years earlier.

As he drew closer to the other sailboat he tried to read the name on the back, but through a mask and without prescription glasses, his long distance vision was just not good enough for more than guesswork. A little word and a longer word, three letters and six or seven letters. He had to get within a few feet before he could confirm what he had suspected.

Sea Urchin. Tucker's boat. His breath was quick and shallow as he grabbed hold of the bottom rung of the ladder, pulled his mask up and rested, assessing the situation. Where was Tucker and why had T-Ron tied off to the yacht's railing? A few other questions nettled his subconscious – what had happened to Lucy... and what was going on with Kay...

A flurry of movement on deck made him freeze and then silently sink lower in the water. T-Ron was dragging first one black garbage bag and then another towards the railing before heaving them both over into his own boat. Tyler had no idea was what going on here, but he knew that it was not right. When T-Ron went into the cabin again, Tyler slipped off his fins and stealthily hauled his dripping body up the ladder, hesitating at the top.

He needed a plan, but nothing came to mind. He'd only actually met this guy in person once, at the poker game, where he'd proven himself an impulsive and avaricious opponent. But right now he was trespassing on family property, there was no other motive for intervention needed.

Quietly setting down his snorkeling gear, he inched himself sideways along the railing until he was safely on the opposite side of the cabin from where the motorboat had tied up. He could hear T-Ron inside, flinging open cupboard doors and throwing crockery against the floor. 'Piracy' was all he could think of. Grabbing hold of the frame of the opening, he pulled himself forward to peer around the edge.

The next thing he knew he was flat on his back against the deck, the tip of a knife poking into his chin and a foot resting heavily on his abdomen. A narrow fox-like face leered close to his own, sneering with satisfaction. "And just like that. The other parent."

Tyler gasped a little as he felt a small trickle of warmth run down his neck and then T-Ron stepped back and held the knife up so they both could see the blood shining on the edge of the blade. "I could just kill you now. But I'd love to have a conversation with you first."

Tyler tried to remember the last time he'd been so viscerally close to death. "Well, I've got some questions for you too." He tried to sit up, but the foot on his chest pressed down more heavily.

"I'm sure you do. We've got a few things in common now, don't we."

"Such as..." He was playing for his life here, buying precious seconds.

"We've both had our dicks inside Lucy. Although I am guessing she was somewhat tighter back in your day." He laughed as Tyler tried to stare him down without reacting to this statement. "And we're both looking for your son. Where do you think that boy is, anyway?"

For once he was glad he had no idea where Tucker was if it meant this lunatic was as much in the dark as he was.

"Oh, come on now. He can't be very far away. He left everything he owns and more on this boat. Like things that were never his to begin with. I'm sure he'll be back soon." Tiburon's lips twisted into an uneven smirk. "I can barely wait for you two to see each other again. This should be a family reunion like no other."

Tyler glanced down at where a slow trickle of blood from his chin was dripping onto his chest. He wasn't going to bleed out, at least not at the moment. Clearing his throat, he said, "I'm assuming that what he doesn't own belongs to you?"

"Damn right, earned fair and square. Worked hard to accumulate my wealth. Enjoyed taking a lot of bastards down a notch for a bunch of years. But that last one was a bugger, infiltrating my own family like he did. Thought I had him safely out of the way until a hurricane undid my work. And then another brought him right into my waiting arms." T-Ron's voice sounded hoarse and he spat a wad of something foul looking over the railing, before quickly training his eye and his knife back on Tyler. "He was a piece of cake, a pushover, until somehow your son ended up in the picture."

Tyler had only an inkling of what the man was talking about, but it seemed important. Too important really, the kind of confession you told someone who would never have the opportunity to reveal it to another.

A sudden thwack from behind startled both of them, but the knife only inches from his face kept Tyler from moving more than his eyes towards the noise.

"Well, look who it is, always bullying someone he doesn't like. Which is pretty much everyone." Kay was wielding her own weapon, the one Tyler had been unable to locate earlier.

A flood of relief washed over him. "Kay, thank god you're—"

"I believe you've met my baby brother before. Tommy, you remember Tyler, don't you? From the last local poker game you crashed." Kay waved her knife from one to the other as though introducing them. But what had she just said – he must have heard her wrong.

"Kelley." T-Ron nodded tersely at her. "You must be losing your touch – how'd this fish get away from you?"

Tyler stayed frozen, and although his body language did not give away his shock, he was sure his complexion had faded to several shades whiter.

"He's a slippery one." She stayed by the ladder, not moving any closer. "And what about your catch of the day?"

"All taken care of. But you..." He shook his head in mock disapproval. "You get a D minus."

"Oh, the best laid plans..." For the first time she actually looked at Tyler. "And sadly, he was the best laid. You were a good time, Tyler Mackenzie."

"I still can be." He hadn't felt this desperate in decades.

"Too bad you are always so damn curious. This could have been much more pleasant." From his prone position he noticed that she was still wearing her flippers, perhaps unable to remove them because she was holding onto the railing with one hand and onto her knife handle with the other.

"I don't get it, Kay. What's in this for you? Everybody here likes you, even trusts you. You've got a perfect life, what more could you need?"

"My share of what has become a legendary family fortune, I guess. Before my thieving sister with the heart of gold stole my husband and lost her share in a card game. Never knew how to hedge her bets, that one. So wholesome, wasn't really cut out for anything but farming." Kay laughed coldly and Tyler now realized that the sound was an uncanny echo of T-Ron's deeper bellow, just at a higher pitch.

"She was always such a poor loser," agreed T-Ron almost sentimentally. "Just like your ex."

"Just a loser, period. I can't believe she really thought she'd get away this."

Tyler was already having trouble comprehending the fact that these two schemers were related, he couldn't imagine a third sibling thrown into the shady mix.

"Yeah, well, you can blame this on that dreamer Flush. Maggie would never have—"

"Tommy, for fuck's sake, just get it over with. Before the other two get back." Kay averted her eyes, gazing back towards her boat. "This is actually a little hard for me."

"Aww, sis. I always said you were too soft for this line of work. You even fell in love with some of the turtles. Maybe a few tender last—" There was a whistling sound and, as T-Ron turned toward the noise, his nose seemed to explode in a mass of blood. "Argh – what the—" Reflexively

302

he raised his hands to his face, the blade of his knife glinting in the sun. Almost immediately there was another woosh and then a clang as something struck the weapon knocking it to the ground inches from Tyler's shoulder.

Amazingly, his reflexes were still quick enough that he was able to react before his wounded attacker could retrieve the knife. He'd never stabbed anyone, had no idea what it felt like to thrust sharp metal into flesh, but it seemed like a primal instinct. As he brought the sharp point downward into Tiburon's foot another projectile whizzed through the air, striking the man in the middle of his chest and in seconds he was down, screaming with pain and confusion.

A few feet away there was a loud splash and Tyler glanced up to see that Kay had disappeared. Seconds later, a lithe figure swung herself from the ladder to the deck, tossing a bush of damp auburn curls out of her eyes, holding tightly to something made of sticks and leather.

"Are you okay?" Fiona came forward breathlessly and then backed off as Tiburon raged at her, baring his teeth like a rabid injured animal.

Again instinct took over as Tyler whacked him hard on the side of his neck with the back of the blade. As he fell again, Tyler shouted, "Get something to tie his hands with!"

But Fiona was already kneeling beside him, suddenly bare-breasted, lashing something black and nylon around T-Ron's wrists and then hog-tying his ankles.

Tyler was breathing so heavily that his chest hurt and he had to lean against the side of the cabin, but Fiona was buzzing around like an insect. "There's no time for you to have a heart attack! Grab that blue line and help me drag him below. And where's your phone? We need to call for help."

"My phone?" Everything was in his day pack, back on Kay's boat; he'd probably never see it again.

"Shit." She realized that he was wearing only his wet swim trunks and a T-shirt, that all of them had come directly from the water, not one of them had a cell on them. "Wait, there must be something on his boat." She looked over the railing. "We'll take it, lash the kayak to it, it will be much faster."

Although he had no idea where they were headed and why, he followed her directions as they hauled the semi-conscious bleeding man down to the floor of the galley, dropping him unceremoniously on the broken dishes he himself had tossed from the cupboards and then lashing him tightly him to a post with the blue rope. Tyler wished there was time to stop and admire this dynamo of a young woman, wearing only a striped bikini bottom and water shoes, taking charge of a life-threatening situation, but her sense of urgency was contagious.

"Maybe he'll bleed out. But who cares." Somehow in the disarray of the cabin she found a purple tank top and pulled it over her head. "We'll lock the door from the outside too, I don't trust the fucker. Do you know how to run a powerboat?"

"I can figure it out, but you'll have to drive. I can't see well enough without my glasses. Where are we going?" Suddenly he had a fearful thought. "Where's my son? Is Tucker okay?"

"He's fine. And keeping his mother alive. Let's go."

CHAPTER EIGHTEEN

July 2018
Luis Peña Island, Puerto Rico

Every minute seemed as long as a day. Tucker's back hurt and the pebbles on the beach were killing his butt, but he tried to stay still and not change the angle of Lucy's head. This was not the way he had envisioned a reunion with his mother, he had not really pictured ever seeing her again at all, but any time his imagination might have strayed to that uncomfortable possibility, he had pictured it happening in Vermont not on a deserted beach on an uninhabited out island of the Caribbean.

Now and then his eyes strayed to the garbage bags strewn on the nearby rocky shore. First and foremost in his mind for months, and yet now less than a hundred feet away and no longer his top priority. Most important was 1) Fiona, 2) the Sea Urchin, 3) the trip, 4) saving his mom. Shit, that should be at the top of the list. Okay so, 1) Lucy, 2) Fiona... it didn't seem right to put his mother first and not even mention his father. Guilt overshadowed all other feelings now – his parents had not even ranked in his priorities for years. Not since he'd pushed away all emotions about Chloe and his past life. And now, what about those twins?

Shit, if only he could turn the clock back two days, when he knew none of this and the future was just another vagabonding adventure on open seas.

As he stared down angrily at Lucy's slack and ashen face, her eyes slowly opened and blinked twice, pale blue irises staring at him unseeingly.

"Mom?"

Her mouth opened as though she were about to say something. Then her lids dropped and as quickly as she had been there she was gone.

"Mom! It's me. Can you hear me?"

Her eyes flew open again and he could see the effort it was taking to focus. He took her hand and held it to his cheek. "I'm here. Look at me."

"Tucker?" Her whole body tensed with fright and then let go with some sort of acceptance. "When did you grow this beard? You need a shave." She seemed to pass out again, but this time her lips curved almost involuntarily, like a newborn baby's smile.

He felt as though he needed to keep her conscious. "Mom. Lucy. How did you get my earring?"

Her expression seemed to twitch uncontrollably from smile to frown and back again. "He put it there. Probably so you would recognize me when you found me. And you did. And you do."

Tucker tried not to shudder at the suggestion of what this could have actually meant if they had not come across her when they had. "Why were you with him, Mom? Didn't you know he was dangerous?"

"Oh, sweetie." Her hand waved as if searching for something and then dropped to the ground. "He was following you. I had to watch him. He was even tracking..."

"Tracking?"

"Your little girlfriend there. You know her name, I can't recall it now. My god, I feel like bloody shit. Where are we?" Her eyes flew open suddenly. "Have you seen your father yet?"

"Tyler? No." Thinking again about both his parents looking for him made all of his itchy places flare up as if cued by a band leader. He wanted to scratch the inside of his ears and his ankles and his elbows but he couldn't do it unless he let go of Lucy.

"Oh, good." She sank back against him, her body heavy with relief. "Then I found you first."

306

"What the hell – was this some kind of contest between the two of you?"

"You know how competitive we are." Then abruptly she convulsed and began coughing. "Bloody hell, I'm going to be sick again."

"I still can't believe they are all related. How did I not see that?" Tyler wiped his hands on his shorts, leaving a trail of brownish-red finger tracks.

"You ought to do something about that cut. That's not just his blood on you." Fiona had to shout to be heard over the roar of the powerful engine. "Maybe there's a first aid kit down there." She nodded to where two black garbage bags blocked the opening to a storage compartment in the forward part of the boat.

"I saw him toss these over. What's in them?" Pushing aside the heavy sacks, Tyler crawled into the dim cramped space. Out of the corner of his eye he saw a quick movement. Were there rats on a boat this size, he wondered for an instant before a hand clapped over his mouth and once again a cold blade pressed against his flesh.

The loud noise of protest he made in his throat was not audible over the deafening motor housed inches from his face. "I don't want to have to hurt you, but if you fight me I will. And pretty Turtle Girl too." Kay's strong fingers squeezed his cheeks tightly as she held her knife flat against his bare back.

"What do you want?!" He could only make the sounds of the words but she knew what he was asking.

"What the hell do you think I want – those two bags out there are only the tip of the iceberg. Wherever Wonder Woman is taking us will lead to your son and I know that he knows where the rest of the stash is."

"You find anything?" Fiona called. "Because we'll be there in a minute and I'm going to need your help."

"When she stops this boat, we are going out there just like this," Kay hissed. "And don't think I don't know how to use this baby. I grew up with lessons from an expert."

307

She was some kind of desperate to believe she could pull off a stunt like this; he had no idea what she was thinking. He'd dealt with crazy women on numerous occasions in his life, too many actually, but now was not the time to dwell on that. She was working on more than the usual adrenalin rush – he could not believe how much his face hurt where her fingers were digging in, but he forced himself to think.

Where had he left T-Ron's knife... he must have put it down on the dashboard shelf in front of the passenger seat. He had to believe that Fiona might be as swift and skillful with it as she'd been with everything else he'd witnessed in the last hour.

The boat started to slow down and Fiona called his name again.

"Tell her you're coming." Kay released the hold on his mouth and wrapped her arm around his throat.

"You're a fucking idiot," he hissed at her, working his jaw. "You could have gone back to your own-" He arched his back away as she angled the blade so he could feel the edge. "Coming up now!"

The engine cut off suddenly and Fiona shouted, "Tucker! We're coming with the kayak!" She was already at the railing ready to lower herself down. "Tyler, grab those life vests and the preserver...oh!" She gasped as Tyler emerged from the storage cubby in Kay's stranglehold, a terrified but determined expression on his face. He seemed to be leaning his head to one side and nodding.

"Why don't you tell Fiona what your plan is, Kay?"

"You mean how I'm going to cut your freakin' dick off if she doesn't do exactly what I say." He had no idea how to predict what she might actually do or say next; even her voice sounded different from the person he'd sailed through the rain with just a few short hours ago. Although he realized now that her personality had definitely been shifting during the journey to Luis Peña.

"I'm sorry what we did to... to your brother." Fiona's tone was timid but apologetic and caught them both off guard before Tyler realized what she was doing. "I know that must have been hard for you to watch."

Tyler could not see Kay's face but he sensed a brief short circuit in the strength of her hold. "He's a son-of-a-bitch, but he's family."

"And were you involved with the turtle-selling business too?" Somehow Fiona managed to infuse this loaded question with youthful innocence.

"You can't possibly know about that." Kay's shock was real and her inflection sounded almost normal, but she quickly regained her composure and reined the emotion in. "And that business is none of your damn business. Now, sweetheart–"

A cry from the shoreline stopped her from finishing the command. All eyes went to the tableau on the rocks – a woman's figure sprawled awkwardly across the rough ground and a thin young man with sun-bleached curls waving long arms at them in a classic distress sign. To Tyler he wasn't much more than a fuzzy blur, but a tremor of emotion at the first sighting of Tucker in nearly two years threatened to undermine his last shreds of internal fortitude.

But then, once again Tyler could feel the change in Kay's energy, this stranger whose physicality he'd recently been so intimate with. He could not let himself get bogged down in that now; later he could chastise himself for letting his sexuality cloud his sensibility one more time, but right now he was suddenly aware that she'd really had no idea where they'd been headed, or that Lucy was still alive.

Her grip around his neck tightened sharply, enough to force a cough from his throat and Fiona stared in alarm. "Here's the deal. You, Turtle Girl, are going to take that kayak into shore and return to me with the rest of that money. Don't look at me like that – I can see all those bags piled up there and waiting. I'll be watching and if you do not come directly back, my dear boyfriend is going to suffer the consequences."

Tyler tried not to flinch as he felt the point of the blade run lightly from his temple to his jaw. He hoped it was sweat and not blood that he felt dripping off his chin, but the wideness of Fiona's eyes and the color draining from her face made him guess otherwise.

"Go. Just do it."

'Get the knife' he mouthed silently but Fiona was already backing away, lowering herself into the kayak. Tyler began to feel panic setting in as she paddled away; he was alone now with a diabolical persona and a danger he had never seen coming until it was too late. Not for the first time, his entire family was at risk because of his poor judgment. "Kay, can we at least sit down?"

"No, I've got to be able to watch her. Move over to the railing there." She nudged him portside and he feigned a stumble so that he could get a look at the console. There it was, right where he remembered leaving it, and he hoped she wouldn't notice. He needed to distract her somehow so that he could get there. It was a weak strategy, she was no doubt more skilled than he was with a knife. An absurd image of a 'Pirates of the Caribbean' style sword-fight showdown flashed through his mind. Well, Kay was not going to do anything to him until Fiona returned with the bags of cash. He just had to survive until then.

"So..." He needed to keep the conversation going, just to steady his own nerves. "This is some family rivalry you've got going on. You and your brother, Tommy Ron, against your sister, Maggie. Whom, by the way, you have no resemblance to." This was obviously not the best topic, but it was the only thing that came to mind.

"She's always let herself go natural, in a granola way. I spray some peroxide on my roots to keep the blonde thing happening." She laughed bitterly. "You have no idea how useful it is to be blonde sometimes; there are so many stupid men out there."

Present company included, he thought. "She seemed nice enough to me." Then again so did you, he inserted silently. "But very different."

"Yeah, well, farmer versus sailor. You become more of whoever you are, when you're old. In her case, a back-stabbing, two-faced thief."

Feeling the blade against his spine, he wanted so badly to add, '*No pun intended*' but he didn't dare.

"She couldn't sail a boat in a bathtub, but she didn't want to sign the Blue Heaven over to Tommy, even though she owed him more money than she could ever repay. He sailed it to Culebra just to spite her, left the Nico behind and then couldn't get back to it before Irma hit." He could feel her shrug her shoulders and roll her neck from the stiffness of holding onto him in this tense pose and the muscles in the arm around his throat began to relax a little.

"What came between you?"

"My husband. And a couple of high stakes poker games."

"How did I not know you were married to Flush?"

She snorted. "How did you not know I've been using you all this time to get to your son and this money?"

He felt his face grow hot with shame at the truth of her words.

"He's way more devious than you. Been eluding us for months with the help of Supergirl. Oh, my god, she's destroyed so many of my brother's drones. I shouldn't laugh but it has been funny. But then the bold little bitch moved right into the game, too bad she's not into poker, I'd love to play her sometime. Speaking of, why is she not there yet?" Her fingers dug into the back of his shoulder blade impatiently as they watched Fiona in the kayak floating sideways with the current. The wind was picking up and the surf increasing; Tyler prayed she knew what she was doing and then decided she probably had a much better plan than his, which was currently to keep talking.

"Maggie told me about Flush, but she never mentioned that he'd been her brother-in-law."

"Fucking A, I bet she didn't. Two losers who were perfect for each other. Dumb name for a guy who outsmarted us all. Thought we had him when he lost

311

everything in the game on Tortola and Tommy managed to get him locked up. Nobody gets out of that prison for years. Unless there's the biggest hurricane in decades. And then a second one on top of that! Meanwhile I was back in Iowa and got stuck there, ended up working the other end of the business for a while." He could feel her arching her back now, trying to stretch away her stiffness without losing her hold on him.

"What happened to Flush?"

"Snorkeling accident." She made a sympathetic sound and smirked. "Old people with medical conditions like Flush and Lucy should be more careful when they go out on the water." At the mention of Lucy's name, Tyler's gaze searched out her inert silhouette on the beach. Kay leaned against him, the weight of her body pressing his chest uncomfortably against the metal railing. "And then there are old people like you. Who end up unfortunate victims of adventure-related mishaps."

He could see Fiona was just getting to shore, the kayak towline tied to her waist; she and Tucker seemed to be having a high-intensity exchange. Tucker shielded his eyes and peered out towards the boat. Tyler started to speak but Kay shushed him as she concentrated on trying to interpret what was happening on shore.

In his tightly wired state of captivity, Tyler had only been able to look in one direction. His world perspective had narrowed down to the scene before him while keeping the conversation going with Kay in the hopes of wearing her down or distracting her. But now, between the rolling splash of the waves against the hull and the building rustle of the sea breeze, came a sound from somewhere behind them in the channel. The roar of a motor grew louder, followed by another approaching at some distance.

"Shit."

Both of their heads turned automatically to look. Two dive boats full of daytrippers ready for scuba excitement were zooming past, on their way to one of the nearby reefs. Tyler's first thought was overwhelming relief that they were not alone or even that far from civilization. Then, as he felt Kay's stance momentarily ease up because of the distraction, he seized the split second window of opportunity. With both hands he swiftly reached up to pry her arm from around his neck, at the same time pushing back against her with his feet. As she struggled to keep her balance, he catapulted himself over the railing and into the water.

He landed not with the agile dive he'd anticipated, but in an unceremonious backwards somersault that broke his fall with a graceless flailing splash. When he surfaced, he began swimming blindly, hoping he was heading in the right direction. Kay's shrieks disappeared into the repetitive kicking of his legs against the current and the pounding of his lungs as he labored for breath.

He heard shouting and swam towards it, howling when a wave drove his body into a rough coral scree. Then a hand gripped his arm, pulling him into a narrow pass between two reefs and finally onto a solid shore. Tyler collapsed on his elbows and knees, pressing his forehead into the sand and sucking in great gasps of air.

"Dad. Are you okay?"

Four people, one bottle of water and a kayak. And one of the four was barely conscious. It was by no means a perfect scenario, but what family reunion ever was. Tucker was brown and thin and serious-looking, and Tyler was too drained to give him the scolding he deserved for not getting in touch for almost two years. At the moment it was low on his inventory of priorities. He knelt beside Lucy, who gave him a pale, dizzy smile when he squeezed her hand while she visibly shivered in the heat of the mid-morning sun.

"Do you think she's in shock?" He didn't want to ask the real question looming in his mind which had to do with whether she was drunk. "Is there anything to wrap around her?" Tyler looked around, noting the pile of garbage bags and the backpack at the end of the beach. "What's in that pack?"

"Not a blanket," Fiona answered darkly. "Get her to drink the rest of that water and let's go."

"Look!" Tucker was pointing at the boat.

"What is it, I can't see for shit anymore." He peered out to sea.

"She just jumped off with a life vest and is swimming away. Why the hell didn't she just take the boat, I wonder."

"This is probably the reason."

They turned to Fiona who opened her palm. At this short distance, even Tyler could see she was holding a key.

Tucker leaped in the air, waving a fist. "Isn't she brilliant? Can you tell why I love her?" He hugged Fiona around the waist.

Tyler shook his head, trying not to think about how complicated the situation was going to be once they got through this present disaster.

Fiona was all business, as usual. "We've got to get Lucy into the kayak. There's no way we'll be able to get her up into the boat in her state. We'll have to tow her behind us. One of you will have to stay with her."

"Shit, I wish she were still small," Tucker muttered under his breath as he and Tyler hauled Lucy the few feet to the water's edge. "How are we even going to get her into the kayak?" He stopped and gave a longing look at the 'family fortune' they were leaving behind before Fiona urged him on. "I'm coming back here, you know."

Despite the immediate crisis at hand, Tyler found himself more preoccupied with where Kay was going and what she was up to. There was also the fact that they'd left a very wounded Tiburon locked in the cabin of the Sea Urchin.

But events moved along quickly once they were back on the cruiser. When Tyler suggested they use Lucy's phone to call the coast guard for help, Tucker quickly nixed that idea. "These two may be pirates, but we're not innocent. How are we going to explain what's gone down here?"

They argued most of the way back to the sailboat about what was going to happen next. Lucy to the clinic obviously.

314

Snorkeling accident. They would motorsail over to Melones, that was the quickest route for meeting the one ambulance that Culebra operated. But what were they going to do with T-Ron?

"And there she goes." Fiona shouted, pointing to Kay's little ketch as it moved swiftly out to sea, riding the easterly winds.

"With my glasses. And my phone. Oh, shit. And my wallet." It was hard to absorb the impact of all these personal catastrophes with the bigger issues they were facing.

As they clamored aboard the Sea Urchin, Tyler tried to calculate how long it had been since they'd left on this most recent leg of the day's exploits, but his brain was too tired to do any numerical calculations.

"Oh my god, I can't believe you guys did this." Tucker exclaimed as he opened the hatchway and peered into the cabin and then backed away.

"It was self-defense. You would have done the same. He was about to kill your father."

"I would have finished him off."

"Yeah, I don't think so." Fiona the super-hero now sounded like an exhausted and petulant teenager. She sank down on the deck and rested her head on her arms. "Can you guys get him back into his own boat? And then Lucy into our dinghy. I need to take a break, I think."

Bruised, dirty and bleeding, dragging the dead weight of another unconscious body...this was not what Tyler had imagined he would be doing with his son when they finally got together again.

"At some point we need to talk about Athena and Artemis," he muttered through gritted teeth as they strained to cantilever T-Ron over the lashed-together railings of the two boats.

Tucker's answer was an angry surge of energy that finished the job of getting the enemy back onto his own territory.

"Make sure you get all of Lucy's stuff off before you cut it loose," Fiona called weakly. "OMG, not those, please."

Once again the garbage bags of cash were being shifted from deck to deck. "Fuck if I'm leaving these with him, dead or alive. Okay, wait." Tucker stopped and emptied half a bag of banded bills into a pile next to T-Ron. "Enough to make him look as guilty as he is."

It seemed to satisfy Fiona so Tyler didn't say he doubted any of that loose cash would actually make its way into a court case by the time the police and paramedics had done their job.

After another bottle of water, Lucy was roused enough to be able to sit up and assist in her own rescue, at least as far as being moved from the kayak to the dinghy. Then she promptly vomited over the side again and slid to the floor, her head on the seat.

"I'll ride back here with her," Tyler volunteered. "Now please, let's get her to town."

CHAPTER NINETEEN

August 2018
Culebra, Puerto Rico

"At the public dock. Can you come now?"
Tucker resented the intrusion of a text message into his life, but Tyler had insisted on buying them a cell phone when he'd had to order himself a new one. In just a few days they were 'connected' to the world again, which was the exact opposite of the whole point of sailing.

"Yes." Well, a one word answer was as much as he was going to give.

"Hey, my father wants me to meet him," he called to Fiona. "I'll be back soon." At his parents' request, he'd agreed to hang around Culebra a little longer, although he was anxious to be gone. Fiona told him spending time with them was the right thing to do, even if it did make him uncomfortable.

Going out to dinner with both Tyler and Lucy had always been an awkward affair, but the two of them seemed to have buried the hatchet and were getting along now, which was almost weirder than the stupid stuff they usually fought about. They tried to catch him up on the news from West Jordan, and although he pretended to pay attention, it was hard to concentrate on listening to talk about the life he had turned away from. He was especially dispassionate when they brought up Chloe and the twins, and he even caught them exchanging worried looks with each other. He was saddened to hear of his mother's breakdown but had no sympathy for Chloe's bout with drug addiction and sex trafficking. However his lack of emotion was easily covered up by Lucy's horrified reaction to Tyler's tale of what had happened to Chloe; apparently Lucy had

317

missed this event while absorbed in her own self-destructive behavior.

The first time Myles's name came up, Tucker said flatly, "We're not friends anymore. I don't want to discuss him," which led to more secret glances and threatening expressions between the formerly estranged parents, and which caused Tucker to get up and walk out of the restaurant like he was still a sulky adolescent. And he did feel like he was moping.

"What's wrong with you?" Tyler asked as he caught up with him on the street.

"Well, let's see. A) My mother was fucking the man who's been stalking me and tried to kill you, and, oh yeah, B) you were screwing that same man's sister. Who, C) just happened to be the former wife of the guy I sailed here with. Who D) was murdered by that same man. Who, E) was doing her sister. So, yeah, maybe give me a little space, okay?"

"We are not done here!" Tyler called after him. "You can't ignore your responsibilities!"

Responsibilities... that was hardest part of it. Because all of it was his fault. All of it.

At least the further delay had given him time to go back to Luis Peña and recover everything he'd had to leave behind.

"Really?!" Fiona thought he was a greedy miser, but he had assured her that he was doing the right thing and she would soon see what he meant.

Tucker started up the outboard to go the short distance across the Ensenada to where Tyler was waiting. The Sea Urchin was anchored in the harbor like the rest of the other sailboats now. They had no reason to hide out anymore. After an "anonymous tip" to the Coast Guard, T-Ron had been rescued and taken to Fajardo where he was under some kind of hospital arrest. Kay had disappeared and it was doubtful that she would dare resurface again anywhere near Culebra. Lucy was now staying at the same guesthouse as Tyler; they both had tickets off the island late tomorrow afternoon.

As he approached the dock, he could see a group of people gathered there; it looked like a family with small children and he wondered whether he'd read the message wrong and that Tyler had meant the Dinghy Dock. But he recognized Tyler standing there, talking to a younger man who was holding a small child in one arm and hanging onto another livelier child who was jumping up and down.

The sinking feeling in his gut told him to do the cowardly thing and turn around now and speed away, but Tyler had already seen him. He was waving and, in a very un-Tyler-like gesture, had swept up the small bouncing girl and was pointing in Tucker's direction.

He did not look up again until he had tied up the dinghy and climbed onto the cement wharf. Myles was standing directly in front of him; a blonde toddler with curly hair was hiding her face in his shoulder. He looked different, older, dreadlocks gone, hair straight now and tucked behind his ears, eyes wide, a tentative smile on his lips.

"Hey."

"Hey." He glanced around nervously, wondering if Chloe was about to emerge from somewhere as well, wishing he'd brought Fiona for support. But there was no one else there, just the three of them and the two babies.

Tucker turned to Tyler, who could no longer restrain the child who was tugging to get away and who dashed towards Tucker wonderingly. "Artemis! What did we say about being careful? Tucker, grab her before she goes over the edge, will you?"

Clumsily he caught the girl around her waist just as she got to the side of the dock to peer eagerly into the water.

"No! Armis want swim! Swim now, Gampy. Now!"

Tucker had no idea what to do with this little creature kicking her legs and trying to squirm out of his grasp, but neither Tyler nor Myles came to his assistance.

319

"Ummm…"

"Artemis, we're going to the beach soon." Myles spoke up, moving a few steps closer. "Just chill. Can you show Tucker how we chill?"

Artemis was suddenly a dead weight in his hands, eyes closed, limbs limp. Then she laughed and said to Myles, "Good, My?"

"Me chill too!" The little girl in Myles's arms imitated her twin and then looked adoringly at Myles for approval. "Teena good, My My?"

Tucker simply stared, unable to absorb the reality of Athena and Artemis, who were no longer just names of daughters he didn't want to believe existed. Finally Tyler came forward and took the thrashing child from him, tucking her into the crook of his elbow and tossing her over his hip. "We're going to Flamenco Beach. Will you come with us?"

It was not really a question.

Tucker and Tyler sat in the shade watching Myles roll around in the shallow surf with the twins.

"Well, bravo to you, Pops, on setting this one up." There was no mistaking the edge to Tucker's words.

"Had to happen. What do you think?"

"He's really good with them." Tucker was cowed by his childhood friend's skill in wrangling the two wild toddlers. "I don't know fuck-all about kids."

"Well, the first thing is not to use expressions like 'fuck-all' around them. I didn't know anything either, but I learned. Remember I never even met you until you were six. Artemis and Athena were the first diapers I ever changed."

"Diapers." The word was foreign to him, his father could have been speaking Chinese.

"Myles has rearranged his life to help care for them. He came back from New Orleans this summer so I could come down here. He's got a special bond with the girls – he was there when they were born."

"Well, I'm glad at least one of us is responsible." Everything he said came out sounding sarcastic.

Tyler snorted a little. "Oh, he has a story as good as yours to tell. Ask him about his trip to Baja when you get a chance. Both of you boys are vagabond runners. Or rotters, as your mom would say." He nodded towards the entrance to the beach where Lucy and Fiona could be seen making their way through the sand. Tucker didn't ask how he'd managed to organize the whole crowd to be here. The details didn't matter.

"So at what point do you trot Chloe out too?"

"I spared you that reunion; she was as enthusiastic about the idea as you are. I'm pretty sure she hoped I would never find you. She's very happy having Myles play dad to the girls when he's around." Although his body language was relaxed, from behind his dark glasses, Tyler was watching his son pretty closely to see how he was reacting to all this news. "And Myles was there for her after her... ordeal."

Tucker assumed this was the drug and sex thing that had been alluded to in earlier conversations.

Fiona and Lucy would reach them in a minute and Tucker had a few things to say before they arrived. "Look, you aren't really expecting me to come home and live with all of you, right? Sounds like the bedroom has more than maximum occupancy as is."

"Actually that's the last thing anybody wants. Except maybe Lucy might have a fantasy that you and Fiona might move in happily-ever-after with her in Burlington."

They actually shared a chuckle at that idea.

"We just thought you should meet your daughters. Understand what's going on. And face the consequences and responsibilities. And maybe patch things up with Myles. Especially if he's going to be the co-caretaker of your biological offspring."

Offspring. It was a stupid word.

"Did you know that Myles is a rising star in the New Orleans music scene? Someday soon you'll be bragging that he was your best friend when you were growing up in Vermont. The only problem is that Chloe wants to–" Tyler stopped as Lucy made her arrival known to her two tow-headed granddaughters, with the theatrical kind of entrance that few people could pull off on a nearly deserted beach. There were big hugs and lots of jumping up and down and even Fiona knelt on the shore, enchanted by the performance.

Tucker felt so conflicted he wanted to dig a hole in the sand and disappear.

"You know, I didn't know how to do it either." His father just kept talking. "I'm still not very good at it, but they don't seem to care. Just think of it as another puzzle that needs to be solved. Artemis can already do a simple jigsaw, by the way. We have a hard time keeping up with her."

Tucker got up and headed to the water just so he wouldn't have to listen to him anymore. Halfway across the beach, he realized that had probably been Tyler's plan all along.

"Photo op! Photo op!" Lucy sang out. "How long have I been waiting for this picture? Everybody get together, Tucker, you get in the middle."

Suddenly he was there, kneeling in the sand beside Fiona, two wet and sticky little girls climbing all over him. "Oh, my god, it makes me want one!" she whispered as they pressed in together with forced smiles on their faces. "Just kidding, just kidding."

Twenty-four hours later, Fiona and Tucker said goodbye to everyone at the Culebra airport, where the extended family and all their gear were the only passengers on the tiny, single-engine plane. With each grandparent holding the hand of one toddler, Myles was the last to leave, carrying a fiddle case and a giant diaper bag.

"Dude, stay in touch this time." He put down his luggage and embraced the two of them.

"Look who's talking. I heard you disappeared for a year." Tucker couldn't hide the emotion he was feeling. "Thanks for taking good care of them. I'm sorry I've been such a dickhead."

"It's easy. I love all of them. And I'm glad you've got a good support system too." Myles winked at Fiona. "So where are you sailing to tomorrow?"

"We're headed down to the Windwards. But we'll be stopping in the BVIs first."

Fiona's eyes widened. "Why don't I know about this? Where are we going?"

The airline agent was hovering at Myles's shoulder and he hastily turned to go. "These small planes are awesome!" he called as he walked backwards, unwilling to sever the connection between them. "You should try flying sometime instead of sailing!"

"So what's our first port of call, captain? No more secrets. I've met your parents and your kids. And now I insist on knowing everything. In advance." Fiona faced him, her hands on her hips.

"Okay, okay." Tucker had trouble tearing his eyes away from the little plane as it moved toward the end of the runway. "Tortola. We're going to Tortola. There's somebody I need to see there."

"You're sure this is a shortcut?"

As Tucker turned to offer Fiona a hand up the steep trail, he could not help thinking about the first time he hiked up this path with Flush after the hurricane. The trees had been leafless then; now the two of them were beating their way through what seemed like a jungle of growth, struggling to follow the narrow strip of bare earth between the underbrush.

"We should come out onto an actual road soon." He could see she was struggling to maintain her balance under the heavy pack that cut into her shoulders. "Thanks for helping carry the load."

"You know I like doing the right thing." She smiled at him and wiped the perspiration from her face, leaving a streak of grime down one cheek. "How is it we always end up dirty and sweaty on your excursions?"

"It's what we do best together, right?"

A dog started to woof nearby, the barking getting louder as they grew closer to their destination. "It'll be dark soon. What if she's not home?"

"Then we'll take a shower and wait for her." A black lab came suddenly bounding down the trail, wagging his tail and jumping around Tucker's legs. "Boo! You remember me, boy? Good dog!"

He was glad Boo had come to meet them; the change in vegetation was so extreme, he barely recognized the way. But finally there was the derelict jeep marking the end of the driveway. Two goats eating grass in the yard looked up at them, mildly interested in their arrival. A brood of baby chicks followed a mother hen who pecked at the gravel and hard earth.

"Well, the prodigal son returns." Maggie opened the screen door and came out onto the top step. "Is this just a random visit or did your parents actually find you?" She crossed her arms over her ample chest and scrutinized him seriously before peering through her black glasses at Fiona. "And who's this? You trade Flush in for someone cuter?"

It was not exactly the welcome he'd been expecting and he stopped in his tracks, realizing that he hadn't really thought this visit through.

"Hi, Maggie. This is Fiona. And we – uh– we brought you something." Tucker heaved the black plastic bag through the air and dropped it at the bottom of the stairs as Fiona slowly lowered her pack to the ground and backed away.

"Maybe we just ought to go," she murmured.

"Good news or bad news?" Maggie asked suspiciously. "Did you bring my boat back finally?"

"Um, no. Maria took the Nico Tico. And the other one…" Tucker scratched at his shoulder and the inside of his elbow. "Well, your sister is somewhere with that one."

"My… sister? Oh, fuck." Maggie sank down onto the steps and wiped her hands on her overalls. "So I guess you met my brother too."

"Uh, yeah. You might say that." He glanced at Fiona who was standing perfectly still now, in fight or flight mode, and he hoped she wasn't thinking about loading her slingshot.

"Bunch of bad apples, that lot. I'm sorry you ended up in my family's mess, Stoney." She looked sincerely contrite. "Flush had me convinced that you wouldn't have to be involved, that you were just his ride. None of us bet on the second hurricane being worse than the first. But, as you probably know by now, I'm not a very good gambler."

"Yeah, I have heard that. Well, hopefully this makes up for your trouble." He kicked at the bag. "You'll be able to buy a new boat, if that's what you really want. But I've heard you're a better farmer than sailor."

"Is that what those shits told you?" Her snicker was eerily reminiscent of her siblings. "Well, now you've piqued my curiosity." She got stiffly to her feet and peered in the bag. This time she threw back her head and let out a laugh that was purely her own. "Oh, my. Finally got my share back. These are big bills too! Oh, Stoney!" Now she folded him into the warm embrace he remembered her for, motioning to Fiona to join them. "Come here, sweetheart. I've got no hard feelings for you guys."

Still Fiona hung back, not entirely convinced of their safety, even when Tucker shot her a triumphant grin.

"Guess I've got to win her over somehow," Maggie whispered to Tucker. "Unlike your mother – we didn't get along very well. I hope she didn't tell you the details of that. I've been pretty ashamed of my behavior."

Tucker's puzzled look told her all she needed to know.

"Well, you kids must be thirsty and hungry. Why don't you come inside and get something cool to drink and we'll make some food. My refrigerator's working now, unlike the last time you were here." She pulled away to look at Tucker again. "How've you been, boy? I'm guessing you have some tales to tell me. And I'm hoping you have some idea where my friend Flush has disappeared to. They're still looking for him on this island, you know."

Tucker glanced back at Fiona, whose worried eyes had taken on the saucer-like appearance he'd grown to know so well as she mouthed the words, "You are going to tell her, aren't you?"

"Come on, let's go inside where it's cooler. I've even got a fan now. Two fans actually." Maggie disappeared into the house. "And latch that door behind you," she called back. "These days I'm trying to keep the flies and mosquitoes outside where they belong."

"Just get it over with." Fiona pulled her arm away from him and stood her ground. "I'm not going to eat dinner with her not knowing."

"Okay, okay. Jesus. You always have to be so up front about everything right off." He turned and climbed the steps, speaking through the screen door before he entered. "Maggie, um, there's something I need to tell you about Flush."

Maggie wailed and railed as she banged pots around the kitchen, and they left her alone to sort out her grief and anger. Tucker showed Fiona the outside shower and the two of them stripped down and rinsed the salt and dirt off their aching bodies.

"I'm scared. How can you trust her – she's related to *them*."

"Okay, I'm going to say something that's going to make me sound way smarter than I am." He dried her back with a hand towel that was hanging over the shower pipe. "Here goes. You can't pick your family. But you can pick your life."

"Who told you that?" He wasn't sure if her laughter was in admiration or mockery.

326

He shrugged. "Maybe I made it up. Because I want it to be true."

"I've been saving this to share with Flush someday." Maggie produced a bottle of whiskey that Tucker recognized as his favorite brand. So I think it's right that we celebrate his life with it." She pushed the dirty dinner plates aside and set the MaCallan in the center of the table. "Stoney, get me three glasses off that top shelf, will you?"

"We're not big drinkers," Fiona started to protest but Tucker cut her off.

"But we'll do our best, won't we, Fiona?"

The two of them gasped and laughed at the fiery burn of the liquor in their throats, but neither of them objected when Maggie poured second shots all around.

"To John Royal. One of the sweetest men I've ever had." Maggie drank her whiskey like a pro, smacking her lips. "He was such a goofball." Tucker and Fiona held their untouched second glasses as they watched her down a third.

Maggie's eyes grew heavy and her expression softened. Then she laughed and turned to Tucker. "Now what about that good-looking father of yours? I liked him. Does he have a girlfriend?"

ABOUT THE AUTHOR

A lifelong lover of travel, mysteries, and creative expression, Marilinne Cooper has always enjoyed the escapist pleasure of combining her passions in a good story. When she is not traveling to warmer climates around the world, she lives in the White Mountains of New Hampshire and is also a freelance copywriting professional. To learn more visit marilinnecooper.com.

ALSO BY MARILINNE COOPER

Night Heron
Butterfly Tattoo
Blue Moon
Double Phoenix
Dead Reckoning
Snake Island
Windfall
Catnip Jazz
Second Wind

Jamaican Draw

Made in United States
North Haven, CT
10 November 2022

26563337R00183